the
VEGETARIAN
BIBLE

the VEGETARIAN
BIBLE

SARAH BROWN

Reader's
Digest

THE READER'S DIGEST ASSOCIATION, INC.
Pleasantville, New York/Montreal

This book was designed and produced by
THE IVY PRESS LIMITED
The Old Candlemakers
West Street, Lewes
East Sussex BN7 2NZ, U.K.

Creative Director Peter Bridgewater
Publisher Sophie Collins
Editorial Director Steve Luck
Design Manager Tony Seddon
Designer Alistair Plumb
Project Editor Caroline Earle
Photography Mary-Louise Avery, Ian Parsons
Home Economist Jacqueline Clark
Picture Research Liz Moore

READER'S DIGEST PROJECT STAFF
Editorial Director Fred DuBose
Senior Designer Susan Welt
Editorial Manager Christine R. Guido

Contributing Editor Susan McQuillan

READER'S DIGEST ILLUSTRATED REFERENCE BOOKS
Editor-in-Chief Christopher Cavanaugh
Art Director Joan Mazzeo
Director, Trade Publishing Christopher T. Reggio
Editorial Director, Trade Susan Randol
Senior Design Director, Trade Elizabeth L. Tunnicliffe

Library of Congress Cataloging in Publication Data

Brown, Sarah.
    The vegetarian bible : the complete illustrated guide to vegetarian food & cooking/
Sarah Brown.
        p. cm.
    Includes index.
    ISBN 0-7621-0359-0
        1. Vegetarian cookery. 2. Vegetarian foods. I. Title.

TX837 .B87527 2002
641.5´636–dc21   2001034927

Visit us on our website for more Reader's Digest products and information:
www.rd.com (in the U.S.)
www.readersdigest.ca (in Canada)

Originated and printed by Hong Kong Graphics
1 3 5 7 9 10 8 6 4 2

Publisher's Note
To the best of the author's knowledge, the recipe measurements in the book are accurate. The preparation and cooking times given for each recipe are an approximate guide only because these may differ according to the techniques and type of stove used. The author cannot be held responsible for new research or developments or individual circumstances that may invalidate any text, advice, or instructions given.

contents

Introduction

Vegetarian food is food that does not include meat or fish, or any of their by-products, such as lard. From this blunt definition has developed an inspirational and exciting cuisine, which uses a vast array of ingredients, the latest cooking techniques, and encompasses a host of international influences.

This book is written for those who are vegetarian or who are thinking about becoming vegetarian and for those who like the idea of occasional meals without meat or fish. It is intended to be a comprehensive guide to the cuisine, providing reference information and recipes for a complete healthy, enjoyable, and practical vegetarian diet.

All over the world more people than ever before are interested in vegetarian food. There is a great variety of reasons why people decide to follow a vegetarian diet. Some do so because they feel better eating less or no meat, some because they are concerned about the quality and origin of their food. For others, their reasons focus on the plight of the animals reared for slaughter, especially by intensive farming methods, and for experimentation. Many vegetarians eat eggs and dairy products, such as cheese. Those who do not eat these products or any food that involves living creatures, such as honey, are vegans.

Looking to the future, many people feel that a vegetarian diet holds the solution to modern dilemmas about our health and that of our planet, responding to environmental concerns and international food production issues.

The Vegetarian Bible takes into account the huge changes in vegetarian food in the last few years—changes mainly brought about by an enormous increase in accessibility and choice of ingredients. Growers and producers are constantly bringing new foods to our attention. Where there used to be simply hard cheese or soft cheese, for example, there is now a rich diversity of flavors and textures on offer. Similarly, with staples such as grains, legumes, and cooking oils, the variety available is greater than ever before. Gone are the days when a salad meant settling for one type of lettuce. Salad greens alone offer a wealth of flavors from sweet to peppery, and colors ranging from white through green to ruby red. This book details over 350 individual ingredients that can be used in meals and snacks.

Vegetarian cuisine is uniquely different from national cuisines in that it is not bound by one style or set of ingredients. It draws inspiration from cooking styles across the world, making this way of eating both varied and flexible. Once seen as limited, bland, or merely imitative of meat, vegetarian food now includes a spectrum of flavors— such as hot and spicy or aromatic and packed with herbs. Dishes range from the quick, crisp stir-fries of Asia and the aromatic grain dishes from India and the Middle East to the gloriously colored, garlic-rich vegetables of the Mediterranean and the fiery chiles of the Americas. Even in areas such as barbecue food, once thought exclusive to the meat eater, there is now a fund of vegetarian ideas.

If you are already vegetarian, I hope you will find many things to inspire you among both the recipes and the many cooking notes given in the ingredients section. If you are less familiar with vegetarian food, I hope that after looking at this book you can approach vegetarian food with more confidence. I initially enjoyed vegetarian cooking because I felt there was so much opportunity to improvise, create, and be flexible. I have now been a vegetarian some 20 years and have been writing cookbooks for 15 of those years. Yet in researching and developing ideas for this book, I was delighted and surprised by the number of new ingredients and techniques still to discover.

For those wanting to make changes to their diet, there is no right or wrong way to do so. It needs to fit in with you, your lifestyle, and your family. You might decide to give up meat and fish overnight, which is fine, but you will be more successful if the people you cook for are willing to support you in trying a new diet. It may be that you will gradually introduce more vegetables and whole-foods into your diet. One of the best ways is to try out a couple of meat-free recipes each week until you have a good repertoire of favorites. Start by trying familiar styles of meals and introduce the unfamiliar more gradually. Whether you are making big or small changes, remember that preparing new recipes or using new ingredients always seems to take more time initially. I hope the ingredients and recipes inspire you and that you find a glorious and tempting array in the following pages.

How to use this book

What makes this book special is that it is not simply a collection of recipes. It covers all the techniques needed to cook vegetarian food, as well as including a wealth of detail on the many ingredients used. Underpinning this information are valuable nutritional facts and advice to reassure you that your diet is well balanced and healthy.

The book is divided into two main sections—a reference section, which covers all aspects of a vegetarian diet, and a recipe section, which includes over 250 recipes. At the back of the book is a smaller section on menu planning and entertaining, including complete menus, as well as a comprehensive index.

The reference section is split into three parts: nutrition, ingredients, and organization. You can read the reference section in depth or dip into it when you need to look up a particular ingredient, nutrient, or technique.

The nutrition part begins by focusing on food composition and the sources of essential nutrients. It looks at a vegetarian diet throughout the different stages in our lives, explaining what is needed and how this diet can be used to improve our health. There is also information on how you may need to vary your diet to fit in with your lifestyle. This section then goes on to consider other diets or aspects of diet that may affect your health.

The ingredients directory describes over 350 individual ingredients, outlining everything you need to know to make the most of each. To make them easy to find, the ingredients are divided into several broad food groups, such as legumes or nuts and seeds. In this part you'll find notes on how to select and store each ingredient, how to prepare them, and which cooking techniques are the most suitable. There are also cookery notes on each ingredient, enabling you to see easily which flavors or other ingredients go well together.

The final part of the reference section is designed to help you use your kitchen and your time efficiently. It looks at the pantry, gadgets, techniques, and storage, time saving, and meal planning. All the information enables you to cook the recipes with the minimum of fuss.

The recipe section follows the reference section and is arranged in chapters. Starting with breakfast, it then moves onto soups and starters, light meals, main courses, side dishes, salads, and baking. It includes many classic recipes, as well as dishes with a modern flavor and style. Every recipe is photographed and there are step-by-step photographs to help you master important techniques, such as pasta or pastry making. There are also feature pages on Mexican, Indian, and Asian food, as well as a section on easy meals for children. Many of the recipes are dairy-free or have options to make them so.

The final section of the book shows you how to put everything together and cook meals for your family and friends, entertaining formally and informally, both at home and al fresco. There are several complete menus pictured, plus suggestions for many more.

USING THE NUTRITIONAL GUIDANCE

Most of the recipes in this book show the nutritional content of a portion of the dish. You can use this information to help you make sure you get the major nutrients you need—but remember that other items, such as milk, cereals, bread, fruit, and vegetables make an important contribution to your balanced diet, too. If you are new to the science of nutrition, don't be too concerned about details. As a starting point, include as many different foods as possible in your diet.

Calcium and iron Recipes that are marked with the high-in-calcium symbol contain no less than 250mg calcium and those high in iron contain 4g iron or more (about ⅓ of the adult daily requirement). Although iron from vegetable sources is not so well absorbed as iron from animal sources, there is no reason for a vegetarian to be iron deficient for dietary reasons alone. It is a good idea to include recipes that are high in iron and calcium when you can, but remember that many of the other recipes do still provide useful amounts of these nutrients. Milk, cheese, and yogurt are particularly good sources of calcium, so if you prefer to use a nondairy product, such as soy milk, do make sure you choose a brand that has been supplemented with calcium.

Protein It is not difficult to obtain sufficient protein in your vegetarian diet. Try to include at least one dish which provides at least 15g protein every day, but remember that bread, rice, pasta, etc. will also contribute to the protein content of your diet, as will milk, cheese, and yogurt.

Fat Many of us have a high-fat diet, which is bad for health. If you are trying to control the fat content of your diet, choose mostly main-course dishes which contain not more than 15g of fat. For appetizers and desserts, look for 5g fat or less. Of course if you choose a low-fat main course, you could have a higher fat appetizer or dessert.

As well as giving the total fat per portion of a recipe, I have included the amount of saturated fat. If possible, your diet should contain only a small proportion of saturated fat. Try to choose dishes low in saturated fat when you can. The remaining fat in the dish will be either poly- or monounsaturated. These fats contain the same amount of calories as saturated fat, but are less harmful.

Calories Some people think that calories are a physical component of food, like protein or fat, but they are actually a measure of the amount of energy contained in a food.

Using the recipes

The recipes are analyzed per portion, except where stated otherwise—per slice or per muffin, for example.

SYMBOLS USED

Ca	high in calcium (i.e., contains approximately one-third of recommended daily adult needs)
Fe	high in iron (i.e., contains approximately one-third of recommended daily adult needs)
$\mathcal{V}$	suitable for vegans

Measurements are given in cups, where appropriate, followed by imperial, then metric. Please note that you should follow only one set of measurements as they are not exactly compatible but rounded up or down to make realistic quantities. The conversions are standard, but are varied in one or two cases where the ratio of one ingredient to another is important, such as in pastry and bread making.

Standard level spoon measures are used
1 cup = 250 milliliters
Eggs are large unless otherwise stated.

NUTRITION

Food provides the energy and nourishment that is needed to survive and enjoy life. This section looks at nutrition from a general and a vegetarian point of view. Nutrition is a fascinating subject and I am constantly amazed by the body's ability to get the best out of the food we eat.

Nutrition is also a modern subject and while certain facts remain undisputed, new research throws up many ideas and constantly changes our view of what we need and why. It is useful to understand a little about what your food contains and, even if you have been vegetarian for a number of years, it is worthwhile looking at some of the changes in nutritional advice.

This section starts by looking at the composition of foods to see exactly where nutrients come from, why they are needed, and in what quantities. Following this is a summary of today's guidelines for a healthy diet and how this relates to a vegetarian diet. While it is useful to have an awareness of general nutrition, it is also important to think about your own specific situation. How do you make sure you are eating the right things? Are there circumstances where you need to change your diet? The influences of lifestyle and age on diet can be found on pages 21–25.

This section also looks beyond nutrition and diet at modern methods of food production and processing, which are a cause of concern for many people, and at other food issues in order to consider their influence and their relevance to a vegetarian lifestyle.

Protein

Nuts and legumes are
protein-rich ingredients that are
a staple part of a well-balanced
vegetarian diet.

Protein is essential during childhood and adolescence, the principal years of growth and development, but it is also needed in adulthood to help maintain the body. It has two main functions. It builds up body structures, such as cell tissues and bone matter, and is found in muscles, skin, nails, and hair, as well as blood. Protein also maintains supplies of enzymes, hormones, and antibodies. These regulate many of the body's most important functions, such as the ability to digest food.

Protein is made up of amino acids, which are found in many foods. Rather like building blocks, the amino acids are linked together in chain structures that give each kind of protein its specific characteristics. There are 24 known amino acids. Ten of these are called "essential amino acids" because the body cannot survive without them, nor can it synthesize them and so they must be obtained from food.

Some foods contain all the essential amino acids in roughly the proportions that the body needs. Milk, eggs, fish, and meat are good examples of these sorts of food and in the past have been defined as "complete proteins" or "first-class proteins." Plant or vegetable sources of protein, apart from the soybean, do not contain this ideal mixture. Because of this they have sometimes been known as "incomplete proteins" or "second-class proteins." Do not get the impression,

however, that these foods are second rate. During digestion, protein is broken down into the component amino acids, which are then absorbed and rearranged. If essential amino acids are missing from one food, they will be extracted from another. As long as all the essential amino acids are included somewhere in the diet, the body will extract the right mixture. It is not even necessary for foods containing all the amino acids to be eaten at the same meal.

SOURCES OF PROTEIN

While the body can do all the clever stuff of processing and extracting protein, it is still important for vegetarians to make sure that they are getting a good supply of all the essential amino acids by eating a wide variety of protein-rich foods. This is quite straightforward since, apart from dairy products, there are three staple food groups that form the main sources of protein for a non-meat eater. These are legumes (beans, peas, and lentils); nuts and seeds; and grains.

What simplifies matters further is that the amino acid profiles in these food groups complement each other. When any two of the above groups are combined, they make a complete protein. It is like a two-piece jigsaw puzzle—each piece alone is incomplete, but together they make up the whole picture.

Fortunately, from a culinary point of view, it is easy to combine these staple foods together since they are also highly complementary in terms of taste and texture. Popular examples of complete protein meals include chili beans with rice, beans on toast, corn tortilla with refried beans, pasta with pesto sauce, and hummus with pita bread. You can also make combinations of proteins in sweet dishes, for example a nut and oat crisp topping or a mixed granola with oats, nuts, and seeds.

The main point to remember is that you will get plenty of protein as long as you eat a wide range of these staple foods. If you are eating no dairy products at all, you should include food from at least two of the staple food groups every day.

Legumes, such as red beans and lentils, which feature in this delicious main course chili (see page 240), are a good source of protein. The recipe also contains bulgar wheat, which complements the legumes.

Fat

Fat is a highly concentrated form of energy. Foods high in fat contain a lot of calories, so eating too many fatty foods means you are liable to put on excess weight. High-fat diets are also linked with obesity and with heart disease.

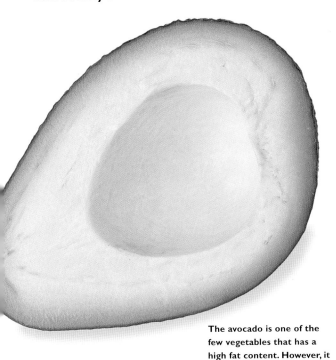

The avocado is one of the few vegetables that has a high fat content. However, it is mostly monounsaturated fat, which helps lower LDL cholesterol levels.

So, should you avoid fat altogether for your health? Certainly not. Fats are vital to the functioning of the body. Fatty tissues store the fat-soluble vitamins, A, D, E, and K, all of which are essential for life. Fat stimulates gall bladder activity, it is needed to produce certain hormones and maintains healthy functioning of the nerves. Fat also helps keep the body warm by being stored in layers under the skin.

There are two fatty acids, linoleic and linolenic acids, which cannot be synthesized in the body and must be obtained from dietary sources. These are called essential fatty acids (EFAs).

Cholesterol is a fat-based molecule, used as a building block for cell membranes and hormones. It is found in the blood in two forms. Low-density LDL cholesterol molecules are small enough to seep into artery walls and begin the process of hardening the arteries. High-density HDL cholesterol molecules are too large to do this and remain in the bloodstream. They help mop up the harmful LDL cholesterol. Cholesterol is produced in our bodies, and the importance of dietary sources of cholesterol are under discussion.

SOURCES OF FAT

There are three main types of fat: saturated, monounsaturated and polyunsaturated. Saturated fats are found mainly in foods of animal origin, such as butter, cream, lard, and fat that occurs in meat. This type of fat stays solid at room temperature. Plant sources of saturated fats are palm and coconut oils. Saturated fats are generally considered unhealthy, since they are thought to increase levels of LDL cholesterol in the blood.

Unsaturated (monounsaturated and polyunsaturated) fats tend to be liquid at room temperature. Monounsaturated fats are found in olive oil and avocados. They tend to be more stable and less prone to rancidity than polyunsaturated fats. They help lower LDL cholesterol levels, raise the levels of the beneficial HDL cholesterol, and are a source of EFAs. Polyunsaturated fats come mainly from plant sources, such as sunflower, safflower, and corn oil, as well as occurring in fish oils. They also supply EFAs. However, polyunsaturates tend to be unstable; they can become rancid quickly and form carcinogenic chemicals. In the process of hydrogenation, which means making the fat solid—for example, some margarines—trans-fatty acids are produced. These are thought to interfere with the functioning of the EFAs and are associated with an increased risk of coronary heart disease.

A constant debate rages as to whether one type of fat is better than another. What is generally agreed, however, is that fat should be eaten sparingly. It is easy to calculate the fat you use in cooking. It is less easy to identify the amount of fat in ready-prepared and processed foods, which is one of the strongest arguments for doing more home cooking.

Simple ways of reducing fat intake include using plain yogurt or silken bean curd instead of cream or mayonnaise, low-fat or skim milk instead of whole milk, and lower-fat cheeses. Choose raw vegetables or fresh fruit instead of high-fat snacks. Broil or bake food rather than fry it and use nonstick pans to cut down on the amount of cooking oil you use.

Sunflower seeds and sunflower oil are good sources of polyunsaturated fats. They also contain essential fatty acids.

Carbohydrate and fiber

Carbohydrate, a major nutrient, comes in three main types: monosaccharides, or simple sugars, which include glucose and fructose; disaccharides, which include sucrose, lactose, and maltose; and complex carbohydrates, which include starch, cellulose, fiber, and glycogen. Dietary fiber is the name given to a number of substances found only in plant foods, which are all constituents of complex carbohydrates. There are several types of fiber, including pectin, gum, cellulose, hemocellulose, and lignin.

Carbohydrate

In a healthy diet carbohydrates are our primary source of energy. Energy is measured in calories and we need calories whether we are working out in a gym or sound asleep in bed. Although all food supplies us with calories, from a nutritional point of view it is best to try and get a good percentage of your daily calorie intake from complex carbohydrate foods or starches. Complex carbohydrates not only supply energy, or calories, but also contain a package of other useful nutrients, such as proteins, vitamins, and minerals. Starches are absorbed slowly into the body, giving sustained levels of energy rather than sudden boosts. They are also bulky to eat and therefore take up room inside you and satisfy you for longer. This leaves little space for the much less healthy, sugary, fatty foods.

Sugar, or sucrose, is also a carbohydrate but while it will certainly give you plenty of calories it provides very little else. Known as "empty calories," sugary foods lack or are very low in the vitamins, minerals, and other nutrients that are needed for health and vitality. Excessive consumption of sugar has many associated health problems, such as tooth decay, diabetes, and high cholesterol levels. Obesity can also

Complex carbohydrates, such as potatoes, give you energy as well as useful nutrients.

Whole-wheat bread is rich in fiber and is a good source of carbohydrate.

become a problem since it is very easy to consume extra calories on a high-sugar diet. Calories not used by the body are stored as fat, so it is best to avoid added sugar.

Fiber

High-fiber diets can help to prevent or alleviate many unhealthy or life-threatening conditions. Fiber stimulates the digestive system and helps reduce the risk of digestive disorders. Soluble fibers, such as gums, act like an internal broom, sweeping away toxins. They also help to lower both blood sugar levels and cholesterol.

All fiber makes food chewy and gives it texture, and as a result you eat less and more slowly. This stimulates saliva production, neutralizing acid formed on the teeth and, in turn, reducing dental decay. Fiber also swells up in the stomach, making you feel more satisfied, so a fiber-rich diet can help counteract obesity.

A healthy vegetarian diet tends to be naturally rich in fiber because there is so much dependence on plant foods for nutrients. To increase your fiber intake, eat more whole-wheat bread and other whole-grain cereals, such as brown rice, whole-wheat pasta, and oats. You should also eat plenty of fresh fruit, salad ingredients, and vegetables with your meals and use lentils, beans, and peas regularly in your diet.

If you are looking to increase the fiber in your diet, it is best to eat a variety of whole grains, which contain beneficial nutrients and fiber, rather than simply adding bran. An acid in the bran called phytate combines with certain minerals in the gut, namely iron, calcium, and zinc, and can prevent them from being absorbed.

SOURCES OF COMPLEX CARBOHYDRATES

In a vegetarian diet there are a wide variety of complex carbohydrates. Good examples are plant-based foods, such as potatoes; legumes (beans, peas, and lentils); all whole grains, such as wheat and rice, and their by-products, such as bread, flour, and pasta.

Antioxidants

These compounds are produced by the body and also occur naturally in many foods, such as broccoli, tomatoes, and spinach. The most common antioxidants are bioflavonoids, which occur widely in green vegetables; carotenes, found in orange and green fruit and vegetables; and vitamins C and E. The minerals copper, zinc, selenium, and manganese also have an antioxidant effect as part of their function. A vegetarian diet will supply more than adequate amounts of these nutrients.

Many claims are made on behalf of antioxidants. It is thought that they may help delay or prevent the onset of cancer and heart disease, slow down the aging process and extend life span, keep the skin young, boost fertility, and reduce memory loss. Many researchers now believe that antioxidants are the medicine of the future, since the body can use antioxidants to boost its own defenses and prevent diseases taking hold.

Include plenty of fruit, such as grapefruit and oranges in your diet, since they are excellent sources of antioxidants and vitamin C.

One way in which antioxidants work in the body is by protecting cells from being attacked by free radicals. Free radicals are harmful substances, which are produced naturally by metabolizing cells. Free radicals attack the genetic material (DNA) in the nucleus of a cell, and resulting changes may cause aging and cancer. Antioxidants work together as a group or, more precisely, they network to mop up free radicals. When the molecules of each antioxidant absorb a free radical they become a weak free radical in the process. They then need help from other antioxidants in order to be recharged or refreshed and change back into the role of a defender. Much is still to be learned about antioxidants, but the evidence of their benefits is impressive and only reinforces the advice that eating plenty of fresh fruit and vegetables is good for your health.

Green vegetables, such as broccoli and cabbage, contain antioxidants that are thought to boost the body's own defense system.

Vitamins

Apricots are a rich source
of vitamin A and iron.

Vitamins are essential chemicals, required by the body in very small quantities
for everyday functions, for its repair and development, and to synthesize other
nutrients. Each vitamin has a slightly different role to play and some vitamins work
in conjunction with each other. Various factors influence the body's daily vitamin
requirements. Growing children, pregnant women, lactating mothers, the elderly,
and those recovering from illness have the greatest need for vitamins. Similarly, those who
smoke, drink, or take regular medication also need to be sure that their food is rich in vitamins.

Vitamins fall into two distinct groups: water soluble and fat soluble. Water-soluble vitamins (B-group
vitamins, folate, and vitamin C) dissolve in the blood and tissue fluids and cannot be stored in the body for
long. Fat-soluble vitamins (vitamins A, D, E, and K) are stored in the liver and fatty tissues. Vitamins can be
destroyed during the storing, preparation, or cooking of food. Water-soluble vitamins are vulnerable to heat;
fat-soluble vitamins are generally more stable but can be sensitive to light and air.

VITAMIN A (*RETINOL*)

Vitamin A is essential for growth and keeps the skin and mucous
membranes healthy. Deficiency in this vitamin can lead to poor night
vision and gradual deterioration in sight, as well as lowering resistance
to infection. Vitamin A can be stored in the body and excessive
amounts can be toxic.

Beta-carotene is a
retinol equivalent; in other
words, the body can
convert it into retinol or
vitamin A. It is now
thought that beta-carotene,
found in orange-colored
vegetables and leafy greens, is also important in its own right.
Research shows that adequate intake of beta-carotene is linked with
a low risk of developing certain cancers.

Good sources
carrots, milk, margarine, butter, bean
sprouts, and bell peppers (especially
red and yellow varieties)

VITAMIN B₁ (*THIAMIN*)

This vitamin is needed to help release energy from
carbohydrates and make sure that the brain and nerves get
enough glucose. A deficiency shows itself in beriberi.

Good sources
germs of grains, such as
brown rice, whole wheat,
and whole-wheat
derivatives (such as cereals
and pasta), and also nuts,
legumes, and milk

VITAMIN B₂ (*RIBOFLAVIN*)

Vitamin B₂ helps to release energy
from protein and fat, and is needed
for healthy skin and mucous
membranes. A deficiency can show
itself in bloodshot eyes, cracked lips,
and sore mouth membranes.

Good sources
yeast extract, eggs,
dairy products
(especially milk),
leafy greens, mushrooms,
and fruit

VITAMIN B₃ (*NIACIN*)

Particularly involved with the
release of energy within the cells,
this vitamin comes from food
sources or can be manufactured
within the body. Deficiency is rare.

Good sources
yeast extract, nuts
(especially peanuts),
legumes, whole
grains, and milk

THE B-GROUP VITAMINS

This is a group of substances involved mainly with the release of
energy from food within the body. B vitamins are required for
the functioning of the immune system, digestive system, brain,
nervous and circulatory systems, the heart and other muscles,
and for the production of new blood cells. They keep the hair,
skin, eyes, mouth, and liver healthy and are important in the
metabolism of carbohydrates, fats, and proteins in the body.
Because they are water-soluble, they are not stored in the body.
Most vegetables contain small quantities of the B vitamins.

While the B-group vitamins work together to a certain
extent, they also each have specific roles to play in the
functioning of the body.

VITAMIN B₅
(PANTOTHENIC ACID)

Good sources
widely found, especially whole-grain products and eggs

This is required for many metabolic reactions within the body and for the synthesis of glucose and fatty acids.

VITAMIN B₆

Vitamin B₆ works best in conjunction with vitamin B₂ and magnesium. It is needed to metabolize protein and for the formation of the protein hemoglobin in red blood cells. Extra amounts of this vitamin are needed by women who are pregnant or who are taking birth control pills. High alcohol consumption also increases the body's need for B₆. Deficiency can cause anemia, fatigue, and depression.

Good sources
cheese, eggs, whole-grain bread and cereals, nuts, and many vegetables

Eggs and dairy products are a major source of vitamin B₆. Vegans should therefore make sure that they take a supplement of this vitamin.

VITAMIN B₁₂

Necessary for the formation of blood cells and nerves, vitamin B₁₂ is generally found in animal products (including dairy products) although there can be traces in some sea vegetables. Some soy products are fortified with B₁₂. Those on a vegan diet (see page 29) must take particular care to get this vitamin, usually in a supplement form. Deficiency can result in pernicious anemia. Low intake combined with low levels of B₆ and folate (see above) have been linked to increased risk of coronary heart disease.

Dairy products provide vitamin B₁₂.

Good sources
dairy products, yeast extract, fortified soy products

FOLATE *(FOLIC ACID)*

Folate is vital for the formation of new cells and therefore for the growth of the baby in the uterus and normal development in children. Women wishing to conceive and those in the early stages of pregnancy should make sure they have adequate quantities of this vitamin since it can help prevent defects, such as spina bifida and hydrocephalus.

Good sources
leafy greens, oranges, whole-wheat bread, whole grains, legumes, and nuts

VITAMIN C *(ASCORBIC ACID)*

Vitamin C is necessary for healthy connective tissues, such as bone cartilage and collagen. It promotes the healing of wounds, increases the absorption of iron, helps the body fight infection, and aids recovery after illness. It is an important antioxidant (see page 15). A deficiency of vitamin C may lead to a lowering of resistance to infection and slowing down of the healing process.

Good sources
citrus fruits, soft fruits (such as black currants and strawberries), kiwi fruits, guavas, potatoes, greens, bell peppers, leeks, and bean sprouts

VITAMIN D

Good sources
dairy products and fortified margarines. It is also formed by the action of sunlight on oils in the skin. Getting out for an hour or so on a sunny day should yield a reasonable amount

Vitamin D is essential for absorbing calcium and phosphorus and making sure of sound formation of bones and teeth. It is especially important for pregnant women and growing children. Deficiency can lead to rickets in children and weakened or porous bones in adults.

VITAMIN E

Good sources
vegetable oils, nuts, avocados, asparagus, whole grains, wheat germ

An antioxidant, vitamin E helps to protect cell membranes from oxidation. It can help prevent the blocking-up of artery walls, and thus protect against heart disease. It also helps boost the immune system, prevents muscle inflammation, and may help reduce symptoms of arthritis.

VITAMIN K

The main function of this vitamin is to aid blood clotting and it is essential for the formation of protein.

Good sources
widely found, particularly dark green vegetables, cereals, and sea vegetables

Minerals

There are a number of minerals in the body, of which about 20 are known or suspected to be essential. Some minerals, such as calcium or sodium, are needed in quite large quantities—more than 100mg per day. Other minerals, for which less than 100mg are needed each day, are referred to as trace elements. They are just as vital even though they are needed in only small quantities.

Minerals have several functions. They are part of the structural framework of the body, as components of bones and teeth; they enable muscles to contract and relax, and impulses to be transmitted through the nerves. In the form of soluble salts, they regulate the composition of body fluids. Minerals also enable many chemical reactions to take place, such as the breaking down and utilization of food.

Plants are the main sources of minerals, which they absorb from the soil. A varied diet of wholesome foods, fresh fruit, vegetables, and nuts should provide an ample supply of all the essential elements. Bear in mind that your need for minerals can be affected by your lifestyle. Living in a polluted area or taking drugs, alcohol, or caffeine alters your mineral requirements. Mineral absorption can also vary according to the presence of certain vitamins. For example, vitamin C enhances the absorption of iron.

CALCIUM

A dietary deficiency of calcium, at any stage in life, may increase the risk of developing osteoporosis. Calcium is also essential for nerve function, for blood clotting, for maintenance of cell membranes, and for the functioning of muscles. Calcium works closely in the body with magnesium and phosphorus.

Both vitamin D and the essential fatty acids (EFAs) can help the absorption of calcium. Equally, certain elements in foods inhibit the process, for example insoluble fiber in whole-wheat bread or brown rice, tannin found in tea, and oxalic acid found in some green vegetables and chocolate. It is therefore vital to eat plenty of calcium-rich foods from a variety of different sources. A deficiency is shown by stunted growth and rickets in young children and by osteoporosis, particularly in postmenopausal women.

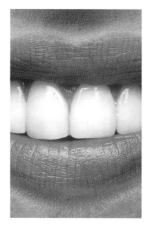

Calcium is a major component of bones and teeth. Deficiency at any stage in life may increase the risk of osteoporosis.

Good sources
dairy products (such as cheese, milk, yogurt), bean curd, nuts and seeds (such as sunflower or sesame seeds), leafy greens, and calcium-enriched soy milks

CHLORINE

Chlorine works in partnership with sodium. It helps remove excess sodium so may be effective in preventing high blood pressure. It is also needed for digesting proteins.

Good sources
widely found. (Most adults consume too much in the form of salt—sodium chloride.)

MAGNESIUM

Magnesium is necessary for metabolizing calcium and potassium. It is involved in energy supply, correct functioning of the nervous system, and helping to regulate temperature. It works with calcium to form an integral part of bones and teeth. Low levels may be associated with increased risk of heart disease. A deficiency is shown by muscle weakness, loss of appetite, and tiredness.

Good sources
nuts, cereals, green vegetables, seaweed, dairy products, soybeans

A varied diet of fruit, nuts, greens, and cereals provides a good supply of minerals.

PHOSPHORUS

Vital for bones and teeth, phosphorus is also important for the release of energy, working in conjunction with calcium. Deficiency is rare.

Good sources
dairy products, eggs, whole-wheat bread, lentils, and yeast extract

Good sources
leafy greens, mushrooms, potatoes, bananas, and dried fruit

POTASSIUM

Potassium is needed for healthy cell function, and also works with sodium in regulating bodily fluids. Diets high in potassium and low in sodium are linked with lower risk of high blood pressure and stroke.

SODIUM

Found mainly in the blood and in fluids surrounding cells, sodium works with potassium to maintain a constant balance of bodily fluids. Deficiency is rare but excessive sodium has been linked to a susceptibility to hypertension.

Good sources
the most common source of sodium is salt

IRON

Iron is necessary for the formation of hemoglobin, which carries oxygen in the blood. Iron can also increase resistance to infection, as well as improving rates of healing.

Although the best source of iron is meat, it is possible to get adequate iron on a vegetarian diet, even though the type of iron found in plants is not so easily absorbed. Vitamin C enhances iron absorption and a trace of copper is needed for the correct functioning of iron in the body. Tannin-containing drinks, such as tea, decrease absorption.

Iron deficiency results in anemia, the symptoms of which include tiredness, breathlessness, and irritability. Women in particular must have adequate supplies to counteract the effect of menstruation.

Dried fruits are good sources of iron. More will be absorbed if eaten in conjunction with food containing vitamin C.

Good sources
leafy greens, legumes (particularly lentils), bean curd, grains (such as wheat and millet), dried fruits (such as apricots and raisins), unsweetened cocoa powder, pumpkin seeds, and nuts

MANGANESE

Manganese is a component of many enzyme systems and important in reproduction. Deficiency is rare.

Good sources
tea, nuts, grains, legumes, and leafy greens

MOLYBDENUM

This helps the functioning of iron in the body and works with fluoride.

Good sources
cereals, legumes, and greens

SELENIUM

Part of the body's defense mechanisms, selenium works with vitamin E as an antioxidant. It helps preserve the structure of membranes and maintain their proper functioning.

Good sources
cereals (especially wheat), cheese, eggs, walnuts, Brazil nuts

ZINC

Zinc is essential for growth, the synthesis of proteins, wound healing, development of reproductive organs, the maintenance of skin, hair, nails, and mucous membranes, and the growth of the fetus.

Good sources
dairy products, eggs, whole grains, pumpkin seeds, legumes

TRACE ELEMENTS

The following minerals are known as trace elements and are required in very small quantities.

CHROMIUM
This is needed for normal metabolism of glucose, fatty acids, insulin, and muscle growth.
Good sources whole-wheat bread, wheat germ, cheese

COPPER
Copper is needed for healthy functioning of many enzymes in the liver, brain, and muscles.
Good sources nuts, dried tree fruit, legumes, greens

IODINE
Very small quantities of iodine are needed for the correct functioning of the thyroid gland.
Good sources kelp and other seaweeds, iodized salt

LIQUIDS

Our bodies are made up of about two-thirds water. Water is continually lost through sweat and waste products so it is vital to drink plenty of fluids, preferably in the form of water.

Water does not contain any nutrients but its purpose is to keep the body hydrated. It helps the body eliminate toxins through waste matter. You should aim to drink between 5 and 10 cups/2 and 4 pints (1 and 2 liters) of pure water a day.

A healthy diet

In the developed world access to foods has improved and conditions caused by dietary deficiency, such as scurvy or rickets, are now rare. However, the growing consumption of processed and packaged foods, together with a change in eating patterns from regular meals to snacking, has led to an increase in a whole host of ailments associated with a poor diet. A modern definition of a poor diet is one that is low in antioxidant vitamins, low in fiber, and high in saturated fats.

Foods such as rice, featured in this **Wild Rice with Hazelnuts, Carrots, and Artichokes** supper (see page 236), are filling but not fattening.

Four Guidelines for a Healthy Diet

We have looked at the individual nutrients and their functions; it is now time to put the jigsaw puzzle together and look broadly at how to achieve a healthy, balanced diet that is also vegetarian. The most important point to remember is that it is vital to eat a wide range of foods, since no single food provides all the nutrients required for the body to remain healthy and function properly. Over and above that, there are four guidelines for a healthy diet. The good news for vegetarians is that all these guidelines fit very comfortably with a vegetarian diet.

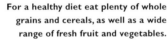

For a healthy diet eat plenty of whole grains and cereals, as well as a wide range of fresh fruit and vegetables.

1 Eat plenty of foods rich in starch and fiber
Foods such as brown rice, whole-wheat bread, and potatoes are filling but not fattening. They are rich in useful nutrients, including vitamins, minerals, and dietary fiber.

2 Eat plenty of fresh fruit and vegetables These provide you with essential vitamins and minerals. There is mounting evidence to show that the biologically active substances in this food group, for example antioxidants, may combat cancer and reduce the likelihood of developing chronic diseases, such as coronary heart disease. Try to have at least five portions per day—not including potatoes—a portion being an apple or a roughly equivalent weight of 4–5 ounces (125–150g) in other fruit or vegetables.

3 Do not eat too many foods that contain a high proportion of fat This is one of the most important recommendations for vegetarians and would-be vegetarians. Dairy products, which are a familiar source of protein, are also high in fat. New vegetarians should be wary of cutting out meat, only to replace it with dairy products. It is important to source your protein and calcium from other food groups, such as beans, nuts, and seeds, in order to have a balanced healthy diet. Nuts and seeds do contain fat but it is largely unsaturated.

4 Do not eat too many sugary foods
Sugar is all calories and no nutrients. Sugary foods are easy to eat—and to overeat. Consumption of sugar is also linked to tooth decay since the bacteria on teeth use sugar to make the acid that causes decay.

Conclusion

To sum up, the best way to be both healthy and vegetarian is to eat plenty of whole foods, such as whole-wheat bread and brown rice; eat a wide variety of fresh fruit and vegetables; and include some dairy products but look broadly for other sources of protein and calcium. Remember, healthy eating is not incompatible with pleasurable eating.

Life cycle and different dietary needs

The following pages look at how our nutritional needs change throughout our lives. Although the principles for a healthy diet remain broadly the same at each stage, there are some extra factors to consider. This section begins with a look at pregnancy, including the months prior to conception, and then takes you through nutritional requirements during weaning, childhood, and adolescence. It is just as important to be nutritionally aware in adulthood, and so nutritional pointers for all age groups are also given.

Pregnancy

Good diet and health are vital during pregnancy for both the mother and the growing baby. However, the months prior to pregnancy are also important and so, if you are thinking about becoming pregnant, it is a good idea to review your diet and increase nutrients as necessary. There is no reason to suggest that a diet free from meat or fish is going to leave you short of any nutrients. In fact, vegetarian foods are good sources of many of the vital nutrients needed at this time.

Pre-pregnancy Follow these general guidelines for good health: eat plenty of unrefined carbohydrates, such as grains and potatoes; reduce your intake of saturated fats but make sure you eat nuts and seeds to give you essential fatty acids; eat a good supply of fresh fruit and vegetables, in particular, foods to give you a good supply of folate (see page 17). This plays a vital role in protecting against birth defects such as spina bifida.

During pregnancy In addition to the basic requirements set by the broad dietary guidelines, the need for certain nutrients increases. Protein is required for the growth of new tissue, and iron is needed for the production of hemoglobin in

both the mother's and the baby's red blood cells (remember that vitamin C helps iron absorption). Calcium is essential for mineralization of the baby's bone structure—most is required during the last three months of pregnancy. B vitamins, which are used in energy production, are also needed, as well as continuing good supplies of folate. Zinc is important for the development of the fetus.

Food safety is an issue during pregnancy. Don't drink unpasteurized milk; do not eat soft ripened cheese, such as Brie or Camembert, and only eat eggs that are thoroughly cooked.

While your intentions to follow a good diet during pregnancy may be good, you may be affected by morning sickness. This usually occurs only in the first few months. Skipping meals can make morning sickness worse, so try to eat little and often. When you do eat, make sure it is a healthy and nutritious food.

Stews, such as this nutritious Sweet Potato Stew (see page 241), are easy to make and freeze for days when you don't feel like cooking.

Post-pregnancy If you are breast-feeding your baby, you will need about 500 extra calories a day because you are really feeding two. Try to eat nutrient-rich foods, following the broad dietary guidelines, and remember that this is not a time to diet.

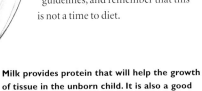

Milk provides protein that will help the growth of tissue in the unborn child. It is also a good source of calcium, which is needed for the baby's bone structure.

Babies and Toddlers

Breast milk or special infant formula contains all a baby needs in the first months of life. For vegan babies or those allergic to dairy products and who are not being breast-fed, a nondairy formula based on soy is available.

Weaning starts at around 4 months. This is an average and much depends on the size of the baby to determine readiness for solid food. First weaning foods are usually vegetarian, for example rice (specially processed for babies), and fruit and vegetable purées, such as carrot, banana, apple, and avocado.

Wheat and wheat products should be avoided for the first 6–9 months in case there is an allergy to gluten. Eggs, too, can cause allergies and are best avoided for the first 6–9 months. Do not add salt or sugar to babies' food. Nuts may cause allergies. Even if your baby does not have an allergy, do not give pieces of nut because the baby can choke. Other foods that can cause allergic reactions, even after 6 months, include citrus fruits, strawberries, and egg white.

Children

Many children do not want to eat meat for a variety of reasons and there is no reason for a child brought up on a good vegetarian diet to be deficient nutritionally. Growing children need plenty of protein and calcium; their need for other nutrients is similar to adults but in smaller quantities. Young children are often very active and require

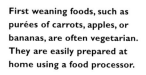

First weaning foods, such as purées of carrots, apples, or bananas, are often vegetarian. They are easily prepared at home using a food processor.

concentrated sources of energy and a whole-food-based vegetarian diet can be bulky in relation to its energy content. To counteract this, if your child has a small appetite, you can vary the types of cereals given, occasionally choosing white rice instead of brown for example. If your child has a high percentage of his or her food as milk, use whole milk rather than skim or low-fat—a low-fat diet may provide too little energy for a small child who cannot eat a bulky diet.

Make sure your child eats a good selection from all the food groups. Legumes, nuts and seeds, and grains, as well as some dairy products will make sure of a good supply of protein, as well as essential fatty acids. Simple food combinations, such as pasta with cheese sauce and beans on toast, appeal to children and are nutritious. Try to make sure children have five portions of fresh fruit and vegetables a day.

Children under three should not be given whole or coarsely chopped nuts because they are a choking hazard.

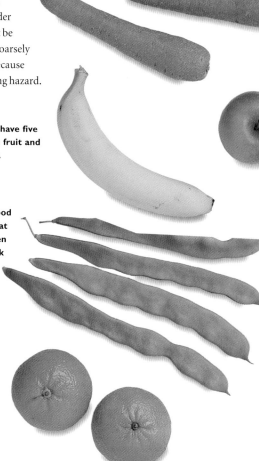

Children should have five portions of fresh fruit and vegetables a day.

Lots of simple food combinations that appeal to children are quick to cook and nutritious. Beans on toast is a classic example.

Adolescence

Adolescence is an important growth period. As well as needing protein, carbohydrates, and fats, youngsters in this age group also need to increase their intake of calcium, iron, zinc, and magnesium. For girls particularly, calcium is accumulated in the bones during the teenage years—adequate storage then can help prevent the onset of osteoporosis later in life. A good supply of iron is also needed at this stage, especially for girls as they begin menstruation.

Adolescence is also a time when eating patterns may become haphazard as teenagers become more independent. If meals are skipped and there is more snacking, it is important to try and make sure that whatever food is eaten, it is nutrient rich. Some teenagers choose to become vegetarian as a way to assert independence, and encouraging some self-sufficiency when it comes to cooking is a positive parental response. There are lots of basic foods, such as pasta and grains, that are not difficult to cook. This may be a good opportunity for your teenager to get involved in the kitchen.

Girls in particular may be attracted to a vegetarian diet as a way of slimming. In general, this is nothing to worry about as long as the food they eat is varied and well balanced. Sometimes this change may be the first step in rejecting food on a wider basis, so it is important to look out for signs of eating disorders. Nine out of 10 sufferers of anorexia are women and for many this condition starts in the teenage years.

Adulthood

For adults who are exclusively vegetarian, the broad guidelines for healthy eating outlined on page 20 should be followed within the parameters of a vegetarian diet. A vegetarian diet is as suitable for men as for women, even though their demand for nutrients, except iron, is slightly greater.

There are lots of basic foods that are not hard for youngsters to cook such as this **Baked Pasta Gratin with Fresh Corn** (see page 203).

Old Age

As we get older, we need fewer calories but we still need protein for repair of cells and tissues. It is just as important at this stage to maintain a good supply of vitamins and minerals. These boost general health as well as the ability to fight infection. If you are house-bound you may need to increase your intake of vitamin D (see page 17 for good sources). However, sitting at an open window may help the natural production of vitamin D.

If raw food is harder to eat, cook vegetables and fruit in the most nutritious way or make more use of purées by serving soup.

Many older people drink less and dehydration can become a problem, with side effects such as constipation. Try to drink plenty of liquids, especially water, fruit juices, and drinks without caffeine. The recommended amount is at least eight large cups of liquid daily.

Yogurt is a good source of calcium, which needs to accumulate in the bones in the teenage years.

Eggs are a useful source of protein and iron.

During adolescence, an important growth period, youngsters should make sure they are getting adequate calcium from nuts and seeds and plenty of iron from greens.

It is vital to drink plenty of liquids to prevent conditions such as constipation.

Lifestyle and nutritional needs

Apart from age and sex, other factors influence your nutritional needs. Your lifestyle plays a significant role and dietary requirements vary according to whether you participate in sport, have a hectic business life, or have to deal with stress. Here are recommendations to make sure that you are aware of how to deal with specific dietary needs you may have.

If you engage in a lot of exercise, you may need to boost your carbohydrate consumption, as well as increase your fluid intake.

Sport

Exercise, even in moderate levels, alters your nutritional needs. The more you train, the more nutrients you need to maintain a good level of red blood cells so that oxygen is supplied during exercise. You also need calories to maintain muscle bulk.

Vegetarians who participate seriously in sport should consider the following:

• Increase complex carbohydrates, such as cereals, root vegetables, and fruits. These foods also contain the sort of carbohydrate that converts quickly to blood glucose.

• Maintain a good level of fluid intake, before and after exercising and during if appropriate.

• Fat is not the best form of energy since the body takes time to mobilize and break down fatty acids. To do this a large supply of dietary carbohydrate is needed. Use monounsaturated fats, such as olive oil, and nuts and seeds for their essential fatty acids.

STRESS

Stress is a term used to describe the symptoms produced by our response to pressure. These symptoms result from high levels of adrenaline, a hormone secreted in response to stressful situations.

There are many ways to deal with stress that are not diet related, such as taking exercise and learning to relax. It is also important to become aware of the situations that cause you stress and find ways to avoid them or lessen their impact.

Vitamin C and the B-group vitamins are depleted under stress. The B vitamins are further depleted by alcohol and sugary foods, which may seem comforting in times of stress. Maintain a good intake of foods rich in B vitamins, such as whole grains. Limit caffeine drinks, such as tea and coffee; try herbal teas instead. Eat plenty of fresh fruit and raw vegetables.

Business Life: Eating Out and Travel

Long hours and business travel make it more difficult to adhere to guidelines for a healthy diet, especially for anyone on a vegetarian diet. Modern working patterns are also often stressful, putting the body under pressure and raising nutritional demands.

It can be difficult to find wholesome food when away from home. Often, airline food has been standing around or is reheated, depleting the nutrients further. Many airlines do offer vegetarian fare; and it is sometimes better to ask for a dairy-free (vegan) meal, which offers a less fatty, grain or legume main course and fresh fruit instead of a sickly sweet dessert. Food offered on railroads or at roadside restaurants varies greatly from one country to another.

In restaurants where there is no obviously suitable main course, consider ordering several vegetable side dishes and salads instead. Try to eat whole-wheat bread instead of white; look for appetizers, such as melon or grapefruit, to enjoy as desserts.

When traveling it is possible to maintain a regular supply of fresh fruit in your diet, even if this does mean going shopping. On long trips away from home it is worth taking with you a few foods to supplement your diet, such as granola or nuts and seeds.

When traveling, it is not always possible to get wholesome food. Fresh fruit should be fairly easy to find and will provide you with useful vitamins and fiber.

Drinking Habits

Whether you are very active or have a generally sedentary lifestyle, it is important to drink plenty of fluid. If you are participating in serious sports or doing a good deal of traveling, it is even more crucial to keep up your fluid intake. Water is the best choice, and there is more information on how much to drink and the benefits on page 19. Stimulants, such as caffeine, and alcohol have both benefits and drawbacks. The effect on your health is examined here with suggestions for alternatives.

Caffeine In small quantities caffeine, which is a stimulant, can get you up and going in the morning or give you a useful boost when you are flagging halfway through the day. However, in larger quantities, caffeine can affect your sleep, digestion, and nervous system. If you have feelings of anxiety, unexplained headaches, or stomach upsets, it is probably worth reducing your caffeine intake. Real coffee has more caffeine than instant coffee and tea. Tea also contains tannin, a substance that can inhibit iron absorption.

To avoid caffeine, decaffeinated coffee is not always an ideal solution, because it sometimes contains chemicals that are used in the decaffeinating process. There are caffeine-free substitutes made from grains, such as barley, but don't expect these to taste like real coffee. Herbal infusions make good hot drinks and some are believed to have additional properties, such as aiding digestion (peppermint), helping relaxation (camomile), and enhancing vitamin C (rosehip). These substitutes may seem insipid at first. They are worth pursuing, however, and within a few days your taste buds will start to appreciate their more subtle quality and the variety of flavors they offer.

Alcohol There is debate as to how alcohol fits in with a healthy diet. Small quantities of alcohol can be useful for relaxation and are also thought to help reduce the risk of heart disease. Red wine is the most beneficial to health, particularly if drunk in moderation with meals. Red wine (and red grape juice) contain unusual antioxidants (flavonoids), which may help reduce the risk of thrombosis and deposits building up inside the arteries. However, these benefits should be seen in a broader context. Alcohol is high in calories and excessive alcohol can cause serious damage to health.

Birth Control Pills

Taking birth control pills for long periods may reduce levels of vitamin B_6, folate, and zinc. If this applies to you, make sure that you include plenty of foods rich in these nutrients in your diet.

Convalescence

If you have been ill or are recovering from surgery, your appetite may be reduced. What you do eat should be nutrient rich. It is often better to have "food" in liquid form and to try to eat little and often. Make fruit or vegetable drinks from juices—freshly extracted if possible—and serve them plain or mixed with yogurt. Use a blender or a food processor to make a good variety of soup-like meals that are easy to digest.

It is worth adding small quantities of wheat germ to savory or sweet meals since this is a light food but very rich in B vitamins and protein, which will help recovery.

Blenders and food processors can be used to make a good variety of easily digestible purées and soups. Food in liquid form is especially good during convalescence.

Red wine, which contains rare antioxidants, may have some health benefits if drunk in moderation.

25

Eat well, stay well

Generally, in the developed world we are sufficiently well nourished, and many serious infectious diseases are a thing of the past. There are, however, several chronic conditions that are thought to be linked to diet. Many of these conditions are more evident in adulthood—some are general, some affect one sex more than another, and some are exclusive to one sex. Although this is not a medical book as such, it is worth looking briefly at some of the more common conditions, the part that nutrients have to play, and the benefits of a vegetarian diet.

Coronary Heart Disease

Coronary heart disease is one of the biggest killers in the Western world, accounting for at least one-third of all male deaths. Dietary advice for reducing the risk of coronary heart disease includes avoiding nutrient-poor processed food and eating whole foods instead; and increasing intake of complex carbohydrates, such as whole-wheat bread and pasta, and brown rice. These foods should account for the bulk of daily calories. In addition, increase the intake of fresh fruit and vegetables, especially raw vegetables. Try to eat roughly 1 pound (500g) per day.

Decrease the total amount of fats eaten. What fat is used should be monounsaturated or polyunsaturated. Switch to skim or low-fat milk. Use olive oil in cooking and for salad dressings. Eat nuts and seeds since these contain essential fatty acids, which have beneficial effects on blood cholesterol. Reduce salt and sugar intake.

Nuts and seeds, such as pumpkin seeds, contain essential fatty acids (EFAs), which may have beneficial effects on the level of cholesterol in the blood.

Starting the day with a good breakfast based on cereal may make all the difference. Complex carbohydrates fill you up and keep you satisfied, meaning there is less room for nutrient-poor, high-fat foods such as candies and cookies.

High Blood Pressure

High blood pressure is a chronic condition that also affects more men than women. Particular advice for this condition is to cut back on salt consumption, remembering that a much higher percentage of salts comes from processed and packaged food than is added in home cooking or at the table.

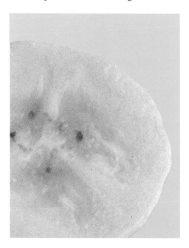

Eat potassium-rich foods, such as all fruit, especially bananas, dried apricots, and vegetables including potatoes, mushrooms, and spinach.

Bananas are rich in potassium. This mineral may help counterbalance a high-sodium diet.

Cancer

Cancer, in all its diverse forms, is one of the most common causes of death affecting men and women. While many factors play a part, medical practitioners do recommend changes in diet as one way of reducing the risk of developing some forms of cancer.

Try to eat more whole-grain cereals and legumes and eat at least five portions of fresh fruit and vegetables a day. Eat food that is high in fiber, and aim for an overall diet that is low in saturated fats.

Obesity

Obesity is recognized as a modern lifestyle problem. Our tendency to become overweight is partly due to the number of high-calorie and rich snacks available, and also due to the fact that many jobs are now sedentary and a vast percentage of adults do not take exercise.

Being overweight makes you more prone to numerous problems—obvious complaints, such as breathlessness, back pain, and heartburn. It also makes you more susceptible to conditions such as high blood pressure, poor circulation, reproductive problems, or certain cancers.

There are many approaches to slimming and the key to success is to find a diet that suits you. A vegetarian diet based around dairy products will not be slimming, nor particularly healthy. Whole-wheat breads and brown rice may seem the antithesis of slimming food but in fact these do not have many calories and will keep you satisfied for a long period. The trick is not to increase calories by smothering these products with butter or rich sauces.

For vegetarians trying to lose weight, try to cut down on fatty foods—the emphasis is on cutting down rather than cutting out. Eat dairy products in moderation, switching to low-fat cheese and skim milk. Use nuts and seeds sparingly. Choose fresh fruit and vegetables as snacks rather than cakes or cookies, and eat complex carbohydrates, such as whole-wheat bread, whole-wheat pasta, and brown rice. Have a nourishing breakfast to sustain you through to lunch, thus eliminating mid-morning nibbles, and take exercise.

Premenstrual Tension

This condition affects many women and the symptoms may be physical or psychological. The problems generally occur in the second half of the cycle when a drop in the level of hormones occurs. Although evidence remains inconclusive, many women feel their well-being is improved by additional vitamin B_6. It is important not to have excessive quantities of this vitamin, however; it may be enough just to include foods rich in B_6 in your regular diet, rather than taking a supplement.

Osteoporosis

This is a degenerative age-related condition affecting both men and women, which begins around the age of 35 but accelerates in women after menopause. It is vital to lay down good supplies of calcium in the teenage years and 20s. A diet that is rich in calcium throughout adult life may slow down the progress of this condition. Doing weight-bearing exercise, such as walking, running, and jumping, during your teens and 20s is also important.

In addition to a healthy diet, enjoying active, healthy leisure pursuits, such as hiking, as well as taking some exercise on a daily basis, will help you to control your weight.

Cheese is an excellent source of calcium. Adequate supplies of this mineral throughout adult life may help to prevent the onset of osteoporosis.

Food Allergies

An allergy is an overaggressive response to a substance by the body's immune system. An allergic reaction may produce a whole range of symptoms, from diarrhea or vomiting to skin rashes and eczema.

Some allergic reactions are so severe as to be life-threatening. This is called anaphylactic shock and can be set off in some instances by having the most casual contact with the allergen. Symptoms include breathing difficulties (because the throat swells), stomach cramps, vomiting, and rashes. For vegetarians, the most common foods to cause this type of reaction are peanuts, other nuts and seeds, and eggs.

Although there is evidence that the tendency to be allergic runs in families, it also seems that food allergies are on the increase. As yet, there is no answer as to why some people are allergic and others are not. Many food allergies do occur in childhood and are outgrown. Some adverse reactions to food are not allergic reactions but a form of food intolerance. It is very hard for a lay person to distinguish between the two.

The most common ingredients to cause allergic reactions or food intolerance are listed below. Remember these may appear in many different foods and are not always readily apparent. For example, wheat is found in pasta and pastry products, and sesame seeds in hummus and burger buns; milk can be present in cereals, cookies, and sauces. It is therefore vital to check labels on food packaging.

Grains and gluten Gluten is a protein found in wheat, rye, barley, and oats, and any foods that contain these ingredients, such as pastry, pasta, or cookies. However, people can be allergic to wheat without necessarily being allergic to gluten.

Milk and dairy products Lactose intolerance is where the sufferer is deficient in the enzyme lactase, which breaks down the lactose found in milk. If lactose is not broken down, it goes into the intestines, causing bloating and diarrhea. Lactose intolerance can sometimes be just a childhood condition and is often outgrown. Some people who can't tolerate cow's milk are able to have goat's milk products.

If you have a wheat or gluten allergy, look for wheat-free breads and pasta made from corn as an alternative.

Eggs Egg white may cause allergic reactions. This is common in preschoolers and can be outgrown.

Nuts and seeds Allergy to peanuts is the most common nut allergy and can be very severe. Peanuts are also referred to as groundnuts, so it is vital to avoid groundnut oil. Other common nut allergens are Brazil nuts, cashew nuts, and walnuts. Sesame seeds can cause allergic reactions, too.

Fermented soy products Intolerance to such foods as miso and shoyu may occur because these products contain yeast or wheat.

A childhood allergy to strawberries may be outgrown. Oranges may also trigger an allergic reaction.

Strawberries and oranges Strawberries can cause a rash. This is often common in childhood and can be outgrown. Oranges have sometimes been found to be a trigger for migraine (as have eggs and chocolate).

Gluten is a protein found in the whole-wheat grain and also in all wheat-based products such as pasta and flour.

Low Sperm Count

Diet is thought to be one of the many factors that will lower sperm count and affect fertility. Research findings have traced a link between low sperm count and diet by showing that 40 percent of sperm damage is due to the harmful effects of free radicals. Make sure you have adequate amounts of antioxidants to absorb free radicals (see page 15).

Different approaches to diet

While a vegetarian diet is strictly defined as being free from meat or fish, there are several different approaches to vegetarian food, which can influence the way that you choose and cook your food. The three most common regimes are vegan, whole-food, and raw food, all of which are outlined here.

Vegan Diet

A vegan eats no animal products at all, nor anything derived from or produced by living creatures, so this diet excludes egg, dairy products, and honey. Those contemplating a vegetarian diet may feel that a vegan diet is extremely restricted. However, thanks to the accessibility of an enormous choice of nuts, grains, fruit, and vegetables, as well as an increasingly imaginative range of soy products, there are a good number of vegan meals possible.

From a nutritional point of view, the consumption of calories on a vegan diet is generally lower. It is also important for vegans to check they are getting vitamins and minerals such as calcium and B_{12}, which are more usually found in dairy products. For alternative sources see pages 17 and 18.

Vegan diets are usually rich in vitamin C and beta-carotene as well as being low in saturated fats and high in complex carbohydrates and fiber. If well balanced and well planned, a vegan diet can amply provide all nutrients for a healthy life.

A healthy vegetarian diet should include a good range of whole-food ingredients such as whole-wheat bread and brown rice. Whole foods are foods that have not been refined or processed in any way.

Whole-Food Diet

Whole foods are traditionally defined as foods that have nothing added and nothing taken away.

Giant Mushrooms Stuffed with Wild Rice and Roasted Onions (see page 173) is one of the recipes suitable for vegans in this book.

This is relevant to vegetarians since many whole foods, for example brown rice and whole-wheat bread, are nutrient rich, whereas their refined counterparts, although suitable for vegetarians, are not of such high nutritional value.

A healthy vegetarian diet should include a good percentage of whole foods, although it needn't necessarily exclude refined ingredients such as white flour or white rice.

Raw-Food Diet

Recognizing the benefits of raw food is not a recent fad. For over 100 years advocates of raw-food diets have researched the possible benefits of eating uncooked food. Arthritis, diabetes, and some forms of cancer are among the serious conditions and diseases that may be helped by a diet high in raw foods. Raw foods are thought to help eliminate toxins because they contain more fiber, can restore a balanced sodium/potassium level, help maintain balance between acidity and alkalinity, and help oxygenation of cells.

Choosing your food

Turning to a vegetarian diet may make you think more carefully about the food you are eating, its source, and its quality. Modern trends in food production have a great influence on our diet. It is useful to be aware of some of these issues so that you can make an informed choice about the best food for yourself and your family, within your lifestyle.

Some foods are now genetically altered to give enhanced resistance to disease, but the long-term effects of this process are not yet fully understood.

Organic Food

In many parts of the world over the past 50 years, farming has undergone huge changes, thanks to the development of machinery, pesticides, and chemical fertilizers. While these developments have positive aspects, such as the eradication of pests or increased yields, there are negative factors, too, such as the worrying traces of chemicals

While research on whether organic food is healthier is not conclusive, it is thought that organic farming is beneficial to the environment.

left behind in the soil and surface water and therefore ultimately in our food. There is concern that high levels of chemical residues in our food may add to the risk of cancer. Vegetables, fruit, and cereals are all crops at risk. As yet, research is inconclusive as to whether organic food is healthier, and there are arguments on both sides. However, you may well be persuaded that buying organic food is a way of limiting exposure to chemical residues.

What is more conclusive is the evidence of the value of organic farming in environmental terms. Organic farmers concentrate on conserving and enhancing the fertility of the soil by natural methods, such as crop rotation. They try to preserve natural habitats and pay

attention to environmental concerns. Organic agriculture conforms to worldwide regulations and there are many certifying organizations. In the USA, large-scale farmers must have state or independent certification through agencies accredited by the U.S. Department of Agriculture. Accreditation of organic products in Canada is a voluntary decision. However, the federal government recently announced a new program that will help organizations that certify organic agriculture products to obtain Standards Council of Canada accreditation.

On the whole, organic food costs more to produce than food from conventional farming methods. Many buyers are prepared to pay more for organic produce. Organic fruit and vegetables tend to be smaller and less regular in shape, but they should still be fresh: never accept substandard produce, even if it is organically grown.

Junk food may look appealing but contains additives such as flavorings, and colorings that can cause behavioral changes.

Genetically Modified Organisms (GMOs)

Depending on where you live in the world, the introduction of genetically modified foodstuffs is either accepted as part of life or is a hotly debated subject. There are powerful lobbies on both sides.

Scientists can now identify individual genes that govern a desired trait. This gene can be extracted, copied, and inserted into another organism. This process is known as genetic modification, or modern biotechnology. As well as being used as a tool in plant breeding, genetic modification is also developing in the animal world as producers look to breed cattle with better milk yields and animals with enhanced resistance to disease.

Proponents of genetic modification argue that this process can be used to make crops disease resistant, increase the amount of protein in low-protein crops, alter the fat content of foods high in saturated fats, and add vitamins to fruit and vegetables. The opponents of genetic modification argue that we do not know enough about the effect of altering genes and what problems it may cause for future generations. There is also concern that copy genes could be accidentally transferred to another species with disastrous consequences, for example accidentally creating a herbicide-tolerant weed or "super weed." A genetic mistake is not an easy one to reverse and the effects on the body are not easy to predict. For example, a Brazil nut gene inserted into a soybean was found to trigger allergies in people who were not previously allergic to soy.

Vegetarians in particular sometimes object to copy genes from animals being used in plant production. They are also likely to be worried about the ethics of creating animals that give higher yields or can adapt to what would normally be alien environments.

The GMO debate is not yet concluded and if any of the above statements make you pause for thought, it is probably worth trying to keep abreast of developments.

Additives

Additives are mostly non-nutritive substances, which are added to food to prolong shelf life, assist in processing, or improve the flavor and appearance of food. They are used universally and it is very hard to avoid them. Additives include flavorings and flavor enhancers, stabilizers, thickeners, emulsifiers, colorings, and preservatives. Different countries have widely differing laws concerning the use of additives. The general rule is that they are supposed to be safe and not used in greater quantities than necessary. The long-term effects of many are not yet known and there is debate as to whether some additives can cause behavioral changes, particularly in children.

The best way to avoid additives is to eat as much fresh food as possible and buy unrefined products, such as whole-wheat pasta and brown rice. Avoid processed and packaged foods; look for additive-free foods.

IRRADIATION

This is a method of food preservation whereby foods are exposed to high levels of radiation. It was introduced as a solution to all our food safety problems because the irradiation process destroys harmful bacteria, such as salmonella. Concerns about irradiation, however, include worries about loss of nutrients during the process and that by making food last longer it will naturally lose more of its vitamins.

INGREDIENTS

This section of the book gives details of over 350 ingredients. For ease of reference, these ingredients are divided into the following food groups: vegetables, fruit, dairy products, grains, legumes, and nuts and seeds. Fruit and vegetables are further divided into family or climate groups, such as the onion family or root vegetables. Following these sections are details of other useful ingredients, such as herbs, spices, oils, and vinegars, as well as a range of further useful flavorings and sweeteners.

Each group of ingredients has a general introduction and nutritional notes, and individual ingredients within the group are also listed. There is advice on what to look for when choosing the product and how to store it, as well as notes on preparation and methods of cooking. I have also suggested ways to use the ingredients and how best to partner them with other ingredients and flavorings—I hope that experienced and enthusiastic cooks will feel confident in improvising new dishes based on these notes.

Vegetables

The success of vegetarian cookery has made everyone, from supermarket buyers to home cooks, realize that vegetables have been seriously undervalued. Vegetables are finally being appreciated for their color and flavor, and, most importantly, for their contribution to our health.

Increasing evidence has shown how vital vegetables are to our well-being. Nutritionists have found strong links between diets high in vegetables and a decreased risk of many life-threatening conditions. The World Health Organization recommends that everyone eats at least five portions of fresh vegetables and fruit per day, excluding potatoes. These recommendations come at a time when, thanks to improved transportation and storage facilities, an impressive range of vegetables is available from all over the world. Freshly picked produce may be available at farmers' markets or pick-your-own outlets.

Vegetables such as winter squash can be stored for several months.

Buying and Storing Vegetables

Buying produce that is fresh is all-important— look for plumpness and a good, bright color; avoid vegetables that are damaged, wrinkled, faded, or limp. This applies equally to organic vegetables. Nutrients are lost in storage, so use vegetables as soon as possible.

Most vegetables are best stored in cool, dark places, such as the refrigerator, since light and heat destroy crispness and nutrients, particularly vitamin B_2 and vitamin C. Green vegetables can lose up to 50 percent of their vitamin C in one day if kept at room temperature.

Nutritional Value

Vegetables are good sources of antioxidants (see page 15), which protect the body by blocking or suppressing harmful substances. The most common of these are bioflavonoids, carotenes, and vitamins C and E. Vegetables also provide important minerals, such as iron, calcium, and potassium and other vitamins, such as the B-group vitamins.

Green vegetables have magnesium, folate, vitamin C, and iron, while many orange-fleshed and red varieties of vegetables, such as bell peppers and tomatoes, supply carotenes. Peculiar to the onion family are sulfurous compounds, which may help protect against gastric cancers; root vegetables supply starch and natural sugars for energy. In addition, vegetables bring roughage into the diet because they are a good source of dietary fiber. They are also generally low in fat (but see avocado, page 43) and cholesterol and also low in calories.

Vegetables are a good source of minerals and vitamins. They also contain antioxidants that boost the body's defense system and help to prevent diseases.

Freezing

Most vegetables—apart from salad greens—freeze successfully. It is best to blanch them first as they will last longer. Prepare the vegetables by peeling, chopping, or slicing as necessary, then plunge into a saucepan of boiling water for 1 minute. Blanch a batch of about 1 pound (500g) at a time so that the water does not cool down too much. Drain the vegetables and plunge immediately into cold water to prevent further cooking. Drain again, using a salad spinner or dryer. Freeze the blanched vegetables on a tray in a single layer covered with a plastic bag. Pack in boxes or bags when frozen. Some varieties will keep for 12 months. Use the vegetables straight from frozen; do not thaw them first or the vitamin content will be significantly reduced.

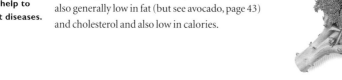

Most vegetables can be frozen successfully. These are good to keep on hand for emergency meals.

Preparation and Cooking

The most nutritious way to eat vegetables is in their raw state, because the more that a food is processed, the greater the loss of nutrients. Wash or scrub vegetables before use but do not soak them since water leaches out the vitamins and minerals. However, raw vegetables are not always appropriate—or even advisable in the case of potatoes— but there are ways of cooking that minimize nutrient loss.

Steaming Steamed vegetables tend to retain their crispness, as well as more of their nutrients, and steaming is an excellent way of preparing simple side dishes. Steamed vegetables cook in the vapor produced by simmering water. You can improvise a steamer by placing a colander over a saucepan, but a stainless steel basket, or a trivet with a lifting handle, or a stack of bamboo steamers are more efficient and easier to use.

Steaming minimizes nutritional loss. Nutrients do not leach out into the cooking water as they do during boiling.

COOK'S TIP

Keep the water at a simmer, not a rolling boil; do not sprinkle salt over the vegetables since this draws out their juices and may discolor them; make sure the saucepan does not boil dry

Sautéing (butter steaming) Sautéing is a similar method to stir-frying in that it is a quick cooking technique done on the stovetop. A sauté pan is wide with high sides so that you can stir the food around without it spilling. It should have a heavy base so that ingredients don't burn. To sauté, melt a small amount of butter or oil in the pan, quickly stir in the vegetable pieces, and sear them by cooking over high heat. Reduce the heat and add just enough liquid to prevent the vegetables from burning, then let them finish off cooking as the liquid evaporates.

Microwaving Vegetables cook very successfully in the microwave and retain their color, flavor, and nutrients since they are cooked quickly in a minimum amount of water. No special equipment is needed other than microwave-safe cookware.

COOK'S TIP

Cut vegetables uniformly so that they cook evenly; pierce the skin of whole vegetables so that they do not burst

Stir-frying This method is a fast, nutrient-friendly way to cook single vegetables or a colorful mixture of several varieties. Stir-frying is best done in a wok, a large rounded-base pan often made of thin metal so that it heats up very quickly and provides a large cooking surface.

A stir-fry is a light, colorful, and nutritious way to enjoy food.

COOK'S TIP

Use a small quantity (1–2 teaspoons) of oil; cut the vegetables into small, even pieces to be sure of quick cooking; prepare and cook the vegetables just before serving to retain their nutrients

Broiling This is a good method for cooking tender vegetables, such as tomatoes, bell peppers, and onions. Brush the vegetables first with oil if you like. Make sure the broiler is properly heated before cooking.

Roasting At one time it seemed that only potatoes were roasted, but now roasting is a popular and delicious way of cooking a variety of vegetables. The long cooking time guarantees the vegetables are really tender and the flavors can often be more intense. However, some vitamins will be lost during the cooking process.

Griddling (char broiling) This is a nutritious way of cooking vegetables and one that uses no oil at all or a minimum amount. The best equipment is a heavy, flat, ridged griddle pan, since the vegetables are seared on the ridges, creating an attractive pattern. A large, heavy nonstick skillet can also be used.

COOK'S TIP

Brush the pieces of vegetable with a little seasoned olive oil; arrange the pieces on the griddle pan in a single layer and don't pack them too closely together

Boiling Of the many different ways of cooking vegetables, boiling is one of the most popular. It is also one of the least desirable, since up to 45 percent of the minerals and 50 percent of vitamin C may be lost.

COOK'S TIP

Use a minimum amount of water and make sure it is boiling when you add the vegetables; never add baking soda since it would destroy vitamin C

Brassicas

This is a large family of vegetables, which includes cabbage, cauliflower, and broccoli, as well as Asian greens such as bok choy and mustard greens. They range in color from white through shades of green to purple. As a group, brassicas are extremely beneficial nutritionally and all brassicas are good sources of vitamin C and a variety of minerals.

PURPLE SPROUTING BROCCOLI AND GREEN BROCCOLI (*CALABRESE*)

Both are good partnered with dairy products; they have a strong enough flavor to counteract the blandness of a soufflé and look good in roulades. They also work well in stir-fries combined with red bell pepper and mushroom, or with pasta when mixed into sauces, or simply steamed and served on the side. Purple sprouting broccoli has a stronger flavor.

All brassicas are good sources of vitamin C and several valuable minerals.

Buying and storing Both should have firm, compact buds or flowers, which should be dark green or dark purple, depending on the variety. Do not buy or use any that shows signs of yellowing. Keep them in the refrigerator and use within a couple of days.

Preparation and cooking Pull off any coarse leaves and trim tough stems, peeling the skin back to the branches. Chop into flowerets. Steam, microwave or boil and be aware that the flower heads can break up if overcooked. Purple sprouting broccoli will leach out color as it cooks and may discolor a dish, its purple overwhelming the colors of other vegetables. If serving in a salad, chill rapidly under cold running water.

Chop broccoli into even-size flowerets. For the best results, steam, stir-fry, or microwave until crisp-tender.

Cabbage heads should have a bright color and feel heavy and solid. When cooking, discard the outer leathery leaves.

GREEN CABBAGE AND KALE

Although they look dissimilar, green cabbage and kale are in fact related. Green cabbage has a heart and kale has looser leaves. For cooking purposes they can be treated in roughly the same way. Cavolo nero (black cabbage) is a variety of kale.

Buying and storing Choose green cabbage and kale with outer leaves since these will help keep the main part of the vegetable fresh. There should be no hint of yellowing or limpness. Cabbage heads should be heavy and feel solid. Keep whole heads loosely wrapped in the refrigerator for several days or longer. Once cut, the vegetable will deteriorate more quickly and lose its nutritional value.

Preparation and cooking Discard leathery outer leaves or any that are damaged and cut out any tough ribs (kale) or core (cabbage). Chop the leaves as necessary and cook in boiling water—uncovered, or the color dulls—for a short time in order to maximize crispness and color. Green cabbage and kale can also be braised in a similar fashion to red cabbage, mixed with onions and spices (see page 37). They can also be stir-fried or sautéed. Young kale leaves can be used in salads; cabbage is good served with butter or cream, or used in small quantities in soups and casseroles. As a side vegetable, cabbage or kale are delicious just lightly steamed and then tossed in butter with plenty of black pepper.

WHITE CABBAGE (DUTCH)

This cabbage has a solid head with pale white to green tightly furled leaves. It is good in salads and forms the basis of traditional coleslaw, a shredded cabbage and carrot salad. There are numerous variations on that theme—the cabbage can be coated with yogurt or crème fraîche, or mixed with grated raw celery root, apple, dried fruits, or fresh herbs.

Buying and storing Select firm heads that feel heavy for their size; the outer leaves should look fresh. Cabbage should keep up to 1 week in the refrigerator, loosely wrapped in plastic.

White cabbage has a nutty flavor with a slightly peppery aftertaste. Great to eat raw, mixed with creamy dressings.

Preparation and cooking To shred cabbage by hand or in a food processor, cut it into fourths first and then remove the inner core if it looks woody. Cut each fourth into fine shreds using a large knife, or chop it into chunks to fit the feeder tube of a food processor and shred using the slicing blade. Finely shredded white cabbage makes a crunchy addition to stir-fries or can be sautéed. Whole leaves can be blanched and stuffed with a filling suitable for a grape leaf.

RED CABBAGE

Similar to white cabbage, this variety also has tight compact leaves and a firm heart. Red cabbage is delicious braised slowly; it can be eaten raw but it tends to be chewy and so is best used in small quantities and mixed with other ingredients, such as slices of orange, walnuts, and wild rice for a great cold weather salad.

Buying and storing The outer leaves may look leathery but they should not be wilted. The cabbage should feel solid. Uncut red cabbage will keep for 1–2 weeks in the refrigerator, loosely wrapped.

Red cabbage is a versatile vegetable that partners well with apple, dried fruits, and sweet spices such as cinnamon.

Preparation and cooking Shred red cabbage as for white cabbage (see opposite). To preserve the red color when cooking, add a little vinegar to the water. Braise slowly, with a minimum amount of water and mix with onion, grated apple, dried fruit, and sweet spices, such as cinnamon. Once cooked in this way, it freezes well. Alternatively, stir-fry or sauté.

BRUSSELS SPROUTS

These look like miniature cabbages but, unlike so many baby vegetables, they don't really seem to have caught on in the cookery scene other than as an accompaniment. They are much too strongly flavored to eat raw. Brussels sprouts are delicious lightly cooked, tossed in butter, and served with roasted almonds, whole or sliced; they also work well with chestnuts.

Buying and storing Choose small ones, smaller than the size of a whole walnut, because they will be sweeter and nuttier. Keep loosely wrapped in the refrigerator for 3–4 days.

Preparation and cooking Trim off outer leaves and woody stalk ends. Cutting a small cross in the stem helps them to cook more quickly. It is best to leave them whole since they have more texture and are less likely to go soggy. Steam, boil, microwave, or sauté. Once cooked, brussels sprouts should be eaten immediately or they come to resemble overcooked cabbage.

Brussels sprouts have a distinctive flavor. They go well with almonds or walnuts.

Cutting a small cross in the stem helps the sprouts cook through more evenly.

CHINESE CABBAGE

This is more delicately flavored than green cabbage. Look for crisp, pale leaves when buying. Keep loosely wrapped in the refrigerator for 3–4 days. To prepare, discard the outer leaves and shred. Serve it stir-fried or sautéed, or use in salads.

Chinese cabbage is good value since there is very little waste in preparation. Use the shredded leaves in salads or add at the last minute to a stir-fry recipe.

CAULIFLOWER

There are many varieties other than the standard white, ranging in color from pale green to near purple. These can be prepared and cooked in the same way. Cauliflower works well in spiced curries and as an ingredient in vegetable fritters. Classically, it is paired with dairy products, particularly cheese and cream sauces. Small pieces can be good in a chunky salad, raw or griddled.

Buying and storing Try to choose cauliflower with plenty of outer leaves because this protects the center flower or "curd." Look for tight heads, which are unpitted with no brown spots. Opened-out curds are a sign that the cauliflower is old or has been exposed to the sun. Avoid outer leaves that look wilted or yellowing. Cut stalks should look moist. Keep in the refrigerator and use within a few days.

Preparation and cooking Chop cauliflower into flowerets, leaving on a little of the stem. If cooking a cauliflower whole, cut a cross through the base of the stem to help the heat penetrate. Remember, the stems taste just as good as the flowers, with a nutty, almost sweet flavor. Slice stems thinly or they will take longer to cook than the flowerets. Steam, boil, or sauté, remembering that overcooked cauliflower goes soggy and smells unpleasant.

If cooking a whole cauliflower, cut a cross in the base to help it cook quickly. Do the same for baby cauliflowers, too.

KOHLRABI

Not one of Nature's beauties, this vegetable is globe shaped with a purple or green skin marked with distinctive slashes where the leaf stalks have been removed. It has a hot, peppery flavor similar to turnip and can be used in a similar way.

Buying and storing Buy small specimens with smooth skins. Kohlrabi will keep in a well-ventilated plastic bag for up to 2 weeks in the refrigerator.

Preparation and cooking Remove the skin with a small, sharp knife rather than trying to use a vegetable peeler. The flesh discolors quickly so have handy a bowl of water with a little lemon juice in it. Try not to leave the cut pieces in the water for too long before cooking. Add raw kohlrabi in small amounts to salads, or steam, boil, or microwave.

Kohlrabi may still have leaf stalks protruding from it. Cut off these and the outer skin with a sharp knife and steam, boil, or microwave.

Look for cauliflowers with plenty of outside leaves since these keep the flowerets fresher.

Leafy greens

Vegetables known as "greens" are not always green but can range in hue from a ruby red or purple through to emerald or bottle green. Many are great to steam, stir-fry, or add to salad. Cooking needs to be light if you are serving greens as an accompaniment. The flavors are intense and you can take full advantage of this by making purées, which can then be used to flavor egg dishes, or for crêpe fillings.

SPINACH AND SWISS CHARD (*LEAF BEETS*)

These greens have an affinity with dairy products, and also go well with Asian flavorings, such as chile, ginger, and shoyu, as well as with herbs, such as basil and oregano.

Baby spinach is great in salads. Swiss chard is like spinach but milder in flavor and with thicker stalks. New varieties of chard are ruby or rhubarb chard, and rainbow chard, which as the names imply are a far cry from "greens!" These leafy greens contain iron, although it is a type that is not easily absorbed.

Buying and storing When buying spinach, look for richly colored, dark leaves without traces of yellowing or slime. Swiss chard should have glossy, dark leaves and heavy white or red stems. Keep in the refrigerator and eat within 2 days.

Preparation and cooking Rinse both spinach and Swiss chard in several changes of water and pat dry; shred larger leaves. Remove chard stems, slice crosswise and cook separately. Steam or stir-fry. The leaves of both contain a large percentage of water so expect the quantity you cook to reduce by about half.

Swiss chard leaves and stems need to be cooked separately.

CHINESE GREENS

These are mostly related to brassicas and tend to be loose-leaved with a prominent central rib and a loosely furled heart. Some of the most common varieties are bok choy, mustard greens, and Chinese cabbage. The stems and sliced leaves are good stir-fried. Once cooked they make an alternative to spinach or Swiss chard for crêpe fillings and savory tarts. These leaves go well with Asian flavorings, such as shoyu and ginger. Young leaves can be eaten raw in salads.

Buying and storing Look for springy, colorful leaves with no curled or wilted edges or blemishes. Keep in the refrigerator and use within a few days.

Preparation and cooking Chop or slice small leaves. With larger leaves, chop the central rib and the leaf separately. Stir-fry, steam, or sauté.

Large leaves from **Swiss chard or Chinese greens** can be shredded and steamed or sautéed, or added to stir-fry recipes.

Stalks and buds

This is a diverse and versatile grouping of vegetables, which includes globe artichoke, asparagus, celery, fennel, and Belgian endive. Flavors range from delicate to nutty or bitter. Some of the vegetables featured here, such as globe artichoke or asparagus, demand a starring role as they are best savored on their own. Celery, fennel, and Belgian endive are delicious eaten raw or cooked. This group can be prepared and eaten in a number of ways. Stalks and buds work well served on their own or mixed with a variety of vegetables.

GLOBE ARTICHOKE

This attractive member of the thistle family is fun and best eaten when you have plenty of time and don't mind there being a lot of mess! If you live in an area where artichokes are plentiful, it is worth cooking them and using just the hearts, which are delicious. Some of us have to settle for canned artichokes, which are perfectly satisfactory. Better still are roasted artichokes, preserved in oil, which are delightful although often expensive.

Cardoons are related to globe artichokes, except that the stems rather than the flowerheads are eaten. They need cooking and can be treated like asparagus.

Buying and storing Choose globe artichokes with firm, tightly packed heads and a good bright color. Brown spots at the base of the head indicate that decay has set in. Eat as soon as possible. If you have to store them uncooked, wrap in damp paper and keep in the refrigerator overnight.

Preparation and cooking As you work, rub all cut surfaces with lemon juice or drop in acidulated water to prevent the globe artichoke from discoloring. To prepare an artichoke for eating whole, break off the stalk and trim the base so that it will sit upright when served. Trim the pointed spines with scissors and cut off the pointed top of the artichoke with a sharp knife. Boil in salted, acidulated water for 30–40 minutes. Lift out with a slotted spoon. If one of the leaves comes away with a gentle pull, the artichoke is ready. Leave upside down to drain. To eat, pull off the leaves one at a time and dip the tiny portion of flesh at the base of the leaf in a sharp, lemony vinaigrette or plain melted butter. Eat this fleshy part and discard the main part of the leaf. When all the outer leaves have been pulled off, you are left with a cone of tiny pale leaves, the choke (a dense mat of whitish fibers) and the base, or heart. Pull off the pale leaves, then slice off or scrape away the choke with a knife to leave the heart, which can be eaten with a knife and fork.

To prepare an artichoke for stuffing, remove the stalk as before and some of the tough lower leaves. Trim as necessary and cut across the top of the artichoke, about a third of the way down. Boil as before. When cooked and cool, pull out the center leaves until you expose the choke. Scrape this away with a teaspoon and knife, leaving a "cup" to stuff.

To obtain artichoke hearts, the artichoke has to be dismantled, as above, before or after cooking.

Baby artichokes are becoming more widely available and can be eaten whole including the stalk and leaves. Cook for 10–15 minutes in boiling water and then serve whole with a vinaigrette, or slice and use in salads or with eggs, or bake in a rich tomato sauce. Young, fresh artichokes may also be eaten raw.

When preparing artichokes, have fresh lemons or lemon juice handy. Rub cut surfaces with a lemon or sprinkle with lemon juice to prevent discoloration.

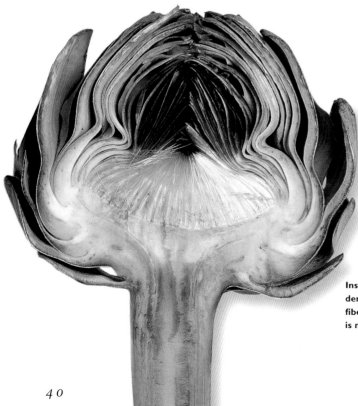

Inside the artichoke is a dense mat of whitish fibers, the choke, which is not eaten.

ASPARAGUS

With its delicate taste, asparagus was traditionally served only with rich buttery sauces. It can, however, take a range of bolder flavorings, such as chile, ginger, and sesame oil, as well as pesto and other Italian flavorings.

Buying and storing Select firm spears with tightly closed tips. Spears can be white or green and are best eaten within 24 hours.

Preparation and cooking Trim off any woody ends. Traditionally boiled upright in bunches in tall saucepans, asparagus is also excellent griddled or broiled, roasted, or stir-fried.

Look for firm spears with tightly closed tips and trim off any woody ends prior to cooking. Asparagus is best cooked in bunches standing upright in a tall saucepan.

CELERY

Not generally served solo, except for crudités, celery is usually used to flavor soups and casseroles. It is also good as a crunchy addition to salads and stir-fries.

Buying and storing Choose crisp, unblemished stalks with leafy tops. Refrigerate for up to 1 week.

Preparation and cooking Separate stalks and rinse thoroughly. Trim as necessary and pull away the coarse outer "strings." Slice or dice to serve raw in salads, stir-fry, broil, or sauté.

Celery adds a good flavor to any slow-cooked dish, such as casseroles or stews. Its texture when raw adds bite and body to salads.

FENNEL

With a distinctive hint of anise seed, this versatile vegetable goes well with all things Italian—tomatoes, basil, Parmesan—but is equally happy with citrus flavors, pears and apples, mild onion, or strong salad greens, such as watercress or radicchio. Despite its crunchy quality, it makes a smooth purée, ideal for soups and sauces.

Buying and storing Look for firm, evenly colored rounded bulbs with feathery, bright green fronds. Refrigerate for up to 1 week.

Preparation and cooking Trim the hard base and cut off any woody stalks. Slice finely to eat raw in salads. Grill, sauté, roast, or steam.

Fennel has a distinctive hint of anise seed. Raw, it has a crisp texture that is good in salads but it can also cook down to a smooth purée.

BELGIAN ENDIVE

This bitter-tasting, crunchy vegetable goes well with butter and cheese. It is also good flavored with herbs and lemon juice and has an affinity with walnuts. It is a useful salad leaf.

Buying and storing Look for crisp heads with pale leaves tinged with light yellow at the tips. Refrigerate for up to 1 week.

Preparation and cooking Discard any outer leaves as necessary. For salads, slice across the vegetable or separate the leaves. For cooking, blanch the Belgian endive whole to reduce the bitterness, then slice to broil, stir-fry, or sauté.

Individual heads of Belgian endive should look crisp with pale leaves lightly tinged at the tips. As with Chinese cabbage, there is very little waste.

Salad greens

Salad greens comprise a virtual rainbow of colors and an equally wide range of texture and flavors. There has been a huge surge of interest in salad greens and consequently a blossoming of varieties.

Salads are a wonderful way to brighten any meal, and they are quick to prepare. More substance can also be added to salad greens by adding chunkier vegetables, such as tomatoes, strips of bell pepper, avocado, slices of fennel, or toasted nuts or seeds, or slivers of cheese. Some salad greens, such as radicchio, arugula, and sorrel, can be served warm, wilted, or finely chopped and used for flavoring rather like an herb. Those with green fingers can grow varieties of salad greens so there is always something fresh at hand.

Buying and Storing

Never choose anything that looks wilted or bruised. Remove tight plastic packaging as soon as possible and keep salad greens in the refrigerator. Eat them on the day of purchase or within a day or so. Ready-mixed salad greens are packed in special bags to keep them fresh. In this case, keep the greens in the bag, but once you have opened the packet use the leaves as soon as possible.

Preparation

All salad greens are fragile and need handling with care. Wash and pat dry. Use a salad spinner if you have one; alternatively, heap the greens into a clean dish towel, gather up the corners, and swing around—preferably outside, unless you want an indoor shower! Tearing greens, rather than chopping, is said to cause less cell damage and therefore preserve more nutrients and also keeps the salad crisper. Some coarser salad greens, such as romaine lettuce, however, do need to be chopped.

Only dress a salad just before serving. Leaf salads are best dressed in vinaigrette-style dressings—not drowned in dressing but very lightly coated so as not to become soggy.

Varieties of Salad Greens

Following is a list of salad greens with a page reference for those mentioned in other sections.

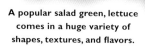

A popular salad green, lettuce comes in a huge variety of shapes, textures, and flavors.

LETTUCE

The lettuce is the best known of all the salad greens. There are many varieties—from hearted to loose-leaved and rosette types.
Butterhead lettuce: a round lettuce with soft leaves and a mild flavor.
Iceberg and crisphead: crisp texture but little flavor.
Lollo rosso: also comes in green; very curled leaves with delicate flavor.
Romaine lettuce: a large-leaved, crisp, and refreshing lettuce.
Bibb lettuce: a crisp, sweet, smaller version of the romaine lettuce.
Mâche (*corn salad*): succulent, mildly flavored leaves with a pretty green hue.
Feuille de chêne (*oakleaf*): a very attractive, loose-leaved variety with maroon edges and dark insides.

CHINESE CABBAGE

More robust in flavor than lettuce but not so much as cabbage, this has good crunchy leaves and a delicate flavor (see page 38).

FRISÉE AND BELGIAN ENDIVE

Greens in this family are known by a variety of names, including escarole, batavia, curly endive, frisée, and radicchio. Some varieties are loosely bunched, some a jagged mass of leaves; they range in flavor from a mild tang to pronounced bitterness. Use in small quantities mixed with other leaves. Radicchio is more distinctive due to its deep red color with contrasting white ribs. Belgian endive has tightly furled heads in pale white tinged with yellow (see page 41).

MISCELLANEOUS GREENS

Mizuna: attractive, dark, green feathery leaves, similar to dandelion, with a spicy, clean taste.
Sorrel: sharp-flavored, dark green leaf. Use sparingly because the tang permeates.
Arugula: attractive, notched leaves with a peppery flavor.
Watercress: a small-leaved plant grown in fresh running water, with a spicy, pungent flavor.
Cress: hot-flavored, delicate leaves on fine stalks.
Baby spinach: soft, dark green leaves with a clean taste (see page 39).

Other salad vegetables

A salad can be made from far more than greens. Radish, cucumber, and avocado are all wonderful ingredients to eat raw. These three are highlighted as salad vegetables because they are seldom cooked, but many other vegetables can also be eaten raw, such as the fruit vegetables and some of the stalks (see pages 40–41 and 54–57).

RADISH

Radishes have crimson red or white roots, which are either finger thick or like small globes. Characterized by a hot, peppery flavor and crisp texture, they make a perky addition to salads. They are also great eaten sliced and salted on lightly buttered bread.

Buying and storing Radishes should look "snappy" in appearance. Refrigerate, loosely wrapped, for up to 1 week.

Radish is characterized by a hot, peppery flavor that perks up salads or sandwich fillings.

CUCUMBER

With its high water content, this is a cooling ingredient. It can be diced, sliced, or cut into sticks. Cucumber is wonderful in a dip mixed with plain yogurt, garlic, and plenty of mint. For recipes like this, it is best to salt it first by sprinkling the chopped cucumber with salt and leaving it in a colander for about 1 hour. This draws out plenty of moisture. Pat dry and then use. Cucumber is good in relishes and can also be stir-fried.

Buying and storing
Cucumbers should feel firm and should be kept in the refrigerator. Only cut as much as you need— once sliced, it dries out quickly.

Cool cucumber is a refreshing salad ingredient that can be served on its own, sliced, or in chunks. When adding to dips, salt first to draw out the moisture.

AVOCADO

Strictly speaking a fruit rather than a vegetable, avocado is pear shaped with knobby or smooth skin, depending on the variety. Organic varieties are also available. Avocado is one of the few fruit vegetables with a high fat content, most of which is monounsaturated.

Buying and storing A ripe avocado will yield gently when pressed. It can be bought unripe and will ripen at home—to speed up the ripening process, place in a paper bag for a day or so. Use avocados when ripe; do not refrigerate them or they will go black. Once cut, the flesh discolors so eat right away or sprinkle the cut surfaces with lemon juice.

Preparation Cut lengthwise around an avocado down to the large pit. Ease the two halves apart and then remove the pit using the tip of a sharp knife.

A ripe avocado will yield very slightly when pressed. They ripen well at home when left in a warm place or put in a paper bag.

Mushrooms

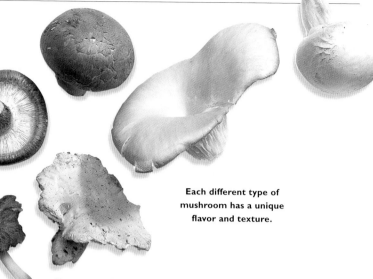

The range of edible fungi available seems to be ever increasing. Fresh mushrooms can either be cultivated or wild and come in an array of shapes, sizes, and flavors. Many species are harvested wild. Some previously wild varieties, such as the shiitake mushroom, are now cultivated, and there are several traditional varieties of cultivated mushroom. Many varieties are sold both fresh and dried.

Mushrooms are not only delicious in their own right but they are also marvelous at adding a wealth of subtle flavors as well as depth of texture to many dishes as diverse as stir-fry, risotto, casserole, or salads.

Each different type of mushroom has a unique flavor and texture.

Fresh Mushrooms

In recent years, there has been a growing focus on foraging for wild mushrooms, a tradition strong in Europe but less common elsewhere. If you intend picking wild mushrooms, it is vital to know exactly what to look for since many varieties that look edible are in fact poisonous. Fall is the main season for mushrooms.

Buying and storing When buying rather than picking fresh mushrooms, look for firm and fresh-looking specimens. Avoid any that are beginning to brown in patches or those with a moist outer skin. Some mushrooms may smell strongly but it should be a pleasant smell rather than an odor. On cultivated mushrooms, pale gills are an indicator of freshness.

Store fresh mushrooms in a paper bag in the refrigerator. Do not keep them in plastic because they will sweat and quickly become pungent. Fresh wild mushrooms deteriorate very quickly so use them as soon as possible.

A little brush is useful for dislodging particles of earth on the cap and around the stalk.

Preparation Cultivated mushrooms need only be wiped. Even if they appear dirty, do not be tempted to wash them because the mushrooms will act like a sponge, absorbing water and becoming soggy. Trim the edges with a knife if necessary.

Fresh wild varieties do need to be thoroughly checked for earthy particles. Gently brush off the dirt and cut away any woody ends.

Dried Mushrooms

You need only small quantities since they should reconstitute to about four or five times their original weight. Wild mushrooms are worth buying for their exquisite flavor, which adds richness and depth to soups, stews, and sauces.

Buying and storing dried mushrooms At first glance, dried wild mushrooms seem very expensive, but it is worth shopping around because you may be able to buy them more cheaply loose rather than pre-packed. Some dried mushrooms have surprisingly short "sell-by" dates. Check that the contents of the packet are not dusty or, if buying loose ones, that the mushrooms are not moist. Store in a cool, dry place. They can have a pungent smell, which may infect ingredients kept nearby.

Preparation Dried mushrooms must always be soaked in some sort of liquid—boiling water, wine, or lemon juice, for example—before they are used. This soaking process helps to clean the mushrooms because earthy particles will float out and can be removed more easily. Soak dried mushrooms for about 15–20 minutes—allow longer if you are using a cold liquid. Don't throw away the soaking liquid—it will be imbued with a rich mushroom flavor. Strain it well, preferably through a coffee filter, and then use as required. Leave the soaked mushrooms whole or chop them finely, depending on the recipe.

Although dried wild mushrooms can be expensive, their exquisite flavor enriches soups and stews.

Varieties of Mushroom

There are many varieties of mushroom, the most common of which are given here.

WHITE MUSHROOM

These are the most immature cultivated mushrooms. Use them whole to make the most of their appearance. They are great in salads, marinades, and stir-fries, as well as in casseroles and soups, although in these instances you may be better off using the stronger-flavored Paris or cremini mushroom.

CHANTERELLE (GIROLLE)

Golden-hued and concave, these dainty mushrooms have a more delicate flavor than cèpes. They are available fresh or dried. Brush off grit rather than washing these mushrooms since they are quite porous, and they do exude a certain amount of water as they cook. This can be poured off if necessary and used as stock.

PARIS AND CREMINI MUSHROOMS

Fresh Paris mushrooms have a good dense texture, which gets darker on cooking, and are excellent in robust stews and rich sauces. They also add a distinctive flavor to savory nut roasts or pie fillings. Paris mushrooms are interchangeable with cremini mushrooms, which are similar in appearance and also have a good flavor and firm texture. Baby cremini mushrooms are also available.

ENOKI MUSHROOM

These little clusters of skinny-stemmed mushrooms with tiny heads have a crisp texture and a slight hint of lemon. They look pretty in soups and can be used in stir-fries and salads.

MOREL

Available fresh and dried, these mushrooms are an exception to the "no washing" rule for mushrooms when fresh. The slim, conical cap of the morel has a honeycomb texture, which easily traps dirt.

Leave morels in salted water for 3 minutes in order to get rid of any insects, then rinse them under cold running water and pat dry with a clean dish towel or paper towel. They can be used whole or finely sliced for sauces.

CÈPE AND PORCINI

Closely related, the cèpe from France and the porcini from Italy are available fresh and dried. When fresh, the mushrooms are quite chunky with a spongy underneath, which is edible. Dried cèpes are sold in thin slices. They are useful for creating instant stock and for imparting a delicious, woody flavor.

SHIITAKE MUSHROOM

Available both fresh and dried, the shiitake mushroom was originally a wild mushroom native to Japan, but is now cultivated in many parts of the world. This mushroom has a fine robust flavor and substantial chewy texture. Occasionally, you need to discard particularly woody stems. Shiitake mushrooms are good for sauces and stir-fries but need to be thinly sliced, or cut up in larger chunks and used in casseroles. Reconstitute the dried variety in boiling water and use the liquid for stock.

STRAW MUSHROOM

This variety of small mushroom is native to China and, as you might expect, cultivated on straw. They can be used as a substitute for white mushrooms, having a similar clean taste and texture.

OYSTER MUSHROOM

Also called pleurotte, this prettily shaped, fluted mushroom is sold fresh, sometimes in small clusters. It is usually pale gray in color, but there are also salmon pink and pale yellow varieties. The flesh of the oyster mushroom is succulent and melting. Oyster mushrooms can be used in most recipes, but take note that they release a lot of moisture during cooking. They are good in soups and sauces as well as casseroles.

PORTOBELLO MUSHROOM

Treat these giants as succulent, edible plates to be served plainly broiled, roasted, or stuffed and baked. Foil wrapped or well oiled, they also make a good addition to the barbecue grill.

Pods and corn

Encompassing a wide range of peas as well as beans, ladies' fingers, corn, and baby corn, these bright, succulent vegetables add a good splash of color to a great variety of dishes and also work well as a quick accompaniment.

Fresh corn on the cob is one of the most succulent and colorful vegetables included in this group.

PEAS

Fresh peas are on sale for only a short period in the year. If the peas inside the pod are very small, they are sweet and delicious to eat raw. Shelled peas work well in spicy curry dishes, as well as with creamy pasta sauces and in stir-fries. They also make a colorful side vegetable. Organic frozen peas are sometimes available.

Buying and storing When buying fresh peas, look for pods that are full, plump, and wrinkle free, and have a bright color. All peas should have a good color, too, and feel squeaky with life. Refrigerate for up to 3 days.

Preparation and cooking To pod fresh peas, press the base to snap open and push out the peas with your thumb. They are best lightly boiled, steamed, microwaved, or added to stir-fries.

Look for fresh peas as they are in season for only a short period. They should be firm and brightly colored.

SNOW PEAS AND SUGAR SNAPS

These are edible pods with immature peas inside. Sugar snaps are plumper than snow peas because they often have some formed peas inside but nevertheless are designed to be eaten whole. These pods are good for stir-fries and salad dishes since they add color and texture.

Buying and storing Look for firm, crisp, bright green pods. Store in the refrigerator for 3–4 days.

Snow peas are slim, edible pods containing minute immature peas. String the pods by breaking off the stalk.

Preparation and cooking String pods before cooking by breaking off the stalk and peeling off the fibrous strings from the sides of the pods. Stir-fry or lightly steam.

BEANS

Each country has its favorite varieties of beans, known variously as green, French, string, runner, bobby, Italian, and wax. Some are as thin as a shoelace, others finger-thick and about as long. There are also lemon-flavored yard-long beans that are used in Asian cookery.

Fresh beans are a good way of adding color to a stew or casserole. They go well with Mediterranean vegetables, such as tomatoes, olives, and bell peppers; they are also great partnered with garlicky Middle Eastern dishes. When served as a side vegetable, beans should be tender yet crisp. They also work well in marinades based on olive oil or with Asian flavors.

Buying and storing Beans should have a good color and all but the youngest and smallest varieties should snap in half easily if they are fresh. Yard-long beans may have patches, which will disappear on cooking. Keep beans in the refrigerator for 4–5 days.

Preparation and cooking String beans were originally named for the fibrous strings running the length of the bean, which were indigestible and needed to be removed before cooking. However, many stringless beans are now available. Chunky, short beans and very fine green beans need trimming but rarely stringing; runner beans are more fibrous and heavily textured, and usually do need stringing. Cut beans thinly either diagonally across the pod or lengthwise. Once prepared, steam, boil, microwave, or stir-fry.

Green beans come in many shapes and sizes, from finger-thick to pencil-fine.

FAVA BEANS

These are the heavyweights of this group. They are bigger in size, coming inevitably from larger pods, which may look swollen and leathery but contain plump beans inside. Fava beans are good with grain dishes, such as paella and casseroles, as well as in hearty, garlic-laden salads. They are also delicious as a simple side vegetable.

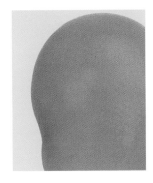

Tasty and substantial, fava beans make a good side vegetable but can also be served with grains or used in salads.

Buying and storing Look for plump pods, not too large, with a good color. Store in the refrigerator for 3–4 days.

Preparation and cooking Open the pods and remove the beans. Really young, small beans can be cooked in boiling water for 5 minutes; older large beans may need up to 15 minutes.

LADIES' FINGERS *(OKRA, GUMBO, BHINDI)*

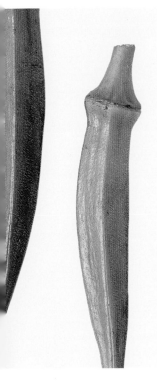

A distinctive, green five-sided slim conical vegetable, about the length of a finger, ladies' fingers are used extensively in the southern states of America, as well as in Indian and African cookery. The pods contain a slippery, gelatinous juice, which is released when the pod is cut. This adds a distinctive quality to a soup or stew as well as thickening it.

Buying and storing The pods should have a good color, be free from blemishes, and firm not floppy. Keep in the refrigerator for up to 3 days.

Preparation and cooking Trim the ends. To release the juices the pods need to be slit. They can then be left whole or sliced and added to soups or stews. If cooking ladies' fingers whole for a dry, spicy dish, typical of Indian cookery, prepare them by trimming both ends but taking care not to split the pods.

Ladies' fingers, sometimes known as okra, gumbo, or bhindi, add a distinctive texture and taste to soups and stews.

CORN

Fresh corn on the cob has a delicate, sweet flavor. It is a versatile ingredient that can be eaten alone but it also adds good color and texture to stews, grain dishes, and salads. Corn is commonly used in Mexican cookery and goes well with sharp flavorings such as lime and chile. The cobs are great to grill on the barbecue whole in the husks. Corn is gluten-free.

Buying and storing Choose cobs that are completely enclosed in green husks because these will protect the kernels and prevent the corn from drying out. If in doubt, peel back the leaves and check that the kernels are still plump. Try not to buy cobs pre-packed because you are unable to inspect them. Once harvested, corn loses its sweetness so eat as soon after buying as possible. If necessary, store in a loose plastic bag in the refrigerator for up to 2 days.

Preparation and cooking Remove the outer leaves and the silky threads. Cook whole cobs in boiling water for 3–5 minutes, or steam them for 8–10 minutes. The individual kernels should be tender when pierced. Kernels can be stripped off the cob. Use a sharp knife and hold the cob at a slight angle, which is safer than balancing it on one end. Scrape off a row of kernels, cutting close to the inner core and working down and away from you. Work your way in this manner around the cob. Each cob should yield about ¾ cup/4 ounces (125g) kernels.

To remove kernels from the cob, hold the cob at an angle and scrape downward with a sharp knife.

BABY CORN COBS

These are finger-length cobs with a sweet flavor and crisp texture. They are good in stir-fries and casseroles; you can also steam or sauté them for a side vegetable.

Onion family

Many varieties of onion are now available, as well as other members of the onion family, such as garlic, leeks, and scallions. This group of vegetables is fundamental as a base flavoring for many recipes. The onion family can also be shown off in its own right when roasted or stir-fried.

Onions form the aromatic base of a huge number of recipes.

ONION

Revered by the ancient Egyptians and favored by the Greeks and Romans, the humble onion is now treated as an essential ingredient in diverse recipes. Many countries grow their own varieties, which range from deep purple-red to pure white, from sweet to pungent, and from bulbous to pencil thin. Onions from colder climates tend to have stronger flavors.

Buying and storing Look for onions with firm bulbs, evenly colored papery skin, and no sprouting. Avoid any that feel spongy or look sooty; a rotting onion will also smell unpleasant. Common onions should last for several weeks, if not months, if they are stored in cool, dark, airy conditions. Red onions and sweet varieties of onion do not last so long.

Once cut, onions should be used quickly. If you have a leftover half, wrap it well before putting it in the refrigerator or the smell will permeate any butter or cheese. Aim to use it the following day.

Preparation and cooking Trim the ends and peel off the skin. Onions have a slippery outer surface so use a sharp knife that won't slide off. Cut the bulb in half and place each half cut-side down. Slice thinly to form crescents. To dice the onion finely, hold the sliced half firmly and cut again—at right angles to the first cuts.

To cut onion rings, trim and peel off the skin as before. Hold the onion carefully because it can be slippery and slice right through, then separate the slices into rings. To make crisp onion rings, dip them in milk and seasoned flour, then deep-fry in hot oil for 2–3 minutes.

ONIONS WITHOUT TEARS

The tears are caused by a chemical reaction when the cells are damaged by cutting the onion. There is no universal remedy although tips are plentiful—from wearing swimming goggles and chewing bread, to soaking the onions in ice water, leaving the root intact, or leaning back slightly as you chop! Remember that some varieties of onion are stronger than others.

COMMON VARIETIES OF ONION

This large family of vegetables forms the flavor base of many recipes. Apart from the common onion you may find some of the following:

Bermuda onion
This is a large, juicy, white-fleshed onion with a mild flavor.

White onion
Pure or pearl white, these onions have a paper-thin skin and crisp flesh. They are good raw or cooked.

Sweet onion
This specially developed species has a sweet flavor and is particularly good in salads. Look for specimens that are firm and shiny with a thin skin.

Red onion
Sweeter and milder than the traditional onion, red onion is good for salads and also for roasting and grilling since its high sugar content helps it caramelize. When selecting a red onion, make sure that its skin is not discolored.

TRANSLUCENT ONIONS

Many recipes start with onions being cooked until translucent. Do not skimp on this stage since when cooked slowly and thoroughly, the onion imparts a subtle flavor to the finished dish. Other ingredients, especially tomatoes, will halt the cooking of the onion, so it is important to have the onions properly softened in the initial stages.

GARLIC

This small but pungent ingredient is used to flavor a diverse range of foods and is popular in French, Italian, Asian, and Indian dishes. Garlic has been credited with lowering blood cholesterol levels and warding off colds. However, in order to get any benefit from garlic, it needs to be eaten regularly and in large amounts.

A fresh head is firm with no slashes or slits.

Buying and storing Look for firm heads of garlic with no slashes or slits. Garlic should last for several weeks in a cool airy place—don't keep it in a steamy kitchen.

Preparation and cooking The traditional method is to chop the garlic and then crush it with the blade of a knife, adding a little salt to prevent the knife from slipping. Alternatively, use a sturdy garlic press. Be careful not to burn or scorch garlic when cooking or it will become bitter. It is best to add garlic once there is another ingredient, such as onion, already cooking in the pan.

Roasted garlic is a wonderful way of adding a very subtle flavor to recipes, especially to raw salad dressing and dips where uncooked garlic might be too strong. Roast plump, firm unpeeled cloves in a preheated oven, 400°F (200°C), for 5 minutes. Let cool, then peel, mash, and use as required.

Garlic can be chopped, sliced, or crushed. To make it easier to chop, smash each clove first with the flat side of the knife.

SHALLOT

This small, brown bulb is related to the onion but has a milder sweeter flavor. The flesh can be pink in appearance. Like onion, it is usually cooked at the beginning of the recipe to add subtle undertones of flavor.

Buying and storing Look for firm bulbs when buying and store in a cool airy place for up to a month. Prepare and cook in a similar way to onions.

Shallots can be used as background flavoring or served as an accompaniment.

LEEK

Leeks are milder in flavor than onions and develop a buttery texture when cooked slowly, which makes them excellent for pairing with cheese. Leeks also have an affinity with potatoes.

Buying and storing It is best to choose medium to small leeks since large ones sometimes have a woody core that is inedible. Look for dark green leaves, which are not dry or wilted. Store leeks in the refrigerator and use within 1 week.

Preparation and cooking Leeks need cleaning thoroughly because dirt is often trapped in the leaves. Remove the outer leaves, trim the green tops, and cut off the bearded ends. Slice twice lengthwise along the green part almost into the white central body of the leek. Rinse under cold running water, fanning out the leaves so that any trapped dirt is flushed away. Cut the leek into slices or chunks.

SCALLIONS (SALAD ONIONS)

These small, immature onions are usually pencil thin with a white base and green leaves. Use them in salads and stir-fries.

Buying and storing The leaves should look bright and springy with no hint of yellowing. Keep in the refrigerator for up to 1 week.

Preparation and cooking Trim the base and any straggly green leaves. Chop, slice, or cut into lengths.

Root vegetables and tubers

This group includes the familiar, such as carrots and potatoes, as well as a large group of lesser-known specimens such as rutabaga, turnip, parsnip, celery root, and Jerusalem artichoke. The poor reputation of some of these vegetables has to do with perception rather than flavor. Cheap root vegetables were often served up as institutional and therefore uninspiring food; other roots were commonly used as animal fodder. It is, however, worth discovering their plus points.

These vegetables are all excellent ingredients to include in casseroles and stews. They work well with each other but also happily partner a broad range of other vegetables, as well as a variety of spices and herbs. They make smooth purées, which can be enriched with cream or soft cheese, and best of all they are delicious roasted, a cooking method that brings out their natural mellow flavor and sweetness. So, if you have always given them a miss, have a rethink!

Parsnips are excellent in slow-cooking dishes such as casseroles. They can also be roasted, puréed, or steamed as an accompaniment.

General Advice

When buying root vegetables, look for wrinkle-free skins with no soft patches or sprouting. Some do have very knobby exteriors but don't be put off; the vegetables should feel firm and heavy. If kept in cool, well-ventilated conditions, most root vegetables will keep for about 1 week and probably longer but they do gradually lose their vitamin C content. They should be used immediately if they start to sprout.

When buying root vegetables, look for wrinkle-free skins with no soft patches or sprouting.

CARROTS

A highly nutritious vegetable, carrots are also a great cooking mainstay, delicious both raw and cooked. Carrots can be teamed with a great variety of flavors—from the mildest dairy product to spicy Indian or Asian flavorings.

Carrots should have a crisp texture and are great eaten raw or cooked.

Buying and storing Carrots should be crisp with a smooth surface. Avoid any that are limp or have damaged skins. Keep them in a cool airy place for about 1 week.

Preparation and cooking Peel carrots thinly to remove any chemicals, but if they are organically grown, this is not necessary. Cut off tops and root ends, and slice, dice, or cut into strips. Boil, steam, microwave, roast, or stir-fry.

Try not to take off more than a thin strip of peel as much of the nutritional value is just below the surface of a carrot.

POTATOES

This is now one of the world's most widely grown vegetables. Potatoes fall into two categories—waxy or mealy—although some all-purpose varieties are midway between the two. Waxy potatoes have a high moisture and low starch content, and are better for sautéing, boiling, and salads. New potatoes tend to have a waxy character. Mealy potatoes have more starch and a lighter texture and are good for baking and mashing.

Potatoes are available worldwide and can be waxy or mealy, depending on the variety.

Buying and storing Potatoes belong to the nightshade family, a group of plants in which all, apart from the tubers, are poisonous. Exposure to light and sprouting, can cause a concentration of poisons—visible as a green hue, so it is vital not to buy or eat green potatoes or sprouting potatoes. A small patch of green can be cut away but discard any with a heavy green tinge.

Do not store potatoes sealed in plastic since this will create condensation and the moisture will cause them to spoil. Stored in a dry, dark place with good ventilation, potatoes will keep for at least 2 weeks, maybe longer. Don't store them with onions.

Preparation and cooking Scrub well to remove most of the pesticides or peel thinly. Potatoes can lose up to 25 percent of their protein if peeled too coarsely and much of their vitamin C content is close to the skin. Boil, roast, or bake whole.

SWEET POTATOES

Sweet potatoes have light brown, orange, or purple skins and bright orange flesh. Their sweetness makes them less versatile than ordinary potatoes, but this quality can be used to advantage when making root vegetable purées, or when adding them to casseroles and roasting.

Sweet potatoes have a marvelous cheerful color and go well with a variety of herbs and spices.

Sweet potatoes team well with a variety of spices and herbs. They are not related to the ordinary potato or the yam but are often interchangeable with the latter.

Buying and storing Check for rotten or soft spots. Store in a cool, dry, dark place and eat within 1 week.

Preparation and cooking Scrub and bake whole, or peel and slice thinly for baking as "chips," or cut into chunks for casseroles. Sweet potatoes can also be boiled and mashed.

YAM

These tropical roots are more starchy than the sweet potato. They are important ingredients in recipes from West Africa, the Caribbean, and Southeast Asia.

Buying and storing Look out for rotten or soft patches. Store in a cool, dry, dark place and eat within 1 week.

Preparation and cooking Scrub, rub with oil, and bake whole. Peel and slice or mash.

Yams are similar to a sweet potato but more starchy. Check carefully for soft patches before buying.

PARSNIP

A long white root, the parsnip is similar in shape to a carrot but with creamy-white flesh and a strong, sweet flavor. Parsnips are not edible raw but can be cooked in a number of ways. They go well with a variety of herbs and spices, as well as flavorings such as orange and lemon. Once cooked, parsnip purées easily, making it highly suitable for soup making.

Roasted parsnips make a delicious accompaniment to pies and roasts. This cooking method brings out their mellow flavor.

Buying and storing It is best to choose small smooth specimens with firm flesh; large parsnips tend to be woody in texture. Store in a cool dry place for about 1 week.

Preparation and cooking Scrub and peel parsnips thinly. Trim tops and root ends and slice or chop into lengths. Boil, steam, sauté, or roast.

BEET

Beet is cultivated for both the root and its greens (see page 42). The roots can vary in color from red and gold to white, although the flavor is roughly the same. The main difference is that golden beet doesn't bleed in the way that red beet does. The flavor of beet is sweet and earthy. It is great with onion or citrus flavors, as well as with sour cream, tangy goat cheese, and hot condiments, such as mustard and horseradish.

Look for turnips the size of golf balls. Their peppery flavor is great in casseroles or mashed with other root vegetables.

Buying and storing
Choose firm, smooth bulbs with the leaves attached. Separate the leaves before storing. Keep beet in a ventilated plastic bag in the refrigerator for some weeks.

Preparation and cooking Red beet will stain everything crimson, so consider carefully what you wear, where you prepare them, and what other ingredients you mix them with. Sadly, the dramatic crimson color can turn rather easily to an unattractive pink. Beet is easier to peel once it has been cooked. Scrub the roots and then boil for 35–40 minutes, or until tender. Remove the skins with a sharp knife when the beet is cool enough to handle. Beet is good roasted or baked. It can be eaten raw and is then best grated or cut into thin slivers.

Beet has a sweet, earthy flavor that goes well with sour cream and tangy cheese.

WHITE-FLESHED TURNIP

The best turnips are no bigger than a golf ball with a greenish white or purple skin. They have a slightly peppery flavor, which works well with dairy products, as well as with pungent herbs, such as thyme or tarragon.

Buying and storing Look for small smooth-skinned roots with creamy flesh. Avoid shriveled or cracked roots. Turnips will keep for up to 2 weeks in the refrigerator.

Preparation and cooking Small young specimens do not need peeling—simply scrub them under running water. They can be added to casseroles, mashed with other root vegetables, steamed, sautéed, or stir-fried.

JERUSALEM ARTICHOKE

These nutty tubers grow beneath yellow flowers related to the sunflower, hence the name "sunchoke." They have a crisp flesh and a sweet flavor, a little like water chestnuts. They are great for soups and stews and can also be partnered with dairy products, such as crème fraîche or sour cream, or with spices.

They cause flatulence due to an indigestible carbohydrate, which eventually causes a build-up of gas in the colon. It is therefore best to eat small quantities at a time.

Jerusalem artichokes have a nutty-flavored, crisp flesh.

Buying and storing Look for firm unblemished tubers. Store in the refrigerator for up to 2 weeks. However, you must check them and use immediately if they begin to sprout.

Preparation and cooking The knobby surface needs a lot of scrubbing and sometimes careful peeling. Some commercially grown varieties now have much smoother skins, which are easier to deal with. Once peeled, the flesh discolors quickly so have a bowl of water containing a few drops of lemon juice at hand. Try not to leave the cut pieces in the water for too long before cooking. Bake, roast, boil, steam, or sauté.

Carefully peel the knobby exterior of Jerusalem artichokes. Since the flesh discolors quickly, drop the cut pieces into a bowl of water with a few drops of lemon juice added.

CELERY ROOT

The knobby, shaggy exterior of celery root can be off-putting, but do persevere. Celery root has a flavor and aroma akin to celery. It is delicious cooked in wine or puréed with butter, cream, or soft cheese. It is also good raw in salads.

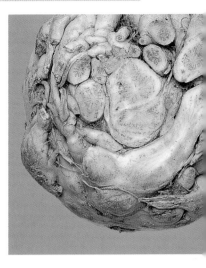

Buying and storing Buy medium varieties because older, larger specimens may have a woody texture or, worse still, may be hollow. Celery root should feel heavy for its size.

Preparation and cooking Remove the skin with a small sharp knife, rather than trying to use a vegetable peeler. The flesh discolors quickly so, as with Jerusalem artichokes, have a bowl of acidulated water at hand. Try not to leave the cut pieces in the water for too long before cooking. Boil or sauté.

Celery root has a knobby exterior concealing a crisp celery-flavored interior.

RUTABAGA *(YELLOW TURNIP)*

Once used almost exclusively for animal fodder, new varieties of rutabaga are being grown specifically for home cooking. These tend to be smaller and not quite so hard, with yellowish-orange flesh that has an attractive, warm appearance. Rutabaga is useful in soups and casseroles and also extremely good when roasted. It goes well with ginger or nutmeg.

Buying and storing Look for smaller specimens with smooth skins, which feel firm and heavy. Store for several weeks in cool, dry conditions.

Preparation and cooking Peel thickly with a sharp knife, exposing the yellowish-orange flesh. Because it has a high water content a simple mash can be rather tasteless. Rutabaga is better roasted, steamed, or microwaved.

Rutabaga has a warm yellowish-orange flesh and is good in casseroles or roasted with other vegetables.

Fruit vegetables

Describing vegetables as fruits may seem a contradiction in terms, but the classification distinguishes the group from flowering vegetables and from roots or shoots. This diverse group includes brightly colored bell peppers, the purple-hued eggplant, tomatoes, and a vast range of squashes. All members of the group are extremely versatile—many can be eaten raw as well as being roasted, broiled, fried, baked, or puréed.

BELL PEPPER (*PIMENTO*)

Bell peppers are related to the chile family, but have a mild rather than hot flavor and they sweeten as they ripen. They are marvelous vegetables, adding plenty of color to all manner of dishes. They can be eaten raw or cooked in a variety of ways and are ideal for stuffing.

Bell peppers come in a dazzling array of colors, the most familiar being red and green but increasingly orange, yellow, and even white and purple are on sale. These are all similar, but warmer colors indicate riper specimens, thus yellow is the sweetest of all while the green bell pepper has a fresh, almost grassy flavor. Look, too, for baby bell peppers, which can be used whole in a dish of marinated vegetables or stuffed for cocktail snacks. Red and yellow bell peppers are very good sources of carotenes and vitamin C.

Buying and storing

Choose bright, firm specimens with smooth skins, which should not be wrinkled or soft. It doesn't matter if the red ones have a touch of green, or vice versa, since this is part of the ripening process. Bell peppers don't have to have a regular appearance, unless you are intending to stuff them. Store them in the refrigerator and they will last for up to 1 week.

This slow-cooked Caponata of Roasted Vegetables (see page 176) includes many different fruit vegetables.

Preparation and cooking The easiest way to prepare bell peppers is to cut a slice off the top, thus removing the stalk and part of the core. Then cut a small slice off the base. (Use these trimmings if appropriate.) This leaves you with a neat, open-ended box. Remove the core, seeds, and membranes. Slice the bell pepper in half, then hold with the inside of the bell pepper uppermost, since this part is less slippery, and cut the flesh into long strips or dice.

To stuff a bell pepper, slice off the top and pull out the core. Shake out any remaining seeds, and then cut out the white membranes.

Bell peppers are fine to eat raw and can also be cooked in casseroles or stir-fries without being skinned. However, some people find the skin indigestible and bell peppers are easily skinned.

ROASTING BELL PEPPERS

This is done most efficiently in the oven since you don't have to stand over them. Wash and wipe the bell peppers and leave them plain or coat lightly with oil. Place on a baking sheet and roast in a preheated oven, 400°F (200°C), for 25–30 minutes, or until the skin chars and blisters. Let cool slightly, then peel off the skin. Don't rinse the bell pepper because you will lose much of the flavor. The cooking juices have a good flavor, too. Once roasted, bell peppers can be kept in the refrigerator for up to 1 week. Roasted bell peppers have a mellow, sweet flavor and soft texture.

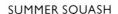

EGGPLANT

The most widespread variety is the purple-hued eggplant. It is a versatile vegetable and features throughout the world in many classic dishes, such as Greek moussaka, Turkish Imam Bayaldi (stuffed eggplant with cooked onions, tomatoes, and garlic), and Baba Ghanoush (roasted eggplant creamed with tahini) from the Middle East.

Eggplant should be smooth and glossy and feel heavy so that the inner flesh is still dense in texture.

Buying and storing Eggplant should look smooth and glossy and feel heavy for their size. If they are big yet weigh little, the insides may be spongy and past their best. Be careful when touching the cap because it can be prickly. Store eggplant in a cool place or they will quickly shrivel.

Preparation and cooking Wipe the eggplant and trim off the cap. Cut into slices or dice as required, using a very sharp knife since the outer skin can be slippery.

To roast and purée an eggplant, wipe it and leave it whole and then place in a roasting pan. Roast in a preheated hot oven, 400°F (200°C), for about 40 minutes, until the eggplant has collapsed and is very soft. Allow it to cool then scrape out the flesh. The purée can be mixed with all manner of spices or herbs, plain yogurt, tahini, or bean curd (see page 83).

SALTING EGGPLANT

This process is used to draw out bitter juices. It is not strictly necessary now because modern varieties of eggplant have been developed to be less bitter. However, salting does help prevent the eggplant from absorbing so much oil when fried. If you have time, therefore, it is worth doing. To salt an eggplant, cut it into slices or cubes, place in a colander, and sprinkle lightly with salt. Leave for at least 20 minutes or longer, then rinse, pat dry with paper towels, and use as required.

SUMMER SQUASH

This group includes zucchini, patty pan, baby patty pan, and yellow crookneck squash. Squashes are popular in America and around the Mediterranean but, apart from the green and gold varieties of zucchini, are lesser known in Northern Europe. Summer squashes are characterized by thinner skins and they tend to be less watery than winter varieties. They often have colorful flesh and roast and purée well, making a good base for soups, sauces, and ravioli stuffing. Squash goes well with many flavorings, including sweet spices such as cinnamon and nutmeg, pungent herbs such as basil or marjoram, walnuts, and some other fruit vegetables.

Large zucchini or marrow has a thick skin and somewhat watery flesh. Large zucchini is best sautéed with spices, such as paprika, cumin, or caraway, or pungent herbs such as thyme. Finish off by adding a splash of wine.

Summer squash can be stuffed with a variety of flavorsome fillings and served either hot or cold.

Buying and storing
Look for firm, glossy vegetables that are not too large—especially zucchini, which are at their best when they are young and small. They should be heavy for their size and have no wrinkled or brown patches. Store them in the refrigerator, loosely covered, for 3–4 days.

Preparation and cooking Do not peel summer squashes because you will lose flavor and texture. Wipe or rinse and trim the ends as necessary. Chop large specimens.

Summer squashes are good stuffed, lightly steamed and marinated for salads served at room temperature. They add bulk and substance to stews and casseroles, and are useful for barbecues and griddling, as well as stir-frying.

Fruit vegetables range from the tough, durable winter squashes to the most delicate of tomatoes. They work well in their own right, but can also be used together or with numerous other vegetables, grains, and legumes.

SQUASH BLOSSOMS

Squash blossoms taste delicately of the parent vegetable and should be used the day they are picked. They can be stuffed, dipped in batter and fried, or eaten raw. Wash first, remove the stamen, and trim any prickly stalk or sepals. They go well with dairy products.

WINTER SQUASH AND PUMPKIN

Don't be put off by craggy skins or monstrous-sized specimens because they will still be delicious. Winter squashes add good color to soups and casseroles. The purée can be used for stuffing vegetables or pasta, as well as for flavoring risotto (see pages 227 and 229). Winter squashes go well with cheese, fiery spices, such as chile or ginger, and pungent herbs and garlic.

Winter squash adds a good color to soups and casseroles and can also be puréed.

Buying and storing Avoid any with damaged skins or definite blemishes. Winter squashes can be stored whole for months in a cool, dry place with plenty of ventilation and away from frost. Once cut, use quickly or wrap and keep in the refrigerator for a few days only.

Preparation and cooking Some varieties, such as butternut squash, have very thin skins, which can be left unpeeled in casseroles and soup, but thicker-skinned varieties will need peeling, which is hard work. Chopping large ones into pieces can also be tricky. Use a good, large sharp knife or cleaver and don't try to cut through the stem for a perfect half. Roasted or baked halves or segments are easier to peel once cooked. This is useful to know, especially if you are making a purée.

Bake winter squash whole and unpeeled, or peel and cut into cubes, then boil, steam, or bake.

The pale orange flesh of butternut squash goes well with fiery spices such as chile or ginger.

TOMATOES

While numerous varieties abound, tomatoes are difficult to find. Many commercial varieties are grown in engineered conditions and do not have much flavor. Vine tomatoes are matured on the vine for the best flavor. There are both cherry and standard tomatoes sold in this form. If you can't buy good tomatoes locally, it is better to use good-quality canned tomatoes or sun-dried tomatoes instead.

Buying and storing Buy local varieties when you can. They should be firm but not rock hard, and have good shiny skins, and a rich color, although this isn't always an indicator of flavor. Smelling them is sometimes a better test.

Keep tomatoes at room temperature since refrigeration deadens the flavor. Keep vine tomatoes on the vine. Ripe tomatoes will keep for a few days and unripe ones can take a week to develop a good flavor.

Preparation and cooking Wipe the tomato, then chop, slice, or cut in wedges, depending on the recipe. Served as a side dish, tomatoes are good broiled, griddled, or baked.

SKINNING TOMATOES

Score a cross in the top of the tomato. Place in a large bowl, cover with boiling water, and leave for 1 minute. You should then be able to peel off the skin very easily. If the finished recipe is to be quite juicy, you can leave the seeds in as well. Removing the seeds is a cosmetic touch and often you lose much of the flesh.

When chopping pumpkins, use a good, large sharp knife and don't try to cut through the stem.

VARIETIES OF TOMATO

Plum tomatoes: not so juicy as the standard tomato, these are good for pulping. Baby plum tomatoes are sometimes available, and they are good in salads and for roasting.

Cherry tomatoes: as you would expect, these are small, very sweet tomatoes, which are pretty left whole in salads or when roasted.

Beef, slicing, or Italian tomatoes: these giant tomatoes look impressive, thickly sliced for a simple salad. They can also be stuffed, or halved and baked, then drizzled with olive oil and balsamic vinegar.

CHILE PEPPERS

Fresh chile peppers range in heat from mild to blisteringly hot. As a rough guide, the smaller and narrower the chile and the darker its color, the more powerful its heat. The hottest chile peppers are the habanero and tiny bird's eye; the mildest include the sweet banana and tapering green Anaheim. Red chile peppers are riper than green and can taste slightly sweeter.

It is not a question of going for the burn! Chile peppers can add a wonderful dimension to your cooking, creating sensations from a rich warmth to a dramatic heat. Counteract their effects with dairy products or beer; surprisingly enough, a glass of water seems to intensify the heat instead of assuaging it.

Fresh chile peppers not only come in a range of shapes and sizes, but they also vary in heat, from being almost as mild as a bell pepper to blisteringly hot. Large green chile peppers are milder, while small, narrow dark-red chiles are at the hottest end of the spectrum. Choose an appropriate variety and they can add an underlying warmth rather than a dominating heat.

Buying and storing Look for bright, glossy skins and avoid any chile peppers that are bruised. Chile peppers can be stored for up to 3 weeks in the refrigerator. If there is any trace of mold, separate the chile peppers out and remove the culprit since the mold spreads quickly. If stored in oil, chile peppers will keep even longer.

Preparation and cooking Always treat chile peppers with care because they contain oils that can permeate the skin. After chopping a chile pepper, never touch your eyes or mouth; wash your hands thoroughly, as well as the knife and cutting board. A good precaution is to wear gloves. The skin, seeds, and membrane are the hottest parts, so discard those if you wish, reserving only the flesh.

SKINNING AND ROASTING CHILE PEPPERS

This can be done in the oven or under the broiler. Cook until the skin is charred. If the skin is thin and doesn't come away easily, place the chile pepper in a plastic bag and let steam in its own heat for 10 minutes. It should then be easier to peel.

Note: *if broiling chile peppers, do so only in a well-ventilated room since the chile pepper can release volatile oils that may sting your eyes.*

Rehydrating dried chile peppers: cover dried chile peppers with boiling water and leave for 30 minutes. Drain then crush with a pestle and mortar or purée in a blender. (Reserve the soaking water for adding to a stock.)

Fruit

To benefit from the valuable, health-giving properties of fruit, try to eat some every day.

Refreshing, colorful, versatile, aromatic, nutritious, exotic, juicy, perfumed—the adjectives that apply to fruit must be as numerous as the varieties of fruit found today in shops, markets, gardens, and greenhouses around the world. Look out for your own local delicacies, such as Scottish raspberries, Californian peaches, Indian mangoes, or Italian grapes.

As with vegetables, better transportation and storage makes sure that we now have access to a wider range of fruit at all times of the year. The downside of this is that many of these fruits may have to be ripened artificially or else never achieve ripeness. You are sometimes better focusing on locally grown produce bought in season and adapting recipes accordingly.

Fruit is an ingredient that fits well into any meal of the day, in both sweet and savory recipes, as well as being delicious as a snack or drink.

Nutritional Value

Fruit has long been valued for its health-giving properties. Fruit provides energy in the form of fructose or fruit sugar; it also contains carbohydrate and fiber. Most fruits are low in fat and therefore low in calories. Fresh fruit, preferably eaten raw, is an important part of any healthy diet. Most fruit contains vitamin C, an important antioxidant which cannot be stored in the body and so needs topping up daily. Some fruits, notably orange-fleshed varieties, such as apricots, mangoes, and peaches, also contain carotenes. Several varieties of fruit are a rich source of many essential minerals.

Buying

If you can, choose fruit from a loose display rather than pre-packed so that you can inspect each piece. Choose fruit that is bright and fresh, avoiding any with bruises or shriveled skins. In general, fruit should feel heavy for its size since this is an indication of a good moisture content.

When choosing fragrant fruits, such as melons, peaches, nectarines, strawberries, and pineapples, be guided by their aroma because this should be a good indication of their ripeness. If they have no smell at all, they may have been picked too early or have been over-refrigerated in transportation. Although some types of fruit may continue to ripen, they may never develop their full flavor.

If a piece of fruit smells almost sickly sweet and rather overpowering, it will be turning from ripeness to overripeness and may taste fermented or fizzy. Ripe fruits will spoil very quickly so handle them as little as possible. If you can taste before you buy, so much the better.

Storing

Fruits with a good protective skin, such as citrus fruit, kiwi fruit, apples, pears, and bananas, can be kept at room temperature. As fruit ripens, it gives off a natural gas, ethylene, which triggers the ripening process in other fruit. This is why fruit displayed in a fruit bowl will ripen slightly more quickly. Use this effect to ripen hard fruit—for the quickest result, put the fruit inside a brown paper bag together with an apple.

If you have a ripe piece of fruit to preserve, it will need to be refrigerated to slow down the ripening process. It is also best to keep it away from other fruit.

Some fruit, such as bananas and apples, can be stored at room temperature. They will ripen slightly quicker if kept in a bowl together.

Combining a variety of ripe, raw fruits makes an enticing fruit salad.

Preparation

With the exception of a few varieties of fruit, such as gooseberries and rhubarb, which need cooking before eating, most fruit can be eaten either raw or cooked. Wash fruit if you think that it needs it and peel it only if necessary.

Once fruit is peeled or chopped it can discolor. Have ready a freshly squeezed lemon or lime or some orange juice. As soon as you peel or cut the fruit, toss it in citrus juice. When presenting individual pieces of fruit, such as a pear fan, use a pastry brush to coat each piece with citrus juice.

Fruit salads can be delicious. Keep them simple—a combination of three or four fruits at the most can show off each to advantage. Contrast tastes and textures and mix the commonplace with the exotic. Rather than swamp the fruits in a sweet syrup, add a dash of liqueur or sparkling wine. Remember to prepare fruit salads at the last moment because cutting exposes more surfaces to the harmful effects of air, and discoloration and vitamin losses result.

Cold deadens the flavor of fruit, so if you are eating fresh fruit it is best at room temperature. Exceptions to this are very sweet melons and watermelons, which are wonderful cold, as are segmented oranges.

Cooking and Serving Fruit

In addition to being eaten raw, fruit can be cooked in several different ways. These methods are described here.

Poaching Many varieties of fruit are delicious served lightly poached. Once cooked, the fruit can be served hot or cold with a choice of accompaniments, from a plain yogurt to a luxury ice cream. Poached fruit can be kept in the refrigerator for several days. Poaching is a useful way of dealing with a sudden glut of a home-grown crop. Fruit can be poached in fruit juice, wine, or sugar syrup.

For a light sugar syrup, use generous ½ cup/4 ounces (125g) sugar to scant 1 cup/500 milliliters) water. Place the sugar and water in a saucepan and heat. Always make sure the sugar is completely dissolved over very low heat before bringing the syrup to a boil. Then boil the syrup for about 1 minute. Reduce to a simmer and add the fruit. Use enough syrup to cover the fruit. Once the fruit is cooked, any remaining syrup can be reduced to a thicker consistency.

Syrups can be flavored with vanilla beans or preserved ginger, as well as spices, such as cloves or cinnamon. Lemon or orange zest also makes a good addition.

For a wine syrup, follow the method for sugar syrup, making sure that the sugar is dissolved before being brought to a boil. Poach the fruit for about 15–20 minutes, depending on its size. Red wine will color the fruit and is the classic French technique for poaching pears.

Many varieties of fruit are delicious lightly poached and this is also a good method for preserving a glut of a home-grown crop. The poaching liquid can be a light sugar syrup flavored with vanilla or ginger.

Poached fruit can also be puréed and used in sauces or they can be mixed with plain yogurt, cream, or soft cheese in order to make a more substantial dessert.

Broiling, griddling, and grilling Most firm fruit broils or grills well in just a few minutes. These techniques can be used to make speedy simple desserts or to provide contrast to savory ingredients. Try using apples, pears, pineapple, plums, figs, nectarines, or apricots.

For broiling, cut the fruit of your choice into suitable chunks or pieces, thread onto skewers, and coat well with citrus juice. Just before cooking, coat the fruit with softened, sweet butter or a light brushing of sunflower oil. Broil for 1–2 minutes, scooping up any of the cooking juices and drizzling these over before serving. The sweet butter can be softened and mixed with flavorings, such as maple syrup, honey, or liqueurs.

Large pieces of firm fruit grill well, especially chunks of pineapple, bananas, and mango. Brush the fruit with citrus juices or honey. Oil the barbecue first so that the fruit does not stick, then cook the fruit until slightly browned on each side.

For griddled fruit, heat a large, preferably ridged, griddle or skillet. When hot, sear the fruit and cook for a few minutes on each side.

Baking This cooking technique brings out the natural sweetness of the fruit and cooks it to a melting texture. It is extremely easy to do and needs little preparation. The fruit can be cooking in the oven while you eat the main part of the meal. Fruit can be baked whole, in large pieces, or individually wrapped in baking parchment or foil.

Apples work well whole. Core them, then pierce the skin in a continuous line around the middle to allow the flesh to expand during cooking. Softer fruits, such as peaches and plums, are good if halved, their pits removed, then stuffed, and baked.

Baking fruit in wax paper or foil packets is a good way of cooking mixtures of large and small fruits, for example red currants and pears, or cranberries with orange and apple. Butter, honey, soft cheese, and a variety of flavorings such as spices can be added to the packet. The fruit retains all its flavor and cooks in its own juices.

Baked fruits are easy to prepare and can be cooked in foil or baking parchment.

An apple corer is a useful tool for preparing baked apple or making apple rings.

Orchard, pitted, and vine fruit

Orchard fruit (namely apples and pears) and pitted fruit (such as apricots and peaches) are grouped here. While distinctly different in flavor, both these groups of fruit are good to eat raw and are surprisingly versatile when cooked. Many can be stewed, broiled, puréed, or poached as a basis for a simple, nutritious dessert. Grapes, classed as vine fruit, is discussed at the end of the section.

Apples are delicious when combined with vegetables in salads or cooked dishes, such as with red cabbage.

APPLE

The apple has long been cherished as a health-giving, nutritious food. Despite the rise in popularity and availability of many exotic fruits, the apple still holds a special place. There are numerous varieties grown around the world with flavors that range from sweet or floral to spicy and aromatic. Apples can be eaten as a snack, are great cooked with dried fruits, used in cakes and pies or in relishes and chutney. They work well in salads, too.

Buying and storing Look for firm, unblemished fruit with smooth skins and a good color. For long-term storage, keep apples in cool conditions, separated from other fruit and vegetables. Apples give off ethylene gas, which can turn root vegetables bitter; apples will also absorb the flavor of onions.

Preparation and cooking Wash apples just before eating. Eat them whole or chop, slice, or dice for salads and fruit salads. The flesh will discolor quickly when cut so brush well with citrus juice.

There are some varieties of apple grown specifically for cooking, for example the Bramley from Britain, which reduces to a soft purée when cooked. This variety is also delicious when baked. There are lots of dessert varieties, however, that are also good to cook. On the whole, tart apples with crisp flesh work best.

Many fruits add a surprising, mellow sweetness to cooked dishes.

Both fresh and dried fruit make tasty purées, such as in this Apricot Lattice (see page 328).

PEAR

Some pears are plump and bell shaped, others are slim and conical, ranging in color from dark green to yellow. Some varieties have a crisp flesh with a grainy texture, others are distinctly buttery in flavor, are juicy, and melt in the mouth. Pears are delicious poached or stewed for pie filling and served with plain yogurt or cream. They work well with other fruits in fruit salads and also combine with savory ingredients, such as blue cheese, peppery salad greens, and avocado.

Buying and storing Pears are best bought unripe since they do bruise very easily. Once ripe, however, they may last only a day or so before developing an unpleasant woolly character. If you need to ripen pears in a hurry, put them in a paper bag with apples and leave them to ripen at room temperature.

Preparation and cooking Eat pears raw, washed and unpeeled. Alternatively, dice and stew, broil, or poach them whole (see page 59). The flesh will discolor quickly when cut so brush with citrus juice immediately if preparing for a salad.

Because pears bruise easily once ripe, it is better to buy firm specimens and give them time to ripen at home.

APRICOT

This small, smooth-skinned, orange-colored fruit has a good flavor only when fully ripe. It is then delicious eaten as it is or served in fruit salads. Apricots poach well, holding their shape, and once cooked can be used in pies, cakes, and crisp-topped desserts. They are excellent with savory foods, especially grains and nuts, and go particularly well with Middle Eastern flavorings, such as coriander or cinnamon.

Buying and storing Choose apricots that are firm and unwrinkled with velvety, pale orange skins. When ripe, they should just yield in the palm of your hand. If you cannot buy good ripe apricots, use dried ones for both sweet and savory recipes.

Preparation and cooking Wash apricots before eating. Slice, remove the pit, and add to fruit or savory salads. Poach, broil, or stew and purée.

COOK'S TIP

An easy method for skinning apricots and peaches is to pour boiling water over them and let them soak for about 1 minute. The skin can then be removed easily.

PEACH

This is an attractive, orange-yellow fruit with a downy skin. It is good served fresh, on its own or mixed with other fruit. Peaches can also be used in savory salads mixed with vegetables or grains such as rice, nuts, or cheese. They are also delicious baked or grilled.

Buying and storing Peaches should be firm, but not rock hard, and certainly free from soft patches. They will ripen after a few days in a warm place.

Preparation and cooking Peaches can be eaten fresh, simply washed and unpeeled. Poach, grill, broil, or stew and purée.

Peaches are gorgeous on their own as well as when mixed with other fruit or added to a savory salad.

NECTARINE

This smooth-skinned member of the peach family has sweet, juicy flesh. Nectarines are extremely easy to broil or grill; they can be eaten as they are, or mixed with other fruit in sweet and savory salads.

Nectarines go well with other types of fruit. They are easy to broil or grill and are delicious with creamy cheese.

Buying and storing Look for firm, but not rock-hard fruit. Avoid any that are bruised or damaged. They can be left to ripen for a while in a warm place.

Preparation and cooking Nectarines can be eaten fresh, simply washed and unpeeled. Poach, grill, broil, or stew and purée.

PLUM

This thin-skinned fruit can be large and black or small and purple, red, or yellow. Some varieties of plum are grown for eating fresh while others are best cooked. Plums are often served for dessert, baked in pies or with a sweet crisp topping. They can also be served with savories as a chutney or relish.

Ripe plums should just yield to the touch and may have a distinctive bloom on their skin.

Damsons and greengages are other pitted fruits that can be treated in a similar way to plums.

Buying and storing Plums should be quite firm and have a distinctive bloom on their skins. Unripe plums can be left to ripen in a warm place.

Preparation and cooking Dessert varieties can be eaten fresh, simply washed and unpeeled, or peeled and sliced. Plums can be broiled, poached, or stewed and puréed.

CHERRY

Light to dark red in color, cherries are a firm, succulent fruit with a sweet flavor. They can be eaten fresh, added uncooked to cakes, muffins, and strudels, or cooked in a light syrup for a purée or sauce.

Buying and storing Select firm, well-colored fruit that is not bruised or split. Store in the refrigerator for a few days.

Preparation and cooking Wash cherries before eating. Pit them before adding to fruit salads or sauces, or before baking.

GRAPE

Grapes range in color from pale green to deep red. Seeded grapes contain small bitter seeds; there are also many varieties of seedless grapes, widely available.

Buying and storing Look for plump specimens; the darker varieties will often have a natural bloom. Once grapes are ripe they do not last long. You can store them in the refrigerator but allow time for them to come to room temperature before eating.

Preparation Wash grapes just before eating. Eat them raw whole, or halve or chop them into sweet and savory salads.

There is an enormous variety of grapes grown throughout the world ranging from pale green to black.

Berry fruit

This colorful group includes strawberries, raspberries, red, white, and black currants, blueberries, blackberries, cranberries, and gooseberries. Soft fruits should be eaten within 1–2 days of purchase. Avoid any that are seeping juices or show any sign of mold. Delicate berries should be washed only just before using since water encourages them to rot.

Berry Fruit Purées

Strawberries and raspberries can be puréed without cooking. Hull and halve strawberries, but leave raspberries whole. Process in a blender or food processor then rub through a fine strainer to remove seeds. Add a fine sugar, such as confectioners' sugar, to taste, and add a little liqueur, such as kirsch, if liked.

If making a purée with red and black currants or blueberries, these need to be cooked first. Poach the fruits in a little sugar syrup (see page 59). Cool, then purée as above.

STRAWBERRY

This bright red, fleshy fruit is still seen as the epitome of summer, although strawberries are frequently available in many countries all year round. They can be served plain or lightly dusted with sugar. Strawberries make good sauces to accompany other fruit and can be used to flavor yogurt, ice cream, or other desserts. They also go well with cucumber, avocado, and salad greens.

Some people have an allergy or intolerance to strawberries, which can cause various symptoms, including a rash or swollen fingers.

Buying and storing Look for dry berries with a good color. Avoid any that have been squashed or show signs of mold. Keep strawberries in the refrigerator in a covered container or their smell will permeate other ingredients.

Strawberries are marvelous served plain or lightly dusted with sugar.

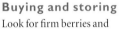

Soft fruit such as strawberries, raspberries, and black currants can easily be puréed.

Preparation Remove the leaves by twisting gently and pulling or cutting out with a knife. Try to avoid washing strawberries since they will become very watery.

RASPBERRY

The raspberry is a fragile, soft fruit containing many tiny seeds. They can be served plainly or with sugar, cream, or yogurt for a simple dessert. They are also a great treat with morning cereal. If the fruit is damaged or beyond its best, purée with some sweetening (see above) and blend with cream or ice cream.

Buying and storing

Look for firm berries and watch out for seeping juices at the bottom of the carton. Eat raspberries as quickly as possible. If necessary, they can be stored overnight in the refrigerator. Frozen raspberries are a good buy if you are intending to purée the fruit.

Preparation and cooking Avoid washing raspberries or they will turn to a mush. Pick over to remove any stalks.

Hull strawberries by gently twisting off the leaves or use a small sharp knife and cut out a conical section.

A few raspberries sprinkled over a plain cereal turn your breakfast into something special.

Red, white, and black currants are all tiny fruits with a distinctive tart flavor. Look for firm bright berries and store them in the refrigerator.

Buying and storing Select dark blue, large berries with a natural blue bloom. Blueberries keep better than other soft fruit and can be stored in the refrigerator for several days.

Preparation and cooking Serve as they come with a little orange or lemon juice and sweetening if you like. Alternatively, they can be added raw to cake and muffin mixture or cooked to a sauce, sweetened with sugar, and then thickened with cornstarch.

A few blueberries added to a muffin mixture keeps the texture moist and adds both color and flavor to the finished product.

BLACKBERRY

Blackberries can be eaten raw but unless they are truly ripe, they will be on the sour side. They are best cooked with a little sweetening and used for pies and sweet, crisp-topped desserts.

Buying and storing Blackberries do not keep well so aim to use them as soon as possible. Store them overnight at most in the refrigerator.

Preparation and cooking Pick over blackberries and, if you have picked them wild yourself, check carefully for insect life. Avoid washing or the fruit will turn to a mush. Stew with a little sugar or fruit juice.

RED, WHITE, AND BLACK CURRANTS

These tiny, round, shiny fruits have a tart flavor. They all look very attractive as an uncooked garnish served with other fruit, as a topping on pavlova and cheesecake, or in tiny fruit tarts. They cook down to a sauce that can be sweet- or sharp-tasting.

Buying and storing Look for firm, brightly colored berries that are moisture free. They can be stored for a day or so in the refrigerator.

Preparation and cooking String currants by pulling small groups through a kitchen fork. Cook them with water and a little sweetening to make the basis of a sauce. They are also good mixed with other soft fruits and stewed to make a richly colored compote, which can be served hot or cold.

BLUEBERRY

The blueberry is the cultivated form of the wild bilberry. It is popular in America but lesser known in Europe. Blueberries can be eaten raw, sweetened with sugar or spiked with a squeeze of lemon or lime, and served with yogurt or cream. Lightly poached with sweet spices, they can be used in pies and crisp-topped desserts or made into sauces for ice cream or sherbet.

After picking wild blackberries, check carefully for tiny spiders or grubs. Cultivated blackberries are more reliable but often have less flavor. Blackberries are best used as soon as possible.

Some soft fruits are better cooked than raw; for example, cranberries, gooseberries, and blackberries. Use a little sugar to bring out their flavor.

GOOSEBERRY

Gooseberries can be pale green or deep red in color. They need cooking and sweetening. Because they are so often watery, they are often underrated. The trick is to cook them whole with a minimum amount of water—generous 1 cup/7 ounces (200g) gooseberries with 1 tablespoon water.

Buying and storing Smaller, green gooseberries generally have the best flavor. Look for firm dry fruit. Gooseberries will keep for several days in the refrigerator.

Preparation and cooking Trim gooseberries, then cook gently until the skin splits. Cool and sweeten with fine sugar, such as confectioners' sugar. Push the cooked gooseberries through a fine strainer if you want a smoother texture—if you are going to strain them, then you needn't trim the fruit first.

CRANBERRY

Cranberries are deep red, round fruits. They can be used to make sauces and relishes, which go well with savory dishes, such as nut roasts or root vegetables. They can also be mixed with other soft fruits to make sweet purées suitable for dessert. Commercially produced cranberry juice is tasty and widely available.

Cranberries are thought to help prevent or treat urinary tract infections and cystitis.

Soft berries can be used in a number of ways. They make easy colorful garnishes, tasty purées, and simple sauces to accompany other fruit.

Buying and storing
Pick firm berries, hard enough to bounce off a counter. They should keep well in cool dry conditions.

Preparation and cooking Place the cranberries in a little water or orange juice in a saucepan, cover, and cook until the berries have popped—this takes 3–4 minutes. Sweeten to taste. The sauce can be served with savory dishes, or used for pie and pastry fillings.

Cranberries are small, deep red berries that are rock hard, so don't be put off if they bounce off the counter.

Citus fruit

This group includes the familiar lemon, lime, orange, and grapefruit, as well as the more unusual Ugli fruit and kumquat. Citrus fruits are often sprayed to give them a healthy shine. This should not affect the flesh inside, but if you are going to use the zest or eat the fruit whole, they will need to be scrubbed or look for unwaxed citrus fruit and for organically grown specimens instead.

The citrus family is a juicy range of fruits and good source of vitamin C. Look out for unwaxed and organically grown varieties.

Juice and Zest

Citrus fruits are frequently used for their juice. To get more juice from a fruit, roll it on the counter a few times before halving and juicing. Alternatively, place it in the microwave on HIGH (650W) for 30 seconds, because this also releases more juice.

Use citrus juice, especially lemon, when preparing apples and pears, and vegetables such as celery root and Jerusalem artichoke, to stop them from going brown on exposure to the air. Citrus juice is delicious in vinaigrette dressings as well as in creamy dressings made with tahini or bean curd (see page 317). Add the juice to soups and stews to lift earthy flavors or counteract sweetness. Oranges, lemons, and grapefruit can all be cooked. Whole pieces can be added to casseroles, sauces, and chutneys. Whole oranges can be baked, and oranges and grapefruit can be dusted with sugar and broiled.

Zest is the colored part of the peel, which is full of flavor, as opposed to the white pith which is bitter. Scrub the fruit if necessary to remove any wax coating, then use a zester, a gadget designed to strip off very fine slivers of peel. Alternatively, use a vegetable peeler or small sharp knife. In this case, if the strips of peel are a little thick, simmer them in boiling water for 4–6 minutes to soften. Drain, refresh in cold water, and use as required.

For grated zest rub the fruit lightly over a grater. Brush out the grater with a pastry brush to get the maximum amount of zest.

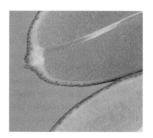

Zest of lemon or lime can be added to cake mixes, salad dressings, or sauces.

LEMON

Fragrant and acidic, lemons are used widely in vegetarian cuisine for both sweet and savory dishes.

Buying and storing
Lemons should have an even color and be free of blemishes. With some varieties a smoother skin indicates a thinner skin. Left whole, a lemon will keep for several days at room temperature or up to 3 weeks in the refrigerator. Once cut, it should be used as soon as possible.

Lemons are widely used to lift sweet and savory dishes.

Preparation Scrub waxed lemons if adding whole pieces to a recipe or if using the zest.

LIME

This fragrant citrus fruit has a distinctive tang. Use the juice and zest to flavor salad dressings and stir-fry sauces. It goes well with other fruits, especially papaya, and is often used in cheesecakes and sherbets.

Buying and storing Look for dark green fruit, shaped like a lemon but generally smaller. As it ripens a lime may turn more yellow in color. Buy firm specimens and store in the refrigerator for up to 1 week. Once cut, use as soon as possible.

Fragrant limes have a distinctive tang. Once cut, use as soon as possible.

ORANGE

The three main varieties of orange available are the smooth, thin-skinned oranges, such as the sweet Valencia and blood oranges; thicker-skinned seedless navel oranges; and bitter oranges, like the Temple, which is used for marmalade and other cooked dishes. The blood orange, so-called because of its distinctive ruby flesh, is more strongly flavored than a standard orange—use it in fruit salads or to make richly colored sherbet.

Oranges can be eaten as they are, squeezed for their juice, segmented and mixed with other fruit, or used in savory salads made with greens or legumes and grains.

Buying and storing Look for oranges with a blemish-free skin and a good orange aroma. They should keep for about 1 week in a cool place.

Preparation Scrub if necessary, peel, and segment, or squeeze and use the juice.

For really attractive segments, do not peel the fruit by hand. Cut the peel away using a serrated knife instead, making sure in the process that you remove the bitter white pith. Once peeled, cut down between the membrane and the flesh on both sides of each segment so that you can ease it out. Continue working around the fruit in this way. Work over a bowl to catch the juice.

Blood oranges have eye-catching ruby flesh and are slightly stronger in flavor than their orange cousins.

Relatives of the orange Tangerines, clementines, and mandarins are all related to the orange. These varieties tend to be easier to peel and have much thinner skins. They are not usually used for zesting or for their juice. Eat as they come, or use in fruit salads or as toppings for cheesecake or frozen desserts.

To make attractive segments, cut away all the pith and peel as well as the membranes on either side of the orange.

GRAPEFRUIT

The grapefruit is larger than the orange with a pleasant but sour taste, which some people can only tolerate when counteracted with sugar or honey. Lightly broiled, grapefruit makes a good appetizer or special breakfast dish. Grapefruit can have a pale yellow flesh or delicate pink, which is sweeter but less juicy. Segmented grapefruit pieces are good in fruit salads.

Close relatives to oranges, tangerines and mandarins. have thinner skins and are easier to peel.

Buying and storing When buying grapefruit choose heavy fruits and avoid any with loose or puffy skin because the flesh inside will be dry. Grapefruit should be stored in the refrigerator and, like the orange, still tastes good when chilled.

Preparation and cooking Cut in half, grapefruit can be eaten straight out of the peel as it is, or sweetened with honey or sugar. Broiled grapefruit works well—simply place the cut half, well sprinkled with sugar, under a preheated broiler for a few minutes. Segment grapefruit as for oranges (see left).

Relatives of the grapefruit The pomelo is the largest citrus fruit and has a bitter fibrous flesh, similar to grapefruit. The tangelo is a cross between a grapefruit and a tangerine. The Ugli fruit, too, is a hybrid, similar in appearance to the grapefruit but smaller and with sweeter-tasting, orange-colored flesh.

KUMQUAT

This small, oval fruit with a sweet-flavored, edible skin has a sharp, citrus-flavored flesh. Beware the seeds, which have an unpleasant taste. Use kumquats sliced as a garnish, with grains such as rice or couscous, and in savory salads.

Ripe kumquats should be soft to the touch. Store in the refrigerator for up to 1 week. Eat them whole, including skin.

Kumquats are roughly the size of a whole pecan nut. Sliced, they make an attractive garnish.

Tropical fruit

Although these fruits are becomingly increasingly accessible, the price and quality may well depend on where in the world you live. For the purposes of making exotic fruit platters and unusual savory salads, it is probably best to see what is available first, then adapt accordingly. Here are some of the best-known and most useful tropical fruits.

BANANA

Once considered exotic, bananas are now commonplace. They are usually eaten raw but are also good baked in their skins or grilled. They make a nutritious drink or meal when blended with milk, coconut milk, or bean curd. Use citrus juice to stop them from going brown. Don't throw out overripe bananas—they make great bread or cake.

The banito is like a miniature banana but with a sweeter flavor.

Bananas do not travel well and are best ripened at home on a hook.

Buying and storing Bananas do not travel well and are therefore picked unripe and then ripened later or during transit. Choose those with a green to yellow skin and do not pack them at the bottom of your shopping because they bruise easily. At home, store them on a hook.

Preparation and cooking Peel and eat raw, or bake with butter and honey, or bake in their skins.

PAPAYA (*PAWPAW*)

This is a large pear-shaped fruit with a yellow skin with a green blush. Slice one in half and you'll find orange-pink, perfumed flesh with tiny black seeds. Papaya is great served just with lime juice (or lemon as a second choice) to bring out its flavor. Use papaya with savory ingredients, such as chile, cilantro, and avocado. When chopped, it can make an unusual salsa or sauce.

Papaya contains an enzyme, papain, that helps digestion and is thought to have useful properties as a general cleanser and detoxifier.

Buying and storing Ripe papaya will feel very slightly soft to the touch. Avoid any with soft patches and check for bruising. Store at room temperature.

MANGO

There are many different types of mango, with skin color ranging from green—even when ripe—to red. It is worth making a note of your favorite variety. The flesh has a wonderful flavor, and is richly perfumed and creamy. Mango is delicious eaten on its own, mixed with other fruit, or used raw in savory salads, particularly those with rice.

Mango is highly regarded as a systemic cleanser especially for the skin and kidneys.

Buying and storing A ripe mango should be well scented and will yield slightly when pressed. Look carefully for bruising and other damage. For this reason try to buy mango that is displayed loose rather than shrink-wrapped.

Preparation Remember that the pit is oval in shape. Cut down the side of the mango, going as close to the pit as possible, using a small sharp knife. You will be left with two shallow cheeks. Score the flesh carefully with crisscross lines while it is still in its skin, then invert the skin so that the flesh stands proud, and slice the cubes off. Remove the flesh left around the pit.

For a mango fan, which is more elegant, use a fruit that is on the firm side. Peel the mango first, then holding the fruit carefully because it can slip, make a cut down to the pit from one end to the other. Make a second cut next to this at a slight angle to give a V-shaped wedge. Ease this out with the knife, then continue to cut thin wedges around the pit.

Tropical fruits can add a touch of the exotic to fruit platters and savory salads.

Mango cubes are easy to make by scoring the flesh while it is still in the skin.

This headily scented guava has a high vitamin C content. When ripe it should just yield to the touch.

GUAVA

This small tree fruit has yellow skin and a pulpy sweet pink flesh and can be large or small in size.

Buying and storing

Ripe guavas are highly scented and slightly yielding. Don't store guava near other foods since the smell may permeate. The smell of the flesh, however, is stronger than its taste. Slice in half and eat the firm flesh, or chop it and mix with soft cheese or cream. Cook guava with apples and pears to make a tasty pie or crisp-topped dessert. Guava has a particularly high vitamin C content.

KIWI FRUIT

The kiwi fruit is an egg-sized fruit with a brown hairy exterior. Inside, the flesh is a jewel-green color with a ring of minute black seeds. Kiwi fruit can taste like melon or gooseberry, depending on its ripeness. Its vitamin C content is higher than that of oranges.

Buying and storing When ripe, the fruit should give slightly when pressed. It can be stored in the refrigerator or ripened by being stored with an apple or banana. Organic varieties are usually smaller.

Preparation Cut in half and eat straight out of its skin with a teaspoon. For other uses, remove the skin with a sharp knife or vegetable peeler, then slice, and use in fruit salad, as a cheesecake or pavlova topping, or with savory salads. If the skin is difficult to peel, drop the kiwi fruit in boiling water for a few seconds.

Kiwi fruit can be eaten straight from the skin as a nutritious snack or peel first and then slice or chop.

PASSION FRUIT AND GRANADILLA

Ripe passion fruit has a hard, purple-brown wrinkled skin, inside which are hundreds of edible black seeds, which are sweet yet sharp in taste and invariably crunchy. The pulp is a golden color and deeply perfumed.

The granadilla is similar to the passion fruit but is larger with a gray-green flesh. Its buying, storing, and preparation guidelines are just as for passion fruit.

Buying and storing It is difficult to tell much about the passion fruit before buying since the exterior is hard and wrinkled. Do not buy specimens with soft patches. Use within 1 week.

With their wrinkled skin, passion fruit may not look very enticing at first glance but inside is a deeply perfumed golden flesh and hundreds of edible black seeds.

Preparation and cooking Cut the fruit in half and eat straight out of its skin with a teaspoon.

Make the most use of its intense flavor by mixing the juice with other ingredients. To extract

To get the most out of a passion fruit, scrape the pulp into a small saucepan and heat gently adding a little sugar. Then press the pulp through a fine strainer. The resulting juice has an intense flavor.

the maximum amount of juice, scrape the flesh into a small saucepan, add a little sugar—about 1 teaspoon—and heat gently. Then strain the seeds and leave the juice to cool. A small amount of juice will flavor a fruit salad or fruit drink. It is also delicious used in sweet sauces.

PERSIMMON (*KAKI FRUIT*) AND SHARON

The persimmon is a large orange-red fruit, about the size of a slicing tomato, with a very tough skin. The sharon fruit is very closely related but is seedless and contains much less tannic acid, so it can be eaten when still firm.

A ripe persimmon may be extremely soft to touch but it is then that it is at its best.

Buying and storing The persimmon has to be eaten in a very soft condition when the jelly-like, dripping flesh is sweet and succulent. Unripe, it can taste bitter and drain the moisture from your mouth. Leave unripe fruit in a plastic bag until the flesh looks translucent and the fruit is soft to the touch. Store ripe persimmons in the refrigerator.

Preparation Slice the fruit in half and scoop out the flesh. Serve fresh or use the pulp as the basis for a sauce or fruit dessert.

PINEAPPLE

One of the best-established tropical fruits, pineapple goes well with other fruit, as well as with savory ingredients in salads, or in stir-fries.

Buying and storing Pineapples do not continue to ripen once picked, so select carefully. A ripe pineapple should yield to gentle pressure applied at the stem. It should be more golden than green, have a good, full scent, and leaves that can be pulled off without much struggle.

Preparation and cooking Cut off the leafy plume and remove the base so that the pineapple will stand upright. Then cut down through the fruit to remove the skin but not too much of the flesh. Remove the "eyes" with the point of a small knife. Serve pineapple in slices, cubes, or fourths, removing any woody core. It is good broiled or grilled.

Ready-to-eat pineapples should be golden with a full scent.

LYCHEE, RAMBUTAN, AND MANGOSTEEN

These are three fairly similar fruits with crisp to hard skin. Not very appealing to look at, these fruits contain a translucent, pearly white flesh with a distinctive, almost grape-like flavor.

Look for firm and dry skin with no bruising, when buying these fruits. They can be cracked or cut open. Discard the brown pit.

MELON

Good in fruit salad, melon also combines savory ingredients, such as avocado, for appetizers. There are a number of varieties of melon available with different levels of sweetness, ranging in color from amber and orange to pale green.

Buying and storing Melons need to smell ripe. Check that they feel a little soft at the stalk end. Store melon in the refrigerator unless it needs extra ripening.

Preparation Serve melon chilled, left in the skin in wedges or halves with the seeds removed. It can also be served in chunks, slices, or balls, and mixed with other fruit or salad ingredients.

Melons come in a number of different varieties from golden fleshed through to orange and green. Most have a thick skin but if you get a good specimen, it will smell ripe.

VARIETIES OF MELON

Cantaloupe: a small, round melon with salmon-colored flesh and a very craggy outer skin. Serve ripe. It is from the same family as the ogen and chanterais.
Chanterais: sweet, succulent, perfumed orange flesh and green or bluish striped skin.
Honeydew: yellow skin with pale green, sometimes white, flesh when ripe. It is not always easy to pick a good specimen.
Ogen: green flesh, which can be very juicy.
Casaba: juicy, cream-colored flesh; slightly wrinkled yellow rind.
Watermelon: the giant of the melon family. Smooth, dark green outer skin, watery, pink inner flesh, and a plethora of inedible black seeds.
Pineapple melon: orange, netted skin and juicy orange flesh with a distinctive scent of pineapple.

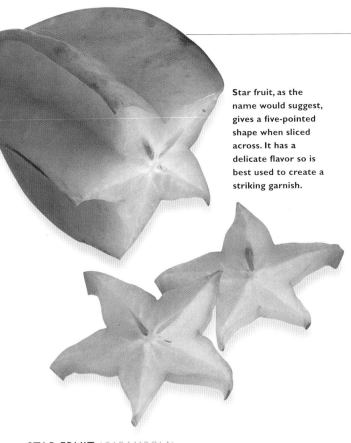

Star fruit, as the name would suggest, gives a five-pointed shape when sliced across. It has a delicate flavor so is best used to create a striking garnish.

STAR FRUIT (CARAMBOLA)

Prized more for its shape than its flavor, this angular, waxy, yellow fruit has a cross-section like a five-pointed star, hence the name.

Buying and storing Look for firm, unblemished fruit. As it ripens, a brown line develops along its ridges.

Preparation and cooking Wash, thinly slice, then use the star shapes as a garnish.

DATE

Fresh dates can be eaten as they are, or pitted and stuffed with sweet or savory fillings. Served like this they make tasty finger food.

Storing Keep in the refrigerator. Fresh dates also freeze well.

Preparation To remove the papery skin, pinch off the stalk end and then squeeze from the opposite end. To remove the pit, halve the date or pull the pit out from the stalk end.

Fresh dates served with nuts or cheese make a quick dessert or nutritious snack. Once pitted, they can be stuffed with sweet or savory fillings.

FIG

There are many varieties of fig, ranging in color from cream and yellow to deep purple and black. Not all varieties are available in every country. Unless you can get local or almost local types, dried figs may be a better option as you are guaranteed sweetness and flavor (see page 73).

Buying and storing A ripe fig should be unbruised and just soft when pressed. Although the skin may look tough, it is edible. The inner flesh is pinkish-brown and full of edible seeds. Store figs in the refrigerator.

Preparation and cooking Wash before eating. Leave whole, or cut in half and macerate in alcohol or fruit syrup, or bake or stew.

Ranging in color from deep purple to cream, ripe figs are sweet and full of flavor.

PHYSALIS (CAPE GOOSEBERRY, GROUND CHERRY)

This unexpected, sweet, orange berry is enclosed in an attractive lantern-like case of papery sepals. The fruit can be eaten raw—simply fold back the casing—or dipped in chocolate to serve as an after-dinner petit four.

The papery sepals hide a sweet orange berry.

POMEGRANATE

This tough, leathery, red-skinned fruit, the size of an apple, contains tightly packed seeds enclosed in a perfumed ruby flesh. The pith and membrane are bitter and should not be eaten.

Buying and storing Look for firm fruit and store for up to a week in the refrigerator.

Preparation Cut through the skin to mark out four segments. Using a sharp knife, cut around the raised end so that you can lift out the hard "button" or tuft. After peeling back the skin in sections, you can separate out the pomegranate without breaking the seeds. To extract the juice, roll the fruit over a counter, then make a hole in the skin, and squeeze out the juice.

Inside the tough leathery skin of the pomegranate is a mass of seeds surrounded by translucent ruby flesh.

Dried fruit

An extremely versatile ingredient, dried fruit
can be used in sweet and savory dishes,
served hot or cold, as well as being eaten as a
healthy snack. It falls into two categories—
vine fruits (raisins and currants) and
tree fruits (apples, apricots, dates,
figs, peaches, pears, and prunes).
Other dried fruit available includes
cranberries, kiwi fruit, blueberries,
and cherries.

It takes some 4 pounds (2kg) of fresh fruit to
produce about 1 pound (500g) raisins or currants
and nearly 6 pounds (3kg) of fresh fruit to produce
1 pound (500g) dried tree fruit, such as apricots
and peaches. The nutritional value of these fruits is
therefore highly concentrated but so, too, is their
sugar content, so they should be eaten in
moderation, especially when unsoaked.

Because they provide a
good number of minerals
and some vitamins, dried
fruit makes a nutritious
and tasty snack.

NUTRITIONAL VALUE

Dried fruits are excellent sources of many nutrients because they
are high in dietary fiber and a good source of energy. They also
contain minerals, such as iron and potassium, as well as some
vitamins—notably vitamins A, B_1, B_2, and C. In addition, they are
rich in fruit sugars, fructose and sucrose, yet they contain virtually
no fat or cholesterol.

Some dried fruits are treated with sulfur dioxide—added in
order to preserve color and maintain water content, thereby
keeping the fruit plumper. It also prevents fermentation and decay
and, while it helps to preserve vitamins A and C, it does destroy
the B vitamins. It is believed that this is not a harmful additive if
eaten in only small quantities.

Buying and Storing

Choose good-looking dried fruit. If it is rock hard or shows any sign
of crystallization, it is old. Once the packet is open, store it in an
airtight container. Keeping a piece of lemon or orange peel in the
container helps keep the fruit moist. Except for apples, most varieties
should keep for up to 1 year. As dried fruit ages it may develop a
sugary coating. This can be removed by soaking in warm water
for a few minutes.

Preparation and Cooking

Rinse dried fruit under warm
running water to remove traces of
preservative. Most fruit these days
is sold ready cleaned.

To plump raisins and currants
soak them in warm or hot liquid
such as water, fruit juice, or alcohol.
Leave for 5–10 minutes, then drain
if necessary.

To reconstitute larger dried
fruits, such as apricots, pears, and
apples, leave them to soak for
several hours using plenty of
liquid—water, fruit juice, or wine.
A quicker method is to cover the
fruit with liquid and bring to a boil.
Simmer, covered, for about 10–15 minutes, then let soak. Leftover
juice can be boiled further until syrupy.

Larger dried fruits, such as
apricots, benefit from being
soaked so that they soften and
swell prior to cooking.

Once soaked and cooked, the fruit can be eaten as it is or easily
puréed using a blender or food processor. Add a little of the soaking
or cooking liquid as necessary.

Vine Fruit

All dried vine fruits are good in baking and can be added to biscuits,
bread dough, strudels, flapjacks, or cookies. They make excellent
additions to breakfast cereals, such as granola or porridge. Dried vine
fruit also works extremely well with many savory dishes, particularly
with grains as a stuffing for grape leaves, bell peppers or zucchini, as
well as in many salads.

GOLDEN RAISIN

Golden raisins are soft, juicy, amber- or golden-colored fruits, with a sweet flavor.

RAISIN

Ranging in color from dark brown to almost black, raisins have a wrinkled skin and a sweet mellow flavor. They are lightly oiled to prevent them from sticking together once dried.

CURRANT

The smallest of the dried vine fruits, currants are dried, black seedless grapes of the Corinth variety. They are the least sweet and are used in many savory recipes, particularly dishes from Greece and the Middle East.

Tree Fruit

These larger dried fruits can be eaten as a snack, snipped raw into cereals and salads, or soaked and mixed with other dried fruits. Once reconstituted and puréed, they make great fillings for pies and tarts, or can be stirred into yogurt, cream, or bean curd to make simple fruit desserts. Use a sweet purée, such as date or apricot, to replace some of the sugar required in a recipe.

Hunza apricots are smaller in size than a regular apricot and have a honey-like flavor. Here, they are shown being dried on a roof in the Hunza valley, Pakistan.

DRIED APPLE

Dried apples are sold ready-peeled, cored, and sliced or in rings. They are chewy and have a mild taste with a slight tang. They are best mixed with other fruits.

DRIED APRICOT

Their rich, mellow flavor is best savored in apricots that are dried whole. For making purées buy halves or pieces of dried apricot. Hunza apricots are beige-brown, small apricots, dried whole, and must be soaked before eating. They have a honey-like flavor once soaked and, if stewed, produce a rich liquid.

DRIED DATE

The date is an extremely sweet fruit once dried. Beware of mixing the purée into anything light colored because it will turn everything else very dark.

DRIED FIG

Another very sweet fruit once dried. When soaked and lightly cooked, dried figs produce a sweet, mellow liquid, which is good for flavoring fruit salads and compotes.

DRIED MANGO

Despite the difficulty of choosing fresh mangoes, the dried fruit is quite reliable in its sweetness and flavor. It is good for a snack—rich but not cloying.

DRIED PEACH

Dried peaches are sold in halves or slices. Some varieties can be extremely sweet, and the orange-colored ones have the most tang.

DRIED PEAR

Sold in halves, this fruit is sweet and chewy with a slightly granular texture. Dried pears have a beautiful, clear, golden-yellow color.

PRUNE

The prune is a dried plum, which is sold whole with a pit or pitted. It has a rich flavor and makes an excellent purée that can be used in baking or mixed with cream, yogurt, or silken bean curd to make a fruit dessert. Prunes can also be eaten just as they come or soaked.

Prunes have a laxative action, partly due to their fiber content but also to the presence of diphenylisatin.

Milk and cream products

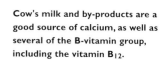

Milk, cheese, and eggs play an important role in a vegetarian diet since they are versatile and nutritious ingredients. If you are new to a vegetarian diet, their familiarity makes them a comforting and accessible source of protein. However, it is important to eat these excellent foods in moderation because of their high saturated fat content.

Cow's milk and by-products are a good source of calcium, as well as several of the B-vitamin group, including the vitamin B$_{12}$.

Organic Dairy Products

Recent concern about the use of growth hormones in dairy farming and how this may affect milk and milk products has raised the profile of organic milk and milk products, such as butter, yogurt, and cream. Although more expensive, they may well be worth the investment.

Strict rules govern the production of organic milk. In general, the animals must be fed on a high percentage of organic food matter with the remainder being natural foodstuffs, rather than food concentrates or animal protein. The use of preventive antibiotics and other medicines is not allowed. In the USA there has been widespread use of the growth hormone referred to as rBGH or rBST. However, many smaller dairies in the USA do not use this hormone and they are allowed to print that information on their cartons of milk. In Canada, the use of these growth hormones is not allowed.

NUTRITIONAL VALUE

Cow's milk and cow's milk products are a good source of protein and calcium—1¼ cups/½ pint (300 milliliters) whole or skim milk provides over half the daily calcium requirements for a child under 10. Milk is also a good source of vitamin B$_{12}$, and provides riboflavin, thiamin, niacin, and folate. Fortified milk contains vitamin A and vitamin D. Milk also supplies zinc, potassium, and phosphorus. The fat content per scant ½ cup (100 milliliters) of cow's milk is 3.9g for whole milk, 1.6g for low-fat, and 0.1g for skim. This fat content is largely saturated.

Other milk products, such as cream, yogurt, and buttermilk, contain similar nutrients. If you are trying to eat less saturated fat, look for lower-fat versions of these products, but read labels carefully since gelatin is sometimes added to enhance the texture.

Butter, although a product of milk, contains no calcium or protein but it is a source of the fat-soluble vitamins A and D.

Goat's milk has a similar nutritional profile to cow's milk but is lower in protein and lower in calcium. It is useful for people who cannot tolerate the protein in cow's milk. For alternatives to milk and milk products see page 83.

Storage

Milk, cream, yogurt, and other milk products must be kept in the refrigerator and consumed within a few days of their "sell-by" date. Make sure the products smell fresh and there is no yellowing or dryness. Milk should also be kept out of the light since this destroys vitamin A.

CRÈME FRAÎCHE

This French version of sour cream has a pleasing delicate tang and tastes rich, thanks to its high fat content. It works well with hot and cold dishes, both sweet and savory. At its simplest it can be spooned over baked potatoes, served with

Cheese can be served as a course in its own right. Choose a combination that gives appealing contrasts in textures and flavors.

chili, or used on fruit. It can also be used with confidence when making sauces and enriching soups since its high fat content means that it can be boiled without separating. There are also low-fat versions of crème fraîche—use these only in cold dishes because they may separate if heated.

BUTTERMILK

Once the liquid whey that was left over from the butter-making process, buttermilk is now more commonly made from low-fat or no-fat milk with added cultures, and it is these that give it a tangy flavor and also thicken it slightly. Buttermilk is excellent used in pancakes and soda breads and other quick breads made with baking soda because acids in the buttermilk react with the baking soda in order to make the dough rise. Buttermilk provides calcium but none of the fat-soluble vitamins.

YOGURT

Yogurt can be made from cow's, ewe's, or goat's milk or even from soybeans. Whether it is thin and sharp-tasting or thick and rich depends on the individual maker. It is a matter of personal taste as to which type of yogurt you use for various dips and dressings. Take care when cooking with yogurt, because it tends to curdle very easily. Some commercial yogurts have vitamin D added to them.

Making your own yogurt Commercial yogurt makers for use at home come with useful size containers and thermostatic controls to keep the yogurt at the right temperature. These are good if you want to make all your own yogurt. For the occasional batch, however, you could simply use a wide-necked vacuum flask. Heat 2½ cups/1 pint (600milliliters) milk to 110–113°F (43–45°C). Stir in a yogurt starter—either 2 tablespoons of plain live yogurt or a culture powder, stir well, then pour the mixture into a clean warmed vacuum flask. Leave overnight or until set, then transfer to a clean container and refrigerate.

Yogurt is made by fermenting milk with bacteria, resulting in a thickened mixture with a distinctive tang.

Yogurt makes a good base for a low-fat salad dressing, or a sweet or savory dip.

Strained or set yogurt As the name suggests, these yogurts have been strained so that some of the whey is removed and the yogurt is thicker and richer. Used on their own, strained yogurts make good salad dressings and combine well with herbs, such as chives, cilantro, and parsley or finely snipped scallions. Lebneh is yogurt cheese made from strained yogurt.

SOUR CREAM

Sour cream has a spooning consistency and is great as a last-minute topping for a spicy casserole or served with potato or red cabbage. It is not of a sufficiently high fat content to be stable at a high heat so add it only to warm soups and sauces.

CLOTTED CREAM

This traditional English product is made by heating cream to make a crust. It is generally used in sweet dishes, for example with fruit or with jelly and biscuits for a traditional English cream tea. It is also good with waffles and pancakes.

Sour cream is ideal for enriching a baked potato or as a last-minute topping on spicy casseroles and refried lentils.

BUTTER

Butter is suitable for vegetarians, and organic varieties are increasingly available. (See pages 114–16 for oils, margarine, and cooking fats.)

GHEE

This is a clarified butter from which the milk solids and sugars have been removed. It adds a rich flavor to cooking and has the advantage of not burning so quickly as other fats. It is widely used in Indian cookery.

Cheese

Taste a fresh soft goat cheese, a mature Parmesan, or a pungent Roquefort and you get some idea of the wide range of flavors and textures within this family of ingredients. The difference between cheeses depends on many factors—the length of aging, the manufacturing process, and the type of milk used.

For lots of everyday cooking, a standard hard cheese is fine. Choose a brand with a reasonable depth of flavor. It is worth gradually trying a variety of cheeses since these will add an extra dimension to your cooking. The majority of cheese is made from cow's milk. Goat cheeses are characterized by sharp clean tastes with a pungency developing as the cheese matures. Ewe's milk cheeses are sometimes mild, the notable exceptions being Roquefort and feta.

Some hard cheeses are encased in protective wax coatings.

NUTRITIONAL VALUE

Cheese provides excellent amounts of protein and is an extremely good source of calcium. A quantity of 1 ounce (25g) Cheddar cheese provides about 20 percent of the daily requirements of calcium for a man and 25 percent of the requirements for a woman. Cheese is also a good source of vitamin B$_{12}$, as well as containing other B vitamins and zinc. The fat content varies considerably from one cheese to another, but it is usually saturated.

Goat cheese has a similar nutritional profile to that made from cow's milk. The main difference is that goat cheese can be tolerated by some people who have an intolerance to products made from cow's milk.

Rennet

Why aren't all varieties of cheese labeled as being suitable for vegetarians? The answer is that many cheeses, especially some traditional varieties, such as Parmesan, are made using animal rennet, an ingredient that helps to curdle the milk and separate it into curds and whey. Rennet is a substance that comes from calf's stomach and is therefore not eaten by strict vegetarians. Fortunately, there are increasing numbers of cheeses that are produced with a plant-derived alternative rennet and these are the cheeses that are labeled as suitable for vegetarians. Soft cheese on the whole does not contain any sort of rennet.

Some cheeses are labeled "GMO-free." This is because they do not contain a type of vegetarian rennet used by some large manufacturers that is a genetically engineered copy enzyme called chymosin. (See page 31 for more on genetically modified food.)

Buying Cheese

It pays to choose cheese for both cooking and eating from somewhere reliable and where you can taste before you buy, especially when looking for unusual and interesting varieties. Choosing cheese for eating is a matter of flavor first. Look for contrasting tastes and textures if you are serving a number of cheeses as a course. When choosing a cheese for cooking you need to consider not only its flavor, but also whether it will melt well, can be grated, and so on.

As a general rule, the longer a cheese has been matured, the stronger its flavor, the drier its texture, and the longer it will keep. Mild, soft, snow-white, fresh cheeses have short "sell-by" dates and

So many varieties of cheese are now available, it is useful to shop somewhere where you can taste before you buy. If you are buying for a cheese board, aim to get a contrast of texture as well as flavor.

delicate tastes, whereas the well-aged Parmesan has a dry, hard granular texture and powerful flavor and can be kept for months.

Hard and semihard cheeses, such as Cheddar, should look smooth without discoloration and mold, unless of course this is part of the character of the cheese. The rind on a hard cheese should not be too dry or cracked, nor should the cheese itself be sweaty. Be guided, too, by the smell. An odorless cheese probably lacks character and flavor, while one smelling of ammonia should be avoided.

Blue cheeses are made with a culture that gives them their characteristic blue or blue-green veining. There should be no sign of pink or beige among the blue, and nor should the cheese be wet. The flavors may be strong but should not be over-salty or chalky. Try to taste before you buy.

Storing Cheese

It is best to wrap hard or semihard cheese and blue cheese in wax paper. Do not use plastic wrap or similar, since this will not let the cheese breathe. If kept well, these cheeses should remain in good condition for some time. Soft, fresh cheeses, creams, and yogurts will not keep for any length of time. Store them in the refrigerator and use within days of the "sell-by" date.

On the whole, all cheeses should be kept in, and used straight from the refrigerator. The exception to this rule is when serving cheese as a course during a meal—make sure that you bring the cheese out of the refrigerator at least 2 hours before serving. The flavors will have time to develop and will be more pronounced.

Wrap a hard or semihard cheese in wax paper to allow it to breathe.

Cooking with Cheese

Always melt cheese slowly over low heat. If you try to do this too quickly, the cheese may separate or become stringy. Cheddar, Gruyère and other Swiss-style cheeses melt very well. Mozzarella is the classic cheese for pizza toppings as it melts evenly, producing long, sinuous strands.

Goat cheese softens and browns beautifully under the broiler, while haloumi cheese is good for barbecues as it softens only slightly as it gets hot.

When melting cheese, do this slowly over gentle heat or the result may be stringy.

For a pizza topping, choose a cheese that melts well, such as mozzarella.

Pungent blue cheese, melting Brie, and nutty-tasting Cheddar show the range of tastes and textures available in cheese. It is worth experimenting with different types of cheese to appreciate the variety.

Varieties of cheese

Add to all the different types of **N**orth **A**merican cheeses, hundreds of European varieties and there is an almost overwhelming selection, too numerous to mention here. The following pages detail a selection of 20 of the most readily available and the most useful cheeses. For the purposes of this book, cheeses are listed under three broad categories: hard and semihard cheese, such as **P**armesan, **C**heddar, **S**wiss, and feta; blue cheeses, such as **S**tilton, **G**orgonzola, and **R**oquefort; and soft cheeses—ripened cheeses, such as **B**rie and **C**amembert, and fresh cheeses such as goat cheese (chèvre).

Cheese is definitely a vegetarian fast food when used in a quick sauce to make a nutritious topping for pasta.

Hard and Semihard Cheeses

These cheeses do not change in consistency once purchased (other than becoming moldy or drying out if you don't get around to eating them). Hard cheeses should grate or slice well, hold their shape in a salad, and may melt to make toppings and sauces.

CHEDDAR

This versatile cheese is good for both eating and cooking. Dense in texture, Cheddar can range in flavor from mild to tangy, and in color from white to deep gold. Much Cheddar is industrially produced and lacks real character, but there is a renaissance in handcrafted Cheddar cheeses, which can be bought in good cheese shops and delicatessens.

PARMESAN

Properly aged Parmesan is labeled "Parmigiano Reggiano" and is rigorously protected by Italian law. It is made to a strict set of standards that have not been altered for 700 years. Aged for a minimum of two years, generally longer, this cheese has a slightly gritty texture, a rich aroma, and complex flavors. Strict vegetarians will not be able to use this as there is no vegetarian version of the true Parmesan, but there are now several vegetarian varieties of a Parmesan-style cheese which, although not so complex in flavor, have a reasonable taste and good texture.

EMMENTAL

Ivory-colored, with a fairly firm, slightly oily texture, this Swiss cheese is characterized by large holes, which are the natural consequence of the cheese-making process. This type of cheese melts and broils well.

GRUYÈRE

Also from Switzerland with a warm yellow color, gruyère is pockmarked with little holes, and characterized by a sweet fruity flavor. It, too, melts and broils well.

FONTINA

Fontina is an ivory-colored Italian cheese with a nutty flavor and sweet aroma. It melts well and, when mature, can be grated.

HALOUMI

This semihard Cypriot cheese is made from ewe's milk, and is used frequently in Turkish and Lebanese cuisine. It is delicious warmed in pita bread. Since it softens, rather than drips or oozes when melted, it is extremely useful for making kabobs for barbecues.

FETA

Traditionally from Greece, this ewe's milk cheese is now produced in several countries. Feta should be snow-white, moist, and crumbly. Its salty, sharp, almost sour tang is accentuated when cooked. In the process of making feta, the curds are salted and then covered with whey and brine. Its strong flavor marries well with strong herbs, such as oregano and marjoram, as well as with many Mediterranean dishes using olives and tomatoes.

Feta will not melt or brown in the way that other cheeses do, but it can be crumbled for use in quiches and pies. It can also be marinated in a good-quality olive oil, which acts as a preservative. Add fresh herbs, peppercorns, chile peppers, sun-dried tomatoes, or even lemon zest to get flavorsome results. Leave refrigerated in jars for a week or so then serve as a cocktail snack and filling for bread.

Blue Cheeses

These cheeses range from surprisingly mild flavors and very creamy textures to strong, salty tastes.

ROQUEFORT

Made from ewe's milk, this is a robustly flavored, slightly crumbly cheese.

DOLCELATTE

Sweet, soft, and creamy, this type of Gorgonzola is good for savory dishes as well as partnering fruit for dessert.

STILTON

One of the few English cheeses that is manufactured under strict conditions, Stilton can be produced only in the three shires of Leicester, Nottingham, and Derby. A good Stilton should be smooth and creamy, rather than dry or crumbly.

GORGONZOLA

An Italian alpine cheese made from cow's milk, Gorgonzola is blue veined with a mild tang. It should not be too salty.

Ripened Soft Cheeses

These cheeses have a high percentage of moisture. They are easy to spread—indeed some fully ripened ones may gently spread over the plate if left at room temperature. Ripened soft cheese should be slightly springy to the touch, the outer bloom should look even, and the inside should look evenly creamy. Avoid any with a firm-looking, chalky white center.

If the cheese is overripe, a thin rind may develop or the crust may split.

The inside should not sink down or look withered. Some of these cheeses are "washed" in brine or wine, a process that helps maintain internal moisture for fermentation. These cheeses often have a strong piquant flavor and aroma.

BRIE

Brie is a classic French cheese that needs to be just ripe to be appreciated. Look for a pale yellow center, which is soft but not running. It is always made as a large cheese and once cut will not ripen.

CAMEMBERT

Originally made in the small village of that name but now manufactured as far afield as America, Camembert should have a light orange-yellow rind, a pale yellow center, and be slightly springy to the touch. The cheese has a slight tang.

Fresh Soft Cheeses

These cheeses range in texture from the very creamy, with a spooning consistency, to those with firmer curds, such as ricotta. They can be between 2 and 10 days old. There should be no yellowing and the curds should look moist, not dry.

RICOTTA

This is another traditional cheese from Italy. Made from whey, it has a snow-white appearance and light texture. It is often used as a filling for ravioli, since it can be packed densely and doesn't ooze when cooked.

FRESH CHÈVRE

Fresh and ripened soft goat cheeses vary greatly in appearance because they can be sold in logs, pyramids, or rounds, wrapped in leaves, or coated with peppercorns or ash, to name but a few varieties. What they have in common is a clean tangy taste, but nothing overpowering. The flavor will develop with age. Goat cheese has a smooth texture and a wonderful capacity to melt.

More mature goat cheese is firmer in texture and more powerful in flavor, with a rind or outer mold that may develop considerably. The mold is bluish-gray and, although visually off-putting, it does not mean there is anything wrong with the cheese.

FARMER'S CHEESE

Made from cow's milk, this soft unripened cheese has a slightly sharp taste. It is beaten until very smooth and in some cases mixed with cream giving it a consistency rather like a set yogurt. The fat content of farmer's cheese varies from brand to brand.

MOZZARELLA

The finest mozzarella is made from buffalo's milk, which has a higher fat content than cow's milk. Since this is hard to come by, much modern mozzarella is made from cow's milk. This snow-white cheese is firm enough to cut and is sold in balls or blocks, usually packed with a little liquid, which should be drained off. When very fresh, it is delicious uncooked in salads with tomato or avocado. It is also excellent on pizzas and broiled vegetables since it melts beautifully.

COTTAGE CHEESE

Made from whole or skim milk curds, cottage cheese has a mild flavor and slightly coarse texture. It is good for using in salads and sandwich fillings, and for blending into low-calorie creamy dressings.

MASCARPONE

This high-fat, soft Italian cheese is made from fresh cream, which is whipped to give it a very smooth texture. In Italy, mascarpone is principally used as a dessert cheese, spiked with liqueur and served with fruit. It can also be added to soups and sauces to give them a velvety texture, and can be the basis of a rich dip or dressing.

QUARK

A low-fat smooth-textured soft cheese made from skim milk, quark can be used in the same way as cottage cheese and natural farmer's cheese.

Eggs

This extremely versatile food can be used in a multitude of ways for making meals. Many eggs are labeled euphemistically as "farm fresh," "barn," or "hens fed on a vegetarian diet" to hide the sorry truth of intensive production, where hens are crammed into dark spaces and kept in squalid conditions. Many vegetarians concerned about animal welfare use only free-range eggs. Free-range birds must have access to runs and a variety of vegetation.

Nutritional Value

Eggs are an excellent source of protein, as well as vitamins A, the B group, D, E, and K. They also contain iron, calcium and iodine. Eggs are high in dietary cholesterol—all of which is in the yolk—and have a low level of saturated fat. New research suggests that pre-formed dietary cholesterol has little impact on the amount of cholesterol in your blood, but it is still wise to moderate your consumption of eggs. They are fiber-free.

The size of an egg is actually its weight. There are several grades of egg, which go up in ¼-ounce (5-g) intervals. The largest eggs weigh around 2½oz (65g).

Salmonella

Salmonella is a particularly unpleasant bacterium, which can cause severe illness. It is endemic in chickens and therefore common in eggs. Since bacteria are killed in the cooking process, egg dishes should be cooked thoroughly—until the white is set and the yolk has thickened and is firm. Do not eat raw egg. Salmonella also multiplies with age. Very fresh eggs, even if contaminated, will have lower levels of the bacteria. Look at the expiration or "use-by" date and do not use eggs beyond this date.

The other danger can come from the egg shell itself. Do not use chipped or damaged eggs, and always wash your hands before and after handling egg shells.

Those most at risk from the effects of salmonella are children, the elderly, pregnant women, and anyone whose immune system is deficient, for example when recovering from illness.

Because egg shells are porous, eggs can pick up odors from other foods stored nearby.

Buying and Storing

Avoid buying eggs with chipped, cracked, or damaged shells. Store eggs in the refrigerator, preferably in their containers. Since their shells are porous it is best to keep them away from strong-smelling food. They should be stored pointed end downward, which keeps the yolk roughly in the middle of the egg. Always use eggs by the expiration or "use-by" date, preferably before. If the eggs have no date, then test them for freshness.

The basic test for freshness is to see if the egg floats or sinks. The older the egg, the lighter it will be, since it will have lost water through its shell during storage. Thus, a fresh egg will sink in a bowl of water and a stale egg will float. The appearance of an egg once cracked is also an indication of its freshness. A fresh egg white is thick and gelatinous, supporting the yolk, which rests on top. Separated whites and egg yolks must be kept in airtight containers. Use yolks within 2 days and whites within 1 week.

Fresh eggs always sink to the bottom of a bowl of water; stale eggs will float.

TECHNIQUES WITH EGGS

It is best to separate eggs taken straight from the refrigerator because the yolk is firm and less likely to run into the white.

Whisking egg whites
Egg whites should be at room temperature for whisking, so leave in a covered bowl for about 1 hour. Use only clean utensils

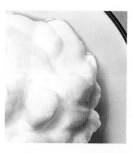

since any grease will prevent the whites from expanding. Whisk in a medium to large bowl, and for small quantities, use a balloon whisk. For larger quantities, use an electric whisk but start on the lowest speed setting and then increase the speed once the whites start to foam. The term "soft peak" describes whisked egg whites that will lift in peaks but the top of the peak will gently tip over. A "Stiff peak" is when the egg white holds its shape completely.

Nondairy alternatives

There are many reasons why people choose not to eat dairy products, or to cut down on them. If you cannot or do not want to have milk, cheese, or yogurt, there are now many straightforward alternatives, generally made from soy milk. You may also find milk made from rice and oats. These can be used for cold drinks as well as served with cereals, but are not so suitable for cooking since they can curdle. For more information on soy alternatives, see page 96.

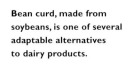

Bean curd, made from soybeans, is one of several adaptable alternatives to dairy products.

SOY MILK

A vegan alternative to milk, made from soybeans, soy milk does not taste like cow's milk, but is perfectly acceptable as a drink or liquid for cereals. It does have a tendency to curdle when added to hot liquids and also to separate in sauces, so it is less versatile. Soy milk is rich in protein and low in fat. Some varieties are enriched with calcium and B_{12}. It is sold unsweetened, or sweetened with sugar or fruit juice concentrates.

Soybeans are used to produce milk, cheese, yogurt, and flour.

SOY CHEESE AND YOGURT

Soy cheese can be firm, with the consistency of a processed cheese. It does have a flavor although it can seem rather fatty to eat. Soy yogurt can be flavored or plain. If you already drink soy milk, you will find these products quite acceptable.

TAHINI

Tahini makes a great binding ingredient for burgers and baked dishes. It will thicken any moisture in the mixture prior to cooking. Be sure to handle it carefully when you are cooking, since it may curdle a mixture.

BEAN CURD

Bean curd makes a good mayonnaise—blend soft or silken bean curd with oil and flavorings to make a rich, creamy dressing. Silken bean curd can also be scrambled to make a savory topping for toast.

Milk, yogurt, and cheese can all be made from nondairy sources. They do not taste the same as their dairy equivalent, nor do they behave in exactly the same way when heated, but they are useful sources of protein. This range of products is continually improving and expanding.

Alternatives to Eggs

If for some reason you cannot eat eggs, there are several alternatives for use in cooking.

SOY FLOUR

Soy flour can be used to enrich mixtures, such as a cake or a savory baked dish, although it won't help lighten the mixture.

Grains

Such is the versatility of grains that they and their derivatives appear in various guises in thousands of dishes around the world—in paella, pasta, crêpes, or enchiladas to name a few. Since ancient times, cereals or grains have been staple foods—wheat, rye, barley, and oats in the temperate climates; rice, corn, and millet in the tropics and subtropics.

In addition to traditional grains, there are lesser known varieties such as quinoa. Included in this group, too, are buckwheat and wild rice. Neither is strictly a grain, but they have similar nutritional properties and are interchangeable with some other grains. Grains come in many different forms besides whole grains, which adds to their versatility as cooking ingredients. They are frequently processed as flakes or cracked grains and partially cooked, as well as being ground into flour.

NUTRITIONAL VALUE

Each whole grain is a seed and contains many nutritional elements within its protective outer layers. These layers include the germ, which is an important source of oils and carbohydrate, and bran, a valuable source of fiber. The starches in grains are broken down during digestion to form glucose, which gives the body a sustained and steady supply of energy. It is important to chew grains thoroughly because it is an enzyme in the saliva that begins the digestion of these starches.

Grains are a rich source of many essential amino acids and should be eaten in conjunction with legumes or nuts to provide complete protein. They are also a good source of minerals, as well as vitamins, particularly the B-group vitamins.

Once a whole grain is processed for flour or flakes, the outer layer is cracked and the oil in the germ begins to oxidize and lose its nutritional value. Although flour and flakes are useful cooking ingredients, it is important to use some whole grains in a well-balanced vegetarian diet. Refined whole grains, such as white rice, and their products, for example white flour or white bread, are nutritionally inferior. The bran and germ have been removed and therefore many of the valuable nutrients lost.

Buying and Storing

Even though whole grains have a long shelf life, they inevitably harden as they age and can take longer to cook. They keep indefinitely in cool dry conditions. They are best stored in airtight containers. Processed grains, such as flakes and flour, do not keep as long so it is best to buy them as fresh as possible. It is possible to find organically grown grains, flakes, and flour but you may need to seek out a specialist outlet for these.

Flakes and flours should be kept away from any heat so that the oils they contain do not go rancid.

Cooking Whole Grains

These are general guidelines for cooking all whole grains (rice, wheat, barley, buckwheat, millet, and quinoa). The basic method remains much the same but the water quantities and the time needed for cooking will vary with each grain (see opposite). First, rinse the whole grains if necessary to remove surface dust.

Whole grains can be stored for a long time in cool, dry conditions. Processed grains such as flakes or flour need to be used more quickly.

Absorption method This is best if you work by volume, for example 1 cup of rice should be cooked in 2 cups of water. Choose a saucepan with a close-fitting lid, or use a pressure cooker. Rub a little oil around the pan to prevent the grains from sticking—this will also make the pans easier to clean. Bring the right quantity of water to a boil, quickly tip in the grains, then stir once. Bring back to a boil, reduce the heat to a simmer, cover the pan, and cook for the required length of time until the grain is tender and

Each whole grain is a seed and contains many useful nutrients. They are a good source of amino acids, minerals, and vitamins, especially the B-group vitamins.

all the liquid has been absorbed. Do not stir since this tends to make the grains sticky. Do not add salt because this toughens the grain.

Toasting grains before cooking helps to bring out their flavor. Use about 1 teaspoon of oil to 1 cup of grain. Heat the oil in the saucepan and gently toast the grain, then pour in the water and cook as normal. This works particularly well for millet, quinoa, and buckwheat. For more flavor, spices such as cumin, coriander, or chile can be lightly toasted and cooked with the grain.

Note, a standard 8-fluid ounce (250-milliliter) cup filled to the brim will hold about 7 ounces (200g) rice or other grain. This is enough for 4 as a small side serving, or it will make a one-pot dish, such as paella or risotto, for 4 with other ingredients added. (Recipes in the book are generally based around this measurement.) If you are serving hungry adults, you may prefer to double the quantity.

Hot water or free simmer method Bring a large quantity of water to a boil in a saucepan. Add the grain and bring back to a boil, then simmer very gently until the grain is tender. Turn into a colander or strainer and drain well. The advantage of this method is that the grain is unlikely to catch on the base

Grains vary enormously in size and appearance, from the slender mahogany-colored wild rice to the chunky, round risotto rice.

of the pan. The disadvantage is that some of the nutrients will be lost as they leach into the cooking liquid and are then thrown away.

Microwave Grains can also be cooked in the microwave but it takes virtually the same length of time. The advantage is that the grains do not stick or boil over. For microwave cooking, use an exact quantity of water because excess water increases the cooking time.

Risotto method This method of cooking is particularly suitable for risotto rice, millet, and short-grain rice. It involves patience and stirring, which gives the grain the creamy, slightly sticky quality of risotto. For 1 cup/7 ounces (200g) grain, use about 4 cups/1¾ pints (1 liter) stock. Using oil or butter, cook chopped onion and garlic, then add the grain. Add one-third of the stock and, stirring constantly, bring to a boil so that the mixture is bubbling gently. When all the stock has been absorbed, repeat the process with the next third, and finally the last third of stock. The whole process will take around 20–30 minutes.

Some grains benefit from being toasted first in a little oil to bring out their flavor. Spices can also be added.

COOKING WHOLE GRAINS BY THE ABSORPTION METHOD

Type of grain in standard measuring cup	Pre-cooking instructions	Amount of liquid per 1 cup of grain	Average cooking time (minutes)
1 cup rice	—	2 cups	25–30
1 cup wheat	Soak overnight	3 cups	50–60
1 cup barley	—	3 cups	50–60
1 cup buckwheat	Toast	2–2½ cups	15–20
1 cup millet	Toast	2½–3 cups	20
1 cup quinoa	Rinse well and toast	2 cups	12–15

Whole grains and flakes

O f all the whole grains, barley, millet, quinoa, buckwheat, oats, rice, and wheat are the most widely available. Many of these grains are also sold in flake form, which makes them more versatile. For cooking instructions see the previous page and for recipes see pages 222–29.

Some grains, such as rice, are predominately used in their whole form, whereas barley or wheat may be used whole, flaked, or in flour.

BARLEY

Barley was popular in ancient times, but is now less widely used. Rarely served on its own, it is more commonly added to soups and casseroles, thickening and flavoring them. Once cooked, it is light and chewy. Barley flakes can be used in baking and added to breakfast cereals.

MILLET

Native to Africa and Asia, millet comprises round grains of golden yellow. It can be served with stews and casseroles, or cooked with vegetables for a pilaf or risotto style of dish. Millet tends to cook unevenly so some of the grains will be crunchy while others are soft.

Also, the grains will stick together if left to stand once cooked. Millet has a milder flavor and less texture than rice. It also combines well with sweet ingredients to make a dessert similar to a rice pudding. Millet flakes and flour are available and can be used in baking, breakfast cereals, and crisp topping mixtures. Millet is gluten-free.

QUINOA

Pronounced "keenwa," this grain has a delicate, grassy flavor. It is somewhat similar in appearance to millet—gold in color with minute round grains. It must be washed thoroughly before cooking because the outside is coated with bitter chemicals. It is important to keep a check on quinoa at the end of the

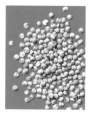

suggested cooking time because the grains are easily overcooked and lose their texture. In the center of each grain is a tiny spiral thread, which is visible when cooked.

BUCKWHEAT

Buckwheat is an attractive angular seed with a distinctive strong flavor. If unroasted, the grains have a greenish tinge; once roasted, they turn a dark reddish-brown. Toasted grains are sometimes called kasha. Buckwheat goes well with cold weather vegetables, such as root vegetables, and with mushrooms and dark green vegetables. It is gluten-free.

OATS

Once the staple food of Northern Britain, oats are rarely sold as whole grains but are used mainly when processed into meal and flakes. Use as the basis for breakfast cereals such as granola and for porridge (see page 134).

Oat flakes are good for thickening soups or casseroles or for adding bulk to burgers or savory baked dishes. When mixed with a little flour and fat, oats make a good crisp topping—either sweet, with added sugar, or savory, when flavored with herbs. Oat flakes and oatmeal can also be used in bread making and for cakes and cookies such as flapjacks (see page 327). Oats contain a soluble dietary fiber that is thought to lower cholesterol levels in the blood.

Rice

Widely available in many different varieties, this is a popular and versatile grain. Fortunately, its long shelf life means that you can store several types and choose the most appropriate for the particular recipe.

Rice is grown in many parts of the world and each variety lends a distinctive character to dishes, such as risotto or pilaf.

Short-grain
This type is suitable for desserts, savory stuffings, and risotto-style dishes since it comprises plump small grains that stick together once cooked.

Glutinous rice
Also called sweet rice or sticky rice, this is a polished rice with round pearl-like grains. Although called glutinous, this grain—like all rice—is gluten-free. Once cooked, the grains tend to stick together. The rice is used for sushi (see page 281), in which cooked rice, sometimes seasoned with vinegar, is wrapped in sheets of nori.

Long-grain
The long, slender grains hold their shape once cooked. Long-grain brown rice has a nutty flavor and is good for accompanying chilies, stir-fries, and curries, and makes a good base for salad. Pre-cooked white and brown rice are available—these have shorter cooking times. Pre-cooked white rice is steamed under pressure when unmilled, then milled afterward, which helps to retain some of the nutrients.

Basmati rice
This fragrant rice with long, slender grains is native to India and Pakistan. Once cooked, the grains separate easily. Cooked plainly, it can accompany a range of dishes from curries to stir-fries.

Jasmine rice (fragrant rice)
Jasmine rice is similar to basmati rice but has a slightly soft and sticky texture when cooked. It has a milder flavor than basmati rice, but still has a distinctive aromatic smell when cooking.

Risotto rice
Usually a polished grain of a medium size, risotto rice gets its creamy quality since some of the starch breaks down as it cooks. It also absorbs about five times its weight in liquid. Some superior varieties of risotto rice are sold by name—look for Arborio, Carnaroli, and Vialone Nano. More nutritious risotto can be made with brown short-grain rice.

Red Rice
This unusual rice from California has medium, russet-colored grains, which are light and chewy when cooked, with a nutty flavor. It can be mixed with ordinary rice, but also works well on its own with sautéed or griddled vegetables. Cooked in a similar manner to long-grain rice. It takes about 20–25 minutes.

Wild Rice
Originally native to the Great Lakes of North America and only found wild, this rice is now cultivated more widely. It is not a true rice but an aquatic grass with thin and slender grains colored a dark chocolate-brown. As it cooks it splits and curls slightly. Wild rice has a distinctive, nutty flavor and works well on its own or mixed with ordinary rice. It can be served hot or cold, it makes a dramatic stuffing for vegetables. Cook as long-grain rice. It takes about 35–40 minutes.

Wheat

The whole grain of wheat, known as the wheat berry, is sweet and chewy with a springy texture. It adds texture to casseroles and can also be used in savory baked dishes and salads. In its other forms, wheat is used in many dishes.

Wheat is widely available and it is processed in a number of ways, making it an extremely versatile ingredient.

Cracked wheat
This is made by cracking whole wheat berries between giant rollers so that the cooking time is reduced.

Bulgur
Bulgur is made from whole wheat that has been cooked, dried, and then cracked. Depending on the brand, it needs little or no cooking, merely soaking in boiling water. Organic varieties of bulgur can take longer to soften.

To soak bulgur, measure it into a large bowl, add a little salt, and pour in twice its volume of boiling water. Let stand for 10–15 minutes. If still chewy, bulgur can be cooked briefly in the microwave. Bulgur can be used as a quick accompaniment, cooked like a pilaf or served cold as the basis for a salad (see pages 230 and 299).

Couscous
North African in origin, couscous is made from the inner layers of the wheat grain and is therefore slightly less nutritious than bulgur. It has the appearance of tiny golden balls. Depending on the

variety, couscous can be lightly steamed or simply soaked in boiling water for 5 minutes. Organic varieties may need more cooking. It makes a quick accompaniment for casseroles, but is also delicious as a salad base.

Semolina
Produced from the starchy part of the grain, semolina can be used for desserts or as an ingredient of gnocchi. It is also used for making commercial pasta.

Wheat flakes
Coarser in texture than oat flakes and not so creamy once cooked, these are useful for thickening soups and stews and also provide a contrasting texture to oat flakes in granola.

Wheat germ
This is the embryo of the grain, containing valuable nutrients such as protein, fat (mostly unsaturated), vitamin E, and B-group vitamins. It is important to store wheat germ in the refrigerator since its high fat content means it can go rancid very easily. Even when stored properly, wheat germ should be used within weeks rather than months. For a nutritional boost, add wheat germ to breakfast cereal, bread or pastry dough, grain salads, and savory baked or crisp-topped dishes. Use only small quantities since it does have a distinctive flavor.

Bran
Comprising the outer layers of the whole grain, bran is a useful source of fiber, but it does need to be combined with flakes or added to savory mixtures or it is unpalatable. It contains phytic acid, which can interfere with the absorption of certain minerals.

Flour and Pasta

Flour is an essential ingredient in many dishes such as pastry, pasta, cakes, and cookies, as well as a thickening agent in sauces. All grains can be made into flour, but many are low in gluten or gluten-free, which makes them less versatile. This section concentrates on wheat and corn flour, which are probably the most widely used.

WHEAT FLOUR

Many varieties of wheat flour are available and it is worth stocking several types so that you can choose the most appropriate flour for the recipe.

Flour from hard wheat, often described as strong flour, has a high gluten content and is good for making bread. Flour from soft wheat, with a low gluten content, is better for cakes, pastry, and baking.

Whole-wheat flour is made from the whole-wheat grain and can vary considerably according to the way in which it has been milled. Some varieties are extremely fine, while others contain visible flecks of bran. The texture of the flour will affect the end result: coarser flour absorbs more liquid.

Unbleached flour is a refined flour—it has had the bran and germ removed but has not been subjected to chemical whitening.

Whole-wheat flour can be finely ground to give a beige appearance flecked with bran.

CORNMEAL

Native to America, corn appears in a variety of forms as diverse as a fresh vegetable, a sweetener, and an oil.

Dried corn is ground into a distinctive yellow meal or flour. The result may be sold as maize meal, cornmeal, corn flour, or polenta, the Italian name. The texture varies from fine to coarse. Once cooked, cornmeal is delicious layered with

Cornmeal can be coarsely or finely milled.

OTHER TYPES OF FLOUR

Here are some types of flour that are not so commonly used, but are still useful, especially the gluten-free varieties.

Buckwheat flour
This pale gray, tasty flour retains the distinctive dry taste of buckwheat. It makes excellent crêpes and is also used commercially to make Japanese soba noodles.

Rice flour
A gluten-free flour that can be used for baking and thickening sauces, or for fine batter.

Rye flour
With a pleasant tang, rye flour does contain gluten but it is the type that does not leaven bread. Generally rye is mixed with wheat for bread making. A spoonful or so of rye flour can add a nutty flavor to pastry.

Quinoa flour
Low in gluten, this flour needs to be mixed with wheat flour for baking because it is a soft flour.

vegetables, cheese, or tomato sauce. It can also be pan-fried or griddled. (See pages 222–24 for cooking instructions and recipes.)

Cornmeal is found in numerous Mexican dishes, such as enchiladas and tortillas. These go well with all the foods popular in that cuisine, such as avocado, chiles, and cheese.

Cornmeal can be mixed with wheat flour to make a golden corn bread or a savory topping for vegetable stews.

PASTA AND NOODLES

Dried pasta and noodles are godsends to busy cooks. Easy to have at hand because of their long shelf life, they can be served with a huge range of sauces, vegetables, or even just plain olive oil or butter. Pasta and noodles may once have been most popular only in Italy and the Far East but their use in cooking now far exceeds these international boundaries.

Look for a range of flavors and different thicknesses. Pasta can be made from wheat, corn, buckwheat, or even quinoa flour; it may be flavored with tomato, spinach, basil, chile, egg, and a host of other flavorings.

Pasta is extremely adaptable. As a rough guideline, fine pastas are best served with lighter, smooth sauces, while larger pastas, such as shells, curls, or broad noodles work better with chunky sauces, making sure that the dish looks more balanced.

Pasta is made from a variety of flours and can have numerous different flavorings.

Legumes

Beans, peas, and lentils, collectively known as legumes, are the edible seeds of leguminous plants. They are a vital group of foods for vegetarians, being both highly nutritious and extremely versatile. They have the added advantages of being readily available and storing well, and are cheap to buy.

Most of the world's cuisines contain a traditional dish featuring a bean or lentil—consider fiery chiles with red kidney or pinto beans from Mexico, spicy samosa from India made with mung beans, Asian stir-fries with bean sprouts, classic baked beans in tomato sauce from Boston, and hearty soups containing split peas from Northern Europe. These and many other recipes show the versatility of these ingredients.

Beans and lentils can be the basis for excellent soups, stews, and casseroles. Puréed or mashed, they are good in dips, pâtés, and burgers or savory baked dishes; freshly cooked and marinated, they work well served cold in substantial salads.

While the flavor differences between varieties of legumes are small, they do come in a wide range of shapes, colors, and sizes. Mixing two contrasting legumes together in the same dish is an excellent way of adding interest in terms of color and texture.

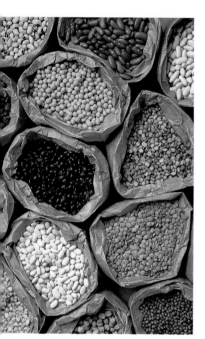

Look for beans and lentils that are plump and glossy with bright colors, and store them in a cool dry place.

Legumes are a good source of protein as well as supplying useful amounts of many vitamins and minerals.

Buying and Storing

Shop for beans and lentils where you know the turnover is brisk. Although they all have a long shelf life, it is better to try to use them within a year of the harvest. Look for beans and lentils that are plump or glossy with bright colors. Avoid any that are wrinkled, chipped, or cracked, because these have probably been around some time. Keep dried legumes in a cool pantry in an airtight jar.

NUTRITIONAL VALUE

Legumes are important in a healthy vegetarian diet because they are a good source of many of the essential amino acids, the building blocks for protein. Eaten in conjunction with grains or nuts they provide high-quality protein.

Legumes are a good source of fiber and starch. They tend to be low in calories since, with the exception of the soybean, they are low in fat. Rich in vitamins B_1, B_2, B_3, and calcium, they also contain some iron, phosphorus, and manganese. Whole, dried legumes are easy to sprout (see page 93). Their vitamin content then increases dramatically and they become an important source of vitamins C and A.

On the minus side, legumes contain phytic acid, which can inhibit the absorption of some minerals.

Preparing Dried Legumes

It is vital to prepare legumes properly because they contain the toxin, lectin, which is only rendered harmless during the soaking and cooking process.

Before using dried beans and lentils, they should be picked over for small pieces of grit, tiny sticks, and ungerminated seeds. Next, put them in a strainer and rinse thoroughly to remove any surface dust or dirt. Lentils are now ready to cook (see below) but larger beans need soaking.

Soaking beans gives them time to swell so that the final cooking time is reduced. It also means that immature or overdry beans, which won't cook properly, float to the surface where they can be removed. Soaking beans before cooking also helps them become more digestible since the soaking process removes some of the complex sugars, which cause gas to build up in the gut. There are two soaking methods that you can use.

When using dried legumes rinse them first. Larger legumes need soaking before cooking.

Long-soaking method Put the beans in a large bowl and cover with four times their volume of cold water. The harder the bean, the longer the soaking takes. Soybeans may need to be left for 8 hours or overnight. Garbanzo beans, too, take several hours; red kidney beans, pinto, and black beans may well be ready after a couple of hours—you can check to see whether the beans look plump or the skin is still wrinkled.

Quick soaking method Bring the beans to a boil in a saucepan containing four times their volume of water. Boil fast for 3–5 minutes then turn off the heat, and let stand for 1 hour.

Cooking Beans

Once the beans are soaked by one of the above methods, drain, and rinse them again. Then bring them to a boil in plenty of fresh water. Use enough water so the beans are covered and have another 1–2 inches (2.5–5cm) depth above them. Boil them at a fast, rolling boil for at least 10 minutes, to make sure that any toxins on the outside skins of the beans are completely destroyed. Then reduce the heat to a

COOK'S TIP

If you are soaking beans in hot conditions, they may start to ferment and you'll see the soaking water start to look frothy. In this case, put the beans to soak in the refrigerator.

simmer, partially cover the pan, and continue cooking the beans until soft (see table, below, for individual timings). Remember the timing can vary from batch to batch. During the boiling process, scum frequently forms on the surface—just skim this off. Adding a little oil to the cooking liquid can help prevent the scum from forming. The beans are cooked when soft to the bite and evenly colored all the way through—test at the end of the suggested cooking time. If the beans are not cooked, continue simmering as necessary—it is better to overcook rather than undercook legumes.

If you use a pressure cooker, the cooking time is generally reduced by at least half. Do not be tempted to cook too many beans at once because the scum that forms may clog the pressure gauge.

Beans must be fast-boiled for at least 10 minutes to destroy any toxins present on the outer skin.

COOK'S TIP

Do not add salt to the cooking water because this toughens the outside skins of the beans and means they will take longer to cook.

COOKING TIMES FOR BEANS

These timings are a guideline only since length of cooking time will vary from one batch to another and may differ according to the quantity of legumes cooked. For all beans, soak them in plenty of water; drain, rinse, and fast-boil for 10 minutes, then cook for the following suggested times, or until tender.

Type of bean	Suggested cooking time
Mung	45–50 minutes
Small navy	45–50 minutes
Adzuki	50–60 minutes
Black-eyed peas	50–60 minutes
Borlotti	50–60 minutes
Cannellini	50–60 minutes
Navy	60–70 minutes
Pinto	50–60 minutes
Black	60–90 minutes
Brown	90–120 minutes
Lima	60–90 minutes
Garbanzo	60–90 minutes
Ful (or foul) medames	60–90 minutes
Red kidney	60–90 minutes
Soy	up to 4 hours

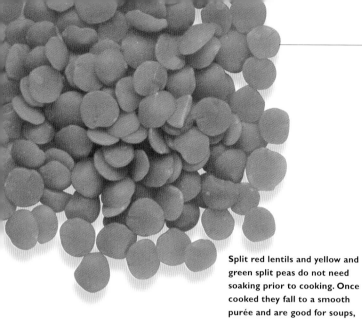

Split red lentils and yellow and green split peas do not need soaking prior to cooking. Once cooked they fall to a smooth purée and are good for soups, pâtés, and fillings for pasties.

Cooking Lentils

Once lentils have been picked over and rinsed, they are ready to cook. For whole lentils, bring them to a boil in plenty of water and cook until just soft. For split lentils, when trying to make a purée—for baked dishes, burgers, and pâtés—you must measure the water exactly, otherwise it is easy to end up with a mixture that is too sloppy to use. As a rough guide, the volume of water should be double the unit of measurement of the weight of the lentils, for example 1 cup/8 ounces (250g) lentils to generous 2 cups (500 milliliters) water.

Whole lentils need to be boiled in plenty of water. Cook until they are soft enough to bite through and then use in soups, stews, or salads.

Quantities

Dried legumes will roughly double in weight once they are soaked and cooked. Generally, it is worth cooking a large batch of beans at a time and then storing them in usable quantities. Recipes in this book either use a ready-cooked weight or give clear instructions for using an uncooked weight.

Canned beans and lentils are pre-cooked by the manufacturer. The advantage is that you don't have to cook them and they are ready to use right away. The disadvantage is that they are generally more expensive and you do have to check the labels for additives. Be aware that many varieties will have salt or sugar added.

Freezing Beans

If you have cooked a large quantity of legumes, it is worth freezing some for future use. They can be frozen in their cooking liquid or drained and stored in a plastic container. Freeze them in shallow blocks for easy storage and fast thawing. Make your blocks of beans a suitable weight for a recipe—for example, a casserole for 4 people needs 2⅗–3¼ cups/13–16 ounces (400–500g) cooked weight. Beans will freeze for up to 6 months.

Thaw overnight in the refrigerator, or for 2–3 hours at room temperature, or defrost them in a microwave.

Beans freeze well either in their cooking liquid or drained and portioned out into suitable plastic containers or bags.

Once soaked, beans will roughly double in weight.

PREPARING AND COOKING LENTILS

Type of lentil	Soaking instructions	Cooking time
Split red	None required	20–30 minutes
Continental	Optional but recommended	30–40 minutes
Puy lentils and lentilles vertes	None required	10–25 minutes
Brown lentils	Optional but recommended	30–40 minutes
Yellow split peas	None required	30–40 minutes

MAKING BEANS MORE DIGESTIBLE

A well-known side effect of beans is flatulence and some people are more affected than others. A golden rule is that legumes must be very thoroughly cooked. Here are a few more tips that may help to make beans more digestible:

• Change the water once or twice during the soaking process; the long-soaking method seems to work better
• Sprout the beans for a day or so before cooking
• Add a strip of kombu (seaweed) to the cooking water
• Cook the legumes with spices, such as cumin or caraway, which aid digestion
• Introduce legumes gradually into your diet
• Start by eating lentils and smaller beans, such as adzuki beans, which are thought to be easier to digest

Growing Bean Sprouts

Although often categorized as bean sprouts, sprouts can be grown from grains, vegetables, or legumes. Useful and nutritious ingredients for salads or stir-fries, they can be grown at any time of the year. It is easy to grow your own bean sprouts, requiring very little equipment.

Mung beans and alfalfa seeds are probably the best choice for beginners as they grow quickly and have an excellent flavor. Sprouts can be grown in a variety of containers, but drainage is essential. The simplest method is to use a wide-necked jar with a porous cover, such as cheesecloth, but colanders, fine strainers, or mesh trays can be used instead.

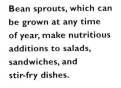

Bean sprouts, which can be grown at any time of year, make nutritious additions to salads, sandwiches, and stir-fry dishes.

Bean sprouts can be grown in wide-necked jars and covered with cheesecloth or a lid pierced with several holes to make draining easy and let air circulate.

1 Pick out any grit, sticks, or damaged specimens and wash the beans or seeds thoroughly.

2 Put 2 tablespoons of beans or seeds into a jar, fill with lukewarm water, and let stand overnight. This soaking process helps break down the outer shell so that the growth is quicker.

3 The next day pour off the water and leave the jar in a warm place. If bean sprouts are grown in the dark they will contain more vitamin B_2; if grown in the light, there is more vitamin C.

4 Every night and morning, until the sprouts are ready, rinse the beans or seeds in the jar with lukewarm water. Shake them gently, so as not to damage the delicate sprouts, and drain them thoroughly. It's best to turn the jar upside down so that all the excess water drains away since if too much moisture is left, the sprouts may go moldy. If the weather—or your kitchen—is warm, you may need to rinse the sprouts an extra couple of times each day to prevent them from drying out. Most sprouts take about 4 days to grow. They will keep fresh for 4–5 days in the refrigerator.

Grain and vegetable sprouts need no cooking but if you have particular trouble digesting legumes, it is worth cooking sprouts from peas and beans for a short time. As well as using sprouts in salads and stir-fries, you can knead them into bread dough or add them to breakfast cereals and sandwiches. For use in casseroles, don't sprout the beans fully—a couple of days should be enough.

RED KIDNEY BEAN

Glossy red and named for their shape, these beans are best known for their use with chile. They go well with hot spices and are great in casseroles and salads. Mashed and reheated for refried beans (see page 191), they are also popular in Mexican cookery.

ADZUKI BEAN

Small, maroon beans from China and Japan, these are small enough to go into pie fillings and savory baked dishes, and make an excellent substitute for ground meat in dishes such as lasagne or moussaka. Adzuki beans go well with rice dishes, mushrooms, and eggplant; for a gourmet treat, cook them with red wine. They are also good when sprouted.

GARBANZO BEAN

Pale gold in color with a nutty flavor and crunchy texture, the garbanzo is also known as chickpea, ceci, and chana dhal. They are popular in Middle Eastern cookery, where they are served toasted and salted or puréed with garlic, oil, lemon, and sesame to make hummus—a delicious soft pâté or dip (see page 167). They are also cooked and ground with spices, then deep-fried to make little savories known as falafel (see page 174). Garbanzo beans make a good contrast with dark-colored beans, both in salads and casseroles.

Gram flour is the powder that is made from grinding garbanzo beans. This flour makes a light batter for vegetable fritters (see page 168) and is used extensively in Indian cookery.

BLACK-EYED PEA

This legume is similar in size to the navy bean but with a distinctive black spot, hence its name. They were introduced to America from Africa and are now popular in the southern states of America, as well as in the Caribbean, because they go well with flavorings from those regions. They are particularly useful in soups and casseroles and make a good contrast with red kidney beans or garbanzo beans.

PINTO BEAN

Originally used in Mexican and South American cookery, pinto beans are a variety of navy bean but speckled pink. In flavor and appearance they are similar to the Italian borlotti bean. They hold their shape well once cooked, and are good for soups, stews, and salads. They can also be mashed to make refried beans (see page 191) and work well with hot and aromatic spices.

SMALL NAVY BEAN

These beans are an attractive pale green color and have a delicate flavor. Very tender when cooked, they are quite digestible. They are good served with butter and herbs, such as chervil or chives, as well as with tomato-based sauces. They are often only available canned.

BORLOTTI BEAN

Light brown or pink with deeper red speckles, these beans cook to a soft texture and are good for pâtés or for mashing into savory baked dishes or burgers. They go well with mild spices, such as nutmeg and cinnamon, and can also be served with Parmesan.

MUNG BEAN

Native to tropical Asia, mung beans are especially popular in Indian and Chinese cookery. Their small size makes them easy to mash into hot spicy snacks, such as samosas. They have a slightly sweet flavor, which is more noticeable once they are sprouted. Sprouting also means they have a very high vitamin content (see page 90). Use the sprouts in stir-fries or spring rolls, in salads, and for sandwich fillings.

LIMA BEAN AND BUTTER BEAN

These are similar beans, the butter bean (top picture) being the larger. They are a traditional ingredient in succotash, a stew made with corn, molasses, and paprika. The smaller lima bean (bottom picture) also looks attractive in salads. Butter beans can be puréed with milk or cream and served as a side vegetable.

CANNELLINI BEAN

This white variety of kidney bean is used in Italian cookery and is good with typical flavorings of the cuisine, such as basil, oregano, and thyme. It also works well in soups, casseroles, and salads.

SOYBEAN

The soybean stands alone as the only bean that provides all the essential amino acids. Although of great value nutritionally, it takes a long time to cook—up to 4 hours—and is thus rarely used as a bean in its own right. Soy products, such as bean curd (tofu), tempeh, miso, soy flour, and soy sauce, are more common (see page 96).

FUL (OR FOUL) MEDAME

This small version of a fava bean is popular in Egypt. The beans are traditionally served boiled and mashed with spices, such as cumin, garlic, and pepper, and sometimes accompanied by eggs, onion, and lemon.

NAVY BEAN

A small, oval bean with a creamy, white color. It is most widely used for "baked beans," but is also useful for casseroles and bean salads where it makes a good contrast with red kidney beans and garbanzos.

BLACK BEAN

These dramatically colored beans are frequently used in central and South American dishes. They go well with cumin, chili, and tomato, as well as with citrus flavors. They are good served as refried beans (see page 191).

SPLIT RED LENTIL

Bright orange in color, despite their name, these lentils are exceedingly versatile and highly nutritious. They disintegrate during cooking, which makes them ideal for soups and for changing the texture of casseroles. They combine well with tomatoes, eggs, and cheese. Once cooked, the purée makes a good base for savory burgers and baked dishes, or a filling for pies.

CONTINENTAL LENTIL

These lentils, the largest of the lentil family, hold their shape once cooked. They make a good textural contrast when served with larger legumes in dishes such as chili. They also go well in salads dressed with yogurt and plenty of garlic, parsley, cilantro, or mint.

PUY LENTIL AND LENTILLE VERTE

These tiny gray-green lentils becoming increasingly easier to find. They have the advantage of being very quick to cook—some varieties in about 10 minutes. Excellent in casseroles, they work well in salads mixed with creamy ingredients, such as cheese or a yogurt dressing. They can also be used for refried bean dishes and go with both hot spices and aromatic herbs.

BROWN LENTIL

This is virtually interchangeable with the larger continental lentil or the Puy lentil. It is good for casseroles and soups as well as pie fillings.

YELLOW SPLIT PEA

This can be used in similar ways to the split red lentil, although it is slightly more robust to cook. Split peas make a good basis for soups, pâtés, and purées. Their earthy flavors work well with spices and herbs and they can be made into dhal (see page 250).

Soybean products

Soybeans are rarely cooked at home, because they require a long cooking time. However, they come into their own when processed as either bean curd or tempeh, or fermented to make the marvelous savory flavorings of miso, shoyu, or tamari. These forms bear very little resemblance to the original bean in either color or flavor.

BEAN CURD (*TOFU*)

Bean curd is a nourishing food made from soybeans, which originated in the Far East. It is worth trying to introduce into your diet because it is a quick cooking ingredient with terrific nutritional value. It contains eight essential amino acids and is low in calories, saturated fat, and salt. It is particularly rich in iron and the B vitamins. Since it is a good source of calcium, it is very useful for anyone with allergies to dairy products.

Regular or firm bean curd can be sliced or cubed, stir-fried, and baked, despite its fairly fragile texture. Bean curd is virtually tasteless and so needs a chance to absorb other flavors. Do this by marinating for an hour or so—Asian-style marinades are particularly successful—or cook the bean curd in a richly flavored casserole or sauce, such as a barbecue or chile sauce.

In Japan, bean curd is often served plain, sprinkled with shoyu or soy sauce and finely chopped scallions.

Bean curd also comes in a smooth variety known as silken bean curd. It is easy to blend into soups, sauces, and drinks, giving them a creamy consistency. If you cannot get silken bean curd, use regular bean curd but add enough water so that the bean curd blends to a consistency similar to strained plain yogurt: about 5 tablespoons water to 6 ounces (150g) regular bean curd. Drain, rinse, and coarsely chop the bean curd and place with the water in a blender or food processor. Process together for a minute. Add more water if necessary.

Buying and storing

Bean curd is generally found in chilled cabinets in stores and supermarkets or from specialist Asian shops, sold either boxed or in plastic packets. It is worth trying different brands since they can vary in both texture and flavor. It is possible to buy bean curd made from organic soybeans, as well as smoked or ready-marinated varieties.

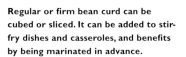

Firm bean curd is sold in small blocks. The texture may vary from one brand to another.

Bean curd will keep for several days in the refrigerator but is not suitable for freezing. Once the packet is open, any leftover bean curd should be covered with fresh water, which must be changed daily. The remaining bean curd should be eaten within a few days. Silken bean curd will keep for months in its packet, but once opened should be eaten within 24 hours.

Regular or firm bean curd can be cubed or sliced. It can be added to stir-fry dishes and casseroles, and benefits by being marinated in advance.

TEMPEH

Tempeh is another high-protein food made from soybeans, which have been cooked, fermented, and mashed into blocks. It is rich in protein and fiber, a good source of the B-group vitamins, and low in fat. Although it can have a rather unappetizing, mottled appearance, it has a slightly nutty, almost dry taste and a good capacity to absorb flavors. It is more robust than bean curd and can be thinly sliced. If sold uncooked, it needs to be steamed or simmered—preferably in a marinade—for about 20 minutes. Tempeh can then be fried, crumbled, or added in pieces to casseroles. When it is sold pre-cooked, it is usually flavored with other ingredients such as garlic.

Buying and storing Keep tempeh in the refrigerator and, once opened, use within a few days. It can also be frozen. It is found in chilled cabinets in supermarkets and specialty stores.

MISO

This savory paste is made from fermented soybeans. It comes in a variety of colors and flavors, depending on which other beans or grains it is mixed with. The most common varieties are mugi miso (soy and barley), hatcho miso (soy only), and genmai miso (soy and rice).

Miso is a living food containing good bacteria, in a similar way to live yogurt. These bacteria are destroyed by boiling so it is common to add miso at the end of cooking. Miso can be a source of vitamin B_{12}.

Miso can easily be made into a nourishing soup mixed with water or Asian stock (see page 145), and garnished with vegetables, such as fine asparagus, roasted seaweed, thinly sliced carrots, or mushrooms. Miso will add a savory flavor to soups, stews, pie fillings, or purées. Since it is often very dense, it is best to thin it down with water or stock to make it easier to mix. Miso can also be mixed with tahini to make a savory spread or dip.

Buying and storing Miso is sold in jars or sturdy plastic packets and will keep for months. It is best stored in the refrigerator.

SHOYU, TAMARI, AND SOY SAUCE

These are names for naturally fermented sauces that are made from soybeans. Shoyu can contain some wheat, whereas tamari is usually wheat-free and has a slightly stronger flavor. Both are dark black in color and have strong, salty flavors but, unlike some other salty flavorings, they seem to enhance food rather than overpower it. Use shoyu or tamari as a flavoring in all robust savory dishes, as a seasoning in stir-fries, or sprinkle it directly over freshly cooked vegetables.

Buying and storing Try to find authentic shoyu or tamari sauce that has been made in the traditional way. These may be sold as soy sauce. Cheaper varieties of soy sauce sometimes have additional flavor enhancers and colorings, and do not have nearly such a good flavor. It is best to keep shoyu and tamari in a cool pantry and they will last a long time.

TEXTURED VEGETABLE PROTEIN (*TVP*)

This high-protein product is used to make meat-like sausages, meatless meatballs, and ground "meat." It is useful for imitating conventional meat meals. If you are a user of TVP, you will be able to add it to many of the casseroles or savory pie recipes featured in this book.

SOY MILK

See "Nondairy Alternatives," page 83.

Nuts and seeds

The classic nut roast may once have been the mainstay of vegetarian cooking but the use of nuts is now more imaginative and more subtle. Nuts and seeds are an invaluable part of a balanced vegetarian diet. Highly nutritious, they can be used to great effect in both savory and sweet dishes.

There are numerous varieties of nuts and seeds to choose from and many ways to present each type, be it whole, sliced, ground, or as a milk, cream, or flavored oil. Nuts and seeds add texture, flavor, and color to many recipes. They go well with the other main food groups, particularly grains, and they also complement vegetables and fruits. They are also great for nutritious snacks, they add crunch to salads and stir-fries, and can easily be cooked into soups and stews.

NUTRITIONAL VALUE

Nuts are a concentrated source of food energy, filled with nutrients essential to a healthy diet. They are a good source of protein and have a reasonable fiber content. Their calorie content is high as a result of the high fat content. However, most of the fat is unsaturated and contains vital essential fatty acids (EFAs). All nuts have useful levels of iron, zinc, and magnesium and many nuts contain traces of other minerals.

Seeds, too, are a good source of protein, minerals, and polyunsaturated fats. Again, they have a high calorie content because of their fat content.

Buying and Storing

For everyday cooking, it is best to buy whole, shelled nuts since they are likely to have a better flavor. Look for long "use-by" dates and check that the contents of the packet don't look dusty or broken. It is now possible to find some varieties of organically grown nuts.

If you intend keeping nuts in a bowl as a nibble or snack, it is good to buy nuts in their shells—these protect the kernels and keep them fresh. The downside is that you can't see what you are buying. It is very disappointing to crack open a shell and find nothing but a little dust. Buy from somewhere with a good turnover so that the stock is fresh.

Nuts are packed with protein and useful quantities of some minerals, although they have a high fat content.

Seeds are generally available whole. Again, check the "use-by" date and the appearance of the contents of the packet.

Nuts and seeds have a high oil content and can go rancid if exposed to warm conditions. They are best stored in a cool place, even the refrigerator if you have room. Keep nuts in airtight containers and try to use whole nuts within 3 months. Split, chopped, or ready-ground nuts will go stale more quickly and should be eaten within 4–6 weeks. Shelled nuts will also keep in the freezer for up to 1 year.

Nuts and seeds aren't just for nibbling. They are good in salads and stir-fry recipes and can be added to risotto or crisp toppings. Store in a cool place and do not keep too long.

Roasting Nuts and Seeds

Roasting or broiling nuts brings out their flavor. Spread out the shelled nuts or seeds in a single layer on a shallow baking sheet or in a roasting pan. Leave as they are or brush with a very little oil. Place the tray in a preheated oven, 400°F (200°C), for 6–10 minutes, shaking the baking sheet or pan two or three times during cooking to make sure that the nuts brown evenly. You can also toast nuts and seeds under the broiler but watch them carefully since they can burn more easily using this method.

Roasted nuts and seeds make a delicious, nutritious snack and are ideal for sprinkling over salads.

Chopping and Grinding

Many recipes call for nuts to be finely chopped or ground. For small quantities, it is best to chop nuts by hand because it is hard to get even size pieces when using a food processor.

Start by chopping individual nuts roughly and then pile them together and chop as you would for quantities of herbs, using a large knife and working the blade forward and backward.

If you want a few slices, cut the nuts by hand using a small sharp knife. Nuts can be ground easily with the right equipment— use an electric nut mill or food processor depending on the quantity you need. Process in bursts several times until you get an even texture.

Use a large, sharp knife for chopping nuts by hand. Keep the nuts close together in a pile, then work the blade across the nuts, cutting as you would for herbs.

Nut Creams and Milks

The best nuts for these are almonds, cashew nuts, and coconut. Use the milk or cream as an alternative to dairy cream or yogurt and serve with hot or cold fruit, cereal, or waffles.

ALMOND OR CASHEW NUT MILK AND CREAM

To make the milk, use a blender or food processor, and blend together 1½ tablespoons ground almonds or cashews with ¾ cup (175 milliliters) water, and sweeten to taste. To make the nut cream, start with half the quantity of water. Blend until smooth, then add more water until you get the desired consistency.

COCONUT MILK OR CREAM

To make coconut milk, grate fresh coconut into a bowl. Cover with boiling water and let stand for 30 minutes. Strain through cheesecloth or a fine strainer, extracting as much liquid as possible. Alternatively, use a block of coconut cream. Chop roughly and then dissolve in boiling water. Add water until the mixture has the consistency you require— thicker for coconut cream, thinner for milk.

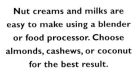

Nut creams and milks are easy to make using a blender or food processor. Choose almonds, cashews, or coconut for the best result.

PEANUT

Although grouped with nuts, strictly speaking the peanut is a legume. Because many people have an allergic reaction to them, it is vital not to serve peanuts—or any of the by-products such as peanut oil—unless you are sure there will be no problems. For those who can eat peanuts, they are a good source of protein and go well with spices and citrus flavors. They are also an ingredient of the Indonesian salad Gado Gado (see page 306).

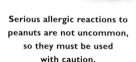

Serious allergic reactions to peanuts are not uncommon, so they must be used with caution.

Peanut butter Peanuts can be puréed with oil and salt to make a spread the consistency of butter. Always read the label since several commercial varieties also contain sugar. Peanut butter makes a nutritious sandwich spread; it can also be mixed into sauces and stews to add flavor and give a thicker consistency. Use peanut butter to make a simple pâté by mixing it with cooked lentils and seasoning with herbs, spices, or citrus flavors.

PISTACHIO

Pistachios have a brilliant green color and slight almond flavor. Although they are often eaten roasted and salted as a cocktail snack, they work well, unsalted, in savory grain dishes and salads, and are delicious in ice cream.

Pick pistachio nuts with a half-open shell. If the shell is closed, the nut is not fully ripe and the shell will be very hard to remove.

To blanch and skin pistachios, put them in a bowl, cover with boiling water, and leave for a few minutes. Lift out of the hot water with a slotted spoon, then pinch the softened skin. The nuts should pop out of their skins when pressed—if they don't, leave them in the hot water a little longer. Skin them while warm or the skin becomes harder to remove.

Pick pistachio nuts with a half-open shell as they are fully ripe. Unsalted nuts are good in both sweet and savory dishes.

WALNUT

Strongly flavored, this nut is very useful as the basis for a nut roast or burger. Walnuts work well when mixed with other milder-flavored nuts, such as almonds or cashews, so that the walnut flavor isn't overpowering. Walnuts also combine well with grains such as bulgur, couscous, buckwheat, or rice. They have an affinity with fruit, especially pears, and also with creamy cheeses such as goat cheese and blue cheese. Use walnuts in desserts, cakes, cookies, and sweet and savory breads.

Toasted and chopped walnuts in small quantities make substantial and nutritious garnishes. For a robust and healthful salad dressing use roasted walnuts as the basis for a vinaigrette (see page 313). See page 116 for walnut oil.

Walnuts work well with a good range of flavors in both sweet and savory foods.

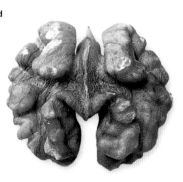

Smooth or chunky, peanut butter makes a delicious spread but it can also be used for dips and sauces.

Nut roasts such as this Spiced Hazelnut and Quinoa Loaf (see page 267) are delicious when well-flavored and moist. They benefit from being served with a sauce or chutney.

PINE NUT

These slim, oval seeds have a distinctive, subtle flavor and can be eaten cooked or raw. Serve them lightly toasted in salads or with roasted vegetables. Alternatively, cook them in sauces, casseroles, and grain dishes. Pine nuts have a particular affinity with many Mediterranean ingredients, such as tomatoes and bell peppers, and are a vital component of the classic Genoese sauce, pesto (see page 211).

The distinctive, delicate flavor of pine nuts goes well with many Mediterranean vegetables such as bell peppers or tomatoes.

BRAZIL NUT

Brazil nuts are delicious to eat raw, with a rich creamy quality. They are frequently sold in their shells and can be at their best when bought like this because they retain their moisture and freshness and make a nutritious snack. Paradoxically, they can be very bland once cooked and are therefore best mixed with other nuts for savory baked dishes and burgers. Lightly toasted, they are delicious in salads—leave them in chunky pieces for the best effect. Skin Brazil nuts as for hazelnuts.

Brazil nuts contrast well with the more strongly flavored walnut or drier hazelnut.

Nuts feature in many different dishes from morning cereals through cakes, stir-fries, and salads. Their crunchy texture goes well with raw ingredients in salads and provides a protein boost.

HAZELNUT

Equally good in savory or sweet dishes, hazelnuts go well with many grains, as well as with pasta, and are delicious in salads or stir-fries. See page 116 for hazelnut oil. They are lower in fat content than other nuts. It is worth toasting them lightly before use to bring out their flavor.

To skin hazelnuts, bake the nuts in a preheated oven, 400°F (200°C), for 5–6 minutes. When the skins are quite brown or even slightly burned, remove the nuts from the oven. Let cool slightly, then rub the nuts in your hands or in a clean dish towel. This will remove most of the skins. There may be the odd stubborn patch that remains but this shouldn't spoil the overall flavor. This method of removing the skins also roasts the nuts lightly.

Toasting hazelnuts really brings out their flavor. They can then be added to salads and savory toppings or mixed into a breakfast cereal.

CASHEW NUT

These useful nuts, with their distinctive mild flavor, work well in both sweet and savory dishes. They are good with many grains, particularly rice and bulgur. They are also delicious in stir-fries and are great flavored with hot or aromatic spices.

Cashew nuts grind easily to a powder and work well as a base ingredient for nut roasts and burgers. They make very good sweet or savory nut milks or creams (see page 99), which are useful for those allergic to, or not wishing to, eat dairy products.

PECAN

For those who find walnuts bitter, the pecan is the answer. This nut is richer and more subtle in flavor, with an oilier texture. Pecans are delicious in salads and with pasta, as well as being suitable for nut roasts. When using pecans in nut roasts, leave some whole since this highlights the flavor and creates an attractive garnish. Pecan pie is a classic sweet pastry dish.

ALMOND

Highly versatile, almonds are sold in a variety of forms—whole, blanched, sliced, slivered, and ground. They are one of the few nuts you should buy ready-processed since their sale turnover is quick, although you should still look for long "use-by" dates.

Almonds can be used in both savory and sweet dishes. When ground, they make a base ingredient for nut roasts and burgers (see page 99); left whole or sliced, they are good with grains, in stir-fries, salad, or with pasta. Lightly salted or spiced, they make a great snack (see page 364).

Blanch and skin almonds as for pistachios (see page 100).

CHESTNUT

This nut is quite starchy compared with other nuts and has a low fat content.

Chestnuts are useful for grinding into nut roasts and baked dishes, but also work well with vegetable mixtures, particularly leeks and mushrooms, to make savory fillings for pies. They have a surprisingly sweet flavor; counteract this in savory dishes by seasoning well with herbs or spices or using shoyu or soy sauce.

Chestnuts are available fresh and dried—both need preparing before use (see below). Ready-cooked chestnuts are often expensive, and some brands of chestnut purée are heavily sweetened.

Fresh sweet chestnuts need to be peeled before use. Slit the pointed ends with a sharp knife and place them in a dish with a little water. Cook in a preheated oven, 400°F (200°C), for about 8 minutes. Let cool slightly, then peel off the shell and skin. Cook the peeled chestnuts in boiling water and simmer for 45–60 minutes. Drain and use as required.

To roast chestnuts in the oven, slit the pointed ends and spread out on a baking sheet. Roast in a preheated oven, 400°F (200°C), for about 20 minutes, or until the shells split open and the chestnuts look golden brown. Let cool slightly, then peel off the shell and skin—they are now ready to eat.

Dried chestnuts, which can be good value, need soaking before use. Soak them in a bowl containing twice their volume of water and leave for 1–2 hours. This should give the chestnuts a chance to swell to their original size. Then cook the chestnuts in their soaking water, adding a little more water if necessary. Bring them to a boil, partially cover the pan, and cook gently until just tender—30–40 minutes. Drain and use as required. Do not throw away the chestnut stock. It can be used instead of vegetable stock, although it has a sweet flavor. The chestnuts and their stock will keep for 3 days in the refrigerator or can be frozen for several months.

COCONUT

While fresh coconut is fun and a treat to eat, ready-prepared block coconut and coconut milk (see page 99) are more useful cooking ingredients. These add an authentic flavor to Asian and Indian dishes. Coconut milk provides a velvety, creamy texture and is especially useful for those who do not want to eat dairy products.

Nuts are an invaluable part of a vegetarian diet and can be used in many sweet and savory dishes.

SUNFLOWER SEEDS

These highly nutritious seeds make useful garnishes and crunchy additions to salads, especially those with creamy dressings, such as coleslaw. Sunflower seeds also go well with grain dishes, particularly those based on wheat, rice, or millet. Add the seeds to breakfast cereals or to cake and muffin recipes, and a handful of seeds added to a basic bread dough will enrich the texture as well as boosting the nutritional content.

Toasting brings out their flavor—do this in the oven or use a dry skillet. To make a quick nutritional snack roast the sunflower seeds in a hot oven, 400°F (200°C) for 2–3 minutes, then toss the hot seeds in a little soy sauce, and roast again for 2–3 minutes more.

Sunflower seeds are also made into sunflower butter—similar to peanut butter—which makes a nutritious spread. Sunflower oil (see page 115) is another by-product and is a very useful, pleasantly flavored oil.

To make a quick nutritious snack, roast sunflower seeds in soy sauce.

SESAME SEEDS

These tiny seeds with a distinctive flavor are an excellent source of calcium, which is better absorbed if the seeds are ground or made into tahini (see above). Toasted sesame seeds make a great topping for bread, pizza, savory baked dishes, and crisps, and are also delicious mixed with grains such as couscous.

Tahini This is the name for the butter, or spread, made from crushed sesame seeds. It has a smooth consistency, rather like a peanut butter, and there is usually a layer of oil on the top, which should be stirred in before use. Tahini can be light or dark, depending on the character of the seeds used, with the dark variety having a slightly stronger flavor. Use tahini to make very quick dips—mix it with a little water, then add oil, lemon juice, garlic, shoyu, or soy sauce to taste. Once mixed, it also blends very well with yogurt. For a sweet spread, mix tahini with water, then honey or syrup. In cooking, tahini can be mixed with bean or lentil purées to thicken them for burgers or patties.

Tahini will keep for several months. It does not need to be refrigerated.

Tahini can be used alone or mixed with lemon juice, garlic, and other flavorings to make delicious dips and savory spreads.

PUMPKIN SEEDS

These distinctive, smooth, green seeds work well in salads and stir-fries, as well as in breakfast cereals, such as granola. They feature in Mexican cookery— often ground into pastes and sauces. Pumpkin seeds can be eaten straight from the packet, but they are also delicious lightly toasted. Do this in a dry skillet or in the oven, but watch them carefully because they will color quite quickly. You could also toss them in a little shoyu or soy sauce. Pumpkin seeds contain polyunsaturated fats as well as vitamins and iron.

Herbs

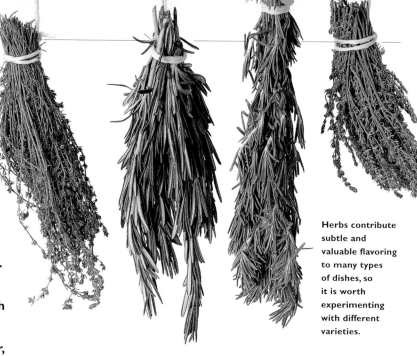

Vital to good vegetarian cooking, herbs are a small but invaluable part of many recipes, adding flavor and aroma to an enormous variety of dishes. There are no hard-and-fast rules as to which herbs to choose as a flavoring. Some clearly have a natural affinity with certain ingredients, for example basil with tomato, or marjoram with mushrooms. Many cuisines favor one herb in particular, as with the widespread use of basil in Italian cookery, parsley in many British recipes, and cilantro in both Indian and Mexican dishes.

It is worth trying out a wide range of herbs and there are numerous ways to incorporate them into your cooking. Use them to highlight a flavor, give a subtle undertone, or even take a leading role.

Herbs contribute subtle and valuable flavoring to many types of dishes, so it is worth experimenting with different varieties.

Buying and Storing Fresh Herbs

The cheapest way to obtain fresh herbs is to grow your own. Even if you don't have access to a yard, many herbs can be grown in pots on windowsills or in tubs in courtyards or on patios. The next best source of fresh herbs is the growing pots found in some larger stores or supermarkets. A wide variety of cut fresh herbs is also available. Look carefully through the packets or bunches for signs of damage or wilting, since herbs, being in the main leafy, are generally fragile.

In the short term, cut fresh herbs should be stored in the refrigerator. Delicate varieties benefit from being wrapped in damp paper towels. The alternative is to chop their stems and stand them in water like a bunch of flowers. Either way they will last for 2–4 days.

For longer-term storage try the following ideas.

Freezing Fresh herbs are suitable for freezing, which works well for more fragile specimens. Freeze whole leaves of basil, chervil, parsley, and tarragon. Wrap in plastic and store for up to 3 months.

Herb oil A good use for herbs is to put them in oil. Use a good-quality sunflower or olive oil. Lightly crush the leaves of the herbs of your choice, put them in a jar or bottle, and cover with oil. Refrigerate for 1–2 weeks, shaking the jar occasionally. Strain into clean jars and use the oil within a day or two. Good herbs for flavoring oil are basil, thyme, rosemary, and marjoram.

Growing your own herbs in pots or buying them already potted is an easy way to have a ready supply.

Herbs can imbue olive oil with their flavor. After a couple of weeks the oil will take on a delicate hint of their taste.

Herb vinegar Use the same process as for making herb oils. It takes about 3 weeks for the flavor to develop. Good herbs for flavoring vinegar are tarragon, which is particularly good, dill, bay, thyme, and garlic.

Home-dried herbs If you have a glut of home-grown herbs, you can dry them easily. Spread out the sprigs on a rack and leave them in a dry, airy place. Once dried, strip off the leaves, and store in airtight jars.

In many cases the flavor of a fresh herb is superior to the dried varieties but there are some herbs that still have a good flavor when dried. Good herbs to dry include bay, marjoram, oregano, rosemary, thyme, and sage.

For home-dried herbs, spread out individual sprigs or leaves on a rack or hang bunches in a dry, airy place.

PARSLEY

Parsley is a splendid, versatile herb with a fresh, slightly spicy flavor. It is robust enough to be added to soups and casseroles to give a good undertone, as well as being suitable for use in large quantities for grain and pasta dishes, or with cooked vegetables, and salads. Parsley also works well with mildly flavored egg dishes.

SAGE

Sage has a powerful flavor, which can overwhelm, so use it with caution. It works well in soups, stews, risotto, and pasta dishes. When dried it can have a slightly musty flavor.

ROSEMARY

This is a pungent aromatic herb with a strong flavor. It goes well with food from the Mediterranean, as well as with starchy foods like bread and potatoes. Dried rosemary needles can be quite sharp so be sure to chop them well before using.

THYME

An intensely aromatic herb that needs to be used in small quantities, thyme is useful for adding depth of flavor to soups and casseroles. It can work well with roasted vegetables and tomato-based dishes, and goes with oregano and marjoram. Add small quantities to bread dough or savory crisps or pastries.

MARJORAM AND OREGANO

These two herbs come from the same family, both native to the Mediterranean and so a perfect foil to foods typical of that region, such as tomatoes, eggplant, and olives. Both herbs are robust enough to stand a certain amount of cooking and can therefore be used to flavor soups, sauces, and stews, as well as grain dishes.

BAY

Bay leaves add a spicy, almond flavor to food. This robust leaf does not break down during the cooking process and is therefore excellent to use in soups and stews. It is best to rub the leaf before adding it to release more flavor—remember to remove it before serving. Bay leaves are also good with grain dishes such as paella or pilaf.

BASIL

This vibrant herb is best known for its use in Italian and Mediterranean cookery. The most familiar variety is sweet basil with its fresh green appearance, soft leaves, and evocative, aromatic, slightly spicy flavor. Look, too, for the anise-flavored and lemon-scented basils, as well as purple basil, which is good for salads.

Basil combines particularly well with tomatoes, mushrooms, beans, and soft cheese. It is also a central ingredient in the classic Genoese sauce, pesto (see page 211).

MINT

A strongly flavored herb with a clean refreshing taste, mint works well with starchy foods such as potatoes, as well as with grains like bulgur and rice. It is also delicious in yogurt and, combined with cucumber, makes the classic tzatziki salad. Add mint only at the last minute because its flavor disappears rapidly when subjected to heat. Also look for mint varieties, such as peppermint or spearmint.

CILANTRO

Fresh cilantro is used widely in Mexican, Turkish, Indian, and Asian cuisines. It is an herb that goes well with strong flavors such as garlic, ginger, and chiles, as well as with milder ingredients, such as avocado. Its heady scent is released the moment you begin chopping, but despite its powerful character the flavor is ruined if subjected to prolonged cooking. It is best to add fresh cilantro toward the very end of cooking, or be bold in its use as a garnish.

CHIVES

Chive blades should be springy in texture with an intense green color. They are members of the onion family and have a very delicate flavor, which disappears on cooking. They are best snipped straight into cold soups and salads or used as a garnish. Chives are versatile but are particularly good with potatoes, cream-based soups and sauces, eggs, and cheese.

TARRAGON

This herb tastes slightly of anise seed and it is much more potent when used fresh rather than dried. It works well in egg dishes, as well as with cream sauces for pasta, or with creamy risotto. It is also good for herb oils and vinegars. Tarragon is also part of the classic fines herbes mixture where it is combined with chives, chervil, and parsley.

Even if you don't have a garden, you can grow herbs in terra cotta pots. If you put them by your doorstep they will reward you with their delicious aromas every time you walk past.

Herbs can be used alone, with spices, or, in many instances, mixed with other herbs to give some wonderful flavors. Classic groups of herbs include bouquet garni with thyme, bay leaf, parsley, and rosemary tied together, which can be added to many slow-cooking dishes such as casseroles or soups.

DILL

This feathery, fragrant herb is from the same family as fennel, caraway, and anise, all of which have a delicate anise seed flavor. Dill works best if added to cooking at the last minute. It is particularly good with cucumber, and with cream cheese and other mild-tasting dairy products.

CHERVIL

This is a pretty herb with delicate leaves and a flavor similar to anise seed. It has an affinity with eggs, and also acts as a refreshing foil to rich creamy sauces and soups.

SUMMER SAVORY

With its lemony tang, this pungent herb is good with green vegetables, such as green beans, fava beans, and asparagus. It partners legumes well, counteracting their earthy quality.

HERB MIXTURES

These are groups of herbs that work extremely well together.

Bouquet garni
Bouquet garni comprises bay, thyme, parsley, and rosemary. These herbs can be tied together or wrapped and tied in a leek leaf. Bouquet garni is especially good in slow-cooking dishes, such as soups, casseroles, and homemade stocks.

Fines herbes
This is made up of equal quantities of chives, chervil, parsley, and tarragon. The mixture has a natural affinity with eggs, so is delicious in soufflés, omelets, and quiche fillings.

Herbs de Provence
Herbs de Provence is a combination of thyme, rosemary, bay, basil, and savory—and occasionally lavender—and, as you would expect, works well with vegetables from the Mediterranean.

Parsley mixtures
These last two mixtures are based around parsley, with garlic or both garlic and lemon added. Persillade comprises garlic and parsley, which are chopped together and added at the end of cooking. It is good for pepping up a soup, stew, or sauce. Gremolada, or gremolata, contains lemon zest combined with the garlic and parsley and is used in the same way as persillade.

Spices

The bark, seeds, stems, roots, and leaves of various aromatic trees and plants are used for spices. With a few exceptions, spices are mostly sold dried. Unlike herbs, the drying of spices tends to concentrate, rather than diminish, their flavors. Using spices will not automatically result in hot, fiery dishes. Some spices, such as ginger and chile, do have exceedingly fiery characters, but there are also sweet, aromatic, and mild spices—cinnamon, cumin, and paprika, for example.

Aromatic and exotic, spices can be bought ready-ground or whole and are sourced from all around the world.

Buying and Storing

Although fresh spices, such as ginger, lemongrass, and chiles, are available, dried spices are more common.

Look for whole rather than ground dried spices wherever possible. These will generally have a better and longer-lasting flavor, even though they take an extra minute or so in preparation. Although not necessarily altering in appearance over time, whole spices become stale and it is best to use them within a year. Buy spices from somewhere that has a good turnover and look for long "use-by" dates.

If you buy ready-ground spices, do not keep them too long because their flavor diminishes over 3–6 months. It is best to have an annual clear out of your pantry and start again.

Store all spices, whole or ground, in airtight containers away from heat and light, which will diminish their strength.

Spices come from the seeds, roots, stems, bark, and leaves of aromatic trees and shrubs.

Cooking with Spices

While some recipes in this book use only a single spice, it is more usual for spices to be used in combination. Certain blends are favored by a national cuisine, for example lemongrass and ginger in Asia, cumin and cinnamon in Middle Eastern cuisine, and chile and coriander in many Mexican dishes. Occasionally, a spice can be added at the last minute, such as a dusting of cinnamon, but most spices benefit from being cooked at the start of a recipe so that they release their flavors.

Spices, whole or ground, can be fried with garlic and onion at the beginning of a recipe or simply in the oil before other ingredients are added. It is important to have enough oil so that the spice doesn't scorch. An alternative is to make a spice paste by grinding and mixing the spices with 1 tablespoon of water. Add this paste to hot oil and cook gently so that the spices release their flavors.

When spices are added at the beginning of the cooking time, they blend in and release their flavors fully into the dish.

Dry-Roasting Spices

Dry-roasted spices are doubly useful because they can be added at either the beginning or the end of cooking. They can be used to flavor uncooked dishes such as salsa, which can be pepped up with a little toasted cumin, or a yogurt sweetened with cardamom and coriander. Dry-roasting takes only a few minutes.

To dry-roast spices, heat a skillet, add the whole spices, and keep shaking the pan because the spices toast and darken. Be careful not to scorch them or they will be bitter.

If dry-roasting in the oven, you need to spread out the spices in a single layer and then shake the baking sheet frequently as they darken. Let cool, grind with a pestle and mortar or electric nut mill, and use as required.

CUMIN

This pungent, warming spice is extremely versatile, teaming up well with coriander for mild spice combinations, but also complementing chile for fiery hot dishes. Dry-roasted cumin makes a good addition to cooked vegetable and grain salads.

ALLSPICE

These small, round berries taste like a mixture of cloves, cinnamon, and nutmeg. They can be used in savory dishes—especially those of Caribbean origin—as well as sweet recipes, such as cakes and cookies.

CARAWAY

A strong. aromatic seed, caraway works well on its own but is also good mixed with paprika. Cook caraway with legumes, cabbage, and other brassicas, because it aids digestion.

SAFFRON

These orange-red threads constitute the most expensive spice in the world. They yield a warm yellow color to food, as well as a distinctive aroma. Saffron is used in Spanish and Mediterranean food, as well as in Middle Eastern and Indian cooking. It is good with rice dishes, such as paella and risotto, and with vegetables like fennel and onions. It can also be used to flavor bread and cakes.

FENNEL SEED

With its sweet flavor, this tiny, pale green seed is similar to anise seed. It can be used in curry dishes as well as in marinades for vegetables and bean curd.

Whole spices keep longer than ready-ground. Store them in airtight containers away from heat and light.

CLOVES

Cloves have a penetrating flavor so the tiny buds must be used sparingly. Cloves are mostly used in sweet dishes and with fruit, but are also good with the onion family and with sweet potato and squashes.

CAYENNE PEPPER AND CHILE POWDER

Cayenne pepper is a very hot, powdered chile, which needs to be used sparingly. Confusingly, chile powder is not just ground chiles (see page 57) but contains other spices as well as cayenne pepper. It, too, can be very hot.

CINNAMON

A popular and versatile spice used in both savory and sweet cooking, cinnamon goes well with grain dishes, such as bulgur and couscous, as well as with vegetables such as eggplant and zucchini. It is also delicious with chocolate and can be used for spicing fruit dishes.

HORSERADISH

This is most readily sold creamed, although in this form it often contains a long list of unwelcome ingredients, such as emulsifiers. Look instead for flakes or dried horseradish, which can be reconstituted with a little water. It is a fiery, powerful seasoning, which works well with creamy ingredients, as well as with walnuts, beet, and onion flavors.

GALANGAL

A member of the same family as ginger, and sharing a similar form and flavor, galangal is used extensively in Indonesian and Southeast Asian cookery.

GINGER

This pungent, fiery root is available fresh or ready-ground. Both fresh and dried ginger are used widely in sweet and savory dishes, especially those from India and Asia. Look for plump, fresh root ginger. It will keep in the refrigerator for at least 2 weeks and even longer, although it may begin to dry out. Peel the root before chopping or grating it. The grated pulp can also be squeezed to get drops of the fiery juice. Dried ground ginger should be used sparingly.

PAPRIKA

A brick-red, sweetish, hot spice, generally sold ground, paprika imparts both flavor and color to food. Its mildness makes it versatile in that it works well with numerous vegetables, as well as with legume and grain dishes.

CORIANDER

This spice goes well with cumin and cinnamon, creating the mild aromatic flavors of Middle Eastern and Indian dishes. Coriander is good with both grains and legumes, and adds spicy-sweet flavor to marinades used for carrots and other vegetables.

JUNIPER

These sweet pine-scented black berries go well with pungent flavors and can cut through oiliness. Juniper berries combine well with bay, garlic, and thyme for a powerful marinade for barbecues.

LEMONGRASS

Lemongrass is commonly used in Southeast Asian cooking. Sold fresh, it is about the size of a pencil and has a delicate hint of lemon. It should be kept in the refrigerator and used within 2 weeks or it becomes very dry. To use, pull off the papery outside leaves, then chop finely or pound to a paste. It can also be used whole to add flavor and should be removed before serving.

Dried lemongrass can be substituted for fresh. If sliced, it needs to be soaked for about 1 hour before use. In powdered or flaked form, it can be used right away.

A pestle and mortar is the best tool for grinding single spices or mixtures. It does take a little effort but is worth it for the intense flavors it releases.

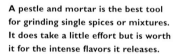

LIME LEAVES

Lime leaves for culinary use come from the Kaffir lime, and the fresh leaves give off a citrus-like scent once bruised. Dried leaves are also available in Thai and Southeast Asian grocery stores because this flavoring is used in dishes originating from those regions. Use lime leaves like bay leaves and remove before serving.

CARDAMOM

Cardamom is a mild, perfumed seed used extensively in Indian and Middle Eastern cooking. It is an important component of garam masala, a mellow spice combination used in many savory dishes, but can also flavor sweet dishes such as cakes and yogurt. Whole cardamom pods are pale green. Before use, crush them with a pestle and mortar and remove the green husks to leave the black seeds, which can be ground more finely.

MACE

This spice is the outer part of the nutmeg seed and is similar in flavor to nutmeg but more powerful. Mace has an affinity with creamy dishes and is commonly used to flavor milk when making béchamel sauce.

MUSTARD

The mustard seed most commonly used as a cooking spice is brown mustard, also known as black mustard. Dry-roasted seeds are less fiery and are good with many vegetable combinations, as well as with grains. There are a huge number of prepared mustards available (see page 112).

NUTMEG

A warm, nutty flavored kernel, nutmeg is best bought whole and grated as needed. It can be used in combination with cumin and coriander for mild savory dishes, and with paprika and caraway for Eastern European mixtures. It is also used in sweet baking.

PEPPERCORNS

Black, white, and green peppercorns are all fruits of a tropical climbing vine. Ready-ground, pepper quickly loses its flavor. It is best to keep peppercorns in a mill ready to grind freshly as a seasoning as required.

POPPY SEEDS

Poppy seeds, which can be white or blue in color, are used widely in Eastern European baking, crushed and soaked in milk or water, and add a dry nutty taste to many cakes, strudels, and cookies. They make a pretty decoration for bread and can also enliven a salad with a creamy dressing.

STAR ANISE

Used extensively in Asian cookery, this attractive spice yields a distinctive anise seed flavor. It is best to dry-roast it before grinding. Star anise is one of the ingredients in the classic Chinese five-spice powder.

TAMARIND

The dried pods produce a sour lemony-flavored pulp, which is used in Indian, Asian, and Caribbean dishes. The pulp is often sold dried. To use, break off a walnut-size piece and soak it in warm water for 10 minutes, then strain, and use the resulting murky liquid. Ready-prepared tamarind is also available from specialist stores and large supermarkets.

FENUGREEK

A powerful, penetrating seed used widely in Indian cookery, fenugreek can also be sprouted and used in salads. Fresh fenugreek leaves are small and oval in appearance with a spicy fragrance and pungent flavor. The leaves should be used as soon as possible as they wilt quickly.

TURMERIC

Used for both its color and flavor, turmeric imparts a yellow hue and a pungent taste. It needs to be used sparingly and is good with grains and legumes, as well as in hot, curry-style dishes.

VANILLA

This spice has a wonderful, floral, spicy sweetness and is used to flavor many sweet dishes, especially those with cream or chocolate. Whole beans can be buried in sugar used for baking to add flavor. Otherwise, buy a pure vanilla extract—beware of vanilla flavorings, which are chemically produced.

Flavorings

Some of the major food groups that are used in a healthy vegetarian diet, particularly legumes and grains, benefit from the addition of extra flavorings. As well as the herbs and spices that have been featured on previous pages, there are a number of other miscellaneous flavorings described here that are well worth getting to know. The plus point of many of these is that you need only small quantities. Because these ingredients have a long shelf life, they are easy to have in stock.

CAPER

Capers are the tiny, unopened green flowerbuds of a shrub grown in southern Europe and North Africa, which are picked and packed into jars filled with salt or wine vinegar. They have a piquant flavor, which can counteract oiliness. They go well with garlic and lemon and are great with roasted or griddled vegetables, as well as with pizza.

Caper plants grow all around the Mediterranean. The buds are either preserved in vinegar or packed into jars with salt.

OLIVE PASTE

Olive paste is handy for adding to pasta, for spreading on bread, croûtons, or hot toast, for mixing with roasted, broiled, or griddled vegetables, or for serving with mozzarella or goat cheese.

To create a simple homemade paste, use a blender or food processor to process 2 cups/8 ounces (250g) pitted olives with about 1–2 tablespoons olive oil. Add 1 tablespoon capers, 2 crushed garlic cloves, 1 tablespoon coriander seeds, and salt and pepper to taste. Spoon into clean jars and cover with extra olive oil. The paste should keep in the refrigerator for 3–4 weeks.

MUSTARD

This huge range of condiments is prepared from combinations of different types of mustard seed.

Hot mustard
This powder has turmeric added to give it its characteristic golden color. Quite fiery, it is useful for adding to cheese or milk-based sauces to enhance the flavor.

Dijon Mustard
Made from black mustard seeds blended with spices and white wine, Dijon mustard ranges in flavor from mild to hot and is classically used in vinaigrette dressing.

Meaux mustard
This crunchy mustard is traditionally sold in pottery jars. It is made from crushed seeds and has a fairly hot flavor. It is good with creamy dressings and sauces, and for adding to marinades and tomato sauces.

German mustard
A smooth mustard made from black seeds, it is often flavored with tarragon. It is particularly good with green vegetables.

Yellow mustard
A sweet, mild, mustard with a sauce-like consistency, yellow mustard is great with broiled and roasted vegetables, as well as for barbecue marinades.

BOUILLON CUBES AND POWDER

A wide range of bouillon cubes and powders suitable for vegetarians can be found in the health food store. They are useful for flavoring soups, sauces, and casseroles. Some are saltier or have an aftertaste and it is worth trying several brands to find one you like.

YEAST EXTRACT

This highly flavored ingredient is made from yeast broken down by its own enzymes. It will keep for several months. It can be used as a spread on crackers or bread or to flavor sauces or casseroles, although use it with a light hand because it imparts a strong, distinctive flavor, which may overpower everything else. It is a useful source of B-group vitamins, including vitamin B_{12}.

GOMASIO (*GOMASHIO*)

This seasoning is made by grinding dry-roasted sesame seeds with salt. If you make your own, alter the ratio to your taste, reducing the salt content to as little as 1 part salt to 10 parts sesame seeds. Gomasio has a good nutty flavor and can be used to season or garnish. It is especially good with grains. For a variation, add crumbled dry-roasted seaweed, such as kombu (see opposite).

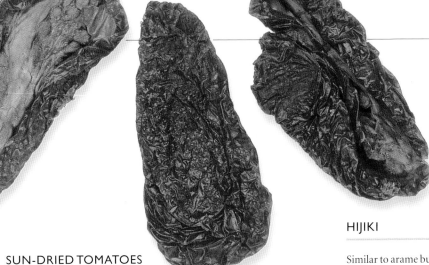

Sun-dried tomatoes may be sold loose in whole pieces. They benefit from an hour's soaking in a warm liquid to make them more tender.

SUN-DRIED TOMATOES AND SUN-DRIED TOMATO PASTE

Sun-dried tomatoes, whether whole, preserved in oil, or in the form of a paste have become a real boon in these days of the flavorless hothouse tomato. These products can add body to a sauce, be finely snipped for a delicious chewy mouthful in a salad, or simmered slowly in a casserole.

Those sold in packets without oil are more leathery, although the flavor is the same, but they do need time and liquid to soften them so add them with the liquids at the start of a recipe. Alternatively, soak for about 1 hour in warm liquid.

TRUFFLE

This highly prized, walnut-size fungus has an intense but elusive flavor. Truffles are often sold finely sliced or grated. Use small amounts to flavor sauces and soups, pasta, and rice dishes.

Sea Vegetables

The sea's rich harvest plays a central role in Asian—particularly Japanese—cookery, but the use of sea vegetables is spreading as their nutritional value and flavoring quality becomes increasingly appreciated elsewhere. Today's dried seaweeds need brief soaking, little or no cooking, and have a pleasant salty tang. Seaweed condiments are increasingly available. They can be used to make a quick stock or as a low-sodium alternative to salt.

ARAME

This grows in delicate black fronds and looks very appealing. Soak the arame in warm to hot water for 4–5 minutes. Arame goes well with some of the sweeter vegetables, such as bell peppers. It is good for stir-fries, salads, pasta, and casseroles, or as a dramatic garnish.

DULSE

With purple-reddish fronds, dulse has a salty, slightly spicy flavor. It goes well with both red and green cabbage, and also works well in salads and stir-fries. It can also be crumbled and dry-roasted as a condiment.

HIJIKI

Similar to arame but with thicker fronds and stronger in flavor, hijiki takes 15–20 minutes to soak and should expand to three times its original volume. Sauté or stir-fry it with vegetables.

KOMBU

Used to make clear soup, this has fairly wide black stems when fresh but can look rather gray when dried. Rinse well and use in small pieces to flavor soups, stews, and casseroles. Remove before serving.

WAKAME

This mildly flavored seaweed has long green fronds and a silky texture. It can be used in soups or salads or mixed with a variety of cooked vegetables. It can also be dry-roasted and crumbled, then crushed with seeds or nuts to make a condiment. Rinse wakame well, then soak in cold water for 4–5 minutes before using.

NORI

Grown in tidal waters on nets, this seaweed is sold in sheets. It can be toasted until it changes color and then crumbled and used as a seasoning or garnish. It is also wrapped around rice to make sushi, a tasty Japanese finger food (see page 281).

AGAR AGAR

Sold in flakes or powder, this can be used in virtually the same way as powdered gelatin, but it must be boiled or it won't set. Use 2 teaspoons to set approximately 2½ cups/1 pint (600 milliliters) liquid. Agar agar will not set recipes that contain egg white.

NUTRITIONAL VALUE

All sea vegetables are rich sources of minerals, especially potassium and sodium. More unusually, they contain a significant amount of the mineral iodine. This mineral is important for the functioning of the thyroid gland, and also thought to be beneficial for other glands, too.

Oil

Oil is more than just a cooking medium, it also adds flavor, acts as a seasoning, and can be nutritionally beneficial. There is a huge range of culinary oils, extracted from a number of plants and seeds, now available. Unrefined, or cold-pressed, and refined, or pure, are some of the terms used to describe oils. These terms refer to the process of extraction, rather than quality.

NUTRITIONAL VALUE

Oils are fats that remain liquid at room temperature. When unrefined they contain vitamins and minerals, especially vitamin E. The fat content of most vegetable oils is polyunsaturated, or monounsaturated in the case of olive oil. Sunflower and safflower oil are high in polyunsaturated fats and are good sources of vitamin E; coconut and palm oils are saturated fats, while peanut oil is about 50 percent monounsaturated and 30 percent saturated fat.

Unrefined Versus Refined Oils

Unrefined oils have not been subjected to any more processing than is needed to extract the oil from the nut or seed. Nor have they been subjected to chemical treatments. Consequently, they often have a stronger taste and smell. They are sometimes called cold-pressed oils, which refers to the method of extraction.

In contrast, a selection of chemicals is used to extract and produce refined oil. The resultant oil has also been bleached and deodorized and has, in effect, become a virtually tasteless, colorless product of little nutritional value. The flavoring is put back afterward.

Buying and Storing

Oils are best stored in cool dry places, away from heat and sunlight. Heat, light, and oxygen can all oxidize oil, causing it to smell sour and taste rancid. Rancid oil should be thrown away. If you use up oil fairly quickly, it shouldn't become rancid but treat precious oils, which you won't use so frequently, with great care.

Keep a small container with your favorite cooking oils near your stove. Refill as necessary. If you keep an oil in the refrigerator, it will congeal to a certain extent and then need time to warm up before it can be properly mixed into dressings.

OLIVE OIL

The versatility of olive oil makes it ideal for all sorts of culinary purposes. It heats well for frying and cooking and tastes good enough to mix into dressings and dips. Olive oil is produced in many countries and one variety can taste and look quite different from another. It is certainly worth trying several varieties as you may prefer one flavor to another. Because olive oil is monounsaturated, it is more stable and less vulnerable to rancidity than polyunsaturated oils.

A huge number of oils extracted from different sources such as olives, sunflower seeds, or nuts are now available. They each have distinctive, subtle flavors. Some can be used in all types of cooking; others are best used as flavorings.

Buying and storing Olive oil is commonly categorized as virgin, extra virgin, or pure oil. Virgin and extra virgin olive oil have not been treated, heated, or chemically processed and are graded according to acidity—the highest grade has the lowest acidity and is therefore the best oil. This is known as extra virgin. Virgin olive oil is slightly more acidic. The cheapest olive oil is called pure olive oil and is generally of a lighter color. This is made from refined olive oil mixed with some virgin oil to give a little color and flavor. This type of oil is suitable when you need a bland cooking oil.

You may come across very expensive estate-bottled olive oil made from olives grown on a single estate and therefore, like wine from a particular vineyard, having a unique flavor. It is certainly worth using in recipes where the flavor will shine through, as in a salad or a dressing. Do not cook with it, however, because any heat will alter the flavor.

As mentioned above, store olive oil in cool conditions.

The seeds of the cheerful sunflower provide a good all-purpose oil that is light with a pleasant flavor. Use it for both cooking—it will stand heating to high temperatures—and for salad dressings or drizzling over food as a flavoring.

SUNFLOWER OIL

This all-purpose oil can be used for cooking, as well as for making dressings and vinaigrettes. It is good for frying because it has a high smoking point and resistance to oxidation. Refined versions of this oil have a delicate flavor, while unrefined, or cold-pressed, oils have more character but not one that will overwhelm the dish.

PEANUT OIL

This is commonly sold as a refined oil and therefore lacks character, although it is possible to find roasted peanut oil, which has more flavor. It can be used rather like sesame oil and drizzled over hot vegetables as a seasoning.

It is thought that the process of refining oil removes the peanut protein believed to be responsible for triggering an allergic reaction. However, should you be allergic to peanuts, it is important to read labels carefully because peanut oil is widely used in processed foods. If in any doubt, avoid these products.

SAFFLOWER OIL

Pale in color with a delicate nutty flavor, this is interchangeable with sunflower oil, although not widely available. It is used for frying and, unrefined, can be good as a base ingredient for salad dressings. The oil is high in polyunsaturated fats.

CORN OIL

Cheap to produce, corn oil is almost tasteless. Occasionally, you may find an unrefined version, which has a hint of corn. Corn oil is very popular in Mexican cookery for frying tortillas; it can be used in cooking generally, particularly where corn is one of the ingredients.

NUT OILS

Use these oils for seasoning rather than for general-purpose cooking, since they are expensive and their flavors are lost when heated to any degree. The best way to savor them is to drizzle them over fresh vegetables or mix them into dips, dressings, and vinaigrette.

Nut oils are made from roasted nuts, which are pressed in order to release their flavor. The color of the final oil will depend on the degree of toasting. As with most oils, it is worth looking around to discover your favorite.

Treat nut oils as a seasoning rather than a cooking ingredient. Their flavor is shown off best when sprinkled over salads or lightly cooked vegetables.

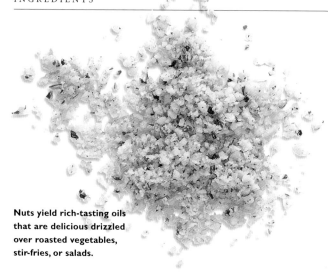

Nuts yield rich-tasting oils that are delicious drizzled over roasted vegetables, stir-fries, or salads.

HAZELNUT OIL

This rich, heavy oil is gold or deep gold in color with the sweet, strong accent of the hazelnut.

WALNUT OIL

Walnut oil is bronze-gold in color with a rich fragrance. You can mix a small quantity of walnut oil with other oils and still get a walnut flavor coming through.

SESAME OIL

This is sold both toasted and untoasted. The untoasted has a pale color and a delicate flavor. Toasting the sesame seeds prior to extraction intensifies the flavor and the oil is consequently darker with a stronger flavor—ranging in color from russet to deep brown. Use sparingly as a garnish for grains and vegetable dishes. Sesame oil has a natural affinity with ginger, lime, and soy sauce.

Other Oils

There are always new products to be found. Oils are no exception and you may find avocado, pumpkin seed, or truffle oil. It is worth experimenting with these as flavorings, especially if you can buy them in small quantities.

MARGARINE

It is important to check labels carefully when buying margarine since many contain animal fat or fish oil. Some additives used in margarine are also not from sources acceptable to vegetarians. Margarines are generally about 80 percent fat, much of which is polyunsaturated but it depends on the processing and types of oil used.

There is debate about the healthiness of margarine because during its manufacture, liquid fats have to be hydrogenated to become solid. Some scientists believe this process turns relatively healthy polyunsaturates into trans fats, which are thought to be as harmful as saturated fats.

STEEPED OILS

Flavored oils are very simple to make—simply steep oil with your chosen flavoring. The best results are achieved by using olive oil for its strong, aromatic undertones and very fresh seasonings. Use a clean, sterilized bottle with a cork or screw-top. Always refrigerate flavored oils and label them with the date they were made. The flavors will take a week or so to develop. Use flavored oils within 1–2 weeks.

Garlic oil
Mince 3–4 garlic cloves. Cover with oil and refrigerate for 1 week. Garlic oil is good with pizza (see page 196) and pasta.

Chile oil
Use 3–4 red or green chiles in generous 2 cups (500 milliliters) oil. You can also add whole, peeled garlic cloves and peppercorns for extra zip. Refrigerate for 2 weeks. Chile-flavored oils are great used with barbecue food or for perking up a casserole or grain dish.

Herb oil
Use 6–8 tablespoons chopped herbs to flavor generous 2 cups (500 milliliters) oil. Refrigerate and use within 2 weeks. Thyme, marjoram, oregano, parsley, and bay all work well (see also page 104). Herb-flavored oils are marvelous in salads.

Steeping oils with different flavorings is extremely easy to do. Garlic, chiles, and various herbs can be used and the process takes a week or so.

Look for brands of margarine with a "no trans fat" label and check whether hydrogenated or trans fats are listed.

WHITE VEGETABLE SHORTENING

White vegetable shortening is a vegetarian alternative to lard. It is, however, a saturated fat and should be used only sparingly. It is most suitable for making pastry.

Vinegar

Vinegar works well with many vegetarian recipes. It is commonly used to counteract oil in a vinaigrette, but it is also used in marinades, for enhancing sauces, and for complementing the earthy flavors of beans and grains, or for sprinkling over food as a seasoning.

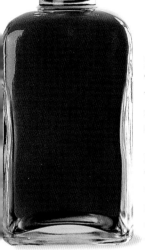

Vinegar is a versatile flavoring that also contains useful enzymes.

Nutritional Value

Vinegar contains some useful enzymes and minerals. It is also reputed to have antiseptic and antibiotic properties.

Buying and Storing

There is a wide range of vinegars to choose from and it is handy to have at least two different flavors in your pantry. Luckily, vinegars are designed to keep for at least 6 months, if not longer. Try to keep them away from heat and light, both of which elements will gradually cause the flavor to deteriorate.

RED AND WHITE WINE VINEGAR

Wine vinegars will vary in character depending on how they are made. Traditional methods take longer and are more expensive; faster processes usually involve heat and inevitably some of the flavors are lost. A good wine vinegar will bear some resemblance to the wine from which it comes so you can find full-blown red wine vinegar at one end of the flavor spectrum and a delicate champagne vinegar at the other end.

APPLE CIDER VINEGAR

Low in acidity, this gentle mild vinegar should have a delicate apple undertone. It is worth looking out for organic, unfiltered varieties. These have a more lively, fruity character, which can make all the difference to a dressing. Use cider vinegar in barbecue or tomato sauces. When used with honey it is a good remedy for a sore throat.

BALSAMIC VINEGAR

Balsamic vinegar has not been allowed to ferment and therefore stays comparatively sweet. It is made from the juice of Trebbiano grapes, with a vinegar "mother"—the technical term for a starter—and some wine vinegar added. It is then stored in wooden barrels. At the end of a year, the vinegar is moved to barrels of a different wood. It loses some of its volume but also takes on some of the flavor of the wood. This aging process can go on for more than 20 years, the liquid gradually reducing to a thick, syrupy consistency. A good balsamic vinegar is usually aged for at least 5 years—the longer the aging time, the more potent the flavor. Cheaper balsamic vinegar has more wine vinegar added.

Balsamic vinegar can be mixed with oil to make a dressing, or used on its own to add a delicious sweetness to vegetables and salads. It is particularly good with the sweeter vegetables, such as tomatoes or bell peppers because it doesn't overwhelm them.

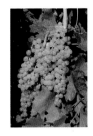

Trebbiano grapes provide the basis for balsamic vinegar.

SHERRY VINEGAR

This is an aromatic sweet vinegar from Jerez in Spain. Like balsamic vinegar, sherry vinegar is mellow enough to be used alone on vegetables. It is particularly good with sautéed mushrooms, roasted bell peppers, and zucchini.

RICE WINE VINEGAR

This vinegar comes in a range of colors and flavors, depending on its country of origin and whether the rice is white or brown. It is generally on the sweet side, the brown rice varieties being fuller in flavor.

Steeped Vinegars

Since vinegar is an excellent medium for preserving delicate flavors, it is hardly surprising that all sorts of fruit and herb vinegars can be found, or indeed made at home. The most common are perhaps raspberry and tarragon.

RASPBERRY VINEGAR

Use roughly 2⅔ cups/1 pound (500g) fruit to generous 2 cups (500 milliliters) white wine vinegar. Crush the fruit gently, pour over vinegar, then cover with a cloth. Refrigerate for 1 week, stirring daily, then strain by allowing the mixture to drip through a cheesecloth-lined strainer rather than pressing it, and bottle.

TARRAGON VINEGAR

Put several sprigs of tarragon in a bottle of good-quality white wine or cider vinegar and refrigerate for 1–2 weeks. If the herb starts to look a little gray-green, strain into a clean bottle.

Sweeteners

Sweeteners are not a mainstay of a vegetarian diet but they are useful ingredients for home baking, as well as being used in many desserts. There are a whole family of sweeteners from pure white sugar to black molasses. Because many vegetarians are concerned about the healthiness of their diet, they tend to favor less refined sugars over pure white sugar and also to look for sugar substitutes that have more flavor and a little more to offer from a nutritional point of view. These include syrups, malt extracts, and fruit concentrates, all of which are described here. This section also includes a look at chocolate and carob.

NUTRITIONAL VALUE

In general, sweeteners offer mostly calories and little else. Much "brown" sugar is merely white sugar colored with caramel or a little molasses.

Unrefined cane sugar is between 87 and 96 percent sucrose and retains some useful B-group vitamins and minerals. It also has a perceptible flavor. Molasses contains small amounts of some minerals and vitamins. Syrups, such as maple syrup and malt extract, also contain minerals. Honey has a slightly different composition from cane or beet sugar but is no better as a source of nutrients.

Remember, food high in sugar should make up only a small part of your overall diet. In many recipes you can cut down the quantity of sugar you use as you gradually become accustomed to a less sweet taste. You can also try sweetening with purées made from dried fruit or using fruit juice concentrates instead of sugar, although these are not appropriate in every recipe. If you like sweet cakes and desserts, try cutting down by alternating them with fresh fruit.

SUGAR

Sugar ranges from fine, powdery confectioners' sugar to dark brown crystals. Fine sugars blend or dissolve more easily; coarse sugars can add crunch to cookies and flapjacks.

Granulated and superfine sugar Granulated sugar is a light, free-flowing sugar used to sweeten sauces and cereals; golden granulated has a slightly buttery taste. Superfine sugar is fine grained and free-flowing and can be used extensively in baking. Golden superfine sugar has a similar taste to golden granulated sugar.

Brown sugars Raw brown sugar has large crystals. It is slightly sticky and has a rich aroma. It is delicious as a sweetener and can be used in baking when the sugar is melted.

Light molasses is a pale brown, soft sugar with a fudge-like flavor. Dark molasses is a sugar rich in natural molasses, which gives the sugar a sticky texture and rich flavor. It is very good for strongly flavored cakes, such as fruit cake or ginger cake, or for sweetening dark sauces.

Molasses is the residue from the sugar-refining process. It has a powerful flavor but is not particularly sweet.

HONEY

Honey is twice as sweet as sugar, so you should use less of it. The best honey comes from a single named flower or a small producer. The darker and more aromatic the honey, the stronger its flavor. Much commercial honey has been overheated to keep it runny, a process that can reduce the flavor and nutrients.

Honey keeps well, but it may crystallize, in which case you can simply heat it gently before using.

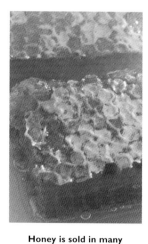

Honey is sold in many different forms, some of which include the honeycomb as an indication that the product has not been processed.

MAPLE SYRUP

Maple syrup is a delicious sweetener, which can be used in all kinds of recipes, sweet and savory. It comes from the sugar maple tree. It takes some 50 gallons (227 liters) of sap to make 1 gallon (4.5 liters) of syrup so it is a very concentrated form of sweetening. Make sure you get the real thing, rather than a maple-flavored syrup, which will contain only a percentage of maple syrup. Store it in a cool place.

MALT EXTRACT

Sometimes known as barley syrup, this is not so sweet as sugar. It has a pleasant but distinctive flavor and can be used for baking and flavoring hot drinks.

PALM SUGAR (JAGGERY)

Tasting rather like a molasses sugar, jaggery is the name given to a range of sugars used in India and Southeast Asia. Many are made from sugar cane but the palm sugars are highly flavored and quite aromatic.

Sugar-free jellies and spreads are sweetened with concentrated fruit purées and contain no added sugar.

SUGAR-FREE JELLY AND FRUIT SPREADS

These are available in specialist stores and are often simply highly concentrated fruit purées. They can be used in place of ordinary jelly as a spread but also used to sweeten fruit sauces, or creamed into margarine as a sugar substitute when making cakes or cookies.

CONCENTRATED FRUIT JUICE

Apple is the main variety of fruit juice concentrates but there are several different flavors available, such as orange and grape. Highly concentrated with a syrup-like texture, these are very useful for sweetening dressings and sauces and for using in fruit salads and compotes, as well as for baking and bread making.

CHOCOLATE

Good-quality chocolate usually has a high percentage of cocoa solids and consequently fewer additions, such as vegetable fat. The high cocoa solids content also means there is less room for sweetening so this sort of chocolate can be quite bitter.

Chocolate will vary from one brand to another. Much will depend on how it is made, how the cocoa beans are selected, dried, and roasted and, finally, how they are ground and mixed to make the chocolate. The slower the final grinding and mixing, the smoother the final texture will be. There should be no powdery aftertaste.

Store chocolate properly in a cool dry place at about 57–61°F (14–16°C).

Bittersweet chocolate has a higher percentage of cocoa solids and consequently less sweetening so it may taste more bitter than milk chocolate.

CAROB POWDER

Carob powder comes from seeds contained in large pods the size of a banana. Carob is naturally sweeter than cocoa powder, has no caffeine, and also a lower fat content. Carob powder can be substituted for unsweetened cocoa powder—start by using about half the amount since it tends to turn mixtures dark. Carob chocolate is also available.

Carob beans come from pods almost the size of a banana. The beans are finely ground and the resulting powder can sometimes be used as a substitute for unsweetened cocoa powder.

THE VEGETARIAN KITCHEN

This section looks at ways to make vegetarian cooking as simple as possible—whether on a daily or weekly basis. There are three main factors that help make organizing, planning, and cooking vegetarian food much easier. First, it is useful to have the right ingredients at hand, be it in your pantry, refrigerator, or freezer; second, it is good to have the right equipment, and, finally, it helps to have a sense of how you are going to organize a recipe in terms of choosing a suitable technique and knowing some shortcuts. This next section covers these three points, as well as looking at specific situations you may want to cater for on a day-to-day basis.

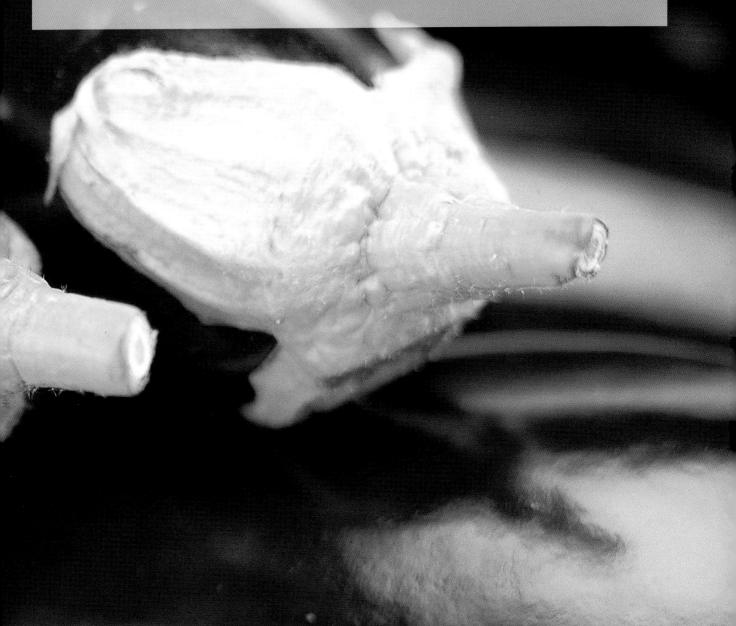

The pantry

It is worth taking the trouble to build up a comprehensive store of staples, as well as some more unusual items that can be stored indefinitely. If you refer to the descriptions of individual ingredients, you'll see that many of the basic foodstuffs will keep for several months.

Once you have plenty of ingredients at hand, you can choose from a wider variety of recipes, introduce variations, and improvise if necessary. This takes some of the headache out of meal planning. Basic stocks also save you from having to make frequent shopping trips.

Essentials

The following checklist of useful ingredients with a long shelf life is meant to give you an idea of some of the most useful items to have at hand, rather than being a definitive list of items to keep in stock. Remember to check on your stocks occasionally, restock any items that are low, and always check the "use-by" dates so that you use your supplies in the right order.

Whole grains Have a choice of rice, such as a basmati and a risotto rice, and at least one other whole grain, such as buckwheat, millet, or quinoa.

Processed grain products Bulgur, couscous, and polenta are all worth keeping in stock. Not only are they quick-cooking staples, but they can also be presented in numerous ways and work well with a great variety of ingredients.

Flakes These are useful for breakfast cereals, crisp toppings, and baking. Oat flakes are the most versatile.

Pasta A variety of shapes and flavors is appealing, and you need only a quick sauce to make a meal.

Flour It is useful to have a strong flour for bread making and an ordinary flour for making pastry, cakes, and sauces. Cornmeal is useful for biscuit topping, polenta, and cornbread. Buy specialist flour, such as gram flour, only when needed and then don't forget to use it up.

Legumes Quick-cooking legumes that don't need soaking, such as Puy and split red lentils, are certainly handy for last-minute meals. A selection of canned beans—garbanzos, red kidney, and pinto beans—for making quick casseroles or substantial salads is useful. Dried legumes have a long shelf life and are also worth cooking in bulk and freezing (see page 92).

Many of the staples of a vegetarian diet have a long shelf life if kept appropriately.

Nuts and seeds Keep two or three of your favorite varieties in stock. Whole cashews, hazelnuts, almonds, and walnuts are all good for savory dishes, salads, and in baking and desserts. Seeds, such as sunflower seeds, make good toppings and add extra protein to salads and breakfast cereals.

Dried or vacuum-packed chestnuts have a long "use-by" dates; ground almonds are useful for pâtés, sweet baking, and in savory mixtures. Nut butters, such as tahini and peanut butter, are good for dips, dressings, and sauces.

Oils Keep a good-quality olive oil and a sunflower oil for general-purpose cooking and making salad dressings. Have smaller quantities of specialist oils, such as sesame or walnut oil, and unusual olive oil, for flavoring for special occasions.

Tomatoes It is useful to have a choice of tomato products at hand, such as canned tomatoes, stewed tomatoes, tomato paste, and sun-dried tomatoes—in oil, dried, or as a paste.

Miscellaneous flavorings As well as a selection of your favorite dried herbs and spices, keep some shoyu or soy sauce, dried mushrooms, pesto, black peppercorns, and at least one mild vinegar, such as red or white wine vinegar. These are all essential flavoring products.

Sweeteners Fruit juice concentrates such as concentrated apple juice are useful for both sweet and savory recipes. Other sweeteners to keep in stock are honey, good-quality unrefined sugar, maple syrup, and preserved ginger.

Dried fruit and nuts are great both for nutritious nibbles and for adding to both sweet and savory recipes.

Canned food All canned food has a long shelf life and, in addition to tomatoes, the following are particularly adaptable and can be used in numerous ways—artichoke hearts, olives, water chestnuts, and corn.

Dried fruits Keep a selection of the larger dried fruits, such as apricots, peaches, and pears, as well as raisins, for use in savory dishes, sweet baking, and desserts.

Keeping a variety of fresh
ingredients in the refrigerator
will make it easier for you to
plan and produce meals.

Refrigerated Staples

Although it is best to shop regularly for fresh produce, there are several
items that have a reasonable shelf life in the refrigerator. The following
checklist is of fresh food items frequently used in vegetarian cooking
and handy to have in stock:

• Butter
• Eggs
• Selection of hard and soft cheese
• Crème fraîche/yogurt/sour cream
• Regular bean curd
• Margarine
• Fresh pasta
• Bean sprouts

"Fresh" Produce

Stored properly, using the guidelines in
the ingredients section, the following are
some useful varieties of fruit and
vegetables that should keep for more than a
few days:

• Onions, garlic, and shallots
• Carrots and other root vegetables
• Squash
• Potatoes
• Lemons and other citrus fruit

It is best to eat many vegetables and some fruit as soon as possible after
purchase, but there are exceptions and you can use this to your
advantage in terms of having ingredients in stock. Plan to use
ingredients such as avocado, bananas, pears, tomatoes, and mango
or papaya several days after
you buy them to give
them a chance
to ripen
properly.

USING THE FREEZER

When used well, a freezer can not only save you time and money but also act as an extension to your pantry. Below is a reminder of some ingredients that freeze well.

- Nuts—up to 1 year
- Ready-cooked legumes—up to 6 months
- Ready-cooked grains such as rice—up to 6 months
- Vegetables, such as corn, green beans, and leaf spinach—up to 1 year (if blanched, their freezer life is longer as certain bacteria and enzymes that cause deterioration have been destroyed)
- Fresh herbs—up to 6 months
- Fruits, such as raspberries—up to 1 year; fruit purée of apple or apricot, up to 6 months
- Heavy or whipping cream, frozen in small quantities—up to 3 months (the higher the fat content, the better it will freeze)
- Hard cheese—3–6 months (best frozen grated since it becomes crumbly on thawing)
- Soft cheese, such as Brie—3–6 months (needs plenty of time to thaw)
- Pastry, including phyllo pastry—up to 3 months
- Crisp toppings—up to 2 months
- Crêpes—up to 6 months
- Bread
- Fresh pasta

The following foods will not freeze: *hard-cooked eggs, light cream, salad ingredients, mayonnaise, and cottage cheese. Also be guided by packet instructions on foods.*

COOKING FROM FROZEN

Vegetables are best cooked from frozen. Sauces, soups, and casseroles are best defrosted in the refrigerator or thawed in the microwave. Grains such as rice need to be thawed for about 1 hour at room temperature or thawed in the microwave.

FREEZING COOKED MEALS

In general, most vegetarian dishes are suitable for freezing as long as you bear in mind the following points about storage.

Make sure the quality of the food you are intending to freeze is good. Although freezing is a way of preserving food, it will not enhance a product, so if you have bought too many vegetables or made too much casserole, freeze right away while the food is still in peak condition.

Food to be frozen must be very well wrapped since exposure to the air will cause deterioration. Fatty foods and dishes that have a high fat content should not be frozen for long because they may go rancid.

The flavor of salt becomes stronger on freezing so use a light hand when seasoning foods that you know you are going to freeze. Dishes that are heavily spiced or make plentiful use of herbs may also change flavor if frozen for too long.

When stored properly, there are several varieties of fruit and vegetables that last for more than a few days.

Equipment

Every good cook has his or her own favorite piece of equipment or gadget, and deciding what is essential is a personal affair. It is important to have the right tools for the job, but this has to be set against the storage space you have available and your own budget. This section looks at small- and large-scale equipment, as well as electrical appliances, to help you decide what is most useful and what is good to have if you have the space and finance.

Knives must be kept sharp and used on appropriate surfaces.

Useful Utensils

There are certain essential items in the kitchen. A good knife and solid cutting board are invaluable. A medium-size chef's knife can do many jobs but it is better to own knives of various lengths. A small, sharp knife is useful for trimming, paring, and peeling. A large blade means you can chop and slice a quantity at a time. A serrated blade is useful for slicing and peeling soft fruit and vegetables such as tomatoes, and a large serrated knife slices bread.

Store knives carefully so as not to damage yourself or the blades. Keep them sharp with a steel or have them regularly sharpened. Get a large cutting board but one that you can lift comfortably. If you have chopped strong-flavored items, such as onion, garlic, or chile, make sure the board is very well washed. A second board is a good option.

Other useful, small-scale utensils include the following:

- Measuring cups and spoons
- Nut and cheese grater
- Squeezer and zester
- Salad spinner
- Whisk
- Sturdy garlic press
- Good-size pastry brush
- Pestle and mortar
- An effective vegetable peeler
- Kitchen scissors
- Tongs

Cookware

It is worth spending money on good cookware: a selection of saucepans—including one large enough for cooking family quantities of pasta—and large and small skillets. A pressure cooker is useful if you intend cooking batches of beans and large quantities of soups and stews. The new designs are easier to use than previous ones.

A steamer, a purpose-built pan and steaming basket combination, is useful since it is easy to check that the pan is not boiling dry. Similarly, three-layered bamboo steamers mean you can cook several vegetables at once, adding others as necessary. A trivet or steaming basket that fits inside a saucepan is an inexpensive alternative and electric steamers are available for those with plenty of space.

A wok is great for crisp, quick stir-frying. This wide, round-based pan is made of thin metal, which heats up quickly and provides a good-sized cooking surface. However, you can improvise with a large skillet instead.

Other useful items include a sturdy roasting pan or baking sheet and good-quality bakeware. Nonstick is useful, otherwise, line bakeware with reusable baking parchment to make cleaning easier.

Good-quality cookware is well worth the money because it will last, even if used frequently.

Having the right tools for the job makes preparation and cooking quicker and easier.

Electrical Appliances

These appliances generally make food preparation quicker and easier. In some instances, manually operated machines make a reasonable alternative.

Blender Blenders save a great deal of time, don't take up too much space, and take all the hard work out of making puréed soups and smooth sauces. It is useful to have a separate small mill for grinding nuts and breadcrumbs. A hand-held electric blender is good for puréeing small quantities. Use it directly in the pan or pour the liquid to be processed into a tall pitcher. Nonelectric alternatives include a food mill or grinder.

Food processor In some ways the food processor is the blender's big brother—both size wise and in terms of the number of jobs it can do. Its functions include blending, grating, and slicing, rubbing in fat, and making all-in-one cake mixtures. It is good for processing relatively large quantities. Some processors come with a smaller inner unit to put in place if you are dealing with small quantities. Make full use of your food processor by keeping it somewhere handy, or just the thought of getting it out can put you off using it. Plan your jobs so that you process dry ingredients before wet ones; in this way you'll save time on dismantling, cleaning and reassembling the processor.

Electric juicer This is a costly appliance, but worth it if you have access to good supplies of fruit and vegetables. Really good fruit and vegetable juices are impossible to make any other way.

Pasta maker See pages 208–9 for instructions on making pasta by hand and by machine. Electric machines are expensive and best for pasta devotees, but manual machines are easy to use and achieve good results. They are also not too bulky to store.

Yogurt maker Although you can make yogurt with a vacuum flask, an electric version makes sure that the temperature is constant and more consistent results are achieved.

Microwave Treat your microwave as an appliance that can speed up all sorts of stages in cooking, as well as occasionally being the best way to cook something from start to finish. When tackling a recipe you do not have to stick to conventional methods of cookery, such as the oven or the stovetop, or use the microwave the whole time. Choose the best method at each stage for the recipe and you will end up saving time and making better use of your kitchen equipment.

It is useful to have a microwave where you can choose a variety of temperatures, including one that is suitable for defrosting (see below).

Use your microwave for a whole range of processes. Vegetables cooked in the microwave retain a good proportion of their nutrients. You can steep milk and make stocks and sauces in the microwave; roux-based sauces are less likely to stick or burn, when cooked this way. You can toast nuts and seeds, reconstitute dried fruit, for example plumping up raisins for a salad or cake; and processed cereals, such as bulgur and polenta, cook quickly in the microwave.

The microwave is very good for defrosting, for which most microwaves have a special setting. When freezing food that you might wish to defrost in the microwave, use straight-sided, shallow, rather than deep, dishes, so that the food gets maximum exposure. Round dishes are better than square ones. For easier defrosting of liquids, use a close-fitting container so that the outsides cannot thaw and spread out to overcook or evaporate. Remember, the greater the bulk of food and the more dense it is, the longer it will take to defrost.

Electric blenders save an enormous amount of time when making smooth soups and sauces or quick purées of fruit.

Meal planning

Curiously, the myth still persists that vegetarian food is more complicated or time consuming to prepare. The truth is that there are just as many shortcuts with regard to techniques and ingredients as in any other cuisine. What does take time—and which is true of doing anything new—is unfamiliarity. The more you cook with staple vegetarian ingredients, the quicker and easier it will become. You will start to use foods without thinking and develop an intuitive sense of what you like to serve with what. The following pages provide plenty of tips and advice for planning, preparing, and cooking vegetarian meals. For planning more elaborate meals, see pages 350–77.

Efficient cooking

There are some general principles that underlie all efficient cooking. Bear these points in mind and you will undoubtedly be more organized when you cook.

Read the recipe. It sounds obvious but it is best to check beforehand whether anything needs soaking for a couple of hours, time to chill, and so on. It is also worth seeing if any of the stages can be prepared in advance.

Have all your ingredients within reach before you start. If you are intending to use equipment, have it at hand, not at the back of the cupboard. Make use of food processors and other electrical gadgets for dealing with large quantities. If possible, use equipment in an order that saves you excess washing and drying—generally, this means using dry ingredients first. Using reusable baking parchment to line roasting pans and baking sheets saves washing unwieldy pans.

When preparing food, keep the counter clear so that you can see what you are doing. Have a bowl or bag handy for sticking in all the vegetable peelings and trimmings as you work. While one thing is cooking, be preparing the next. The exception to this is a stir-fry when you need to have everything prepared and at hand, ready to cook.

If you double the recipe quantity it does not take double the time. If you are making a staple recipe, such as tomato sauce or a favorite casserole, make twice as much so that you can freeze or store some for another time.

A vegetarian stir-fry is one of the quickest and most nutritious meals. The possible ingredients are infinitely variable.

Having your ingredients ready before you start and being familiar with the recipe will make a difference to the preparation time. The more you cook, the quicker and more efficient you will become.

Quick Meals

Whether you plan ahead or are a spur-of-the-moment cook, it is useful to have in mind an idea of what can be put together simply and quickly, and where and how to make shortcuts.

Bulgar wheat takes only a matter of minutes to cook.

Certain ingredients and recipe ideas are quick both to prepare and to cook. Most stir-fry vegetables fall into this category—add protein with nuts, bean sprouts, or bean curd, and serve with quick-cooking noodles. Couscous can be flavored with chopped herbs and served with a quick vegetable sauté, or serve pasta with herb butter or oil, or with Asian flavorings. Cook bulgur to serve as an accompaniment or for a pilaf or salad base. Use quick-cooking lentils and serve them refried with tortillas or nachos, or spiced as a dhal with nan bread. Any omelet and basic egg dishes are quick to make, while canned legumes are ready to use and ideal in a number of quick meals.

Recipe ideas that are quick to prepare but take time to cook include most casseroles, baked potatoes, layered vegetable gratin, and one-pot grain dishes, such as paella.

New to Vegetarian Food

Keep in mind the points mentioned earlier and remember that it is a good idea to familiarize yourself with new ingredients gradually. It may take time to adjust to eating whole foods, so vary your diet with some refined products. Don't rely on just eggs and cheese; get into the habit of cooking grains and legumes once or twice a week. You will soon build up a repertoire of favorite dishes—some that you can cook without referring to the recipe!

Nan bread with lentil dhal is a vegetarian favorite.

Cooking for One or Two

Although most of the recipes in this book serve 4, lots of ideas adapt easily for fewer servings. It is little trouble to cook small amounts of pasta or couscous. Stir-fry recipes can be scaled down for one or two; similarly, most of the simple savories recipes (see page 143) can be easily scaled down to serve one or two.

Salads are easy to make in small quantities. Dressings can be more bother in small quantities, but they do tend to keep long enough to be used again. Phyllo pastry sheets make good individual pies without the need for making lots of dough.

Sauces, soups, and casseroles are best made in large quantities and because they usually freeze well, make plenty and then store in suitable portion sizes. If you need to eat the same meal two days running, simply vary the accompaniments.

USEFUL HINTS

- Rub your pan with peeled garlic before cooking to add flavor.
- Use crème fraîche or melt soft goat cheese to make a quick sauce, without lengthy mixing.
- Add a handful of nuts, bean sprouts, or grated cheese for instant protein.
- Bake bean curd in shoyu and oil for 10 minutes to give it a boost of flavor before adding other ingredients.
- Use walnut or hazelnut oil or a good-quality olive oil if you have no dressing handy.
- Serve fruit as an appetizer or dessert.
- Offer specialty breads as a substantial accompaniment.
- Remember that two or three small dishes put together can also make a meal.
- Make simple salads to add color and nutrients or to create a quick separate course.
- Make the most of leftovers by using them as fillings for vegetables, pies, and crêpes if there is not enough to freeze.

The Lone Vegetarian

Catering for one member of the family who is vegetarian while the rest are not is quite a common situation and should not condemn the cook to a life of cooking two separate meals. There are bound to be some vegetarian meals that will be enjoyed by everyone—pies, pasta, and dishes with eggs and cheese usually fall into this category.

Many recipes have a distinct point at which vegetable protein is added. This is the point to divide the meal and make some portion of it vegetarian and add meat or fish to the rest. Soups, stews, and casseroles fall into this category. Again, don't bother to make just one portion—make plenty to freeze in suitable portion sizes.

Putting It All Together

Planning a balanced diet will be different for each individual, couple, or family. Much will depend on your hours of work and proximity to stores. There are some general points to bear in mind, however, whatever your situation.

Simplicity does not equal monotony. A simple meal such as pasta with a sauce or a stir-fry with rice is nutritious, open to many variations, and can be full of different flavors and textures. Build a repertoire of recipes that you and your family like so that you can make them without thinking. These are the ones that you'll be most happy improvising with if you don't have every ingredient on hand.

Plan your weekly menus on firm foundations, using whole-grains and legumes for substance and carbohydrate. Add lots of vegetables for color and vital vitamins and minerals. Use richer ingredients, such as nuts or dairy products, less frequently. Serve fruit for dessert unless you have the time and energy to make something more elaborate. For festive occasions, serve a cheese board laden with dried fruits and nuts.

RECIPES

I am often asked what is my favorite meal, but as I am passionate about such a wide range of flavors and ingredients, I find it is a very hard question to answer. Perhaps the truth is that it is the meal I've just eaten. I hope that you, too, will find plenty of favorites among the 250 recipes in the following sections. There are lots to choose from with something that will appeal for every meal and every occasion.

The recipes are arranged in chapters starting with ideas for breakfast, followed by soups, appetizers, and light meals, then moving on to more substantial main courses. These meals are divided into groups that have in common either ingredients, such as pasta or grains, or are categorized by a style of cooking, such as stir-fry or slow-cooking casseroles. Useful sauces and vegetable accompaniments follow and then there are salads and dressings. Desserts, breads, and baking complete the individual recipe selection. The final part of the book, Entertaining, includes another selection of recipes grouped together in menus suitable for a wide range of occasions, from light suppers and barbecues to formal dinner parties.

Use the notes on ingredients and flavorings in the previous pages to help you make variations that suit your family's taste and lifestyle. Look also at the general notes for planning and preparation since becoming familiar with techniques and having the right equipment and ingredients at hand will make a big difference.

I hope that the tempting photographs will encourage you to try new ideas and I wish you great success with whatever you try.

Breakfast

Breakfast like a king! While it is an easy meal to skip, perhaps grabbing a coffee on the way to the office, it is a time of day when your body needs an energy boost and something substantial enough to stop you feeling hungry an hour later.

Everyday breakfasts need to be nutritious, simple, and fast. For fast breakfasts, go for juices, fruit dishes, cereals, and straightforward egg recipes (see page 178) or Rösti (see page 288). If you decide to have lazy weekend brunches, these can be more elaborate. Treat yourself and your guests to some quick muffins or pancakes with fruit. There are also a number of easy savories that can be prepared ahead during the week.

Many of the egg dishes on pages 178–85 are ideal for brunch, as are the Mexican recipes on pages 190–93. You can also serve grain dishes such as risotto, Red Rice with Pan-Fried Squash, Mushrooms, and Pecan Nuts (see page 229) or Paella with Many Vegetables (see page 233) for brunch. Puy lentils are quick cooking and also make an excellent breakfast dish, mixed with cooked onion and mushroom and well seasoned with shoyu or soy sauce.

fresh pear compote with apricots and prunes

This rich, spiced fruit compote is suitable for brunch as well as a winter dessert—use red wine instead of the grape juice for an alcoholic version, if you like. The finished cooking liquid should be rich and syrupy. It can be reduced further if you wish—remove the pears after cooking, then boil the liquid until it is sufficiently reduced, before continuing with the recipe.

serves 6

preparation: 10 minutes, plus standing

cooking: about 1 hour

v

1 ¼ cups/½ pint (300 milliliters) red grape juice
scant ½ cup (100 milliliters) water
scant ½ cup/3 ounces (75g) sugar or to taste
2 pears
1 bay leaf
1 cinnamon stick
12 peppercorns
1 sprig thyme
½ cup/4 ounces (125g) dried apricots
½ cup/4 ounces (125g) prunes

1 Measure the grape juice and water into a deep saucepan or flameproof casserole. Stir in the sugar.

2 Peel the pears and cut them into eighths. Place immediately in the grape juice and water. Add the bay leaf, cinnamon, peppercorns, and thyme. Bring to a boil, then simmer for 45–60 minutes, or until the pears are just tender.

3 Add the apricots and prunes to the cooked pears and let soak overnight. When cold, adjust the sweetening to taste. Serve with plain yogurt.

nutritional breakdown per serving: calories 178, protein 2g, fat 0g (saturated fat 0g), carbohydrates 44g

fruit and cereals

Fresh fruit is light to eat, provides vital minerals and vitamins, and makes a refreshing start to the day. Fruit platters and fruit salads sweetened with natural juice are colorful to serve. You can also keep to simple combinations of one or two fruits, such as a mixture of fresh apricots and figs served with white grape juice and roasted almonds, slices of fresh oranges served with passion fruit sauce, and the classic combination of papaya and lime.

Dried fruit should be soaked in plenty of liquid before eating. Choose a mixture of peaches, apricots, pears, and prunes. If you cook the fruit it will be softer and the cooking liquid will be more intense. You can add spices during the cooking process, if you like.

While oats and wheat are popular breakfast cereals, millet, rice, and quinoa can all be served, too—especially for cooked cold weather breakfasts. A creamy mixture can be made by cooking 1 part millet to 3 parts milk, bringing the mixture to a boil, and then cooking over gentle heat or in a low oven. Sweeten to taste and add spices, such as ground cinnamon or nutmeg, and dried fruit, such as raisins.

Rice makes a good start to the day either cooked with milk, or cooked as normal (see page 87) and then served with milk, soy milk, plain yogurt, and chopped fruit or roasted nuts or seeds.

The soft texture of quinoa lends itself well to a type of porridge for a hearty, warming breakfast.

toasted granola

Cereals make a wonderful start to the day, providing you with plenty of carbohydrate and fiber, while added fruit contributes essential vitamins and minerals. Many commercial cereals have a high sugar content and contain salt but it is easy to make toasted cereals at home with a minimum of sweetening. The malt extract could be replaced with honey, if you like.

serves 6

preparation: 5 minutes

cooking: 1 hour

𝑣

2⅓ cups/8 ounces (250g) oats
½ cup/2 ounces (50g) blanched almonds
scant ½ cup/2 ounces (50g) sunflower seeds
2–3 tablespoons wheat germ
¼ cup (50 milliliters) sunflower oil
¼ cup (50 milliliters) malt extract
generous ⅔ cup/2 ounces (50g) raisins

nutritional breakdown per serving: calories 373, protein 9g, fat 19g (saturated fat 2g), carbohydrate 45g

1 Combine the oats, almonds, sunflower seeds, and wheat germ in a bowl. Stir in the sunflower oil and malt extract and add a little water to moisten.

2 Spread out the mixture on a baking sheet and bake in a preheated oven, 250°F (120°C), for 1 hour, or until lightly browned and crisp.

3 Let cool before stirring in the raisins.

VARIATIONS
If you prefer a raw cereal, it is a good idea to soak granola overnight. This gives the oats a chance to soften and develop their natural creaminess. For 1 serving use about 4 tablespoons of oats and a similar amount of water. Sweeten with honey or sugar to taste and flavor with orange zest or orange juice. You can also stir in some plain yogurt. Leave this mixture in the refrigerator overnight. The following day, add fruits, such as grated apple, raspberries, sliced strawberries, or seedless grapes, and nuts, such as chopped roasted hazelnuts or almonds. This granola is energy giving and sustaining and provides a good range of vital vitamins and minerals.

blueberry muffins

Wholesome, moist, and delicious straight from the oven,
these muffins are easy to make just before breakfast!

makes 12
preparation: 5 minutes
cooking: 20 minutes
suitable for freezing

2 cups/8 ounces (250g) whole-wheat flour
½ cup/4 ounces (125g) light brown sugar
2 teaspoons baking powder
¼ teaspoon salt
1 teaspoon ground cinnamon
1 egg, beaten
1 cup (250 milliliters) milk
¼ cup (½ stick)/2 ounces (50g) melted butter or
   ¼ cup (50 milliliters) sunflower oil
2 cups/8 ounces (250g) blueberries

1   Combine the flour, sugar, baking powder, salt, and
    cinnamon in a large bowl. Mix the egg, with the
    milk and melted butter or oil in a pitcher.

2   Add the wet ingredients to the bowl of dry
    ingredients and mix together until only just
    combined.

3   Stir the blueberries into the muffin mixture.
    Spoon into 12 paper muffin cases and bake in a
    preheated oven, 400°F (200°C), for 20 minutes
    until risen and firm.

nutritional breakdown per muffin: calories 159, protein 4g,
fat 5g (saturated fat 3g), carbohydrate 27g

VARIATIONS

Once you are familiar with the basic mixture, you can
try many variations. Use ingredients such as bran or
oats instead of some of the flour. Add chopped nuts or
dried fruits, such as dates or golden raisins instead of
the blueberries. Alternatively, change the sweetening
and use honey or molasses instead of the sugar. If you
want a dairy-free version, add 1 tablespoon soy flour
mixed with a little water as a substitute for the egg. Use
soy milk instead of cow's milk.

traditional pancakes

TOPPINGS

Pancakes can be
served with syrup,
maple syrup, or clear
honey and topped
with thick yogurt,
cream, or crème
fraîche.

*These are great for a quick breakfast treat. It is simply
a matter of combining the dry and the wet ingredients.
Make sure the baking powder and baking soda are
evenly distributed through the flour. When mixing the
batter, simply stir until combined otherwise the pancakes
won't be so light.*

*Many variations are possible. Try using different flour,
such as rye flour or cornmeal; add spices, such as ground
ginger, nutmeg, or cinnamon; or sweeten with honey or
molasses instead of sugar for a different flavor.*

makes 12

preparation: 10 minutes

cooking: 10–15 minutes

1¾ cups/7 ounces (200g) whole-wheat flour
2–3 tablespoons light brown sugar
2 tablespoons wheat germ
1 teaspoon baking powder
2 teaspoons baking soda
1½ cups (350 milliliters) buttermilk
2 eggs, beaten
2 tablespoons/1 ounce (25g) butter, melted
¼ teaspoon vanilla extract

1 Combine the flour, sugar, wheat germ, baking
   powder, and baking soda in a large bowl.

2 In a separate bowl, beat the buttermilk with the
   eggs, melted butter, and vanilla extract. Pour onto
   the dry ingredients and stir until just combined.

3 Heat a large nonstick skillet or griddle, pour in
   some of the pancake batter, and shake the pan
   gently so that the mixture spreads out to a round,
   about 4 inches (10cm) across and ¼ inch (5mm)
   thick. Cook for a few minutes then, when well risen
   and full of holes, flip over using a spatula, and cook
   on the other side.

4 Repeat the process with the remaining batter to
   make about 12 pancakes. You can make several
   pancakes at a time.

nutritional breakdown per pancake: calories 102, protein 4g,
fat 3g (saturated fat 2g), carbohydrate 15g

mushroom and olive strata

serves 4

preparation: 15 minutes and standing overnight

cooking: 40–45 minutes

2 tablespoons/1 ounce (25g) butter
3¼ cups/8 ounces (250g) mushrooms
8 ounces (250g) whole-wheat bread, sliced
4 ounces (125g) mozzarella, sliced
½ cup/2 ounces (50g) pitted black olives, chopped
1 teaspoon dried oregano
salt and freshly ground black pepper
4 eggs
2 cups (450 milliliters) milk

1   Use a little of the butter to cook the mushrooms in a skillet or saucepan until soft. Use the remaining butter to spread over the slices of bread and cut the slices in half.

2   Layer the slices of bread and butter in a deep, lightly greased ovenproof dish with the sliced cheeses, chopped olives, and oregano, and the cooked mushrooms, seasoning each layer with salt and pepper and trimming the bread if necessary.

3   Beat the eggs with the milk in a pitcher and pour this over the layers of bread. Cover and refrigerate overnight.

4   The next day, cook the layers in a preheated oven, 400°F (200°C), for 35–45 minutes, or until well browned and crispy on top. The middle should be soft and a little runny.

nutritional breakdown per serving: calories 499, protein 30g, fat 29g (saturated fat 11g), carbohydrate 33g

juices and drinks

It is vital for your health to drink plenty of liquids. Bodily fluids lost through perspiration and even simple activities such as breathing need continually replacing. Liquids also help flush out the system and often form the basis of cleansing and detox diets. The juice and drinks recipes here offer a range of benefits and make very good alternatives to less healthy sweetened drinks or sodas.

Freshly made juices have many benefits, being full of natural sugars and high in vitamins and minerals. Since this is already in liquid form, the nutrients are easily absorbed into the bloodstream. It is best to drink freshly made juices before

a meal so that they have time to be absorbed and there is less chance of feeling bloated.

There are many juices to try. Apple and citrus fruits make a good starting base for fruit juices and carrot, or carrot and apple, makes a good foundation for a vegetable juice. Use strong flavor vegetables such as watercress, spinach, parsley, or beet in small quantities at first. The quality of the juice you make will depend on the raw ingredients. Buy organic or locally grown produce if you can.

For these juices you need an electric juicer to extract the maximum amount of juice possible from the fruit or vegetable.

carrot, apple, and celery juice

serves 1

preparation: 5 minutes

cooking: none

v

2 large carrots
3 celery stalks
2 tart dessert apples (such as Granny Smith)

1 Wash and chop the carrots, celery, and apples.

2 Juice in an electric juicer.

nutritional breakdown per serving: calories 146, protein 2g, fat 1g (saturated fat 0g), carbohydrate 35g

spiced mango juice

serves 1

preparation: 5 minutes

cooking: none

v

fresh ginger to make ginger juice
1 large orange
1 mango
lime juice to taste

1 Grate a small piece of fresh ginger onto a paper towel. Squeeze the juice through the towel into a small cup. Peel the orange and mango.

2 Juice in an electric juicer. Mix in a few drops of ginger juice, then add lime juice to taste.

nutritional breakdown per serving: calories 163, protein 3g, fat 1g (saturated fat 0g), carbohydrate 39g

tomato, cucumber, and watercress juice

spiced mango juice
top **carrot, apple, and
celery juice** center
**tomato, cucumber,
and watercress
juice** bottom

serves 1

preparation: 5 minutes

cooking: none

10 ounces (300g) tomatoes
3 ounces (75g) cucumber
¾–1 cup/¾–1 ounce (20–25g) watercress

1 Wash and chop the tomatoes, cucumber, and watercress.

2 Juice in an electric juicer.

nutritional breakdown per serving: calories 80, protein 4g, fat 2g (saturated fat 1g), carbohydrate 14g

smoothies

These blended mixtures are more of a "meal in a glass" than a drink, as they are based on protein-rich ingredients, such as milk, plain yogurt, bean curd, and nut milk. You can interchange the base ingredient to suit your taste. The drinks are made in a blender or food processor, not an electric juicer, and are a good way of creating a light nutritious meal with little effort.

banana and almond milk

This should not be prepared in advance because, despite the lemon juice, the banana in the mixture quickly starts to go brown. Sweeten with honey instead of sugar, if you like.

serves 1

preparation: 5 minutes

cooking: none

$\mathcal{V}$

⅓ cup/1½ ounces (40g) ground almonds
¾ cup (175 milliliters) water
1 banana
juice of 1 lemon
sugar to taste
1 tablespoon toasted sliced almonds

1 Blend the ground almonds with the water in a blender or food processor.

2 Add the banana and lemon juice and sweeten to taste with sugar. Blend again until smooth. Serve right away, topped with toasted sliced almonds.

nutritional breakdown per serving: calories 466, protein 13g, fat 31g (saturated fat 3g), carbohydrate 36g

savory smoothie

serves 1

preparation: 5 minutes

cooking: none

(Ca)

⅔ cup/¼ pint (150 milliliters) plain yogurt
¾ cup/¾ ounce (20g) spinach or
    watercress, chopped
1 tomato, skinned and deseeded
2–3 teaspoons wheat germ
salt and freshly ground black pepper
sesame seeds, dry-roasted, to garnish

1 Place the yogurt, spinach, tomato, and wheat germ in a blender or food processor and blend until smooth.

2 Season with salt and pepper to taste and serve garnished with sesame seeds.

nutritional breakdown per serving: calories 145, protein 11g, fat 5g (saturated fat 1g), carbohydrate 16g

bean curd and strawberry with vanilla

As before, the sugar could be replaced with honey, if you like.

serves 1

preparation: 5 minutes

cooking: none

Ⓒₐ 𝒱

7 ounces (200g) silken bean curd
1 cup/4 ounces (125g) strawberries
¼ teaspoon vanilla extract
soy milk to thin, optional
lemon juice to taste
sugar or honey to taste

1 Put the silken bean curd, strawberries, and vanilla extract in a blender or food processor and blend until smooth.

2 Add a little soy milk if you want a runnier consistency. Add lemon juice and sugar or honey to taste, then serve.

nutritional breakdown per serving: calories 220, protein 17g, fat 9g (saturated fat 1g), carbohydrate 20g

banana and almond milk left, **savory smoothie** center, **bean curd and strawberry with vanilla** right

Soups and Starters

Soups can make delicate and tempting first courses or, with a few well-chosen accompaniments, they can make substantial and easy meals, which fit in very well with today's informal style of eating. Many staple vegetarian ingredients lend themselves well to soups. It takes no special skill to produce good soup nor is it a lot of work for most recipes.

When serving soup as an appetizer, choose something light if the main course is filling or rich. Remember to aim for a contrast of texture and flavor with the rest of the meal. On the whole, a smooth soup is more elegant than a chunky broth.

Here you will find a range of soups, with something for every occasion. For a substantial soup—a meal in a bowl—try the Chowder with Sweet Potato or Country Vegetable Broth with Barley. If you want an elegant appetizer, make the deliciously creamy Carrot and Parsnip Soup with Coconut and Tamarind. For a quick, exotic meal, choose the Asian Mushroom Soup with Chile and Ginger. And soups are not just for cold weather—there is a selection of refreshing, cold soups to try on summer days, including the glorious Avocado Gazpacho.

avocado gazpacho

It is important to have ripe avocado for this delicately colored soup. It is light enough to make a good appetizer for a lunch or evening party. Follow it with Artichoke and Red Bell Pepper Gougère (see page 259) or Stuffed Italian Tomatoes with Red Pesto and Mozzarella (see page 172). For a simple meal, add finely chopped green bell pepper or very fresh garden peas to the soup and serve it with a good bread, feta cheese, slices of Leek and Fennel Frittata (see page 180), and a tomato salad.

serves 4

preparation: 10 minutes, plus chilling

cooking: none

2 ripe avocados
1¼ cups/½ pint (300 milliliters) plain yogurt
1¼ cups/½ pint (300 milliliters) Vegetable Stock
   (see page 144)
juice and zest of 1 lemon
1 garlic clove
¾ cup/¾ ounces (20g) parsley, chopped
¼ cucumber, finely chopped
2 scallions, finely chopped
2–3 tablespoons finely snipped chives

1 Peel 1 avocado, remove the pit, and place the avocado flesh in a blender or food processor. Add the yogurt, stock, lemon juice and zest, garlic, and parsley. Process until smooth, then pour into a bowl.

2 Peel the remaining avocado and chop into small pieces. Stir this into the soup with the chopped cucumber, scallions, and finely snipped chives, reserving some of these for garnish.

3 Chill well before serving.

nutritional breakdown per serving: calories 190, protein 6g, fat 15g (sat. fat 3g), carbohydrates 8g

stock

Making stock is not difficult—it is merely an extra stage to be considered when planning to make soup. Homemade stock can be quite sweet; to counteract this, add salt or extra herbs or some shoyu or soy sauce. If you don't have time to make your own stock, you can use the soaking water from dried mushrooms, or use a commercial bouillon cube or powder.

basic vegetable stock

makes 5 cups/2 pints (1.2 liters)

preparation: 10 minutes

cooking: 55–70 minutes

suitable for freezing

v

2 tablespoons sunflower oil
1 onion, coarsely chopped
2 carrots, coarsely chopped
1 leek, coarsely chopped
1 celery stalk, coarsely chopped
6¼ cups/2½ pints (1.5 liters) water
2 sprigs parsley
1 bay leaf
6 peppercorns
1 garlic clove, left whole

1   Heat the oil in a large saucepan and cook the onion, carrots, leek, and celery very gently. For a pale-colored stock, don't let the vegetables color although the flavor will be less intense. For a fuller-flavored version, let the vegetables brown.

2   Add the water to the vegetables, together with the parsley, bay leaf, peppercorns, and garlic. Bring to a boil, then simmer for 45–60 minutes. Strain and use as required.

minimal nutritional content

VARIATIONS

Many other ingredients may be added to basic stock. Add parsnips for a good, sweet, nutty flavor, or celery root and fennel for their delicate fragrance. Winter and summer squash, such as butternut squash or zucchini, may be added; another option is scrubbed potato peelings. Avoid whole pieces of potato because they will make the stock cloudy. Spices such as ginger or lemongrass are flavorsome additions, too.

Lemon Stock—add ½ lemon to the basic vegetable stock liquid prior to simmering.

what to avoid

Some ingredients should be avoided when making stock. For example, green vegetables, such as cabbage or broccoli, can give soup a bitter taste; beet will turn the stock red. Very old or moldy vegetables certainly won't do anything for the final flavor, either.

croûtons

These are made from day-old bread that is either cubed or sliced. The pieces can be fried in a mixture of olive oil and butter, or just oil. Add a little walnut oil or hazelnut oil to alter the flavor. Alternatively, the slices can be left plain and toasted or baked until crisp. For a more elaborate version make mini Bruschetta (see page 364).

dark mushroom stock

Dried mushrooms are particularly good as a base for a rich stock with complex flavors.

makes 5 cups/2 pints (1.2 liters)
preparation: 10 minutes
cooking: 1¼ hours
suitable for freezing
𝓋

1 cup/2 ounces (50g) dried wild mushrooms
6¼ cups/2½ pints (1.5 liters) boiling water
1 onion, coarsely chopped
2 celery stalks, coarsely chopped
2 leeks, coarsely chopped
3¼ cups/8 ounces (250g) fresh mushrooms, halved or chopped
2 tablespoons olive or sunflower oil
1 bay leaf
1 sprig thyme

1   Soak the dried mushrooms in a bowl of the boiling water while you prepare the vegetables. Heat the oil in a large saucepan and cook the onion until well browned—this takes up to 10 minutes. Add the celery, leeks, and fresh mushrooms, and cook for 5 minutes.

2   Remove the soaked mushrooms from the bowl with a slotted spoon, reserving the soaking liquid. Strain the soaking liquid, preferably through a coffee filter, to remove the sediment. Then add the wild mushrooms, soaking liquid, bay leaf, and thyme to the pan of vegetables.

3   Bring the stock to a boil and simmer for 1 hour, covered. Strain and use as required.

minimal nutritional content

VARIATIONS

Roast Garlic Stock—Separate 1 small unpeeled head of garlic into cloves. Roast in a preheated oven, 400°F (200°C), for about 5 minutes. Peel and mash the garlic and add to the dark mushroom stock.
Asian Clear Stock—Add a strip of kombu (a dried seaweed) to the mushroom stock liquid prior to simmering. This stock can also be flavored with miso or shoyu or soy sauce

STORING SOUPS AND STOCKS

Always keep soups and stocks in the refrigerator. Bring to a boil to reheat. A soup will generally thicken on standing—add stock, milk, or water to thin down.

good soup making

- Use a good stock.
- Remember there are other liquids apart from stock that make a good flavor base, for example milk or coconut milk.
- Make sure the onions are well cooked before adding other ingredients; otherwise, they may never properly soften.
- Sweat the vegetables when they are added to improve the overall flavor. Make sure you use a big enough pan to do this; a wide pan is better than a tall pan.
- Pasta, rice, and dumplings add body to a thin soup.
- A smooth soup need not be a chore, thanks to blenders and food processors. Always let soup cool before puréeing. Adding a pat of butter, a tablespoon of crème fraîche, or good-quality olive oil will enrich the soup at this stage.
- Many soups benefit from being made in advance and reheated.

garnishes and accompaniments

It is always worth spending a minute or two thinking about and organizing a garnish for a soup. A few green herbs can brighten the muted color of a broth; a julienne of vegetables floating on a smooth purée makes a pleasing contrast in texture; a swirl of cream enhances and enriches. Here are a few ideas:

- *chopped herbs or whole herb leaves*
- *herb butter, chilled and cut into an attractive shape*
- *julienne strips of vegetables such as zucchini, carrot, or celery*
- *roasted nuts, chopped*
- *coarsely crushed peppercorns or coriander seeds*
- *dry-roasted spice seeds such as cumin*
- *blanched zest of lemon or orange*
- *thinly sliced sautéed baby mushrooms*
- *chopped slivers of black or green olives*
- *ribbons of carrots or cucumber*
- *cooked polenta, cut into tiny shapes.*

red lentil soup with cumin

Red lentils are a great ingredient for soups because they turn so easily to a thick purée. Their earthy flavor is best counteracted with spices such as the cumin used here or with citrus fruit.

This soup could be followed by a grain dish such as Sesame Millet with Pan-fried Zucchini, Asparagus, and Avocado Cream (see page 228) or Almond Croustade with Swiss Chard (see page 268).

serves 4

preparation: 5 minutes

cooking: 55 minutes

suitable for freezing

(Fe) 𝒱

2 tablespoons olive oil
1 large onion, finely chopped
1 garlic clove, crushed
1 teaspoon cumin seeds
½ cup/4 ounces (125g) red lentils
2½ cups/1 pint (600 milliliters) Vegetable Stock
　(see page 144)
1 pound (500g) tomato purée
salt and freshly ground black pepper
1–2 tablespoons chopped cilantro, to garnish

1　Heat the olive oil in a large saucepan and gently cook the onion and garlic until soft. Add the cumin seeds and toast for a few minutes until just colored.

2　Add the red lentils to the pan and stir well so they become coated with the onion mixture.

3　Next pour in the stock, bring to a boil, and simmer for 15 minutes so that the lentils have a chance to soften, then add the tomato purée, and bring to a boil. Turn down the heat and simmer, covered, for 30 minutes more.

4　Let cool then, using a blender or food processor, purée the soup until very smooth. Season to taste then heat gently before serving, garnished with chopped cilantro.

nutritional breakdown per serving: calories 196, protein 10g, fat 6g (saturated fat 1g), carbohydrate 27g

chowder with sweet potato

This is a colorful soup with corn, carrots, and sweet potato and a stock base enriched with cream. This soup could be followed by a light savory such as Griddled Zucchini Quiche with Pine Nuts (see page 255).

serves 4

preparation: 10 minutes

cooking: about 1 hour

suitable for freezing

2 tablespoons sunflower oil
1 onion, finely chopped
2 garlic cloves, crushed
1 cup/4 ounces (125g) baby corn cobs, chopped
12 ounces (375g) sweet potato, finely chopped
2 carrots, peeled and finely chopped
1 red bell pepper, cored, deseeded, and chopped
½ teaspoon paprika
2½ cups/1 pint (600 milliliters) Vegetable Stock
   (see page 144)
2 tablespoons finely chopped parsley
1 teaspoon dried thyme
scant ½ cup (100 milliliters) heavy cream
salt and freshly ground black pepper

1 Heat the sunflower oil in a large saucepan and gently cook the onion and garlic until soft. Add all the prepared vegetables and stir them into the onion mixture. Cook slowly for 5 minutes so that the vegetables start to soften.

2 Sprinkle in the paprika and stir it in. Pour in the stock, add the parsley and thyme, and bring to a boil.

3 Remove the pan from the heat, pour in the cream, and mix very well. Return the pan to the heat and simmer the mixture, partially covered, for 40–45 minutes, or until the vegetables are really soft. Season well and serve hot.

nutritional breakdown per serving: calories 277, protein 3g, fat 18g (saturated fat 8g), carbohydrate 27g

puy lentil and mushroom soup

Lentils, mushrooms, and red wine are a wonderful combination, served here as a rich soup. Try to get shiitake mushrooms since they have a distinctive flavor and solid texture; second choice would be cremini or Paris mushrooms. This soup could be followed by a simple Potato and Leek Boulangère (see page 262) or Roquefort and Celery Root Crêpes (see page 187).

serves 4

preparation: 10 minutes

cooking: about 1 hour

suitable for freezing

(Fe) 𝒱

2 tablespoons olive oil
1 onion, finely chopped
1 garlic clove, crushed
1 red chile, finely chopped
1 carrot, finely chopped
1 celery stalk, finely chopped
2 cups/5 ounces (150g) shiitake
    mushrooms, sliced
¼ cup (50 milliliters) red wine
⅔ cup/5 ounces (150g) Puy or brown lentils
4 cups/1¾ pints (1 liter) Mushroom Stock
    (see page 145)
2 tablespoons shoyu or soy sauce
salt and freshly ground black pepper

1 Heat the olive oil in a large saucepan, and gently cook the onion and garlic until fairly soft. Add the red chile and cook for 2 minutes, then add the carrot, celery, and mushrooms. Cook for 5 minutes, or until the mushrooms have begun to soften.

2 Pour in the red wine and increase the heat, then cook until most of the liquid has been driven off. Add the lentils and stir in, then pour in the mushroom stock.

3 Bring to a boil and cook for 45–50 minutes, or until the lentils and vegetables are very soft. Add the shoyu or soy sauce and season with salt and pepper to taste. Serve hot.

nutritional breakdown per serving: calories 198, protein 11g, fat 7g (saturated fat 1g), carbohydrate 23g

roasted yellow bell pepper soup

This simple soup has a good creamy texture and mellow flavor thanks to the roasted vegetable base. It could be followed by a contrasting grain dish such as Layered Bulgur with Tomatoes and Feta (see page 231) or by a pasta dish.

serves 4

preparation: 10–15 minutes

cooking: 35 minutes

suitable for freezing

𝓥

3 large yellow bell peppers, lightly brushed
   with oil
8 shallots, unpeeled
1 large/8 ounces (250g) potato, coarsely
   chopped
2½ cups/1 pint (500 milliliters) Vegetable Stock
   (see page 144)
salt and freshly ground black pepper
freshly grated nutmeg
1–2 tablespoons olive oil

1 Place the bell peppers in a roasting pan and roast in a preheated oven, 400°F (400°C), for 30 minutes. Put the shallots in the oven at the same time and roast for 20 minutes.

2 Once the vegetables are roasted, let cool slightly then skin the bell peppers and remove the seeds. Don't discard any cooking juices. Let the shallots cool slightly before peeling.

3 Meanwhile, cook the potato in a saucepan of boiling salted water for about 10–15 minutes, or until soft.

4 Using a blender or food processor, purée the cooked bell peppers, shallots, and potato with the vegetable stock and any juices from the bell peppers. Season well with salt and pepper and add a generous grating of nutmeg plus up to 2 tablespoons olive oil to give the finished soup a velvety texture. Pour into a large pan and heat through before serving.

nutritional breakdown per serving: calories 118, protein 3g,
fat 4g (saturated fat 1g), carbohydrate 18g

spiced gumbo

This is a wonderful warming meal in a bowl and is especially good when served with Savory Cheese Corn Bread (see page 340). If you want more the look of a stew rather than soup, keep all the vegetables chunky and add less liquid. This soup is best made in large quantities so that you can pack in lots of ingredients.

serves 4

preparation: 10 minutes

cooking: 55–65 minutes

𝓋

2 tablespoons sunflower oil
1 onion, finely chopped
1 garlic clove, crushed
1 red chile, deseeded and chopped
1 green bell pepper, cored, deseeded, and chopped
3 medium/13 ounces (400g) potatoes, finely chopped
4 ounces (125g) okra, thickly sliced
14 ounces (398 milliliters) canned chopped tomatoes
2½ cups/1 pint (600 milliliters) Vegetable Stock (see page 144)
2 bay leaves
salt and freshly ground black pepper

1   Heat the oil in a large saucepan and gently cook the onion and garlic until soft. Add the chile and cook for 3 minutes. Add the pepper, potatoes, and okra, stir well, and cook for 2 minutes.

2   Pour the canned tomatoes and stock into the pan, add the bay leaves and a little salt and pepper. Bring to a boil, then cover the pan, and simmer for 45–60 minutes, or until the vegetables are very soft. Remove the bay leaves, adjust the seasoning to taste, and serve hot.

nutritional breakdown per serving (4 portions): calories 170, protein 5g, fat 6g (saturated fat 1g), carbohydrate 25g

carrot and parsnip soup with coconut and tamarind

Root vegetables such as carrots and parsnips make wonderful, smooth, colorful soups. They can be flavored in many different ways—from a simple grating of nutmeg to this more complex mixture of spices. The coconut milk adds a velvety quality to the finished soup, which is balanced by the slightly sour flavor of the tamarind. This soup can also be made with squash, pumpkin, or sweet potato.

serves 4

preparation: 10 minutes

cooking: 1–¼ hours

suitable for freezing

𝑣

1 teaspoon coriander seeds
1 teaspoon cumin seeds
2 tablespoons sunflower oil
1 onion, finely chopped
2 garlic cloves, crushed
8 ounces (250g) carrots, finely chopped
8 ounces (250g) parsnips, finely chopped
3¾ cups/1½ pints (900 milliliters) Vegetable
    Stock (see page 144)
⅔ cup/¼ pint (150 milliliters) coconut milk
1 tablespoon tamarind (ready-prepared)
salt and freshly ground black pepper

1   In a small skillet, dry-roast the coriander and cumin seeds until lightly roasted, then crush with a pestle and mortar, and set aside.

2   Heat the oil in a large saucepan, and gently cook the onion and garlic until very soft, then add the dry-roasted spices. Add the finely chopped carrots and parsnips to the pan and cook slowly for 10 minutes, then pour in the stock, and cook for 50–60 minutes.

3   Let cool slightly, then place the vegetable mixture in a blender or food processor with the coconut milk and tamarind, and purée until smooth.

4   Season with salt and pepper to taste, return to the pan, and heat through. Serve hot.

nutritional breakdown per serving: calories 154, protein 3g, fat 7g (saturated fat 1g), carbohydrate 21g

garbanzo and celery soup with gremolada

Gremolada or gremolata is a fresh flavoring made from parsley, garlic, and lemon zest. It gives a definite perk to any dish and here counteracts the mellow earthy character of the garbanzo beans and potato.

You could use other legumes such as lima beans or black-eyed peas instead of the garbanzos. Serve this soup with a good bread to make a light meal; or follow it with a simple savory such as Giant Mushrooms Stuffed with Wild Rice and Roasted Onions (see page 173) or Kuku with Spinach (see page 181).

serves 4

preparation: 10 minutes

cooking: about 1 hour

suitable for freezing after step 2

𝒱

2 tablespoons olive oil
1 onion, finely chopped
3 celery stalks, finely chopped
scant 1 cup/7 ounces (200g) garbanzo beans (cooked weight)
1 potato, finely chopped
14 ounces (398 milliliters) canned chopped tomatoes
3¾ cups/1½ pints (900 milliliters) Vegetable Stock (see page 144)
salt and freshly ground black pepper

For the gremolada:
¼ cup/¼ ounce (7g) chopped parsley
zest of 1 lemon
2 garlic cloves, finely chopped

1 Heat the oil in a large saucepan and gently cook the onion. Add the celery and cook for 5 minutes, then add the garbanzo beans, and potato, and cook for 5 minutes.

2 Pour in the canned tomatoes and vegetable stock and bring the mixture to a boil. Cover the pan and simmer for 45–50 minutes. Season well with salt and pepper.

3 To make the gremolada, combine the chopped parsley, lemon zest, and garlic and stir into the soup. Let stand for 1–2 minutes, then serve hot.

nutritional breakdown per serving: calories 170, protein 6g, fat 8g (saturated fat 1g), carbohydrate 21g

asian mushroom soup with chile and ginger

Packed with colorful vegetables, this spiced soup is virtually a meal in a bowl. If you prefer a hotter version, leave in some of the chile seeds.

nutritional breakdown per serving: calories 288, protein 10g, fat 9g (saturated fat 2g), carbohydrate 44g

serves 4

preparation: 15 minutes, plus soaking

cooking: 20 minutes

v

½ cup/1 ounce (25g) dried mushrooms
5 cups/2 pints (1.2 liters) boiling water
2 tablespoons sunflower oil
5 ounces (150g) shallots, chopped
2 celery stalks, sliced
2 teaspoons grated fresh ginger
1 red chile, deseeded and chopped
2 carrots, cut into thin batons
3¼ cups/8 ounces (250g) shiitake and oyster
   mushrooms, sliced
generous ¾ cup/5 ounces (150g) corn
3 tablespoons shoyu or soy sauce
4 ounces (125g) medium or fine egg or
   rice noodles
scant 2 cups/5 ounces (150g) snow peas
1 cup/1 ounce (25g) chopped cilantro leaves
salt and freshly ground black pepper

1   To make the stock, soak the dried mushrooms in the boiling water. Let stand for 20 minutes, then drain, reserving the soaking liquid. Chop the soaked mushrooms coarsely and set aside.

2   Heat the oil in a large saucepan and cook the shallots until soft. Add the celery, ginger, and chile and cook for 3–4 minutes more, then add the carrots, the fresh and dried mushrooms, and the corn. Stir well and cook slowly for 5–10 minutes.

3   Pour in the mushroom liquid and add the shoyu or soy sauce. Bring the soup to a boil. Meanwhile, soak the noodles in boiling water for 4 minutes, drain, and add to the pan with the snow peas and half the cilantro.

4   Bring the soup back to a boil and cook for 2–3 minutes, or until the peas are just tender. Season with salt and pepper to taste and serve immediately, garnished with the remaining cilantro.

celery root and emmental soup

Melted cheese gives this soup a rich texture as well as boosting the nutritional content. Follow this soup with a grain dish such as Mushroom Risotto with Tarragon (see page 226) or with the Roasted Pecan and Cashew Loaf (see page 264). Alternatively, eat on its own, served with walnut croûtons, for a light meal.

serves 4

preparation: 10 minutes

cooking: 1 hour

suitable for freezing (without the cheese)

2 tablespoons/1 ounce (25g) butter
1 onion, finely chopped
1 garlic clove, crushed
1 pound (500g) celery root, peeled and
    finely chopped
3 cups/1¼ pints (750 milliliters) Vegetable Stock
    (see page 144)
salt and freshly ground black pepper
¾ cup/3 ounces (75g) grated Emmental

1 Melt the butter in a large saucepan and gently
   cook the onion and garlic until soft. Add the
   finely chopped celery root and cook slowly for
   about 10 minutes.

2 Pour in the stock, bring to a boil, then cover the
   pan, and simmer for 45–50 minutes. Let cool then,
   using a blender or food processor, purée until
   smooth. Season with salt and pepper to taste.

3 Return the soup to the pan, then stir in the grated
   cheese. Stir over a gentle heat until the cheese has
   melted—you need to melt the cheese slowly or it
   may become stringy. Serve the soup hot.

nutritional breakdown per serving: calories 157, protein 8g,
fat 12g (saturated fat 7g), carbohydrate 6g

caramelized onion soup with brandy

This is a rich vegetarian version of the classic French onion soup. Use a well-flavored dark stock as a base, but also make sure the onions are both well cooked and well browned so that the soup has a good depth of flavor and color. This makes a great party soup followed by a pastry dish such as Chestnut and Cèpe Pie (see page 257), or serve it as a warming lunch dish on a dreary day.

serves 4

preparation: 10 minutes

cooking: 45 minutes

suitable for freezing (without the cheese)

(Ca)

¼ cup (½ stick)/2 ounces (50g) butter
1 pound (500g) onions, chopped
3 tablespoons brandy
4 cups/1¾ pints (1 liter) dark Vegetable Stock
  (see page 144)
1 teaspoon dried thyme
1 tablespoon miso, dissolved in a little stock
salt and freshly ground black pepper
4 slices rustic bread
1 garlic clove, peeled and halved
2 teaspoon coarse grain mustard
1 cup/4 ounces (125g) grated Gruyère

1 Melt the butter in a large saucepan and cook the onions very gently until completely soft—this takes about 20 minutes.

2 Once soft, turn up the heat and cook the onions to a dark brown, stirring frequently. Add the brandy and cook over high heat until reduced.

3 Pour in the stock and add the thyme and miso. Bring to a boil, then cover and simmer for 20 minutes. Season well with salt and pepper.

4 Meanwhile, place the bread in a preheated oven, 400°F (200°C), and bake for 3–4 minutes, until dry but not toasted. Rub with the cut side of a garlic clove, then spread with a little mustard, and cover with grated cheese.

5 Pour the soup into flameproof bowls. Put a slice of bread in each bowl, then place under a preheated broiler until the cheese has melted. Serve the soup immediately.

nutritional breakdown per serving: calories 408, protein 14g, fat 23g (saturated fat 14g), carbohydrate 32g

country vegetable soup with barley

Soups like this tend to be best made in large quantities so that you can include a wide selection of vegetables to give a full flavor and a good mix of colors. Easy to make and suitable for freezing, this soup makes a meal served with a wholesome bread and cheese or a simple dip or pâté such as Oyster Mushroom and Roast Almond Pâté (see page 165) or Roasted Eggplant and Garlic Dip (see page 167).

If you can, make the broth the day before you want to eat it so the flavors have plenty of time to develop. As the soup cooks, the colors will become quite muted. Counteract this by serving it with lots of fresh parsley.

serves 6–8

preparation: 10 minutes

cooking: 1–¼ hours

𝒱

1 tablespoon sunflower oil
1 onion, finely chopped
1 leek, chopped
1 carrot, chopped
1 parsnip, chopped
1 bulb fennel, chopped
10 ounces (300g) squash or rutabaga, chopped
⅓ cup/2 ounces (50g) barley
4 cups/1¾ pints (1 liter) Vegetable Stock (see
    page 144)
1 bouquet garni (bay leaf, 1 sprig thyme, parsley
    tied with string—see page 107)
salt and freshly ground black pepper
2–3 tablespoons finely chopped parsley, to garnish

1 Heat the oil in a large saucepan and gently cook the onion until fairly soft. Add the leek, carrot, parsnip, fennel, squash, and barley and cook slowly for 10 minutes, stirring occasionally, so that the vegetables sweat and start to soften.

2 Add the stock and the bouquet garni and bring to a boil. Season well with salt and pepper, then cover the pan and simmer for 50–60 minutes.

3 Remove and discard the bouquet garni. Adjust the seasoning if necessary, then serve the soup garnished with a good sprinkling of chopped parsley.

nutritional breakdown per serving: calories 88, protein 2g, fat 3g (saturated fat 0g), carbohydrate 15g

chilled bean soup

This is a delicious, refreshing soup to eat on hot days or warm evenings. The flavors will develop as it stands but it is important to use a well-flavored stock as a base. A recipe for stock is included here but if you have stock at hand then use that instead. Follow this soup with Phyllo Pie with Double Mushrooms and Goat Cheese (see page 261).

serves 4

preparation: 15 minutes, plus chilling

cooking : 15 minutes, plus making stock

For the stock:

1 tablespoon olive oil

1 onion, roughly chopped

2 garlic cloves

½ bulb fennel, roughly chopped

1 carrot, roughly chopped

2 celery stalks, roughly chopped

4 cups/1¾ pints (1 liter) water

1 bay leaf

sprigs of parsley and thyme

For the soup:

1 tablespoon olive oil

1 onion, finely chopped

½ bulb fennel, finely chopped

⅔ cup/3½ ounces (100g) green beans, sliced

scant 1 cup/3½ ounces (100g) peas

3½ ounces (100g) asparagus, sliced

1⅓ cups/3½ ounces (100g) snow peas

2–3 tablespoons Pesto (see page 211)

scant ½ cup (100 milliliters) plain yogurt

salt and freshly ground black pepper

basil leaves, to garnish

1 To make the stock, heat the oil in a large saucepan and gently cook the onion, garlic, fennel, carrot, and celery until lightly browned. Add the water, bay leaf, parsley, and thyme. Bring to a boil, then simmer, covered, for 40–60 minutes. Strain and reserve.

2 To make the soup, heat the oil in a large saucepan and gently cook the onion and fennel until soft but not colored.

3 Add 2½ cups/1 pint (600 milliliters) of the vegetable stock and bring to a boil. Boil for 4–5 minutes, then add the prepared beans, peas, asparagus and snow peas and cook for 3 minutes, or until the vegetables are just cooked but still crisp.

4 Remove the pan from the heat and let cool. When the soup is cold, stir in the pesto and yogurt and season with salt and pepper to taste. Chill thoroughly before serving. Garnish with basil.

nutritional breakdown per serving: calories 180, protein 8g, fat 12g (saturated fat 3g), carbohydrate 10g

chilled melon soup with wine and honey

This fragrant chilled fruit soup is great on a hot day, perhaps served as part of an exotic picnic. The refreshing flavors also work well used as a palate cleanser between courses. Vegans can make this dish by substituting sugar for the honey. Make sure the sugar is dissolved before bringing the mixture to a boil.

serves 4

preparation: 15 minutes, plus chilling

cooking: about 5 minutes

3 tablespoons honey
3 tablespoons water
8 cardamom pods, husk removed and seeds
    crushed, or ½ teaspoon ground cardamom
⅓ cup (80 milliliters) white wine
2 small melons
generous ¾ cup/4 ounces (125g) raspberries
2 passion fruit

1 Boil the honey and water in a large saucepan with the cardamom seeds. Simmer for 5 minutes, then add the wine and let cool.

2 Extract the juice of 1 melon with a juicer and add this to the wine and honey mixture. Scoop the remaining melon into balls or cut it into chunks and add to the melon liquid in the pan. Gently mix in the raspberries.

3 Extract the juice from the passion fruit, either by using a juicer or by adding a little sugar to the flesh, and heating it in a small saucepan, then pressing it through a strainer. Add this to the melon and raspberry mixture.

4 Chill the soup thoroughly before serving.

nutritional breakdown per serving: calories 587, protein 2g, fat 0g (saturated fat 0g), carbohydrate 151g

glazed nectarines with gorgonzola

This is an elegant appetizer or light meal, augmented perhaps with a special bread and some extra salad greens. Do make sure you use good-quality ripe fruit.

serves 4

preparation: 10 minutes

cooking: 3–4 minutes

2 tablespoons honey
2 tablespoons lime juice
2 nectarines, halved and pits removed
4 ounces (125g) gorgonzola, thinly sliced
zest of 1 lime
watercress or a dark green or dark red leaf
    (such as radicchio or lollo rosso), to serve

1   Combine the honey and lime juice in a small bowl.

2   Slice each nectarine half into 8 wedges. Lay the
    nectarine slices in a flameproof dish and pour the
    lemon and honey mixture over them.

3   Place the dish under a preheated hot broiler and
    broil for 3–4 minutes, or until the nectarines are
    lightly browned. Baste with any remaining juice.

4   Arrange slices of nectarine alternately with slices
    of cheese on individual serving plates. Sprinkle
    with a little lime zest.

5   Add some dark green or red salad leaves on the
    side. Serve at room temperature.

nutritional breakdown per serving: calories 160, protein 4g,
fat 10g (saturated fat 6g). carbohydrate 16g

griddled leeks and asparagus with cream cheese dressing

This simple appetizer or light lunch is quick to make. As an appetizer it needs no accompaniment and could be followed by Lentil Layer with Red Bell Pepper (see page 266) or Cider Casserole with New Potatoes (see page 243). For a light lunch, serve with a good rustic bread.

serves 4

preparation: 5 minutes

cooking: 5 minutes

For the dressing:

⅓ cup/3 ounces (175g) cream cheese
2 tablespoons white wine vinegar
⅓ cup (80 milliliters) olive oil
salt and freshly ground black pepper

12 ounces (370g) baby leeks
6 ounces (175g) asparagus tips
2 tablespoons blue poppy seeds

1 To make the dressing, use a blender or food processor to blend the cream cheese with the wine vinegar. Then, with the motor running, add the oil in a thin steady stream and blend until smooth. Season to taste.

2 Heat a griddle pan or a large nonstick skillet until very hot.

3 Slice the leeks lengthwise in half if more than a finger width thick. Put the leeks and asparagus on the griddle pan and cook for 4–5 minutes, turning over once or twice during cooking.

4 Remove from the pan and arrange on individual serving plates, then pour on the cream cheese dressing, and sprinkle with poppy seeds. Serve at room temperature.

nutritional breakdown per serving: calories 264, protein 5g, fat 29g (saturated fat 8g), carbohydrate 4g

broiled belgian endive with two cheeses

This is great for an easy lunch or supper snack with crusty bread. Try a range of different melting cheeses.

serves 4

preparation: 5 minutes

cooking: 6–8 minutes

(Ca)

4 heads Belgian endive

scant 1 cup/3½ ounces (100g) grated Cheddar

scant 1 cup/3½ ounces (100g) grated
    smoked cheese

salt and freshly ground black pepper

1 Quarter the heads of Belgian endive and braise in a saucepan containing stock or water for 3–4 minutes until just soft. Drain well.

2 Place the cooked pieces of Belgian endive in a lightly greased flameproof dish and season well. Cover with the Cheddar and smoked cheese and place under a preheated hot broiler. Broil for 3–4 minutes, or until the cheese has melted and is well browned. Serve hot.

nutritional breakdown per serving: calories 190, protein 12g, fat 15g (saturated fat 9g), carbohydrate 3g

poached vegetables with herbs and wine

This is an easy succulent way of serving a variety of vegetables. Use a good-quality olive oil because the flavor will come through. As the colors of the cooked vegetables invariably become muted, add a handful of fresh herbs as a bright garnish, or mix in some black olives and cubes of feta cheese as a colorful contrast.

serves 4

preparation: 10 minutes

cooking: 10 minutes

v

8 ounces (250g) shallots, peeled and left whole
3¼ cups/8 ounces (250g) white mushrooms
8 ounces (250g) fennel, sliced
1 cup (250 milliliters) white wine
1 bay leaf
2 sprigs thyme
1 sprig rosemary
2 garlic cloves, thinly sliced
6 peppercorns
1 cinnamon stick
1½ cups/8 ounces (250g) green beans, sliced
⅔ cup/¼ pint (150 milliliters) olive oil
salt and freshly ground black pepper

1 Put the shallots, mushrooms, fennel, and white wine in a large saucepan.

2 Add the bay leaf, thyme, rosemary, garlic, peppercorns, and cinnamon stick and bring to a boil. Simmer for 5 minutes.

3 Add the green beans, then simmer for 3–4 minutes more.

4 Remove the pan from the heat and let cool slightly. Then stir in the olive oil and season with salt and pepper to taste. Serve at room temperature.

nutritional breakdown per serving: calories 340, protein 4g, fat 28g (saturated fat 4g), carbohydrate 9g

oranges with red onion and black olives in sherry dressing

This is a very simple but effective combination of ingredients that is both refreshing and colorful. It is quick to prepare but do leave time for chilling since the coolness of this appetizer is part of its charm. For a vegan alternative, substitute a concentrated fruit juice for the honey.

serves 4

preparation: 10 minutes, plus chilling

cooking: none

4 large oranges, peeled and thinly sliced
1 small red onion, thinly sliced
¼ cup (50 milliliters) olive oil
1–2 tablespoons sherry vinegar
1 teaspoon honey
1 tablespoon chopped mint
salt and freshly ground black pepper
½ cup/2 ounces (50g) black olives
sprigs of mint, to garnish

1 Arrange the slices of orange on a large plate with the slices of red onion.

2 Combine the olive oil, sherry vinegar, honey, and chopped mint in a pitcher and season with salt and pepper to taste. Pour the dressing over the oranges and chill for at least 1 hour.

3 Sprinkle with the black olives and garnish with sprigs of mint.

nutritional breakdown per serving: calories 204, protein 3g, fat 13g (saturated fat 2g), carbohydrate 21g

COOK'S TIP

To get really attractive slices of orange, cut off the peel with a serrated knife before slicing, making sure all the white pith is cut away.

savory choux puffs with avocado and pesto

Tiny puffs of choux pastry make easy cocktail snacks. The pastry and filling can be prepared well ahead of time, leaving a quick assembly an hour or so before serving. Slightly larger buns can be filled in the same way and, served with salad, make a great light lunch or supper snack. For more on choux pastry see page 258.

makes 14–16
preparation: 15 minutes
cooking: 25–30 minutes
suitable for freezing (see note)

For the choux pastry:
½ cup (125 milliliters) water
¼ cup (½ stick)/2 ounces (50g) butter
⅔ cup/3 ounces (75g) all-purpose flour, sifted
2 eggs
½ cup/2 ounces (50g) grated Cheddar
¼ teaspoon prepared mustard

For the filling:
1 ripe avocado
2–3 teaspoons pesto (see page 211)
1 teaspoon lemon juice
salt and freshly ground black pepper

1 To make the choux pastry, put the water and the butter in a saucepan and bring to a boil.

2 When boiling and the butter has melted, remove the pan from the heat, and add all the flour at once. Beat vigorously with a wooden spoon until very glossy.

3 Beat in the eggs, one at a time. Then add the grated cheese and mustard and beat again.

4 Put dessertspoonfuls of the mixture onto a lightly greased baking sheet and bake in a preheated oven, 400°F (200°C), for 20–25 minutes. The "buns" should be well risen, brown, and firm. It is best to over-bake them slightly so that they won't collapse. Let cool on a wire rack.

5 To make the filling, halve the avocado, remove the pit, and scoop out the flesh. Mash with the pesto and lemon juice and season to taste.

6 To serve the choux puffs, make a slit in the side of each puff and fill with the avocado mixture. Serve within 2 hours or the pastry may become too soft.

VARIATIONS

There are plenty of other options for filling bite-size choux puffs. Try mashed mild goat cheese with lemon and chives; crumbled blue cheese with cream and chopped watercress or arugula; mascarpone cheese with finely chopped walnuts; or Green Olive Tapenade (see page 166).

nutritional breakdown per serving (14 choux puffs): calories 99, protein 3g, fat 8g (saturated fat 4g), carbohydrate 4g

FREEZING CHOUX PASTRY
Choux pastry can be frozen uncooked. Spoon the mixture onto nonstick baking sheets as in step 4, freeze uncovered, then pack the balls into bags or containers. Raw choux shapes should be cooked from frozen. Add an extra 5 minutes or so to the cooking time.

Cooked choux buns can also be frozen. Cool completely after cooking, then pack in containers, putting wax or freezer paper between layers if necessary. Frozen ready-baked choux buns will need 10 minutes in a hot oven to crisp.

oyster mushroom and roast almond pâté

This is a delicious, rich pâté with a delicate blend of flavors. It is easy to spread and goes well with crisp crackers or bread. Alternatively, serve it with raw vegetables.

serves 4
preparation: 10 minutes, plus cooling
cooking: 10 minutes
suitable for freezing

¾ cup/3 ounces (75g) sliced almonds
¼ cup (½ stick)/2 ounces (50g) butter
1 onion, finely chopped
2 garlic cloves, crushed
8 ounces (240g) oyster mushrooms
salt and freshly ground black pepper

1 Spread the almonds on a baking sheet and roast in a preheated oven, 400°F (200°C), for 4–5 minutes, or until light brown. Set aside a few slices for garnish.

2 Melt 2 tablespoons/ 1 ounce (25g) butter in a saucepan and gently cook the onion and garlic until soft. Add the mushrooms and turn up the heat; cook until soft and slightly browned. Let cool.

3 Place the almonds and cooked mushroom mixture in a blender or food processor and blend until smooth, adding the remaining butter. Season well with salt and pepper.

4 Spoon the mixture into an attractive bowl or individual ramekins and garnish with the reserved almond slices.

nutritional breakdown per serving: calories 223, protein 6g, fat 21g (saturated fat 8g), carbohydrate 3g

hummus left, **green
olive tapenade** center,
**roasted eggplant and
garlic dip** right

green olive tapenade

*This lusty dip has a good strong color and flavor to match.
Serve it with crudités or with roasted bell peppers and
eggplant. Spread it thinly as a sandwich filling then top
with a mass of salad and sliced egg or mozzarella for a
substantial snack. Tapenade will keep in the refrigerator
for at least a week.*

serves 4
preparation: 10 minutes
cooking: none
v

1 cup/4 ounces (125g) pitted green olives
2 garlic cloves, coarsely chopped
2 teaspoons capers
½ cup/1 ounce (25g) chopped parsley
½ teaspoon dried thyme
⅓ cup (80 milliliters) olive oil
salt and freshly ground black pepper

1 Put the olives, garlic, capers, parsley, and thyme
 into a blender or food processor. Blend for a few
 seconds, then, with the motor running, add the
 olive oil gradually in a thin steady stream to make a
 thick creamy paste.

2 Season with salt and pepper and add extra garlic,
 capers, or herbs according to taste.

nutritional breakdown per serving: calories 184, protein 1g,
fat 20g (saturated fat 3g), carbohydrate 0g

roasted eggplant and garlic dip

Roasted eggplant with its smoky flavor and creamy consistency makes a wonderful base for a dip or spread. Serve it with raw or broiled vegetables, in pita bread, or simply add to a buffet spread. This recipe goes well with other Middle Eastern-inspired ideas such as Falafel (see page 174), Classic Tabbouleh (see page 299), Stuffed Grape Leaves with Spiced Bulgur (see page 359), and Frittatas (see page 179).

serves 4

preparation: 10 minutes

cooking: 40 minutes

𝒱

2 eggplant
2 garlic cloves, crushed
juice of 1 lemon
½ teaspoon ground cumin
3 tablespoons olive oil
1 small chile, deseeded and chopped
salt and freshly ground black pepper

1 Prick the eggplant in several places and place in a roasting pan. Roast them in a preheated oven, 400°F (200°C), for 40 minutes, or until they have collapsed and are completely soft.

2 Cool slightly, then cut in half and scoop out the flesh.

3 Using a blender or food processor, purée the eggplant flesh with the remaining ingredients.

4 Season to taste and pile into a small bowl. Serve at room temperature.

nutritional breakdown per serving: calories 107, protein 2g, fat 9g (saturated fat 1g), carbohydrate 5g

hummus

This classic dip is not only delicious but also very easy to make. Highlight your favorite flavors by adding more of any of the ingredients. Hummus is great served with crudités or crackers as an appetizer. Use it as part of a buffet spread, especially with dishes such as Classic Tabbouleh (see page 299), Roasted Bell Peppers with Basil Vinaigrette (see page 313), or Greek Potato Salad (see page 301). It is also useful for filling sandwiches or piling into warm pita bread for a nutritious snack. It can be frozen for up to 1 month. For information on cooking legumes see page 90.

serves 4

preparation time: 10 minutes

cooking time: none

suitable for freezing

𝒱

scant 1 cup/7 ounces (200g) garbanzo beans
   (cooked weight)
¼ cup/2 ounces (50g) tahini
¼ cup lemon juice
2 garlic cloves, crushed

3 tablespoons olive oil, plus extra to serve
1 teaspoon cumin seeds, dry-roasted, optional
2 tablespoons chopped parsley or cilantro
   leaves, optional
salt and freshly ground black pepper

1 Using a blender or food processor, purée the cooked garbanzos with enough cooking liquid (or light stock or water) to make a smooth paste.

2 Add the tahini, lemon juice, garlic, and olive oil and process again until smooth. Season to taste.

3 Add the dry-roasted cumin seeds and/or chopped parsley or cilantro, if using.

4 To serve, spoon the hummus into a serving dish. Make a slight well in the center and fill with olive oil.

nutritional breakdown per serving: calories 210, protein 6g, fat 17g (saturated fat 2g), carbohydrate 9g

spiced vegetable fritters

These tasty vegetable fritters make a quick snack served with bread, salad, and a quick yogurt dip or Cucumber Relish with Chile and Lemon (see page 295). As the batter is quite thick, it is best to chop the vegetables finely or even grate them so that they mix well with the batter. Don't worry if the fritters are shaped unevenly; that is part of their charm.

serves 4
preparation: 10 minutes
cooking: 5–10 minutes
$\mathcal{V}$

For the batter:
1 cup/4 ounces (125g) garbanzo bean flour
1 tablespoon vegetable oil
1 teaspoon ground coriander
½ teaspoon ground turmeric
¼ teaspoon chile powder
1 teaspoon salt
⅔ cup/¼ pint (150 milliliters) warm water

8 ounces (250g) mixed fresh vegetables
   (such as chopped onion, grated carrot,
   cauliflower flowerets, finely chopped
   red bell pepper)
vegetable oil for frying

1 Combine the flour in a large bowl with the oil, coriander, turmeric, chile powder, and salt. Pour in the warm water and mix to a smooth batter, using a whisk or a wooden spoon.

2 Prepare the vegetables, grating or chopping them quite finely, and stir them into the batter.

3 Heat approximately 1 inch (2.5cm) vegetable oil in a deep saucepan. Drop tablespoons of the batter into the oil, cooking about 4 at a time for 2–3 minutes until the fritters are golden brown.

4 Drain on paper towels. The fritters are best served when freshly made but they can stand for an hour or so.

nutritional breakdown per serving: calories 258, protein 9g, fat 16g (saturated fat 2g), carbohydrate 21g

roasted peanut and cilantro sambal

This spicy accompaniment is extremely easy to make. Serve it with the Spiced Vegetable Fritters (see above) or use it with spiced rice and curry dishes.

serves 4
preparation time: 10 minutes
cooking time: 5 minutes
suitable for freezing
$\mathcal{V}$

½ cup/2 ounces (50g) peanuts
2 cups/2 ounces (50g) cilantro leaves,
   coarsely chopped
1 small fresh green chile, split and deseeded
4–6 tablespoons water
2–3 tablespoons lemon juice
salt

1 Spread the peanuts on a baking sheet and roast in a preheated oven, 400°F (200°C), for 5 minutes. Let cool.

2 Put the peanuts, cilantro, chile, water, and lemon juice in a blender or food processor. Blend until fairly smooth, then adjust the seasoning to taste. Add more water or lemon juice if necessary.

nutritional breakdown per serving: calories 75, protein 4g, fat 6g (saturated fat 1g), carbohydrate 2g

spiced vegetable
fritters with roasted
peanut and cilantro
sambal

Light Meals

Eating habits have changed enormously in the last few years. Light meals and snacks, particularly in the middle of the day, are a popular alternative to more hearty fare. Generally, these lighter meals are easy and quick to make, use many fresh ingredients, and can be prepared for several people without much trouble. If you are very hungry, try combining several light meals together to make a feast.

On the following pages you'll find several simple vegetable savories such as **Stuffed Italian Tomatoes with Red Pesto and Mozzarella**, or **Leek and Potato Cakes with Gruyère**. There is also a range of egg dishes including the **Herb Soufflé** featured here, as well as classic omelets, frittatas, baked eggs, and roulades. Mexican food is represented by a range of salsas as well as classics such as **Enchiladas**, **Refried Black Beans**, and **Quesadillas**. Pancakes and pizzas are good for light meals and extremely easy to make. You'll find a choice of tempting fillings and toppings to try, such as tangy **Mushroom and Goat Cheese Crêpes**, **Classic Tomato Pizza Topping**, as well as a golden **Saffron Onion Pizza**. Finally, in this section there are some suggestions for simple and tasty meals for children.

herb soufflé

This is a light, simple soufflé, brilliantly colored. It is good to make when herbs are plentiful—try using different combinations. For a slightly more substantial dish, add ½ cup/2 ounces (50g) grated cheese in step 3. This soufflé is ideal as an appetizer for 4 people, followed by a grain or pasta dish; alternatively, serve it with a salad for a light meal for 2 people.

serves 4
preparation: 10 minutes
cooking: 30–35 minutes

2 tablespoons/1 ounce (25g) butter
¼ cup/1 ounce (25g) all-purpose flour
1 cup (250 milliliters) milk
salt and freshly ground black pepper
4 eggs, separated
2 cups/2 ounces (50g) chopped herbs from a
  selection of parsley, basil, chives, rosemary,
  and dill

nutritional breakdown per serving: calories 174, protein 9g,
fat 12g (saturated fat 6g), carbohydrate 8g

1 Grease a 13-quart (900-milliliter) soufflé dish and tie a collar of wax paper around the edge of the dish.

2 Make a white sauce by melting the butter in a small pan. Stir in the flour to make a roux and cook for 1 minute. Add the milk and, stirring constantly, bring the sauce to a boil. then simmer for 2–3 minutes—it should be very thick. Season with salt and pepper.

3 Stir the egg yolks and chopped herbs into the cooked white sauce.

4 Whisk the egg whites in a large bowl until stiff. Stir 1 tablespoon egg white into the white sauce. Then fold in the remaining egg white using a metal spoon.

5 Spoon the mixture into the prepared dish and bake in a preheated oven, 400°F (200°C), for 25 minutes. If you are using a deep dish, the soufflé may take 5 minutes longer. The top should be golden brown and the soufflé well risen and firm on top. Serve immediately.

stuffed italian tomatoes with red pesto and mozzarella

Tomatoes and cheese are enriched here with a heady red pesto sauce. The pesto can be made in advance since it keeps in the refrigerator for at least 2 weeks. Serve this savory with a good bread, such as focaccia, and a crisp salad. For a more substantial meal, follow with a simple pasta such as Tagliatelle with Fennel and Fresh Herbs (see page 207).

serves 4

preparation: 15 minutes

cooking: 15–20 minutes

For the pesto:
2 tablespoons olive oil
1 small red onion, finely chopped
2 garlic cloves, crushed
8 sun-dried tomatoes (in oil)
2 tablespoons freshly grated Parmesan
4 tablespoons chopped basil
¼ cup/1 ounce (25g) pine nuts
salt and freshly ground black pepper

4 large Italian tomatoes, halved
salt and freshly ground black pepper
4 ounces (125g) mozzarella, sliced

1 To make the pesto, combine the olive oil, onion, garlic, tomatoes, Parmesan, basil, and pine nuts in a food processor. Process until finely chopped. Season to taste with salt and pepper.

2 Lightly season the tomato halves with salt and pepper. Divide the pesto between the 8 halves and set them on a lightly oiled baking sheet or in an ovenproof dish. Place 1 or 2 slices of mozzarella on each half.

3 Bake in a preheated oven, 375°F (190°C), for 15–20 minutes, or until the cheese is melted and the tomatoes look well cooked.

nutritional breakdown per serving: calories 487, protein 14g, fat 44g (saturated fat 10g), carbohydrate 9g

giant mushrooms stuffed with wild rice and roasted onions

Three members of the onion family roasted make a colorful and flavorsome addition to wild rice. This mixture is terrific served piled on top of succulent, roasted mushrooms. Serve these as a meal in their own right, accompanied by a salad, or a side vegetable such as Butternut Squash and Carrot Purée with Nutmeg and Mascarpone (see page 286). The rice and onion mixture can be served on its own, but you should increase the quantity of rice.

nutritional breakdown per serving: calories 396, protein 7g, fat 15g (saturated fat 2g), carbohydrate 57g

VARIATIONS

For an extra gourmet snack you can top the vegetable mixture with a slice of cheese and melt quickly under a hot broiler. For a dairy-free treat serve this with Baked Bean Curd and Cremini Mushrooms (see page 175).

serves 4
preparation: 10 minutes
cooking: 50–55 minutes
suitable for freezing (rice only)
v

1 cup/4 ounces (125g) wild rice
6 tablespoons olive oil
2 onions, chopped
2 leeks, sliced
3½ ounces (100g) shallots, quartered
4 very large or 8 medium portobello mushrooms
salt and freshly ground black pepper

1   Put the rice in a large saucepan and bring it to a boil in double its volume of water. Cover the pan and simmer for 35–40 minutes, or until soft.

2   While the rice is cooking, put 4 tablespoons of the olive oil in a large bowl and season well with salt and pepper. Toss in the onions, leeks, and shallots, then spread out the oiled vegetables on baking sheets in one layer. Bake in a preheated oven, 400°F (200°C), for 20 minutes, or until well browned.

3   Meanwhile, remove the stalks from the mushrooms and discard. Using the remaining oil and any residue in the bowl, coat the mushrooms with oil and drizzle more oil on top. Season well.

4   Put the mushrooms in a shallow ovenproof dish and place in the oven with the roasting vegetables. Bake for 15 minutes, or until soft.

5   Drain the rice, if necessary, and toss in the roasted leeks, onions, and shallots and adjust the seasoning. Pile generously onto the cooked mushroom bases and serve immediately.

falafel

This tasty snack is simple to prepare and may be served as part of a buffet meal or in pita bread with salad greens, chopped tomatoes, and a little mild onion. Falafel are traditionally deep-fried or baked but, with care, shallow-frying can produce good results. Baked falafel use less oil and are consequently drier in texture. Counteract this by serving them with a seasoned yogurt dip made with chopped chile, roasted cumin, and lemon juice to taste. Bite-size falafel can be served as appetizers.

makes 20

preparation: 15 minutes, plus overnight soaking and chilling

cooking: 25–30 minutes

suitable for freezing

𝓋

1 cup/8 ounces (250g) garbanzo beans, soaked overnight
1 onion, coarsely chopped
2 garlic cloves, coarsely chopped
2 teaspoons cumin seeds
2 teaspoons ground coriander
2 tablespoons chopped parsley
2 tablespoons chopped cilantro leaves
oil for deep-frying
salt and freshly ground black pepper

1 Drain the garbanzo beans and rinse. Place them in a blender or food processor and grind them into a coarse powder. Scrape the powder into a large bowl.

2 Using the blender or food processor again, process the onion, garlic, cumin, coriander, parsley, and cilantro until finely chopped. Stir into the garbanzo powder and mix well with a spoon. Season well with salt and pepper. Cover and chill for up to 2 hours.

3 To make the falafel, dampen your hands and shape small amounts of the mixture between your hands to make walnut-size balls. Flatten carefully into round patties. (The falafel can be frozen at this point, if you like.)

4 To fry the falafel, heat the oil in a small, deep-sided skillet. When hot, slide in the falafel, about 4 at a time. Cook for 2–3 minutes, then turn over and cook for 2–3 minutes more—the outside should be very crisp. Drain on paper towels.

VARIATION

To bake the falafel, place the cakes on a well-oiled baking sheet and brush or drizzle with oil. Bake in a preheated oven, 400°F (200°C), for 15 minutes, then turn over and bake for 10–15 minutes more, or until they are well browned.

nutritional breakdown per falafel: calories 57, protein 3g, fat 2g (saturated fat 0g), carbohydrate 7g

baked bean curd and cremini mushrooms

This is a tasty snack that can be served on its own, with stir-fry vegetables for a light meal, or with rice, noodles, or buckwheat to make something more substantial. Augment the bean curd with roasted shallots if you like. Alternatively, you could spear pieces of bean curd and mushrooms on cocktail sticks and serve them as miniature cocktail kabobs.

serves 4

preparation: 5 minutes, plus marinating

cooking: 10 minutes

 $\mathcal{V}$

For the marinade:

2 tablespoons lemon juice

1 tablespoon shoyu or soy sauce

1 tablespoon tomato paste

1 garlic clove, crushed

2 teaspoons chopped oregano

2 tablespoons olive oil

7 ounces (200g) bean curd

2¾ cups/7 ounces (200g) cremini mushrooms

1 Prepare the marinade by combining the lemon juice, shoyu, tomato paste, garlic, oregano, and oil in a large shallow dish.

2 Chop the bean curd into bite-size pieces. Stir into the marinade with the mushrooms and let stand for at least 1 hour.

3 Spread out the pieces of bean curd and the mushrooms on a baking sheet and scrape over any residue of marinade. Bake in a preheated oven, 400°F (200°C), for 10 minutes.

4 Serve hot with bread or with cooked rice, noodles, or buckwheat.

nutritional breakdown per serving: calories 100, protein 6g, fat 8g (saturated fat 1g), carbohydrate 2g

caponata of roasted vegetables

Caponata is a classic dish from the Mediterranean comprising sweet bell peppers and eggplant, sharpened with capers, and a dash of wine vinegar. In this version, the vegetables are roasted rather than stewed. The end result has a mellow flavor. This makes an easy lunch or snack served with good bread and crisp salad greens. Serve cubes of feta or haloumi cheese or pine nuts separately to boost the protein content.

serves 4

preparation: 15 minutes, plus salting

cooking: 25–30 minutes

suitable for freezing

𝒱

2 eggplant, cubed
2 red bell peppers, cored, deseeded, and
   thickly sliced
1 onion, thickly sliced
4 tomatoes, halved
½ cup (125 milliliters) olive oil
4 garlic cloves, left unpeeled
2 tablespoons red wine vinegar
2–3 teaspoons capers
salt and freshly ground black pepper

1 Put the cubes of eggplant in a colander and sprinkle with salt. Set aside for 30 minutes, then pat dry with paper towels.

2 Put the peppers, onion, and tomatoes in a large bowl with the salted eggplant cubes. Toss in 6 tablespoons of the olive oil and season well, then spread out in a large roasting pan.

3 Roast in a preheated oven, 400°F (200°C), for 25–30 minutes, or until all the vegetables are well browned. Add the whole garlic cloves for the last 5 minutes of cooking time. Remove the vegetables from the oven and put everything except the garlic cloves and tomato halves in a large bowl.

4 Remove and discard the skins from the roasted tomatoes. Chop the flesh finely, then mix with any oil residue or juices from the roasting pan. Add the remaining olive oil, red wine vinegar, and capers and mix well to make a dressing.

5 Crush the roasted garlic, remove the skin, and mix into the dressing. Season with salt and pepper to taste, then mix the dressing with the roasted vegetables, and serve warm or at room temperature.

nutritional breakdown per serving: calories 268, protein 3g, fat 23g (saturated fat 3g), carbohydrate 14g

leek and potato cakes with gruyère

From surprisingly humble ingredients comes this light and delicious savory. These potato cakes are inspired by the potato gnocchi that feature in northern Italian cuisine. Baked in ramekins, they are a little more sturdy but perhaps more foolproof. Serve with Buttered Shallot and Wine Sauce (see page 290) or Very Easy Tomato Sauce (see page 292).

serves 4

preparation: 20 minutes
cooking: 40–45 minutes
suitable for freezing

1 pound (500g) mealy potatoes
2 tablespoons/1 ounce (25g) butter
2 leeks, finely chopped
2 garlic cloves, crushed
2 eggs, beaten
¾ cup/3 ounces (75g) grated Gruyère
½ cup (125 milliliters) crème fraîche
3 tablespoons chopped parsley
salt and freshly ground black pepper

nutritional breakdown per serving: calories 385, protein 12g, fat 27g (saturated fat 17g), carbohydrate 24g

1 Boil the potatoes in their skins in a large saucepan of boiling water for 15–20 minutes, or until soft. Drain well. Leave until cool enough to handle, then remove the skins and mash the potatoes.

2 Melt the butter in a small skillet and gently cook the leeks and garlic until soft. Stir into the mashed potatoes. Remove from the heat and add the eggs, grated cheese, crème fraîche, and parsley. Mix very well and season with salt and pepper to taste.

3 Grease 8 ⅔-cup/¼-pint (150-milliliter) ramekins. Line the bottoms with waxed paper. Spoon the mixture into these and bake in a preheated oven, 400°F (200°C), for 20 minutes, or until well browned. Turn out and serve hot with a sauce.

VARIATIONS

Potato cakes are popular with children and can be a good way of introducing some different vegetable flavors. Corn, carrot, and finely chopped celery can be added to the mixture. You can also use Cheddar instead of Gruyère. Serve the cakes with a smooth tomato sauce or ketchup.

RAMEKINS

Use cups, deep muffin pans, or individual rings set on a baking sheet if you don't have any ramekin dishes.

eggs

These are genuine fast foods because they can be prepared in numerous simple ways to make a meal in minutes. Included here are all the classic ways to serve eggs such as frittata, roulade, oven-baked egg dishes, and more. First, however, there is a quick look at the many ways eggs can be prepared and served by themselves. Needless to say with many of these recipes, variations are possible by adding simple vegetables and herbs. See page 82 for safety and storing.

fried egg

Heat a little butter or oil in a skillet until hot but not smoking. Crack in the egg and cook for 4 minutes. Baste only the white with oil if you want to keep the yolk runny. Alternatively, baste both. Fried eggs can be turned over so as to cook both sides evenly but take care not to break the yolk.

boiling eggs

Soft-cooked Egg—Start with the egg at room temperature. Put the egg in cold water and bring to a boil. Once boiling, cook for 3–4 minutes, then serve. (Timing will vary according to the size of the egg— allow longer for an extra large egg.)

If you are worried about salmonella when boiling eggs for children, it is a good idea to use an egg coddler. This is a traditional heavy china container with a screw-on metal lid that can withstand boiling water. The advantage is that you can look at the egg prior to cooking and check whether it is done by unscrewing the lid after a few minutes to see if the white has set. A slight disadvantage is that the egg takes a little longer to cook using this method.

Hard-cooked Egg—Start with the egg at room temperature. Put the egg in cold water and bring to a boil. Once boiling, simmer for 8–10 minutes, then plunge immediately into a bowl of cold water to prevent a black rim forming between the yolk and the white. Shell the egg once cold.

scrambled egg

Scrambled eggs should be creamy and fluffy not rubbery or stringy. For perfect results, don't try to scramble the eggs too quickly over too high a heat. Stir all the time.

nutritional breakdown per serving: calories 180, protein 13g, fat 14g (saturated fat 5g), carbohydrate 1g

serves 2

4 eggs
2 tablespoons water or milk
pat of butter
salt and freshly ground black pepper

1 Break the eggs into a bowl, then add the water or milk, and whisk with a fork. Season well with salt and pepper.

2 Melt the butter in a small pan. When sizzling, pour in the egg mixture. Stir constantly over low heat for about 4–5 minutes. Once the mixture no longer has a runny quality, remove the pan from the heat because the eggs will continue cooking. Keep stirring, then serve immediately.

VARIATIONS

Mexican Scrambled Eggs—Make the eggs as in the main recipe but beat in 2–3 tablespoons of Cooked Salsa with Chile (see page 190) as the eggs scramble.

Lots of other ingredients can be stirred into scrambled eggs. Make sure you have them ready first, though. Try adding chopped herbs, such as parsley, chives, or tarragon; 2–3 tablespoons grated cheese; cooked chopped onion or scallion, cooked sliced baby mushrooms, or chopped roasted bell pepper.

The following make good accompaniments to serve with scrambled egg: baked tomatoes, spinach purée, and roasted vegetables, such as roasted bell peppers, onions, or shallots.

poached egg

Aficionados break an egg straight into boiling water rather than cheating by cooking the eggs in a little specially designed metal dish. The texture of the white is softer if cooked straight in the water; however, it can take a little practice to get right. A tip is to create a little whirlpool in the water to try to preserve an oval shape.

1 Use a wide pan, add water to a depth of about 2–3 inches (5–7 cm) plus 1 tablespoon white wine vinegar.

2 Bring to a boil. Stir in the water and crack in an egg and immediately turn the heat to low otherwise violent boiling will disperse the egg white.

3 Cook for 3 minutes until the white is opaque.

> **nutritional breakdown per egg:** calories 75, protein 6g, fat 5g (saturated fat 2g), carbohydrate 0g

omelet

An omelet is a fried mixture of beaten egg. It is important to have the right size pan so that the mixture is not too thick or too thin. A 6-inch (15-cm) skillet works well for a 2–3 egg omelet. Do not overbeat the eggs; otherwise, the texture becomes rubbery. Simply break the eggs into a small bowl and stir with a fork until the egg yolk and white are lightly combined.

serves 1

2 eggs
pat of butter
salt and freshly ground black pepper

1 Break the eggs into a bowl, mix lightly with a fork, and season with salt and pepper.

2 Melt the butter in a small skillet. When it has stopped foaming, pour in the eggs, and tip the pan so that the mixture spreads evenly around the base of the pan. Stir with a fork until the egg starts to set. As the egg sets at the edges, use a spatula to lift up the sides so that uncooked egg in the middle of the pan runs underneath.

3 When the omelet is set, add a filling if using (see below), then fold the omelet in half in the pan, and slide it out onto a plate.

> **nutritional breakdown per serving:** calories 220, protein 13g, fat 19g (saturated fat 9g), carbohydrate 0g

VARIATIONS

Suitable additions to omelets include grated cheese, cooked mushrooms, roasted vegetables, such as bell peppers or onion, and griddled asparagus or baby leeks.

folded soufflé omelet

For this type of omelet, the eggs are separated and the whites whisked until stiff, then folded into the beaten yolks. The omelet is prepared as usual but turns out much lighter.

japanese omelet

These are very thin omelets made with an egg and water batter for lightness. They are briefly fried, then rolled up, and cooked until set.

Other types of omelet

Frittata—a thick Italian omelet, partially cooked in the pan and then finished off under the broiler. Can also be cooked in the oven.

Tortilla—the Spanish name for the thick omelet, usually cooked with lots of onions, potatoes, and bell peppers, all of which are pre-fried in olive oil. The cooked mixture is flipped in the pan so that it browns and sets on both sides.

Eggah or Kuku—a traditional Persian dish where the eggs are baked omelet-style in the oven. It is served cut into wedges, hot or cold.

leek and fennel frittata

Moist and delicately flavored, this is a straightforward savory that can be served hot or cold. Add bread or new potatoes to make a main course of it, or serve as it is for a light lunch or supper.

serves 4

| preparation: 10 minutes |
| cooking: 40–45 minutes |

2 tablespoons olive oil
1 onion, finely chopped
2 large leeks, finely chopped
1 garlic clove, crushed
8 ounces (240g) fennel, finely chopped
2 tablespoons chopped dill
6 eggs
6 ounces (180g) soft goat cheese
1–2 tablespoons freshly grated Parmesan
salt and freshly ground black pepper

1 Heat the oil in a saucepan and cook the onion, leeks, and garlic until soft. Add the fennel and cook for 6–8 minutes, or until lightly cooked and colored. Add the dill and stir well, then remove the pan from the heat.

2 Mix the eggs with the goat cheese in a large bowl and season well. Stir in the cooked vegetables, season if necessary, then pour the mixture into a lightly buttered ovenproof dish.

3 Dust with Parmesan, then bake in a preheated oven, 375°F (190°C), for 30 minutes, or until well browned and firm in the center.

nutritional breakdown per serving: calories 278, protein 17g, fat 21g (saturated fat 8g), carbohydrate 6g

kuku with spinach

This is one of the names given to the substantial, thick baked omelet found in many variations all over the Middle East. It is designed to be served cold so that the flavors can fully develop and is therefore ideal for warm weather suppers. This version is densely packed with spinach and an undertone of herbs and spices that prevents the kuku from tasting bland.

serves 4

preparation: 5 minutes

cooking: 30–35 minutes

(Ca) (Fe)

1 pound (500g) spinach
5 eggs
1 tablespoon chopped mint
¼ teaspoon ground cumin
4 ounces (125g) feta (drained weight), crumbled
salt and freshly ground black pepper

1 Gently cook the washed spinach in a saucepan without adding any extra water for 4–5 minutes, or until soft.

2 Put the spinach in a colander to drain off all the excess water, then press the spinach down with the back of a wooden spoon to squeeze out as much water as possible. Chop the spinach coarsely.

3 Break the eggs into a bowl and stir lightly with a fork to combine the yolks and whites. (Stirring the eggs rather than beating them makes sure that the finished texture is not rubbery.) Add the chopped spinach and mix with the mint and cumin. Stir in the crumbled feta and season well with salt and pepper.

4 Pour the mixture into a lightly oiled ovenproof dish and bake in a preheated oven 350°F (180°C), for 25–30 minutes, or until just set. Leave until cold then cut into squares or wedges to serve.

nutritional breakdown per serving: calories 202, protein 17g, fat 13g (saturated fat 2g), carbohydrate 5g

COOKING WITH FETA

Feta provides a salty tang but it is not a cheese that melts. To create a marbled effect in the finished dish, make sure the cheese is chopped quite small or crumbled.

baked eggs with mozzarella and fresh tomatoes

This is a simple, high-protein supper or lunch dish, which can easily be made in smaller quantities if you are cooking for fewer people. There are obviously lots of variations on this idea—add mushrooms, chopped bell peppers, chile, or corn to the basic sauce. This would also make a good appetizer for a meal such as fresh pasta with a simple sauce (see pages 208–11).

serves 4

preparation: 10 minutes

cooking: 20 minutes

2 tablespoons olive oil
1 onion, finely chopped
4 tomatoes, skinned and chopped
2 tablespoons chopped parsley
salt and freshly ground black pepper
4 eggs
4 ounces (125g) mozzarella, cubed

1 Heat the oil in a saucepan and gently cook the onion until soft. Add the tomatoes and cook for 5 minutes, then add the parsley, reserving a little for garnish, and season well with salt and pepper.

2 Spoon the mixture into 4 lightly oiled ovenproof dishes. Make a hollow in the center of each and break an egg into each dish. Divide the cubes of mozzarella among the dishes.

3 Bake in a preheated oven, 350°F (180°C), for 12 minutes, or until the eggs have set. Serve immediately, garnished with the reserved parsley.

nutritional breakdown per serving: calories 242, protein 15g, fat 18g (saturated fat 7g), carbohydrate 6g

broccoli and stilton roulade

An impressive light lunch, supper dish, or appetizer for a special meal, a roulade is not that tricky to make. It is essentially a soufflé mixture, which is baked in a flat tray, then rolled up around a sauce or filling. You can prepare up to and including step 4 well ahead of time when entertaining guests. Cold roulades are great for buffets and picnics (see page 354).

serves 4

preparation: 10 minutes

cooking: 20–25 minutes

For the sauce:
2 tablespoons/1 ounce (25g) butter
3 tablespoons all-purpose flour
⅔ cup/¼ pint (150 milliliters) milk
2 tablespoons light cream
2 ounces (50g) Stilton, crumbled
salt and freshly ground black pepper

For the roulade:
8 ounces (250g) broccoli
1 tablespoon/½ ounce (15g) butter
4 eggs, separated
salt and freshly ground black pepper

1 To make the sauce, melt the butter in a small saucepan then stir in the flour to make a roux. Add the milk, stirring constantly until it thickens, then bring to a boil, and simmer for 3–4 minutes.

2 Stir the cream and Stilton into the sauce. Season well with salt and pepper and keep warm.

3 Divide the broccoli into small flowerets and chop the stalk finely. Steam over a pan of boiling water until soft. Let cool, then chop finely, and toss in the butter. Meanwhile, line a shallow 8 x 12 inch (20 x 30cm) pan with baking parchment.

4 Beat the egg yolks and mix with the cooled broccoli. Season well with salt and pepper.

5 Whisk the egg whites in a separate large bowl until stiff. Fold into the broccoli mixture.

6 Spoon the mixture into the pan, then bake in a preheated oven, 400°F (400°C), for 10–15 minutes, or until just browned and firm.

7 When the roulade is cooked, remove from the oven and turn out on to a piece of wax paper.

8 Quickly spread the warm sauce over the roulade, then roll it up by folding in one end of the oblong, then, using the underneath sheet of wax paper to help you, ease it into a roll. Transfer to a serving dish and serve immediately.

nutritional breakdown per serving: calories 320, protein 14g, fat 26g (saturated fat 15g), carbohydrate 7g

strata

This colorful dish comprises layers of buttered bread, chopped bell peppers, and tomatoes all doused with a seasoned egg and milk mixture. The strata can be baked right away or chilled for several hours, thus making it a good dish for a special breakfast since it can be assembled the day before, then baked in the morning. Richer versions can be made using extra cheese and vegetables.

serves 4

preparation: 10 minutes, plus chilling

cooking: 35–45 minutes

(Ca) (Fe)

8 ounces (250g) whole-wheat bread, sliced
2 tablespoons/1 ounce (25g) butter
1 red bell pepper, cored, deseeded, and sliced
1 yellow bell pepper, cored, deseeded, and sliced
8 sun-dried tomatoes, finely chopped
3 tablespoons chopped parsley
2 tablespoons chopped basil
4 eggs
generous 2 cups (500 milliliters) milk
¼ cup freshly grated romano
salt and freshly ground black pepper

1 Spread the slices of bread with the butter and cut the slices in half. Layer the slices of bread and butter with the sliced bell peppers, chopped tomatoes, parsley, and basil in a buttered deep ovenproof dish, seasoning each layer as you go with salt and pepper and trimming the bread if necessary.

2 Beat the eggs in a pitcher with the milk and pour the mixture over the layers of bread. Cover and chill for 4–5 hours, or overnight if you wish.

3 Sprinkle with grated cheese and bake in a preheated oven, 400°F (200°C), for 35–45 minutes, or until well browned and crisp on top—the middle should be soft but not runny.

nutritional breakdown per serving: calories 628, protein 23g, fat 43g (saturated fat 12g), carbohydrate 40g

asparagus and pea fricassée with eggs

This fresh-looking dish with shades of green is particularly good with new potatoes and dark salad greens such as watercress and feuille de chêne. Small portions would make an elegant hot appetizer, ideally followed by a simple pasta dish such as Tagliatelle with Fennel and Fresh Herbs (see page 207) or a risotto.

serves 4

preparation: 15 minutes

cooking: 25 minutes

(Fe)

For the sauce:

¼ cup (½ stick)/2 ounces (50g) butter

8 ounces (250g) shallots, finely chopped

3 tablespoons all-purpose flour

scant 1 cup (200 milliliters) white wine

1–1¼ cups (200–300 milliliters) Vegetable Stock
  (see page 144)

salt and freshly ground black pepper

8 ounces (250g) asparagus, halved

¼ cup water, optional

2 cups/8 ounces (250g) peas (shelled weight)

1–2 tablespoons lemon juice

6 eggs

1–2 tablespoons finely chopped mint, to garnish

1 To make the sauce, melt the butter in a medium saucepan and gently cook the shallots until soft. Stir in the flour to make a soft roux. Add the white wine and scant 1 cup (200 milliliters) of the stock, stirring constantly, and gradually bring to a boil, stirring frequently as the sauce thickens. Add more stock if the sauce is too thick. Season well with salt and pepper and keep warm.

2 Microwave the asparagus on High for 2 minutes with 2 tablespoons water or steam over a saucepan of boiling water for 5 minutes, or until tender. Drain and stir into the shallot sauce.

3 Similarly, microwave the peas on High for 2 minutes with 2 tablespoons water, or steam for 3 minutes until just tender. Again, drain and stir into the shallot sauce. Adjust the seasoning and add lemon juice to taste.

4 Bring the eggs to a boil in a large saucepan of water and simmer for 8 minutes. Run the hard-cooked eggs under cold water, then shell while still warm. Cut lengthwise into 4 wedges and reserve 4 wedges for garnish.

5 Stir the eggs into the vegetable fricassée and spoon into a warm serving dish. Garnish with the reserved egg wedges and sprinkle with the chopped mint.

nutritional breakdown per serving: calories 377, protein 18g, fat 20g (saturated fat 9g), carbohydrate 25g

crêpes

Crêpes turn up throughout the world in many guises—from the tiny yeasted blinis made with buckwheat flour to the golden Mexican tortilla. In whatever form, crêpes are an attractive way of serving a variety of fillings.

Crêpes are quick and easy to make and, thanks to food processors, there should no longer be a problem with lumpy batter. It is important to have the right pan, however, which you should keep solely for crêpes and omelets so that it develops a good nonstick surface. A good crêpe pan should be about 7 inches (18cm) in diameter and have curved sides so that the crêpes can be easily flipped or turned over and removed from the pan. Traditional Breton galettes or lace crêpes are much larger and for these you need a griddle or completely flat cooking area on which to spread the batter.

Once cooked, crêpes keep very well. Stored on a plate, interleaved with, and then wrapped in wax paper or plastic wrap, they can be kept for 3 days in the refrigerator. For freezing, place a piece of freezer wrap or plastic wrap between each crêpe, then wrap in foil or use a freezer bag. Filled crêpes (assuming the filling is suitable for freezing) should be kept in rigid containers. Let the filling cool before filling the crêpes; otherwise, the crêpes will get soggy.

Unfilled crêpes can be frozen for 6 months; filled crêpes for up to 2 months. To thaw, separate out and leave at room temperature for 30 minutes. To reheat, stack in a lightly greased ovenproof dish and heat through in a preheated oven, 350°F (180°C), for 15–20 minutes, depending on the number of crêpes. Filled crêpes take longer to reheat.

whole-wheat crêpes

makes 8

preparation: 10 minutes, plus standing

cooking: 10 minutes

suitable for freezing

1¼ cups/½ pint (300 milliliters) milk
1 egg
pinch of salt
1 teaspoon vegetable oil, plus extra for frying
¾–1 cup/3½–4 ounces (100–125g) whole-wheat flour

1 To make the batter using a blender or food processor, put the milk, egg, salt, and oil into the container and blend thoroughly. Then add the flour and blend again for about 30 seconds.

2 To make the batter by hand, put the flour and salt in a bowl. Using a balloon whisk, beat the egg in a pitcher with the milk and oil, then pour this into the flour, and whisk in until the batter is smooth.

3 Let the batter stand for 30 minutes, if possible.

4 To cook the crêpes, heat a little oil in a suitable crêpe pan and, when hot, pour in 2 tablespoons of batter. Tilt the pan so that the batter coats the base of the pan evenly.

5 Cook for about 2–3 minutes, then loosen the edge, and either toss or flip the crêpe over with a spatula, then cook the other side for 1 minute.

6 Keep the cooked crêpes warm while you make more in the same way until all the batter is used. If not eating immediately, cool the crêpes on a flat surface, then wrap, and store (see above).

nutritional breakdown per crêpe: calories 69, protein 4g, fat 2g (saturated fat 1g), carbohydrate 10g

buckwheat crêpes

makes 8

preparation: 10 minutes, plus standing

cooking: 10 minutes

suitable for freezing

1¼ cups/½ pint (300 milliliters) milk
2 eggs
pinch of salt
1 teaspoon vegetable oil, plus extra for frying
½ cup/2 ounces (50g) whole-wheat flour
½ cup/2 ounces (50g) buckwheat flour

1 To make the batter using a blender or food processor, put the milk, eggs, salt, and oil into the container and blend thoroughly. Then add both flours and blend again for about 30 seconds.

2 To make the batter by hand, put both types of flour and salt in a bowl. Using a balloon whisk, beat the egg in a pitcher with the milk and oil, then pour this into the flour and whisk in until the batter is smooth. Let the batter stand for 30 minutes.

3 To cook the crêpes, heat a little oil in a suitable crêpe pan and, when hot, pour in 2 tablespoons of batter. Tilt the pan so that the batter coats the base of the pan evenly.

4 Cook for about 2–3 minutes, then loosen the edge, and either toss or flip the crêpe over with a spatula, then cook the other side for 1 minute.

5 Keep the cooked crêpes warm while you make more in the same way until all the batter is used. If not eating immediately, cool the crêpes on a flat surface, then wrap, and store (see page 186).

nutritional breakdown per crêpe: calories 80, protein 4g, fat 3g (saturated fat 1g), carbohydrate 9g

RICH MIXTURE

For an enriched mixture, use an extra egg. If you make the enriched batter by hand, beat the egg well with the flour to a smooth consistency, then add the milk slowly. This should ensure a lump-free batter.

roquefort and celery root crêpes

This heavenly filling with a rich taste and texture can be prepared well in advance, as can the crêpes, leaving you with just a last-minute assembly job. Serve with a crisp side salad of frisée and watercress.

serves 4

preparation: 10 minutes, plus crêpe making

cooking: 15–20 minutes, plus crêpes

Ⓒₐ

1 quantity Whole-wheat or Buckwheat Crêpe batter (see page 186 and above)
8 ounces (250g) celery root (weight after peeling)
scant ½ cup/3½ ounces (100g) mascarpone cheese
3½ ounces (100g) Roquefort
3 tablespoons chopped parsley
salt and freshly ground black pepper
2 tablespoons/1 ounce (25g) butter, melted
½ cup/2 ounces (50g) chopped walnuts, toasted, to garnish

1 Make 8 crêpes according to the instructions on page 186.

2 Cook the celery root in a saucepan of boiling water for 8–10 minutes. Let cool.

3 Using a blender or food processor, purée the celery root with the mascarpone and Roquefort until smooth. Stir in the parsley and season to taste with salt and pepper.

4 Spoon the filling onto the prepared crêpes and fold or roll up and place in a lightly greased ovenproof dish. Brush each crêpe with melted butter.

5 Cover the dish with foil and heat through in a preheated oven, 350°F (180°C), for 8–10 minutes. Serve the crêpes hot, garnished with toasted chopped walnuts.

nutritional breakdown per serving: calories 504, protein 16g, fat 39g (saturated fat 20g), carbohydrate 23g

mushroom and goat cheese crêpes

Goat cheese and mushrooms are a great combination, being both succulent and tangy, and this straightforward tasty filling is very quick to create. The crêpes make an easy supper dish, or serve with extra salads for a special meal.

serves 4

preparation: 5 minutes, plus pancake making

cooking: 15 minutes, plus pancakes

suitable for freezing

1 quantity Whole–wheat or Buckwheat Crêpe
   batter (see pages 186–87)
6 tablespoons (¾ stick)/3 ounces (75g) butter
2 shallots, finely chopped
1 garlic clove, crushed
8 ounces (250g) oyster mushrooms, thinly sliced
8 ounces (250g) white mushrooms, thinly sliced
4 ounces (125g) soft goat cheese, crumbled
3–4 tablespoons water
salt and freshly ground black pepper
3 tablespoons chopped cilantro
sprigs of cilantro, to garnish

1 Make 8 crêpes according to the instructions on page 186.

2 Melt 4 tablespoons (½ stick)/2 ounces (50g) of the butter in a large skillet, add the shallots and garlic, and cook gently until soft. Add the mushrooms and season well. Cook over high heat for about 2 minutes. Reduce the heat, cover the skillet, and cook for 5 minutes, or until the mushrooms are soft.

3 Add the goat cheese and stir in as it melts; add 3–4 tablespoons of water if the mixture is too thick. It should have the consistency of pouring cream. Season with salt and pepper to taste. Stir in the chopped cilantro.

4 Spoon the filling onto the prepared crêpes and fold or roll up, and place in an ovenproof dish. Melt the remaining butter and brush it liberally over each crêpe.

5 Cover the dish with foil and heat through in a preheated oven, 350°F (180°C), for 8–10 minutes. Serve the crêpe hot, garnished with cilantro.

nutritional breakdown per serving: calories 360, protein 14g, fat 25g (saturated fat 15g), carbohydrate 12g

crespelles

These are crêpes stuffed with Swiss chard, cream, and smoked cheese, then baked in the oven smothered with creamy tomato sauce. The end result is a warming main course suitable for a family meal or, dressed up, for a special occasion. The crêpes themselves can be prepared some time ahead or frozen, as can the tomato sauce, but prepare the filling freshly.

serves 4

preparation: 5 minutes, plus crêpe making

cooking: 65 minutes

suitable for freezing

(Ca) (Fe)

1 quantity Whole-wheat or Buckwheat Crêpe batter (see pages 186–87)

For the filling:
1 pound (500g) Swiss chard, shredded
⅓ cup (80 milliliters) heavy cream
1 cup/4 ounces (125g) grated smoked cheese
salt and freshly ground black pepper

For the sauce:
2 tablespoons olive oil
1 onion, finely chopped
1 garlic clove, crushed
1 bay leaf
generous 2 cups (500 milliliters) tomato purée
½ teaspoon sugar
½ teaspoon salt
¼ cup (50 milliliters) heavy cream
½ cup/2 ounces (50g) grated smoked cheese

1 Make 8 crêpes according to the instructions on page 186.

2 To make the filling, place the Swiss chard in a saucepan and cook without adding extra water for about 5 minutes. Remove from the heat, then stir in the cream and grated smoked cheese. Season well with salt and pepper.

3 To make the sauce, heat the oil in a saucepan and cook the onion until soft. Add the garlic and cook for a few minutes, then add the bay leaf, tomato purée, sugar, and salt.

4 Bring to a boil, then simmer, covered, for 30–40 minutes. Remove the bay leaf, adjust the seasoning, and stir in the heavy cream.

5 To assemble the dish, put a spoonful of filling on each crêpe and roll up. Place the filled crêpes in a lightly greased ovenproof dish.

6 Cover with the tomato sauce, then sprinkle with the grated cheese. Bake in a preheated oven, 400°F (200°C), for 15 minutes, or until heated through. Serve hot.

nutritional breakdown per serving: calories 523, protein 21g, fat 36g (saturated fat 18g), carbohydrates 32g

mexican food—tortillas and fillings

Mexican food has a lot to offer vegetarians with its strong flavors and liberal use of spices and herbs. You can create plenty of variety with a few simple recipes, mixing and matching to make platters to suit everyone. If you are entertaining, highlight these tasty dishes by using brightly colored crockery and tableware to re-create the striking colors of Mexican culture.

OTHER MEXICAN RECIPES

Green Rice with Chile (see page 232)
Pinto Bean Salsa (see page 292)

cooked salsa with chile

serves 4

preparation: 10 minutes, plus soaking

cooking: 25 minutes

suitable for freezing

$\mathcal{V}$

3 chiles, soaked in hot water for 15 minutes
1 onion, finely chopped
1 garlic clove, finely chopped
1–2 tablespoons olive oil
6–8 tomatoes, chopped
salt

1 Lift the chiles out of the soaking water. Remove the seeds and the veins from the chiles. Sprinkle the chiles with salt and pound to a paste, using a pestle and mortar.

2 Add a little of the chopped onion and garlic and pound again to get a coarse paste.

3 To make the salsa, heat the oil in a saucepan and cook the remaining onion until soft. Add the remaining garlic and cook a little longer, then add the tomatoes and cook to soften.

4 Add the 1–2 teaspoons pounded chile mixture and the chile soaking water. Cover the pan and simmer for 20 minutes.

5 Cool slightly then, using a blender or food processor, process until smooth. Season with salt.

nutritional breakdown per total recipe: calories 285, protein 5g, fat 18g (saturated fat 3g), carbohydrate 28g

black beans

serves 4

preparation: 5 minutes, plus overnight soaking

cooking: 50–60 minutes

suitable for freezing

$\mathcal{V}$

8 ounces (250g) dry black beans, soaked overnight
1 onion, cut into 4 wedges
1 garlic clove, chopped
salt and freshly ground black pepper

1 Drain the beans, then bring to a boil in a large saucepan of fresh water. Add the onion wedges and garlic and boil fast for 10 minutes, then cover the pan, and simmer for 45–60 minutes, or until the beans are soft. Season with salt and pepper to taste.

2 At this stage the beans are often served drained as an accompaniment to scrambled egg or with Enchiladas (see page 191).

nutritional breakdown per serving: calories 184, protein 13g, fat 0g (saturated fat 0g), carbohydrate 34g

refried black beans

This is an extension of the previous recipe. It is easier to make refried beans while the beans are warm and freshly cooked.

1 Complete step 1 of the previous recipe. Leave the beans in the saucepan in their cooking water.

2 To make refried beans, heat 1 tablespoon olive oil in a large skillet.

3 Remove several tablespoons of beans at a time from the saucepan, using a slotted spoon.

4 Mash into the hot oil, add a little more olive oil if necessary, and, if the mixture gets too dry, add some of the beans' cooking liquid to get a soft paste rather than a floury mixture. Gradually mash in the rest of the beans. Add more liquid if necessary. Season with salt.

nutritional breakdown per serving: calories 217, protein 14g, fat 3g (saturated fat 0g), carbohydrate 36g

enchiladas

serves 4

preparation: 5 minutes

cooking: 5 minutes

2–3 tablespoons corn oil
12 corn tortillas
1 quantity Cooked Salsa with Chile
  (see page 190)
1 quantity Refried Black Beans (see above)
1 iceberg lettuce, shredded
½ cup (125 milliliters) sour cream
4 ounces (125g) goat cheese, crumbled

1 To assemble the enchiladas, heat the corn oil in a large skillet and quickly fry the tortillas, one at a time, to soften them.

2 Remove the tortillas with a slotted spoon, then dip them, one at a time, in the pan of cooked salsa.

3 Lift out onto a counter and place a generous tablespoon of refried beans on each tortilla. Fold the tortillas in half and arrange singly or grouped together on plates.

4 Top the tortillas with shredded lettuce, sour cream, and crumbled cheese. Serve immediately.

nutritional breakdown per serving: calories 774, protein 29g, fat 36g (saturated fat 13g), carbohydrate 89g

salsa mexicana

This is the classic salsa or relish, so-called because the ingredients echo the colors of the Mexican flag. The onion, tomatoes, and cilantro should be finely chopped to approximately the same size.

serves 4
preparation: 5 minutes
cooking: none
𝒱

1 onion, finely chopped
1 garlic clove, finely chopped
4 tomatoes, finely chopped
¾ cup/¾ ounce (20g) chopped
    cilantro
salt

Combine the onion, garlic, tomatoes, and cilantro in a bowl. Season with salt.

> nutritional breakdown per total recipe: calories 119, protein 5g, fat 2g (saturated fat 0g), carbohydrate 23g

VARIATIONS

Salsa with Chile—Add a fresh green chile (a serrano chile if possible) to create a hotter version. Cut the chile lengthwise into 4 pieces, remove the veins and seeds, and chop finely. Stir into the salsa.
Salsa with Lime—For a more piquant flavor add the juice of ¼ of a lime to the basic salsa.
Chunky Guacamole—This variation is excellent served with Quesadillas (see below). Make the basic salsa mixture and add a finely chopped avocado, 1–2 tablespoons lemon juice, and extra finely chopped garlic to taste.

quesadillas

These easy snacks comprise folded tortillas filled with melted cheese.

serves 4
preparation: 5 minutes
cooking: 10 minutes
(Ca)

2–3 tablespoons corn oil
12 corn tortilla
4–6 ounces (125–175g) goat cheese, crumbled
1 quantity Chunky Guacamole (see above)

1 Heat the corn oil in a large skillet and quickly fry the tortillas, one at a time, to soften them.

2 Lift out with a slotted spoon and place some crumbled cheese on top. Fold each tortilla in half, then return it to the skillet, pressing it down until the cheese melts.

3 Top with Chunky Guacamole and serve hot.

> nutritional breakdown per serving: calories 485, protein 15g, fat 26g (saturated fat 9g), carbohydrate 51g

huevos rancheros

An easy, colorful egg dish which makes a great snack any time of day.

serves 4
preparation: 5 minutes
cooking: 10 minutes

2–3 tablespoons corn oil, plus extra for
  frying eggs
4 corn tortillas
4 eggs
1 quantity Cooked Salsa with Chile (see page 190)
1 yellow and 1 red bell pepper, sliced, then
  broiled or fried

1 Heat the corn oil in a large skillet and quickly fry
   the tortillas, one at a time, to soften them. Lift out
   with a slotted spoon and keep warm.

2 Heat a little oil in the pan for frying the eggs.
   Break the eggs into the pan, 2 or more at a time
   depending on the size of your pan. Cook for
   4 minutes, basting the white, and the yolk, too,
   if you like, with oil.

3 When cooked, put 1 egg on top of each tortilla,
   cover with cooked salsa and slices of cooked bell
   peppers. Serve hot.

nutritional breakdown per serving: calories 273, protein 10g,
fat 17g (saturated fat 3g), carbohydrate 22g

pizzas

Modern, fast-acting yeast and strong flour mean you can put together a pizza base in just 10 minutes. It then has to be left to rest for about 15 minutes, but that time can be used to make the topping. Toppings are simple to make, and you can include a selection of your favorite ingredients, which can be as unusual as you like! For those who don't like tomato, I've created a succulent onion pizza, which makes a great appetizer or easy snack when served in small pieces.

basic pizza bases

Pizza dough is straightforward to make. It is essentially a bread dough, but because it is rolled into a thin crust it needs less time to rise. The dough takes about 10 minutes to make, less than half an hour to rest, 5 minutes to cook, and is then ready for the topping.

makes two 10-inch (25-cm) pizza bases; serves 4–6

preparation: 10 minutes, plus resting

cooking: 5 minutes

suitable for freezing

ⓒⓐ 𝑣

3 cups/12 ounces (375g) white bread flour, plus extra for dusting
1 packet/¼ ounce (7g) active dry yeast
1 teaspoon sugar
1 teaspoon salt
scant 1 cup (200 milliliters) warm water
2 tablespoons olive oil, plus extra for brushing

1 Combine the flour with the yeast, sugar, and salt in a large bowl. Pour in the warm water and add the olive oil.

2 Draw the mixture into a dough and knead well. Add more flour if necessary. Return the dough to a clean bowl and cover with plastic wrap. Let rest for 15 minutes or longer.

3 Turn out the dough onto a lightly floured counter and knead again. Divide in half. Roll out each piece into a round, about 10 inches (25cm) in diameter. Place on a baking sheet and prick with a fork. Let rest for 10 minutes.

4 Part-bake in a preheated oven, 425°F (220°C), for 5 minutes. Brush with olive oil or Garlic Oil (see page 196), before adding topping.

nutritional breakdown per pizza base: calories 1432, protein 38g, fat 27g (saturated fat 4g), carbohydrate 277g

three-flour pizza bases

This pizza dough combines three different flours. The whole-wheat flour adds a nutty flavor and the rye flour has a distinctive tang. Depending on your personal taste, you can alter the ratios of the flours. The technique for making this dough, known as the sponge or batter method, is slightly different from the earlier basic recipe. Initially, only a small quantity of flour (without salt) is mixed with the water and stirred to make a batter similar to a crêpe batter. The advantage of this method is that the yeast gets started very easily with the absence of salt and, as the sponge starts to rise, gluten is formed, thus making the dough more elastic. This method is most appropriate when using heavier flours or flours that are lower in gluten, such as rye.

makes two 10-inch (25-cm) pizza bases; serves 4–6

preparation: 15 minutes, plus resting

cooking: 5 minutes

suitable for freezing

(Fe) 𝒱

1½ cups/6 ounces (175g) white bread flour, plus
    extra for dusting
1 cup/4 ounces (125g) whole-wheat flour
½ cup/2 ounces (50g) rye flour
1 packet/¼ ounce (7g) active dry yeast
scant 1 cup (200 milliliters) warm water
1 teaspoon sugar
1 teaspoon salt
2 tablespoons olive oil, plus extra for brushing

1 Measure the strong white bread, whole-wheat, and rye flours into a bowl. Spoon about one-third of the flour mixture into a separate bowl and sprinkle in the yeast. Add the warm water and mix very thoroughly to form a batter. Cover the bowl with a damp dish towel and leave the batter for about 30 minutes or until it looks frothy.

2 Combine the sugar and salt with the reserved flour, then tip this into the batter. Stir well and add the olive oil.

3 Draw up into a dough and knead well. Add more flour if necessary. Return the dough to a clean bowl and cover with plastic wrap. Leave for 15 minutes or longer.

4 Turn out the dough onto a lightly floured counter and knead again. Divide in half. Roll out each piece into a round, about 10 inches (25cm) in diameter. Place on a baking sheet and prick with a fork. Let rest for 10 minutes.

5 Part-bake in a preheated oven, 425°F (220°C), for 5 minutes. Brush with olive oil or Garlic Oil (see page 196), before adding topping.

nutritional breakdown per pizza base: calories 689, protein 19g, fat 14g (saturated fat 2g), carbohydrate 129g

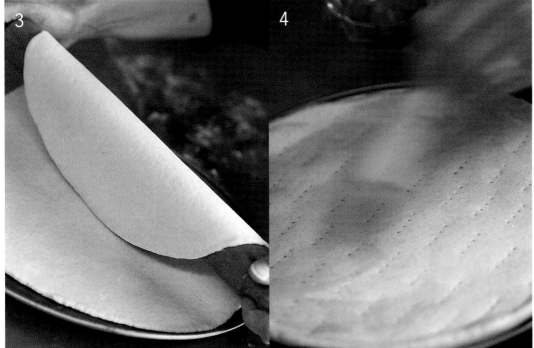

Step 1 Add the oil to the flour and water mixture.
Step 2 Knead the dough until smooth using the heel of the hand.
Step 3 Roll the dough thinly into a large round and place on a baking sheet.
Step 4 Prick well and leave to rest, then bake for about 5 minutes.

classic tomato pizza topping

This simple pizza topping is redolent with herbs and comprises a tomato mixture that is cooked down to a thick pulp.

makes sufficient for 2 x 10-inch (25-cm) pizza bases

serves 4

preparation: 5 minutes

cooking: 15–20 minutes

suitable for freezing

𝓋

1–2 tablespoons olive oil
1 onion, finely chopped
1 garlic clove, crushed
14 ounces (398 milliliters) canned chopped
   tomatoes
1 teaspoon dried oregano
1 teaspoon dried thyme
1 bay leaf
salt and freshly ground black pepper

1 Heat the oil in a saucepan and gently cook the onion and garlic until soft.

2 Add the can of chopped tomatoes, oregano, thyme, and bay leaf and stir well. Bring the mixture to a boil, then simmer, uncovered, over moderate heat for 15–20 minutes, stirring frequently until some of the liquid has evaporated to leave a rich tomato pulp. Remove the bay leaf and season with salt and pepper to taste.

nutritional breakdown per serving: calories 69, protein 2g, fat 5g (saturated fat 1g), carbohydrate 6g

garlic oil

This is a useful infusion to have handy when making pizza or bruschetta.

makes ⅔ cup/¼ pint (150 milliliters)

preparation: 5 minutes

cooking: none

𝓋

4 garlic cloves
⅔ cup/¼ pint (150 milliliters) olive oil

1 Crush the garlic or chop it finely and put in a screw-top jar.

2 Cover with olive oil and refrigerate for 2 days, during which time the oil will take on a subtle hint of garlic. This oil can be kept in the refrigerator for 2–3 weeks.

nutritional breakdown per tablespoon: calories 91, protein 0g, fat 100g (saturated fat 11g), carbohydrate 0g

pesto, plum tomato, and black olive pizza

makes two 10-inch (25-cm) pizzas; serves 4

preparation time: 10 minutes, plus pizza base making

cooking time: 15–20 minutes, plus pizza bases

suitable for freezing

 (Ca) (Fe)

2 tablespoons pesto (see page 211)

2 precooked Basic or Three-Flour Pizza Bases
(see pages 194–95)

1 quantity Classic Tomato Pizza Topping (see
page 196)

8 ounces (250g) plum tomatoes, sliced

12 basil leaves

4 ounces (125g) mozzarella, sliced

¼ cup/1 ounce (25g) pitted black olives

1 Spread the pesto over the precooked pizza bases,
then cover with the tomato topping.

2 Arrange the sliced fresh tomatoes on top of the
tomato sauce and tuck the basil leaves in between.
Cover with the cheese and black olives.

3 Bake in a preheated oven, 400°F (200°C), for
15–20 minutes.

nutritional breakdown per serving: calories 622, protein 22g,
fat 21g (saturated fat 8g), carbohydrate 76g

VARIATIONS

Other additions to pizza toppings could include
artichoke hearts, sliced bell peppers, corn, chopped
cooked broccoli, green olives, mild or hot chiles (with
care!), different cheeses, and pine nuts.

cheese and tomato pizza

makes two 10-inch (25-cm) pizzas; serves 4

preparation time: 5 minutes, plus pizza base making

cooking time: 15–20 minutes, plus pizza base

suitable for freezing

(Ca)

2 precooked Basic or Three-Flour Pizza Bases
  (see pages 194–95)
1 quantity Classic Tomato Pizza Topping
  (see page 196)
4 ounces (125g) mozzarella, sliced
1 tablespoon olive oil

1 Cover the precooked pizza bases with the tomato topping. Cover with the sliced cheese, then drizzle the olive oil over the top.

2 Bake in a preheated oven, 400°F (200°C), for 15–20 minutes.

nutritional breakdown per serving: calories 586, protein 18g, fat 23g (saturated fat 7g), carbohydrate 77g

mushroom pizza

makes two 10-inch (25-cm) pizzas; serves 4

preparation time: 10 minutes, plus pizza base making

cooking time: 20 minutes, plus pizza bases

suitable for freezing

(Fe) (Ca)

2 precooked Basic or Three-Flour Pizza Bases
  (see pages 194–95)
1 quantity Classic Tomato Pizza Topping
  (see page 196)
1 tablespoon olive oil
5¼ cups/13 ounces (400g) white mushrooms,
  very thinly sliced
4 ounces (125g) mozzarella, sliced, optional

1 Cover the precooked pizza bases with the tomato topping.

2 Heat the olive oil in a skillet and cook the mushrooms until soft.

3 Arrange the mushrooms on top of the tomato sauce, then cover with cheese, if using. Bake in a preheated oven, 400°F (200°C), for 15–20 minutes.

nutritional breakdown per serving: calories 578, protein 21g, fat 24g (saturated fat 24g), carbohydrate 76g

saffron onion pizza

makes two 10-inch (25-cm) pizzas; serves 4

preparation: 10 minutes, plus pizza base making

cooking: 30 minutes, plus pizza bases

suitable for freezing

𝒱

2–3 tablespoons olive oil
15 ounces (450g) onions, thinly sliced into rings
¼ teaspoon saffron, steeped in 3 tablespoons
  water
salt and freshly ground black pepper
2 precooked Basic or Three-Flour Pizza Bases
  (see pages 194–95)
1 teaspoon green peppercorns or capers,
  coarsely chopped

1 Heat 2 tablespoons of the oil in a saucepan and gently cook the onions for 10 minutes, or until very soft.

2 Add the steeped saffron and water and cook until the liquid has evaporated. Season with salt and pepper.

3 Brush the pizza bases with a little of the remaining oil, spread on the onion mixture, then sprinkle with the peppercorns. Drizzle with the rest of the oil.

4 Bake in a preheated oven, 400°F (200°C), for 15–20 minutes. Serve hot or at room temperature.

nutritional breakdown per serving: calories 463, protein 11g, fat 14g, (saturated fat 2g), carbohydrate 79g

cheese and tomato pizza (foreground), **mushroom pizza** and **saffron onion pizza**

spinach and chile calzone

Calzone is the term for a folded pizza, a little like a turnover. The advantage of this style of pizza is that you can cook moist fillings without them drying out. The end result is quite substantial but once cooked you can always cut the calzone in half to serve more people. I think it looks quite appetizing to expose the filling.

makes 6

preparation: 15 minutes, plus pizza dough making

cooking: 25 minutes

suitable for freezing

(Ca) (Fe) v

1 tablespoon olive oil
1 onion, finely chopped
1 garlic clove, crushed
1 chile, deseeded and chopped
¼ cup/1 ounce (25g) pine nuts
12 ounces (375g) spinach, shredded
salt and freshly ground black pepper
¼ cup/2 ounces (50g) currants
4 ounces (125g) mozzarella or smoked bean
   curd, cubed
1 quantity uncooked Basic Pizza Base dough
   (see page 194)
flour for dusting

1 Heat the oil in a saucepan and gently cook the onion, garlic, and chile until soft. Add the pine nuts and cook until just lightly browned.

2 Add the shredded spinach and stir-fry until the leaves have wilted—about 3–4 minutes. Remove from the heat, season well with salt and pepper, stir in the currants, and let cool.

3 When cool, mix in the pieces of mozzarella or bean curd.

4 Divide the pizza dough into 6 equal pieces. On a lightly floured counter, roll out each piece to a small round, about 6–7 inches ·15–18cm) in diameter.

5 Divide the filling among the 6 rounds. Moisten the edges with cold water, fold over each piece of dough to make a semicircle, then press the edges together.

6 Place on a baking sheet and bake in a preheated oven, 425°F (220°C), for 15 minutes. Serve hot or let cool on a wire rack and serve warm.

nutritional breakdown per calzone: calories 392, protein 15g, fat 14g (saturated fat 4g), carbohydrate 57g

quick biscuit pizza with broiled vegetables and gruyère

This biscuit base covered with lightly broiled vegetables and cheese makes a quick tasty meal. You could serve individual pizzas as substantial snacks, if you like.

serves 4
preparation: 10 minutes
cooking: 20–25 minutes
suitable for freezing: base only

For the biscuit base:

3 tablespoons/1½ ounces) butter or margarine

2 cups/8 ounces (250g) self-rising flour, plus extra for dusting

1 egg, beaten, mixed with enough milk to make ⅔ cup/¼ pint (150 milliliters)

For the topping:

1 onion, sliced into rings

1 yellow or red bell pepper, cored, deseeded, and sliced

1 zucchini, sliced

1–2 tablespoons olive oil

salt and freshly ground black pepper

2–3 tablespoons ready-made tomato sauce

1 cup/4 ounces (125g) grated Gruyère or other hard cheese suitable for melting

1   To make the biscuit base, rub the butter into the flour until the mixture resembles fine bread crumbs. This can be done by hand or in a food processor. Add the egg and milk and mix quickly to a dough.

2   Turn out the dough on to a lightly floured counter and press it into a round, about 8 inches (20cm) in diameter. Place on a greased baking sheet and bake in a preheated oven, 425°F (220°C), for 15–20 minutes.

3   To make the topping, spread out the onion, bell pepper, and zucchini on a broiler pan. Drizzle with the olive oil and season well with salt and pepper. Place under a preheated broiler and broil for 4–5 minutes, or until well browned, turning them over once during the cooking.

4   Spread the tomato sauce over the cooked biscuit base, arrange the broiled vegetables on top, and cover with the cheese. Cook under the broiler until the cheese has melted. Serve hot.

IN A HURRY

Use a biscuit dough for a classic pizza base when you are in a hurry.

nutritional breakdown per serving: calories 514, protein 18g, fat 26g (saturated fat 14g), carbohydrate 55g

easy meals for children

Including a special section on children's food here is not to imply that they cannot manage to eat the majority of recipes in this book. Children enjoy sophisticated and sometimes strong flavors, proved by the number of children who like spiced foods from Southeast Asia and India, as well as South America.

I've used this section to highlight some simple ideas for quick meals that you might wish to make on occasions when the whole family cannot eat together. Also included is a list of ideas from the book that make good family meals.

I have added here a couple of fried recipes, such as Quick Nut Nuggets, which are on a par with popular fast food. There is also a wheat-free burger and a dairy-free burger, as well as some low-sugar baked beans. These recipes all offer a healthy option when you need fast food.

quick baked beans

Many commercial brands of baked beans have a lot of sugar added so, by making your own, you are more in control of what your children are eating. The final taste will be different, but by juggling around with ingredients you can highlight a favorite flavor. Non-vegans could use honey as a sweetener, instead of sugar.

serves 4
preparation: 5 minutes
cooking: 40 minutes
suitable for freezing
v

1 tablespoon olive oil
1 onion, finely chopped
1 garlic clove, crushed
4 ounces (125g) cooked navy beans or
    black-eyed peas or 15-ounce (450-g) can
    beans, rinsed and drained
1 dessert apple, grated
14 ounces (398 milliliters) canned chopped
    tomatoes
2 tablespoons tomato ketchup

2 tablespoons concentrated apple juice
sugar to taste
salt and freshly ground black pepper

1 Heat the oil in a large saucepan and gently cook the onion and garlic until very soft. Add the cooked beans and stir well, then cook for 3 minutes.

2 Add the apple, tomatoes, tomato ketchup, and concentrated apple juice. Sweeten a little more if necessary with sugar and season well.

3 Cook for 30 minutes, stirring occasionally. Serve hot.

nutritional breakdown per serving: calories 203, protein 9g, fat 4g (saturated fat 1g), carbohydrate 36g

baked potatoes

These are straightforward to make and can easily be filled to suit everyone's taste.

1 Scrub and prick the potato or slash through to make an attractive pattern or hedgehog effect. Bake in a preheated oven, 400°F (200°C), for 1–1½ hours. To keep the skin soft, wrap the potato in foil before cooking.

2 Fill with dips, such as Hummus (see page 167); cottage cheese, soft cheese or grated cheese; cooked mushrooms; simple stir-fry vegetables; or Chunky Guacamole (see page 192).

nutritional breakdown per medium potato including skin: calories 136, protein 4g, fat 0g (saturated fat 0g), carbohydrate 32g

baked pasta gratin with fresh corn

This makes a simple but colorful supper dish, which, although in the children's section, also appeals to adults. Go easy on the herbs if your children's taste buds are quite conservative. You can also use canned corn.

serves 4

preparation: 10 minutes

cooking: about 1 hour

suitable for freezing

(Ce)

2 cups/8 ounces (250g) whole-wheat pasta shells
    or spirals
2 corn cobs

For the sauce:
2 tablespoons olive oil
1 onion, finely chopped
1 garlic clove, crushed
generous 2 cups (500 milliliters) tomato purée
½ teaspoon dried thyme, optional
½ teaspoon dried oregano, optional
1 bay leaf
salt and freshly ground black pepper
5 ounces (150g) hard cheese, such as Parmesan,
    grated, or mozzarella, sliced

1 Cook the pasta in a large pan of boiling water for 8–10 minutes, or until just cooked. Drain and set aside.

2 Meanwhile, strip the corn kernels using a sharp knife. Steam for 6–8 minutes over a pan of boiling water or microwave at medium for 3–4 minutes with 3 tablespoons water. Drain and set aside.

3 To make the sauce, heat the oil in a large saucepan and gently cook the onion and garlic until soft. Add the tomato purée and herbs, if using, and bring to a boil. Cover the pan and simmer for 30–35 minutes. Remove the bay leaf and season with salt and pepper.

4 Mix the cooked pasta and corn with the sauce and spoon the mixture into a lightly oiled ovenproof dish. Cover with grated or sliced cheese.

5 Bake in a preheated oven, 350°F (180°C), for 15–20 minutes, or until the cheese has melted and the pasta heated through. Serve hot.

nutritional breakdown per serving: calories 436, protein 20g, fat 15g (saturated fat 6g), carbohydrate 58g

bean curd fritters

This is a dairy-free recipe for children who cannot tolerate eggs or cheese.

makes 8 small fritters	
preparation: 10 minutes	
cooking: 12 minutes	
𝑣	

8 ounces (225g) bean curd, drained and grated
1¼ cups/5 ounces (150g) short-grain or risotto rice (cooked weight)
2 ounces (50g) carrot, grated
2 ounces (50g) scallion, finely chopped or mild onion, grated
1 tablespoon Gomasio (see page 112)
1 tablespoon shoyu or soy sauce
salt and freshly ground black pepper
1 tablespoon all-purpose flour, optional
1–2 tablespoons sunflower oil

1 Combine the bean curd, rice, carrot, scallion, Gomasio, shoyu, and salt and pepper to taste in a large bowl.

2 Shape into 8 small balls, between 2 spoons or using your hands. Keep them damp and the fritter mixture will be less likely to stick. The mixture will only lightly hold together—for something less fragile add the tablespoon of flour.

3 Heat the oil in a skillet and fry the fritters, 2 or 3 at a time, for about 3 minutes, then turn over. and fry the other side for about 3 minutes. Serve hot.

nutritional breakdown per fritter: calories 110, protein 4g, fat 3g (saturated fat 0g), carbohydrate 18g

quick nut nuggets

This is a very simple idea for children that you can make in a real hurry but you do need a food processor. The mixture is quite soft and needs cooking carefully, which is why I suggest making nuggets rather than larger burgers. Many variations with additional ingredients are possible, such as adding herbs or grated carrot.

makes 10

preparation: 5 minutes

cooking: 15 minutes

suitable for freezing

1 onion, coarsely chopped
2 leeks, coarsely chopped
1 red bell pepper, cored, deseeded, and
   coarsely chopped
1 cup/4 ounces (125g) walnuts
1 cup/4 ounces (125g) almonds
2½ cups/5 ounces (150g) fresh whole-wheat
   bread crumbs
2 tablespoons shoyu or soy sauce
salt and freshly ground black pepper
2 eggs, beaten
vegetable or sunflower oil for shallow-frying

1 Put the onions, leeks, pepper, walnuts, almonds, and bread crumbs in a food processor and process until finely ground. Add the shoyu and blend again. Season to taste with salt and pepper.

2 Add the eggs and blend again so that they are evenly mixed in. Divide the mixture into walnut-size nuggets.

3 Heat a little oil in a skillet and add the nuggets. Once the outsides are crisp, turn down the heat and cook slowly for 10 minutes more so that the nuggets are cooked through to the center. Serve hot.

nutritional breakdown per nugget: calories 244, protein 8g, fat 19g (saturated fat 2g), carbohydrate 10g

other meal suggestions for children

- Pizza (see page 194)
- Pasta with sauce (see page 210)
- Egg dishes such as Strata (see page 184) or Baked Eggs with Mozzarella and Fresh Tomatoes (see page 182)
- Polenta with sauces, as well as Polenta Cheese Squares (see page 222)
- Grain dishes such as Layered Bulgur with Tomatoes and Feta (see page 231),
- Risotto (see page 226), or Paella with Many Vegetables (see page 233)
- Small savories such as Baked Bean Curd and Cremini Mushrooms (see page 175), Falafel (see page 174), or Enchiladas (see page 191)
- Baked dishes and casseroles such as Almond Croustade with Swiss Chard (see page 268), Potato and Leek Boulangère (see page 262), or Country Casserole with
- Spiced Cheese Dumplings (see page 244)

Main Courses

Whatever the taste, occasion, or season, here you'll find a wealth of recipes for a wide range of main courses. This chapter is subdivided into smaller sections to help you find what you want more easily. Each section is either centered around a family of ingredients, such as pasta and polenta, or rice and grains, or takes as a focus a style of cooking, such as casseroles, baked dishes, or stir-fries.

Some of the main courses featured here need little or no accompaniment. Recipes such as Broccoli and Mushroom Lasagne with Almonds, Baked Polenta with Rich Tomato and Mascarpone Sauce, or Paella with Many Vegetables, are meals in their own right. Where main courses need accompaniments, such as Sweet Potato Stew or Red Bean and Lentil Chili, I have given ideas for these in the introduction to the recipe. These are only suggestions, but do indicate either a good contrast in color and texture or flavors that are complementary. There are plenty of quick-to-cook ideas here, especially within the pasta, rice, and stir-fry sections. Layered Bulgur with Tomatoes and Feta is a delicious supper and takes only about 15 minutes from start to finish! Some main courses do take longer to prepare, such as pastry, but many steps can be prepared in advance. I hope that this chapter will add to your repertoire of favorite meals.

tagliatelle with fennel and fresh herbs

Fresh and delicate, this simple pasta makes an easy supper dish or light lunch. A vegan version can easily be made without butter. A mixture of olive oil and walnut oil instead adds an extra dimension to the flavor.

serves 4

preparation: 10 minutes

cooking: 10 minutes

2 tablespoons/1 ounce (25g) butter
⅓ cup (80 milliliters) olive oil
2 garlic cloves, crushed
8 ounces (250g) fennel, finely chopped
1 teaspoon lemon zest
¼ cup/¼ ounce (7g) chopped parsley
¼ cup/¼ ounce (7g) chopped basil
2 teaspoons snipped fennel tops
salt and freshly ground black pepper
2 cups/8 ounces (250g) peas
1 pound (500g) fresh tagliatelle, or 12 ounces (350g) dried
wedges of lemon, to garnish
freshly grated Parmesan, optional

1 Melt the butter in a small saucepan with the olive oil and gently cook the garlic, fennel, and lemon zest for 5 minutes. Stir in the parsley, basil, and fennel tops, remove from the heat, and season well with salt and pepper.

2 Cook the peas in a saucepan of boiling water for 3–4 minutes, until just tender. Drain well.

3 Meanwhile, cook the pasta in a large saucepan of boiling salted water until firm-tender, then drain.

4 Quickly combine the fennel and herb sauce with the cooked peas and pasta. Serve immediately with wedges of lemon on the side and sprinkled with Parmesan, if using.

nutritional breakdown per serving: calories 636, protein 20g, fat 25g (saturated fat 6g), carbohydrate 83g

pasta

Making your own pasta may appear rather daunting, but it is not tricky to do and it is not necessary to purchase special equipment. As with other cooking techniques, such as bread-making or pastry-making, you'll find you get more confident and achieve better results after a little practice.

Once you have learned how to make plain pasta, you can experiment with flavoring the basic dough with lots of different ingredients. You can also make delicious, but simple ravioli and mezza luna (large rounds of pasta stuffed and folded), which can be hard to find in the stores.

Use a strong all-purpose flour, ideally one that is recommended for bread-making. The gluten in it will make the dough more elastic and stretchy, so that it roll outs easily. Strong whole-wheat flour can also be used to make pasta. The fiber in this type of flour absorbs more liquid so it is best to add an extra egg initially. The texture of whole-wheat pasta will be robust, rather than melting, so always serve plenty of sauce with it.

To store homemade pasta, keep it in the refrigerator and aim to use it within 24 hours. Homemade pasta will also freeze and can be cooked from frozen.

basic pasta

makes sufficient for 4 for a light main course

preparation: 40 minutes, plus resting

cooking: none

suitable for freezing

12 ounces (350g) strong white bread flour, plus
    extra for dusting
1 teaspoon salt
3 extra large eggs, lightly beaten
1–2 tablespoons olive oil
1–2 tablespoons water

1   Sift the flour and salt into a large bowl. Make a well in the center and add the eggs. Mix with a wooden spoon to make a dough, then add 1 tablespoon of olive oil and 1 tablespoon of water. Knead again and if the mixture seems too dry, then gradually add equal quantities of olive oil and water, 1 teaspoon at a time, until you have a smooth but firm dough. If the dough seems sticky, sprinkle on a little more flour. Knead the dough until it is smooth and elastic—this can take 5–10 minutes.

2   Cover the bowl with plastic wrap and leave the dough to rest for 30–60 minutes. It is then ready to roll out and cut. (If you have a food processor, you can use it to make the pasta dough, then do the final kneading by hand.)

nutritional breakdown per serving: calories 379, protein 14g, fat 9g (saturated fat 2g), carbohydrate 66g

quantities

For fresh pasta, either bought or homemade, allow 4 ounces (125g) per person for a reasonable main course helping. Obviously, allow less for an appetizer and adjust quantities if you are feeding children. For dried pasta, allow about 3 ounces (75g) per person for a good portion.

Cooking Pasta

Both fresh and dried pasta needs to be cooked in plenty of salted water. Use a large saucepan and allow 4½ quarts/9 pints (4 liters) per 1 pound (500g) pasta. If your pan is too crowded, the pasta will stick together. Add salt to flavor the dough. You can also add 1 tablespoon of olive oil to the water to prevent the pasta from sticking together.

Once cooked, pasta should be eaten right away. It cools very quickly so have warmed plates and your sauce ready before you start cooking the pasta. Some fresh pasta takes only minutes to cook. Filled ravioli take 8–10 minutes; dried whole-wheat pasta takes the longest—up to 10–12 minutes.

To check if pasta is cooked, remove a piece of pasta from the pan. It should be firm-tender— firm to the bite but not hard in the center.

rolling out

A pasta machine will make excellent, evenly thin dough. Small hand-operated machines work on the principle of a wringer. Changing the settings each time the pasta dough is passed through makes it thinner. This is most useful when you want to make long strands of pasta, such as tagliatelle.

If rolling by hand, use a good sturdy rolling pin. Working on a lightly floured counter, use one-fourth or half the dough at a time so that it will be more manageable, and roll it into oblongs. Cut the dough with a pastry wheel or large knife so that you don't drag it out of shape. Once the strands are cut, leave them to dry hanging over a floured broom handle for 15 minutes.

For lasagne and ravioli, roll the dough into large squares or oblongs and cut appropriately sized sheets for lasagne or cut out rounds 4–6 inches (10–15cm) in diameter for mezza luna. Keep the cut pieces of pasta on a lightly floured surface; otherwise, they will stick. For ravioli you can cut small rounds or use a raviolamp (a special ravioli tray divided into sections). Let dry for 15 minutes.

Step 1 Make a well in the flour and add the beaten eggs.
Step 2 Mix with a rounded knife.
Step 3 Add the oil and water, then knead the mixture.
Step 4 Leave the dough to rest for 30–60 minutes. Then roll out and cut.

flavored and colored pasta

Practice making a basic dough before trying variations. Additions will invariably alter the look and texture of the pasta so you must be sure you are going to get it right in the first place. Add dry ingredients, such as herbs, with the sifted flour. Ingredients that contain moisture, such as sun-dried tomato paste or cooked spinach, should be added with the eggs.

The following ingredients can be added to pasta dough:
- 3–4 tablespoons very finely chopped herbs, such as parsley, rosemary, or basil
- Substitute walnut or hazelnut oil for the olive oil
- 2 ounces (50g) very finely chopped raw baby spinach
- For a red pasta, add 2 ounces (50g) finely chopped sun-dried tomatoes, or sun-dried tomato paste to taste
- For green pasta, add 2 ounces (50g) cooked, finely chopped spinach or Swiss chard
- For golden pasta, add a few threads of saffron—grind the threads with a pestle and mortar, then steep in 1 tablespoon boiling water. Let the liquid cool, then add to the dough with the eggs.

savory butters

Savory butters are one of the easiest additions to plain pasta, adding both richness and a subtle flavor. Always start with butter that has been out of the refrigerator for a while so that it is slightly soft but still cool. Allow time for the butter to firm up again once you have added the flavoring.

Flavorings range from herbs and spices to citrus juice. As well as serving with pasta, savory butters can be tossed into freshly cooked vegetables or dotted over vegetables prior to broiling. A nondairy alternative to savory butter is to steep herbs and garlic in a good-quality olive oil.

sage butter

serves 4

preparation: 5 minutes

cooking: none

suitable for freezing

6 tablespoons (¾ stick)/3 ounces (75g) butter
2 tablespoons sage leaves, finely chopped
2 teaspoons lemon juice
salt and freshly ground black pepper

1 Soften the butter in a bowl. Add the finely chopped sage leaves and mix into the softened butter.

2 When creamy, stir in the lemon juice, and season with salt and pepper to taste. Chill until required.

nutritional breakdown per serving: calories 140, protein 0g, fat 15g (saturated fat 10g), carbohydrate 0g

lightly spiced tomato sauce

PEP IT UP

For extra zip add a finely chopped chile to the oil with the garlic and shallots.

This is based on the classic Italian sauce, puttanesca. It is a combination of bold flavors and has a thick and pulpy texture. Quick to make, it is ideal with spaghetti or tagliatelle.

serves 4

preparation: 10 minutes

cooking: 30 minutes

suitable for freezing

v

2 tablespoons olive oil
2 garlic cloves, crushed
2 shallots, finely chopped
1 teaspoon fennel seeds
14 ounces (398 milliliters) canned chopped tomatoes
¼ cup/2 ounces (50g) capers
½ cup/2 ounces (50g) olives, coarsely chopped
salt and freshly ground black pepper
1 tablespoon snipped fennel tops, to garnish

1 Heat the oil in a saucepan and cook the garlic and shallots very gently so that they steep in the oil rather than scorch.

2 Stir in the fennel seeds and cook for 1 minute. Add the tomatoes, capers, and olives and mix well.

3 Bring to a boil, then simmer, semicovered, over medium heat for 25 minutes.

4 Season with salt and pepper to taste and serve hot on your chosen pasta. Garnish with fennel tops.

nutritional breakdown per serving: calories 15, protein 0g, fat 1g (saturated fat 0g), carbohydrate 1g

pesto

Pesto is the classic Genoese sauce, made with basil, olive oil, Parmesan, and garlic. Its color is vibrant and its consistency like that of a thick but smooth vinaigrette. Make this basic pesto and you'll see opportunities for a multitude of variations by changing the type of nuts or cheese used. Pesto goes brilliantly with pasta, making fully flavored but light dishes—simply stir 1–2 tablespoons pesto into freshly cooked pasta. It is also wonderful drizzled over new potatoes, mixed into roasted bell peppers, or added as a flavoring to tomato sauces. The possibilities are endless.

makes about 1 cup/7–8 ounces (200–250g)

preparation: 10 minutes

cooking: none

2 cups/2 ounces (50g) basil
2 garlic cloves, coarsely chopped
½ cup/2 ounces (50g) pine nuts
⅓ cup (80 milliliters) olive oil
⅔ cup/2 ounces (50g) grated Parmesan
salt and freshly ground black pepper

1 Using a blender or food processor, blend the basil, garlic, and pine nuts to make a coarse paste.

2 With the motor running, gradually add the olive oil in a thin steady stream and blend until quite smooth.

3 Add the grated cheese and process briefly. Season with salt and pepper to taste.

4 Store the pesto in a screw-top jar in the refrigerator for up to 2 weeks. Cover with a little extra olive oil if necessary.

nutritional breakdown per 2 tablespoons: calories 32, protein 1g, fat 3g (saturated fat 0.6g), carbohydrate 0g

roast garlic butter

serves 4

preparation: 10 minutes

cooking: 5–6 minutes

suitable for freezing

6 garlic cloves, unpeeled
6 tablespoons (¾ stick)/3 ounces (75g) butter
1 tablespoon lemon juice
salt and freshly ground black pepper

1 Roast the unpeeled garlic cloves in a preheated oven, 400°F (200°C), for 5–6 minutes. Let cool, then squeeze out of their skins, and mash the flesh.

2 Soften the butter in a bowl and mash in the roasted garlic and lemon juice. Season to taste and chill until required.

nutritional breakdown per serving: calories 140, protein 0g, fat 15g (saturated fat 10g), carbohydrate 1g

mushroom sauce with wine and herbs

Richly flavored with wine and herbs, this dark mushroom sauce is good with both whole-wheat and plain pasta. If you can, prepare it well ahead so the flavors have time to develop.

serves 4
preparation: 10 minutes
cooking: 35 minutes
suitable for freezing
V

1 tablespoon olive oil
1 onion, finely chopped
1 garlic clove, crushed
1 pound (500g) mushrooms, thinly sliced
¼ cup (50 milliliters) red wine
1¼ cups/½ pint (300 milliliters) tomato purée
½ cup (125 milliliters) water
1 teaspoon dried oregano
1 teaspoon dried thyme
salt and freshly ground black pepper

1 Heat the oil in a large saucepan and gently cook the onion and garlic until soft. Add the mushrooms and cook for 5 minutes until quite soft.

2 Pour in the wine, increase the heat, then cook over high heat for 3–4 minutes to reduce the liquid.

3 Reduce the heat and add the tomato sauce and water. Stir well, mix in the oregano and thyme, and season with salt and pepper to taste.

4 Bring to a boil, then simmer, semicovered, for 20–25 minutes. Adjust the seasoning and serve hot with your chosen pasta.

nutritional breakdown per serving: calories 75, protein 4g, fat 4g (saturated fat 1g), carbohydrate 6g

gorgonzola sauce with walnuts

A very rich but easy sauce for serving with a pasta such as shells or bows. The walnuts can be toasted in advance but the wine sauce needs to be made just prior to eating.

serves 4
preparation: 5 minutes
cooking: 10 minutes
Ⓒₐ

2 tablespoons/1 ounce (25g) butter
2 garlic cloves, finely chopped
scant 1 cup/3½ ounces (100g) walnut pieces
scant 1 cup (200 milliliters) white wine
8 ounces (250g) gorgonzola, finely cubed
salt and freshly ground black pepper
2–3 tablespoons finely chopped sorrel,
  to garnish

1 Melt the butter in a skillet and gently cook the garlic. Then add the walnuts and cook until slightly toasted and well coated with the butter. Set aside.

2 Heat the wine in a small saucepan and, when warm, add the gorgonzola and melt it gently, stirring constantly. Season to taste.

3 To serve, toss the walnut pieces and sauce into freshly cooked pasta. Serve immediately, garnished with chopped sorrel.

right **gorgonzola sauce with walnuts served on pasta**

nutritional breakdown per serving: calories 426, protein 14g, fat 37g (saturated fat 14g), carbohydrate 1g

mushroom and olive ravioli

makes 48–60 pasta rounds or 16–20 mezza luna; serves 4

preparation: 20 minutes, plus pasta making

cooking: 20 minutes

suitable for freezing

For the filling:

2 tablespoons olive oil

1 onion, finely chopped

2 garlic cloves, chopped

3¼ cups/8 ounces (250g) cremini or Paris
   mushrooms, sliced

¼ cup (50 milliliters) red wine

scant 1 cup/3½ ounces (100g) pitted black olives

salt and freshly ground black pepper

1 quantity Basic Pasta (see page 208)

flour for dusting

2 tablespoons/1 ounce (25g) butter or Very Easy
   Tomato Sauce (see page 292) and grated
   Parmesan to serve

1   To make the filling, heat the oil in a saucepan and
    gently cook the onion and garlic until very soft.

2   Add the cremini or Paris mushrooms and cook
    until soft, then pour in the red wine and increase
    the heat. Simmer the mixture until most of the
    liquid has evaporated.

3   Let cool slightly, then process the cooked
    mushroom mixture with the olives in a food
    processor until finely chopped. If you like a
    smoother texture, process the mixture to a coarse
    paste. Season well with salt and pepper.

4   Roll out the pasta thinly on a lightly floured counter,
    according to the instructions on page 209. Using a
    2½-inch (6-cm) cutter, cut 48–60 rounds or, using a
    4-inch (10-cm) cutter, cut out 16–20 rounds.

5   Fill the small rounds with 1 teaspoon filling or the
    large rounds with about 1 tablespoon filling.

6   Moisten half the edge of each round with water,
    fold over to make a semicircle, and seal the edges
    well. Leave on a lightly floured plate.

7   Cook the pasta for 8–10 minutes, or until firm-
    tender. Drain and serve tossed in butter or sauce,
    with the Parmesan served separately.

nutritional breakdown per serving: calories 530, protein 16g,
fat 22g (saturated fat 6g), carbohydrate 69g

pasta with sauté vegetables and mascarpone

This delightful tangle of fresh vegetables enriched with melting cheese makes a very simple supper dish. Do brown the leeks before adding the other vegetables as this adds to the quality of the sauce.

serves 4
preparation: 10 minutes
cooking: 15 minutes

2 tablespoons olive oil
1 garlic clove, crushed
2 leeks, sliced
8 ounces (250g) oyster mushrooms, sliced
   if large
1 red bell pepper, cored, deseeded, and sliced
⅓ cup (4–6 tablespoons) mascarpone cheese
10 ounces (300g) dried pasta or 1 pound (500g)
   fresh pasta
salt and freshly ground black pepper

1   Heat the oil in a saucepan and gently cook the garlic for 2 minutes.

2   Add the leeks and increase the heat so that the leeks start to brown. Cook for 4–5 minutes.

3   Add the oyster mushrooms and bell pepper. Stir well and cook over moderate heat, until the mushrooms are soft and the bell pepper browned.

4   Season well and stir in the mascarpone, reduce the heat, and keep the sauce warm.

5   Meanwhile, have ready a saucepan of boiling salted water. Add the pasta, bring to a boil, and cook according to packet instructions, or until firm-tender. Drain, toss into the vegetables, adjust the seasoning, and serve immediately.

nutritional breakdown per serving: calories 597, protein 19g, fat 22g (saturated fat 11g), carbohydrate 81g

ricotta, pesto, and herb ravioli

makes 48–60 pasta rounds or 16–20 mezza luna;

serves 4

preparation: 15 minutes, plus pasta making

cooking: 10 minutes

suitable for freezing

(Ca) (Fe)

For the filling:

1¼ cups/10 ounces (300g) ricotta cheese

2 cups/2 ounces (50g) chopped herbs (such as
basil, parsley, marjoram, oregano, thyme)

2–3 tablespoons pesto (see page 211)

salt and freshly ground black pepper

1 quantity Basic Pasta (see page 208)

flour for dusting

2 tablespoons/1 ounce (25g) butter or Very Easy
Tomato Sauce (see page 292) and freshly
grated Parmesan to serve

 Combine the ricotta with the herbs and pesto in a
bowl and season well with salt and pepper.

2 Roll out the pasta thinly on a lightly floured
counter, according to the instructions on page 209.
Using a 2½-inch (6-cm) cutter, cut 48–60 rounds
of pasta or, using a 4-inch (10-cm) cutter, cut out
16–20 rounds.

3 Fill the small rounds with 1 teaspoon filling or the
large rounds with about 1 tablespoon filling.

4 Moisten half the edge of each round with water,
fold over to make a semicircle, and seal the edges
well. Leave on a lightly floured plate.

5 Bring a large saucepan of salted water to a boil,
and cook the pasta for 8–10 minutes, or until firm-
tender. Drain and serve either tossed in butter or a
sauce, with the Parmesan served separately.

> **VARIATION**
>
> Another alternative
> easy filling for ravioli
> is to combine ricotta
> cheese with pesto
> and an equal quantity
> of mashed potato.
> Season well. This
> makes a creamy but
> less rich filling.

nutritional breakdown per serving (without butter or
sauce): calories 602, protein 24g, fat 28g (saturated fat 12g),
carbohydrate 68g

pasta with roasted fennel and patty pans

serves 4

preparation: 15 minutes

cooking: 30 minutes

(Fe)

8 ounces (250g) fennel, chopped
1 pound (500g) patty pan squash, kept whole
   or golden zucchini, chopped
2 onions, sliced
3 tablespoons olive oil
salt and freshly ground black pepper

For the walnut pesto:
½ cup/2 ounces (50g) walnuts
2 cups/2 ounces (50g) basil
1–2 garlic cloves, coarsely chopped
⅓ cup/1 ounce (25g) grated Parmesan
6–8 tablespoons olive oil

12 ounces (350g) dried pasta or 1 pound (500g)
   fresh pasta
freshly grated Parmesan, to serve

1 Toss the fennel, squash, and onions in a bowl with the olive oil and season well with salt and pepper. Spread the vegetables out on 1 or 2 large roasting pans or baking sheets and roast in a preheated oven, 400°F (200°C), for 20 minutes, or until well browned.

2 Meanwhile, to make the pesto, blend together the walnuts, basil, garlic, and Parmesan in a blender or food processor. Then, with the motor running, add the oil gradually in a thin steady stream to produce a sauce-like consistency.

3 When the vegetables are roasted, toss them in 2–3 tablespoons pesto and keep warm.

4 Cook the pasta in a saucepan of boiling salted water until firm-tender. Drain and toss into the cooked vegetables. Serve immediately with extra Parmesan served separately.

nutritional breakdown per serving: calories 900, protein 27g, fat 49g (saturated fat 8g), carbohydrate 90g

pasta with spinach, shiitake mushrooms, and bean curd

This Asian-style dish is a departure from Italian flavorings but is a combination that works very well and produces a robust sauce, which goes perfectly with either whole-wheat or buckwheat pasta. Bean curd boosts the protein content, making this a complete meal, which is quick and simple to make.

serves 4

preparation: 10 minutes

cooking: 20 minutes

(Ca) (Fe) $\mathcal{V}$

2 tablespoons sunflower oil
1 onion, finely chopped
2 garlic cloves, crushed
8 ounces (250g) bean curd, thinly sliced
4 cups/10 ounces (300g) shiitake mushrooms, thinly sliced
2 tablespoons shoyu or soy sauce
1½ pounds (750g) spinach, shredded
1 teaspoon sesame oil
12 ounces (350g) dried pasta
salt and freshly ground black pepper
2–3 tablespoons toasted sesame seeds, to garnish

1 Heat the oil in a large saucepan or lidded skillet, and gently cook the onion and garlic until soft.

2 Add the slices of bean curd and the mushrooms and stir well. Cook slowly until the mushrooms are soft, then add the shoyu or soy sauce. Cover the pan and cook for 4 minutes so that the mushrooms release their juices.

3 Add the spinach in handfuls and stir until it wilts and reduces in size. Cook until soft, then sprinkle with the sesame oil, and season well.

4 Meanwhile, cook the pasta in a large saucepan of boiling salted water until firm-tender. Drain.

5 Pile the cooked vegetables over the cooked pasta, then serve immediately, garnished with toasted sesame seeds.

nutritional breakdown per serving: calories 420, protein 23g, fat 12g (saturated fat 2g), carbohydrate 61g

lentil lasagne

BÉCHAMEL SAUCE

Béchamel sauce is a white sauce made with a flavored milk. It is very easy to do this by first warming the milk in a small saucepan or in a pitcher in the microwave and then adding flavorings, such as onion, peppercorns, and herbs. The steeped milk adds an extra dimension to the sauce but if you are in a hurry, make a plain white sauce.

Lentils make a hearty bolognese-style filling for lasagne. Puy lentils or brown lentils work best since their small size means that they blend well into the sauce. You can also use larger Continental green lentils or adzuki beans for this recipe. The crème fraîche in the white sauce adds a good tang to counterbalance the earthy quality of the lentils. As with any lasagne, try to get as much as possible prepared in advance, leaving just a matter of assembly.

serves 4

preparation: 15 minutes, plus standing

cooking: about 1½ hours

suitable for freezing

(Ca) (Fe)

For the filling:
1 cup/8 ounces (250g) green or brown lentils
2 tablespoons olive oil
1 onion, finely chopped
2 garlic cloves, crushed
2 celery stalks, finely chopped
2 red bell peppers, cored, deseeded, and finely chopped
3¼ cups/8 ounces (250g) mushrooms, chopped
2 tablespoons chopped sun-dried tomatoes
3–4 tablespoons chopped basil
scant 2 cups (500 milliliters) tomato purée
salt and freshly ground black pepper

For the béchamel sauce:
scant 2 cups/¾ pint (450 milliliters) milk
6 black peppercorns
½ onion
1 bay leaf
1 sprig thyme
3 tablespoons/1½ ounces (40g) butter
¼ cup/1 ounce (25g) all-purpose flour
scant 1 cup (200 milliliters) crème fraîche
salt and freshly ground black pepper

6–8 sheets lasagne
1–2 tablespoons freshly grated Parmesan

1 To make the filling, cook the lentils in a large saucepan of boiling water for 15–25 minutes, or until quite soft. Drain and set aside.

2 Heat the oil in a large saucepan and gently cook the onion and garlic until soft. Add the celery and cook for a few minutes, then add the red bell peppers and mushrooms, and cook until soft. Stir in the cooked lentils with the sun-dried tomatoes and basil and mix well.

3 Pour in the tomato purée and season well. Bring the sauce to a boil, then simmer, covered, for 10–15 minutes. Season well.

4 Meanwhile, to make the béchamel sauce, warm the milk in a small saucepan and add the peppercorns, onion, bay leaf, and thyme. Let stand for 15 minutes.

5 Next, melt the butter in a small saucepan. Add the flour and cook over gentle heat for 2 minutes. Strain the steeped milk into the roux and bring the sauce to a boil, stirring constantly. Simmer for 2–3 minutes, until the sauce thickens. Then stir in the crème fraîche and season well with salt and pepper.

6 Prepare the lasagne by covering with boiling water, or according to the packet instructions. Drain and separate the sheets.

7 To assemble the dish, place 2–3 spoonfuls of the lentil and tomato sauce in the base of a large ovenproof dish, and cover with 2 or 3 sheets of lasagne. Cover with half the lentil sauce and spoon on a little of the white sauce. Cover with 2 or 3 more sheets of lasagne, then cover with the remaining lentil and tomato sauce and a little more white sauce. Finish with sheets of lasagne. Cover these with the remainder of the white sauce and top with grated Parmesan.

8 Bake in a preheated oven, 375°F (190°C), for 35–40 minutes, or until browned on the top.

nutritional breakdown per serving: calories 665, protein 30g, fat 25g (saturated fat 22g), carbohydrate 87g

broccoli and mushroom lasagne with almonds

Lasagne is a splendid complete meal in itself and here almonds add texture and protein. Try to make the main sauces used, generally tomato and white sauce, well ahead of time. Both of these can be frozen.

serves 4

preparation: 15 minutes

cooking: 1½ hours

suitable for freezing

(Ca) (Fe)

1 pound (500g) broccoli, divided into flowerets
3 tablespoons/1½ ounces (40g) butter
½ cup/2 ounces (50g) sliced almonds
1 pound (500g) mushrooms, sliced if large

For the tomato sauce:

1 tablespoon olive oil
1 onion, chopped
1 garlic clove, crushed
14 ounces (398 milliliters) canned chopped
 tomatoes
½ teaspoon sugar
½ teaspoon salt

For the white sauce:

¼ cup (½ stick)/2 ounces (50g) butter
½ cup/2 ounces (50g) all-purpose flour
2½ cups/1 pint (600 milliliters) milk (low-fat
 used for nutrient content)
salt and freshly ground black pepper

9 sheets of lasagne (or enough to make 3 layers)
freshly grated Parmesan
salt and freshly ground black pepper

1 Steam the broccoli over a saucepan of boiling water for 2 minutes. Drain and set aside.

2 Melt the butter in a large skillet, add the almonds, and cook until brown, then add the mushrooms and cook until quite soft. Stir in the broccoli with the mushrooms, then remove the skillet from the heat.

3 To make the tomato sauce, heat the oil in a saucepan and gently cook the onion and garlic until soft. Add the chopped tomatoes, sugar, and salt. Bring to a boil, then cover the pan, and simmer for 35 minutes.

4 Combine the tomato sauce with the broccoli and mushroom mixture and season well.

5 To make the white sauce, melt the butter in a saucepan and stir in the flour. Cook for 2 minutes, then pour in the milk, and bring to a boil, stirring constantly. Cook for 2 minutes, then season to taste.

6 To assemble the dish, prepare the lasagne according to the packet instructions.

7 Lightly oil a large ovenproof dish, put in a little of the broccoli mixture, then cover with 3 sheets lasagne, cover with half the remaining broccoli mixture, and cover with lasagne. Repeat this layer with the remaining broccoli and lasagne, then pour the white sauce on top.

8 Sprinkle the Parmesan over the top and bake in a preheated oven, 375°F (190°C), for 35 minutes, or until golden brown. Serve hot.

nutritional breakdown per serving: calories 670, protein 26g, fat 35g (saturated fat 16g), carbohydrate 68g

polenta

Polenta can be served just boiled, although when cooked like this, it is fairly bland and somewhat lacking in texture. If this doesn't appeal, it is worth trying polenta baked or broiled. This type of polenta can then be eaten with any of the sauces at the beginning of this chapter (see pages 210–12).

Polenta can also be layered and baked with sauces in a similar fashion to lasagne. This type of recipe makes a substantial but appealing supper dish, and it is easy to make vegan versions.

Polenta is also good served as a quick snack fried with a cheese filling. This "sandwich" has a crisp outside with a succulent melting center.

Brands of polenta vary in texture and consequently may absorb differing amounts of water. Be guided by the instructions on the packet. The amount you need will also vary depending on whether it is to be the main part of a meal or a snack—150–350g (5–12 ounces) serves 4 people, the smaller quantity for a light meal and the larger amount for a more substantial dish.

polenta cheese squares

These succulent squares can be a snack or light meal for 4 people or a main course for 2. Serve them plainly or with a simple tomato sauce, roasted vegetables, broiled tomatoes, or salad greens.

serves 4

preparation: 15 minutes

cooking: 30 minutes

(Ca)

2½ cups/1 pint (600 milliliters) water
1 cup/5 ounces (150g) medium-grind cornmeal or polenta, plus a little extra for dusting
½ teaspoon salt
2 tablespoons finely chopped sun-dried tomatoes
6 ounces (175g) fontina or Gruyère, sliced
2 eggs, lightly beaten
2 cups/4 ounces (125g) fresh bread crumbs
sunflower oil for shallow-frying

1 To make the polenta, bring the water to a boil in a large saucepan. Stir in the cornmeal, salt, and sun-dried tomatoes. Stir constantly until the mixture thickens, then continue stirring over medium heat for 5 minutes, or according to the packet instructions.

2 Spoon out the cooked polenta onto a large board and flatten with the back of a spoon or a spatula into a rough oblong about 8 x 12 inches (20 x 30cm). The polenta should be slightly less than ½ inch (1cm) thick. Let cool.

3 Cut the polenta into 2-inch (5-cm) squares. Sandwich a slice of cheese between a pair of polenta squares. Dust with a little extra cornmeal, then dip in lightly beaten egg, and coat with bread crumbs.

4 Heat the oil in a large skillet until it will sizzle a piece of bread dropped in. Fry the polenta squares for about 3–4 minutes on each side. Drain on paper towels. Serve immediately.

nutritional breakdown per serving: calories 533, protein 22g, fat 31g (saturated fat 11g), carbohydrate 43g

baked polenta with rich tomato and mascarpone sauce

Both the sauce and polenta can be cooked well in advance, leaving you an easy assembly and a dish that is ready in 20 minutes. This makes a good family supper served with green beans, broccoli, or a colorful salad.

serves 4
preparation: 15 minutes
cooking: 1–1 ¼ hours
suitable for freezing
(Ca)

4 cups/1¾ pints (1 liter) water
1⅓ cups/7 ounces (200g) medium-grind
   cornmeal or polenta

For the sauce:
2 tablespoons olive oil
1 onion, chopped
2 garlic cloves, crushed
1 red bell pepper, cored, deseeded, and chopped
generous 2 cups (500 milliliters) tomato purée
6 sun-dried tomatoes, finely chopped
2 tablespoons chopped basil
½ teaspoon ground cinnamon
½ cup/4 ounces (125g) mascarpone cheese

salt and freshly ground black pepper
2 tablespoons freshly grated Parmesan

1   Bring the water to a boil in a large saucepan, add the polenta with ½ teaspoon salt, and stir well for 5–10 minutes, until the mixture has thickened. Alternatively, follow the packet instructions.

2   Pour the polenta into a greased dish and let cool before cutting into bite-size squares.

3   To make the sauce, heat the oil in a saucepan and cook the onion and garlic until soft.

4   Using a blender or food processor, purée the bell pepper with the tomato purée, sun-dried tomatoes, and basil. Add this purée to the pan of onions, add the cinnamon, and stir well.

5   Bring the mixture to a boil, then simmer, partially covered, for 30–40 minutes over low heat. Cool slightly, then stir in the mascarpone. Season with salt and pepper to taste.

6   To assemble the dish, spoon a thin layer of sauce into a lightly greased shallow gratin dish. Cover with squares of polenta, add another layer of sauce, and more polenta, finishing with the sauce.

7   Sprinkle the grated Parmesan on top and bake in a preheated oven, 400°F (200°C), for 20 minutes, or until the Parmesan is well browned and the sauce heated through. Serve hot.

nutritional breakdown per serving: calories 598, protein 11g, fat 41g (saturated fat 13g), carbohydrate 49g

rosemary polenta with eggplant and gorgonzola

Fresh rosemary makes a fragrant addition to the polenta, leaving it attractively flecked with green. Serve it on its own as an elegant light snack or with Fennel and Red Bell Pepper Salad with Lemon and Oregano Dressing (see page 308) for a main meal.

Although there are quite a number of stages when making this recipe, each step is very simple. The polenta, tomato concasse, and eggplant slices can be prepared in advance, so it can be just a question of assembly and last-minute broiling. If you can't get all the portions under the broiler at the same time, have the oven preheated and keep half warm in the oven while broiling the second batch.

serves 4

preparation: 20 minutes, plus salting

cooking: 30 minutes

nutritional breakdown per serving: calories 400, protein 10g, fat 26g (saturated fat 11g), carbohydrate 33g

1 eggplant, thickly sliced
1 tablespoon finely chopped rosemary
1 cup/5 ounces (150g) medium-grind cornmeal or polenta
3 cups/1¼ pints (750 milliliters) water
1 tablespoon olive oil, plus extra for frying
1 small onion, chopped
1 garlic clove, crushed
4 tomatoes, skinned and chopped
1 tablespoon tomato paste
7 ounces (200g) gorgonzola, sliced
salt and freshly ground black pepper

1 Put the eggplant slices in a large colander and sprinkle with salt. Let stand for 20–30 minutes. Combine the rosemary with the polenta.

2 Bring the water to a boil in a large saucepan, add the polenta with ½ teaspoon salt, and stir well for 5–10 minutes, until the mixture has thickened. Alternatively, follow the packet instructions. Pour the polenta into a greased dish and let cool.

3 To make the tomato concasse, heat the oil in a saucepan and cook the onion and garlic until soft. Add the skinned chopped tomatoes and tomato paste. Cook for 5 minutes.

4 Cool the tomato concasse slightly then, using a blender or food processor, purée until smooth. Strain for an extra smooth finish and season.

5 Pat the eggplant slices dry with paper towels, then fry the slices in olive oil until well browned and soft.

6 To assemble the dish, cut the cooled polenta into large rounds using a (3-inch (7-cm) cutter, allowing for 2 rounds per person for a main course or 1 for a light snack.

7 Top each polenta round with a spoonful of the tomato concasse and 1–2 slices eggplant. Divide the gorgonzola between the portions and place them under a preheated hot broiler to cook until the cheese is thoroughly melted.

8 Transfer the polenta rounds to serving plates, using a spatula, then spoon on any residue of melted cheese. Serve immediately.

potato gnocchi

Popular in northern Italy, gnocchi are a type of dumpling made from a plain potato or semolina base and flavored with spinach, Swiss chard, or ricotta cheese. Gnocchi can be served with flavored butters, pesto, or a rich tomato sauce. They can be a light meal in themselves, especially if accompanied by a salad, or can be served as an appetizer followed by Strata (see page 184) or Mediterranean Galette (see page 358). A vegan version can be made without eggs but the mixture is more fragile.

Gnocchi are very quick to cook, but you must allow time for chilling the mixture and about 30 minutes for making it. It is worth getting the preparation done well ahead of time.

serves 4

preparation: 15 minutes, plus chilling

cooking: 25–30 minutes

suitable for freezing (after step 4)

1½ pounds (800g) mealy potatoes
1 egg, beaten
1¼–1½ cups/6–7 ounces (175–200g) bread flour
1 tablespoon olive oil
salt
flavored melted butter, pesto or a tomato sauce
  and freshly grated Parmesan

1 Cook the potatoes in their skins in a large saucepan of boiling salted water for about 20 minutes, or until soft. Drain. When cool enough to handle, drain and peel, then mash until smooth.

2 Beat in the egg and half the flour. Turn out onto a floured board and gradually add more flour, kneading lightly until you have a soft but not sticky dough.

3 Keep the board well floured while you roll pieces of the dough into long thick sausage shapes about 1 inch (2.5cm) thick. Cut each "rope" into pieces about 1 inch (2.5cm) long to make gnocchi.

4 Press the gnocchi against the back of a fork to make the traditional indentations, then place on a floured tray. Cover with a floured cloth and chill for at least 30 minutes.

5 To cook the gnocchi, bring a large pan of salted water to a boil. Add the olive oil and reduce the heat to a gentle simmer since fast boiling will destroy the shape of the gnocchi.

6 Add the gnocchi to the water in batches, cooking them for 2–3 minutes. They should float to the surface when they are almost cooked. Remove from the water with a slotted spoon and keep warm in a buttered serving dish while you cook the remainder.

7 Have ready a flavored melted butter or sauce. When all the gnocchi are cooked, pour the melted butter or sauce over them and sprinkle with grated Parmesan. Serve hot.

nutritional breakdown per serving (without butter or sauce):
calories 342, protein 11g, fat 5g (saturated fat 1g), carbohydrate 67g

risotto

A good risotto should be creamy but not sticky. This is achieved by cooking the rice slowly and stirring in the wine and stock almost continually until the liquid is absorbed. It is best to use a special type of rice, risotto rice (see page 87), which is a plump robust grain that can withstand a good deal of stirring without breaking down. Although it is possible to make risotto-style dishes using short-grain brown rice, the end result is well flavored but lacks the silky characteristic of classic risotto.

mushroom risotto with tarragon

LEFTOVERS

Leftover risotto is perfect for making into little croquettes. The neatest way to do this is to gather up portions of rice in a little square of plastic wrap and press them into an oval shape between your hands. Alternatively, dampen your hands and shape the rice between your palms. Tuck a small piece of mozzarella inside each croquette, if you like. Roll the croquette in all-purpose flour, then beaten egg, then bread crumbs, and shallow-fry for 4–5 minutes, or until crisp all over.

Dried mushrooms add an intense underlying flavor to this simple risotto, while the tarragon cuts through the richness with a clean tang – a great combination. Serve this as a main course with side vegetables.

serves 4

| preparation: 15 minutes, plus soaking |
| cooking: 35 minutes |
| suitable for freezing |

¼ cup/½ ounce (15g) dried mushrooms
2½ cups/1 pint (600 milliliters) boiling water
¼ cup (½ stick)/2 ounces (50g) butter
2 shallots, finely chopped
1 garlic clove, crushed
2½ cups/6 ounces (175g) cremini mushrooms, thinly sliced
2 cups/8 ounces (250g) arborio rice
⅔ cup/¼ pint (150 milliliters) white wine
salt and freshly ground black pepper
1 tablespoon chopped tarragon
2 tablespoons freshly grated Parmesan

1 Soak the dried mushrooms in a bowl of a boiling water for at least 30 minutes. Drain through a fine strainer or coffee filter to remove any sediment and reserve the liquid as stock. Rinse the mushrooms and chop finely.

2 Melt 3 tablespoons/1½ ounces (40g) butter in a large saucepan or skillet and gently cook the shallots and garlic until soft. Add the sliced fresh mushrooms and cook until softened.

3 Add the rice and chopped dried mushrooms and stir until well coated with the butter. Add the wine and cook over low heat, stirring constantly until the liquid has been absorbed.

4 Add a third of the reserved mushroom stock. Keep stirring and cook until the stock is absorbed, then add a further third of the stock, and repeat this process, before adding the remaining stock. The rice should become thick and creamy but not sticky and should take 20–25 minutes to cook in total.

5 Season well with salt and pepper and add the remaining butter, the chopped tarragon, and grated Parmesan.

nutritional breakdown per serving: calories 383, protein 7g, fat 12g (saturated fat 8g), carbohydrate 59g

risotto with roasted squash

The melting flesh of squash combines brilliantly with creamy rice for a warmly colored risotto. Roasting the squash first brings out a very mellow flavor. This recipe could also be made with other winter squashes or with pumpkin. Serve with buttered leeks or steamed broccoli.

serves 4

preparation: 10 minutes

cooking: 1¼ hours

suitable for freezing

2 pounds (1kg) acorn squash, cut into large
   chunks and deseeded

3 tablespoons olive oil

2 tablespoons/1 ounce (25g) butter

1 onion, finely chopped

1 garlic clove, crushed

2 cups/8 ounces (250g) arborio rice

⅔ cup/¼ pint (150 milliliters) white wine

scant 2 cups/¾ pint (450 milliliters) hot
   Vegetable Stock (see page 144)

salt and freshly ground black pepper

1 tablespoon finely chopped flat leaf parsley,
   to garnish

freshly grated Parmesan, to serve

1 Put 1 tablespoon of the olive oil into a bowl and season well. Add the squash and mix well to coat. Reserve one-fourth of the squash for garnish.

2 Place the remaining squash in a roasting pan or on a baking sheet and cook in a preheated oven, 400°F (200°C), for 40 minutes, or until the outer skin looks brown and the flesh is soft. Let cool, remove skin, and chop coarsely.

3 To cook the risotto, heat the remaining olive oil with the butter in a large saucepan or skillet and gently cook the onion and garlic until translucent.

4 Add the rice, stir well until coated with the butter and oil, then pour in the white wine and cook gently until all the liquid has been absorbed.

5 Add the cooked squash and about one-third of the hot stock. Keep stirring and cook until the stock is absorbed, then add a further one-third of the stock, and repeat the process. Finally, add the remaining stock and stir less often. The whole process takes about 20–25 minutes and the rice should become thick and creamy. Season well with salt and pepper.

6 While the risotto is cooking, roast the remaining squash. Cut into fairly thin slices and coat with extra seasoned oil if necessary. Place in a roasting pan or on a baking sheet and roast at 400°F (200°C) for 25 minutes.

7 Use the slices to garnish the risotto and sprinkle with chopped parsley. Serve the grated Parmesan cheese separately.

nutritional breakdown per serving: calories 478, protein 8g, fat 15g (saturated fat 5g), carbohydrate 78g

sesame millet with pan-fried zucchini, asparagus, and avocado cream

VARIATION

To make a vegan version of this recipe, replace the avocado cream with Salsa Mexicana (see page 192).

This is a dish of wonderful contrasts with lightly textured millet, succulent vegetables, and creamy avocado topping. It stands on its own as a main course but could be served with an appetizer of Oyster Mushroom and Roast Almond Pâté (see page 165). Millet does not cook evenly so expect some crunchy grains when testing for doneness.

serves 4

preparation: 15 minutes

cooking: 25 minutes

(Fe)

1 teaspoon sunflower oil
1 teaspoon cumin seeds
7 ounces (200g) millet
2 tablespoons sesame seeds
3 cups/1¼ pints (750 milliliters) boiling water
salt and freshly ground black pepper

For the pan-fried vegetables:
2 tablespoons sunflower oil
6 scallions, chopped
1 red bell pepper, cored, deseeded, and thinly sliced
8 ounces (250g) asparagus, chopped
4 zucchini, sliced

For the topping:
1 ripe avocado
3–4 tablespoons crème fraîche
2 tablespoons chopped parsley

1 Heat the oil in a large saucepan and lightly toast the cumin seeds. Add the millet and sesame seeds and toast for 2 minutes.

2 Pour in the boiling water. Bring back to a boil, then cover the pan, and simmer for 20 minutes. Season well with salt and pepper.

3 Meanwhile, to cook the vegetables, heat the oil in a large skillet and gently cook the scallions. Add the red bell pepper, asparagus, and zucchini and cook over medium heat, stirring frequently, for 5–10 minutes, or until soft and browned. Season well with salt and pepper.

4 To make the topping, halve the avocado, remove the pit, and scoop the flesh into a bowl. Mash with the crème fraîche and mix in the parsley. Season to taste with salt and pepper.

5 When the millet is cooked, spoon it out onto warmed plates and cover with the pan-fried vegetables. Top with the avocado cream or serve it separately.

nutritional breakdown per serving: calories 373, protein 8g, fat 17g (saturated fat 8g), carbohydrate 45g

red rice with pan-fried squash, mushrooms, and pecan nuts

Warm russet colors and nutty flavors dominate this dish. Serve it on its own for a light meal or serve it with a contrasting green vegetable or salad greens. For a more substantial meal start with a creamy soup such as Celery Root and Emmental (see page 154).

serves 4

preparation: 10 minutes

cooking: 20 minutes

v

2 cups/8 ounces (250g) red rice
2 tablespoons sunflower oil
1 onion, chopped
1 pound (500g) butternut squash, peeled and chopped
1 pound (500g) mushrooms, quartered
1 cup/4 ounces (125g) pecans
salt and freshly ground black pepper

1 Place the rice in a large saucepan and bring it to a boil in double its volume of water. Cover the pan and simmer for 20 minutes or until soft.

2 Meanwhile, heat the oil in a large skillet and cook the onion until soft. Add the squash, mushrooms, and pecan nuts and increase the heat.

3 Cook the vegetables for 5–10 minutes, or until the squash is lightly colored and the mushrooms softened, then turn down the heat, and cook until the vegetables are tender. Season with salt and pepper.

4 Once the rice is cooked, drain well, then toss the pan-fried mixture with the rice, and serve hot.

nutritional breakdown per serving: calories 553, protein 11g, fat 29g (saturated fat 3g), carbohydrate 61g

VARIATION

This recipe could also be made with brown rice but the color is less intense.

bulgur with roasted eggplant, yellow bell pepper, and red onion

This easy supper dish can inspire many variations. Try different vegetables such as red bell pepper, fennel, or zucchini. Bulgur needs a sauce or dressing to counterbalance the dry texture of the grains. In this recipe I've created a quick but nutritious sauce using tahini. You could use Chunky Guacamole (see page 192) or Salsa Mexicana (see page 192), instead.

serves 4

preparation: 15 minutes, plus salting

cooking: 20–25 minutes

(Fe) 𝒱

2 eggplant, cubed
salt
⅓ cup (80 milliliters) olive oil
freshly ground black pepper

2 yellow bell peppers, cored, deseeded, and sliced
1 red onion, sliced
generous 1 cup/7 ounces (200g) bulgur
1¾ cups (400 milliliters) boiling water
2 tablespoons finely chopped cilantro leaves

For the sauce:
¼ cup (4 tablespoons) tahini
¼ cup (50 milliliters) water
juice of 1 lemon
1–2 tablespoons olive oil
1 garlic clove, crushed
1 teaspoon ground coriander, dry-roasted
1 tablespoon shoyu or soy sauce

1 Place the cubes of eggplant in a large colander and sprinkle with salt, then let stand for 20–30 minutes. Pat dry with paper towels.

2 Pour the oil into a large bowl and season well with salt and pepper. Mix the salted eggplant cubes, yellow bell peppers, and onion in the seasoned oil and spread on a baking sheet. Roast the vegetables in a preheated oven, 400°F (200°C), for 20–25 minutes, or until well browned. Turn the vegetables over once or twice during cooking.

3 Meanwhile, place the bulgur in a large bowl, add ½ teaspoon salt, and pour in the boiling water. Let soak for 15–20 minutes. Drain if necessary. Stir in the cilantro and adjust the seasoning to taste.

4 To make the sauce, mix the tahini in a bowl with the water until well blended. Add the lemon juice, olive oil, crushed garlic, dry-roasted coriander, and shoyu or soy sauce and mix well. Season to taste with salt and pepper.

5 Spoon the bulgur into a large shallow serving dish and pile all the vegetables on top. Serve immediately with the tahini sauce.

nutritional breakdown per serving: calories 550, protein 13g, fat 35g (saturated fat 5g), carbohydrate 49g

layered bulgur with tomatoes and feta

This is a very easy meal that takes only a matter of minutes to prepare. Serve with salad greens or steamed green vegetables.

serves 4
preparation: 10 minutes
cooking: 10 minutes
(Fe)

1⅓ cups/8 ounces (250g) bulgur
salt
scant 2 cups/¾ pint (450 milliliters) boiling water
4–5 plum tomatoes, skinned and thickly sliced
freshly ground black pepper
1 small red chile, deseeded and finely chopped
1–2 tablespoons olive oil
6 ounces (200g) feta (drained weight)
6 pitted black olives, chopped

1 Place the bulgur in a large bowl with ½ teaspoon salt. Cover with boiling water and let stand for 5 minutes, then drain.

2 Spoon the bulgur into a lightly oiled flameproof dish. Cover with the tomato slices and season well with salt and pepper.

3 Sprinkle the chile on top, then drizzle with the olive oil. Cook under a preheated broiler for 5 minutes.

4 Crumble the feta on top and sprinkle with the chopped olives. Return the dish to the broiler for 5 minutes more, or until the feta has melted and is well browned. Serve hot.

nutritional breakdown per serving: calories 409, protein 15g, fat 11g (saturated fat 1g), carbohydrate 51g

> **SKINNING TOMATOES**
>
> To skin tomatoes, cut a cross in the end of each tomato and drop them in a bowl of boiling water. Leave for 1 minute, then remove with a slotted spoon and peel off the skins.

green rice with chile

This is a spiced rice with a delicate green color, inspired by Mexican cuisine. It is great as an accompaniment for casseroles such as Red Bean and Lentil Chili (see page 240). Leftovers can be stuffed into green bell peppers and baked with tomato sauce.

serves 4

preparation: 20 minutes

cooking: 55 minutes

suitable for freezing

𝓋

1 large green bell pepper
2 mild green chiles
3 garlic cloves, crushed
1 cup/1 ounce (25g) cilantro leaves
2 tablespoons olive oil
1 onion, finely chopped
2 cups/8 ounces (250g) brown rice
2 cups (475 milliliters) hot Vegetable Stock
  (see page 144)
salt and freshly ground black pepper

1 Place the bell pepper on a baking sheet or in a roasting pan and roast in a preheated oven, 400°F (200°C), for 25 minutes, or until well blistered and soft. Place in a plastic bag, seal, and set aside for 10 minutes, then peel, and remove the seeds.

2 Roast the chiles for 10 minutes at 400°F (200°C). Place in a plastic bag and set aside for 10 minutes, then peel, and remove the seeds.

3 Using a blender or food processor, process the roasted bell pepper, chiles, garlic, and cilantro leaves to make a coarse green paste.

4 Heat the oil in a large saucepan and gently cook the onion until soft. Add the rice and stir to coat well with the oil. Mix in the green bell pepper paste and pour in the boiling stock.

5 Stir once or twice and bring to a boil, then cover the pan, and simmer for 25 minutes, or until the rice is cooked and all the stock has been absorbed. Season with salt and pepper toward the end of cooking.

nutritional breakdown per serving: calories 290, protein 5g, fat 8g (saturated fat 1g), carbohydrate 54g

paella with many vegetables

This may seem a long list of ingredients but this dish is straightforward to make. Do use a range of vegetables as they give the paella plenty of texture, color, and flavor. Saffron, tomato, and paprika create warm undertones. You can, of course, use a number of other vegetables, such as fava beans, fine beans, or colored bell peppers, as well as adding cashew nuts or sliced egg for extra protein. This dish needs serving with nothing more than a crisp salad.

serves 4
preparation: 15 minutes
cooking: 50 minutes
𝑣

2 tablespoons olive oil
1 onion, finely chopped
2 garlic cloves, crushed
1 teaspoon fennel seeds
3 celery stalks, finely chopped
scant ½ cup (100 milliliters) white wine
2 cups/8 ounces (250g) short-grain rice
pinch of saffron, steeped in 2 tablespoons hot
    water for 5 minutes
1 teaspoon paprika
2½ cups/1 pint (600 milliliters) hot Vegetable
    Stock (see page 144) or water
3 tablespoons tomato paste
6 plum tomatoes, skinned and chopped
1¼ cups/5 ounces (150g) peas, fresh or frozen

5 ounces (150g) asparagus, coarsely chopped
5 ounces (150g) baby corn cobs,
    coarsely chopped
2 tablespoons chopped parsley
black olives, to garnish
wedges of lemon, to serve

1 Heat the olive oil in a large saucepan or skillet and gently cook the onion and garlic until soft.

2 Add the fennel seeds and celery and cook for 4–5 minutes. Pour in the white wine and simmer until most of the liquid has evaporated.

3 Add the rice and stir well. Add the steeped saffron water to the rice with the paprika, stock, tomato paste, and fresh tomatoes. Bring the mixture to a boil, then season well, and simmer for 30 minutes, or until the rice is cooked.

4 About 5 minutes before the end of cooking add the peas, asparagus, corn, and parsley.

5 Just before serving, stir in black olives and serve with wedges of lemon.

nutritional breakdown per serving: calories 390, protein 11g, fat 8g (saturated fat 1g), carbohydrate 70g

almond and lemon pilaf

A simple rice dish that can be a meal in itself, accompanied by steamed green beans or peas and a bowl of plain or seasoned yogurt. Alternatively, add extra vegetables to the pilaf itself if you want to keep it a meal in one pan. Mushrooms, bell peppers, or celery could all be added. This recipe also makes a good accompaniment to Mixed Lentil Dhal (see page 250) and Spiced Vegetable Fritters (see page 168).

Although this dish is suitable for freezing, it should not be frozen for more than 1 month because of the quantity of spices, which can deteriorate in flavor.

serves 4

preparation: 10 minutes

cooking: 40 minutes

suitable for freezing

v

2 tablespoons olive oil

1 onion, finely chopped

2 garlic cloves, crushed

¾ cup/3 ounces (75g) blanched almonds, roughly chopped

1 teaspoons paprika

1 teaspoon ground cumin

1 teaspoon ground coriander

½ teaspoon ground cinnamon

2 tablespoons water

2 teaspoons grated fresh ginger

3 carrots, finely chopped

2 cups/8 ounces (250g) basmati rice

2½ cups/1 pint (600 milliliters) boiling water

juice and zest of 1 lemon

salt and freshly ground black pepper

1 Heat the oil in a large saucepan or skillet and gently cook the onion and garlic. Add the chopped almonds and cook until lightly toasted.

2 Mix the paprika, cumin, coriander, and cinnamon to a paste with the 2 tablespoons of water. Add the paste to the pan with the ginger and stir well. Cook for 2–3 minutes.

3 Add the carrots and cook for 2–3 minutes more, stirring well. Then add the rice and stir in.

4 Pour in the boiling water and the lemon juice and zest. Bring to a boil, stirring once or twice. Cover the pan and cook over a low heat for 25–30 minutes.

5 At the end of the cooking time the water should have been absorbed and the rice soft. Season with salt and pepper to taste and fluff with a fork before serving.

nutritional breakdown per serving: calories 415, protein 10g, fat 17g (saturated fat 2g), carbohydrate 56g

spiced mushroom rice

Warm and spicy, this easy rice dish needs little attention once the spices have been cooked. Soaking rice not only shortens the cooking time but also reduces the amount of water needed. Varieties of basmati may differ so you may need to adjust quantities slightly. Serve on its own with a couple of simple accompaniments, such as natural yogurt with cucumber or Spiced Vegetable Fritters (see page 168).

serves 4

preparation: 10 minutes, plus soaking

cooking: 35–40 minutes

3 tablespoons/1½ ounces (40g) clarified butter
1 onion, finely chopped
2 garlic cloves, crushed
½ chile, finely chopped
1-inch (2.5-cm) piece of fresh ginger, grated
1⅔ cups/4 ounces (125g) mushrooms, chopped
salt
2 cups/8 ounces (250g) brown basmati rice, soaked for 2 hours
1¼ cups/½ pint (300 milliliters) boiling water
freshly ground black pepper

1 Melt the butter in a large saucepan or skillet and cook the onion, garlic, chile, and ginger together, stirring well.

2 Add the mushrooms, ½ teaspoon salt, and the drained, soaked rice. Cook for 5 minutes.

3 Add the water and bring to a boil. Cover the pan with a close-fitting lid, turn down the heat, and simmer for 25 minutes without stirring. At the end of this time all the water should have been absorbed and the rice cooked. If necessary, cook for a few minutes without the lid if there is excess water.

4 Stir with a fork, add salt and pepper to taste, and serve immediately.

PAN LIDS

If your pan doesn't have a close-fitting lid, try tying a dish towel around the outside of a lid since this can make it fit more snugly.

nutritional breakdown per serving: calories 308, protein 5g, fat 10g (saturated fat 6g), carbohydrate 52g

wild rice with hazelnuts, carrots, and artichokes

This slender mahogany-colored grain with its faintly salty tang combines well with the sweet nutty flavors of hazelnuts and artichokes. Carrots add a splash of color and the end result is a lightly textured dish, great on its own or served with a frittata for a more substantial meal. Use fresh artichoke hearts if you can. Otherwise, buy good-quality canned or marinated ones.

serves 4
preparation: 10 minutes
cooking: 50–55 minutes
v

2 cups/8 ounces (250g) wild rice
2 tablespoons olive oil
1 red onion, finely chopped
1 garlic clove, crushed
6–8 artichoke hearts, halved, or 10–12 canned
    artichoke hearts
½ cup/2 ounces (50g) roasted hazelnuts,
    coarsely chopped
4 carrots, cut into julienne strips
2 tablespoons shoyu or soy sauce
2 tablespoons lemon juice
2 tablespoons chopped cilantro leaves
salt and freshly ground black pepper

1 Cook the rice in a large saucepan of boiling salted water for 35–40 minutes, or until cooked. Drain and keep warm.

2 Heat the oil in a large skillet and gently cook the onion and garlic until soft.

3 Add the artichoke hearts, hazelnuts, and carrot and cook over high heat until lightly browned. Then reduce the heat and cook for 5–6 minutes, or until the carrots are slightly soft.

4 Stir in the shoyu or soy sauce and lemon juice and season well with salt and pepper. Stir in the warm rice and cilantro. Adjust the seasoning to taste and serve the rice hot or warm.

nutritional breakdown per serving: calories 397, protein 10g, fat 15g (saturated fat 2g), carbohydrate 57g

couscous with spiced bean curd and mixed bell pepper sauce

Couscous is a delicate grain that needs a sauce or moist dressing; otherwise, it can seem dry. Here it is served with a mildly spiced mix of bell peppers and bean curd. A big advantage of bean curd is that it soaks up flavors very quickly, as well as giving a nutritional boost to a dish. Put it in at the beginning so that it can absorb the flavors and always mix it in carefully or the pieces may break up. Serve this dish with a contrasting vegetable or salad.

serves 4

preparation: 10 minutes

cooking: 55 minutes

(Ca) (Fe) 𝒱

2 tablespoons sunflower oil
1 onion, finely chopped
2 garlic cloves, crushed
½ teaspoon cumin seeds
½ teaspoon ground coriander
¼ teaspoon ground cinnamon
8 ounces (200g) bean curd, cut into
　　bite-size pieces
2 red bell peppers, cored, deseeded, and
　　finely chopped
2 green bell peppers, cored, deseeded, and
　　finely chopped
4 carrots, chopped
generous 2 cups (500 milliliters) tomato purée

½ cup/2 ounces (50g) currants
salt and freshly ground black pepper
1⅓ cups/8 ounces (250g) couscous
scant 2 cups/¾ pint (450 milliliters) boiling water

1　Heat the oil in a large saucepan and gently cook the onion, then add the garlic, cumin, coriander, and cinnamon and cook for a few minutes.

2　Add the bean curd to the pan and mix it in carefully but well. Add the red and green bell peppers and carrots and cook slowly for 10 minutes.

3　Pour in the tomato purée, add the currants, and bring the mixture to a boil. Cover the pan and simmer for 35–40 minutes. Season with salt and pepper to taste.

4　Just before serving, tip the couscous into a large bowl, add ½ teaspoon salt, and the boiling water. Soak for 5 minutes, then fluff with a fork, and spoon onto individual plates or a large serving platter. Top with the spiced bean curd and bell pepper sauce and serve hot.

nutritional breakdown per serving: calories 356, protein 13g, fat 10g (saturated fat 1g), carbohydrate 56g

buckwheat with leeks and wild mushrooms

Buckwheat has a distinctive earthy flavor and pleasant character, and this dark robust dish is great on colder evenings. Contrasting vegetables such as steamed carrots or other roots such as beets and parsnips or Butternut Squash and Carrot Purée with Nutmeg and Mascarpone (see page 286) are ideal accompaniments.

serves 4

preparation: 15 minutes, plus soaking

cooking: 35 minutes

suitable for freezing

𝒱

¼ cup/½ ounces (15g) dried mushrooms
1¼ cups/½ pint (300 milliliters) boiling water
1¼ cups/½ pint (300 milliliters) hot water or
    Vegetable Stock (see page 144)
2 tablespoons sunflower oil
1 onion, finely chopped
2 garlic cloves, crushed
1 teaspoon grated fresh ginger
2 leeks, sliced
scant 1 cup/6 ounces (175g) buckwheat
salt and freshly ground black pepper

1 Soak the dried mushrooms in a bowl of a boiling water for 15 minutes. Drain, reserving the soaking liquid, then chop the mushrooms finely.

2 Heat the oil in a large saucepan and gently cook the onion and garlic until soft.

3 Add the ginger and cook for 2–3 minutes, then add the leeks and chopped mushrooms. Cook for 5 minutes, or until the leeks are beginning to soften. Add the buckwheat and stir well.

4 Add hot water or vegetable stock to the reserved mushroom liquid to make 2½ cups/1 pint (600 milliliters) stock. Pour this over the buckwheat and bring to a boil, then cover the pan, and simmer for 20 minutes, or until the buckwheat is cooked and the water has been absorbed.

5 Season well and serve hot.

nutritional breakdown per serving: calories 243, protein 5g, fat 7g (saturated fat 1g), carbohydrate 44g

millet pilaf with pine nuts

Millet works well in pilaf-style dishes although you should eat it as soon as it is cooked since it tends to become rather solid on standing. The grains do not always cook evenly but a light crunchy texture is quite pleasant. Serve this on its own or with Garbanzo Bean Curry (see page 247) or with a stir-fry of contrasting vegetables.

serves 4
preparation: 10 minutes
cooking: 35–40 minutes
𝑣

2 tablespoons sunflower oil
generous 1 cup/7 ounces (200g) millet
½ cup/2 ounces (50g) pine nuts
1 teaspoon coriander seeds, lightly crushed
½ teaspoon cardamom seeds, lightly crushed
1 onion, finely chopped
1 garlic clove, crushed
½ teaspoon finely grated fresh ginger
12 ounces (400g) carrots, finely chopped
3 cups/1¼ pints (750 milliliters) boiling water
1 red bell pepper, cored, deseeded, and
    finely chopped
1½ cups/8 ounces (250g) green beans, chopped
salt and freshly ground black pepper

1 Using 1 teaspoon of oil, toast the millet and pine nuts in a large saucepan for 2–3 minutes, then remove from the pan.

2 Add the remaining oil to the pan, and fry the coriander and cardamom seeds until just toasted. Add the onion, garlic, and ginger and cook until soft, then add the carrot, and cook for 2–3 minutes.

3 Return the millet and pine nuts to the pan and stir well. Pour in the boiling water and bring back to a boil. Cover the pan and cook for 15 minutes over low heat.

4 Add the red bell pepper and green beans to the pan, but do not stir in. Cover the pan and cook for 10 minutes more.

5 Season well with salt and pepper and fluff the millet with a fork, mixing in the red bell pepper and green beans, which should have steamed on the top. Serve the pilaf immediately.

nutritional breakdown per serving: calories 382, protein 7g, fat 16g (saturated fat 1g), carbohydrate 52g

red bean and lentil chili

Chili bean casseroles, with their warm flavors and rich hues, have deservedly become a classic vegetarian staple. The secret is to include many different textures by using a variety of beans and lentils—use more than two types if you like—and a range of vegetables. I add bulgur because it absorbs the liquid and thickens the dish without making it heavy. Be sure to cook the spices well at the beginning, otherwise, the casserole will have a raw taste. Add more chili to suit your temperament! Serve this chili with a choice of the suggested toppings, as well as rice, baked potato, corn bread, or soft tortillas.

serves 4

preparation: 10 minutes

cooking: about 1¼ hours

suitable for freezing

(Fe) 𝒱

3 tablespoons olive oil
1 onion, coarsely chopped
2 garlic cloves, crushed
½–1 teaspoon chili powder
2 teaspoons cumin seeds
1 cinnamon stick
2 celery stalks, sliced
3 carrots, chopped
1 red bell pepper, cored, deseeded, and chopped
2 cups/8 ounces (250g) cooked brown lentils
1⅔ cups/8 ounces (250g) cooked red kidney beans
generous 2 cups (500 milliliters) tomato purée
1¼ cups/½ pint (300 milliliters) Vegetable Stock (see page 144)
1⅓ cups/2 ounces (50g) bulgur
salt and freshly ground black pepper
sour cream or crème fraîche, 1–2 tablespoons chopped cilantro leaves and grated cheese to serve

1 Heat the oil in a large saucepan and gently cook the onion and garlic until soft but not colored.

2 Add the chili powder, cumin seeds, and cinnamon to the pan and fry for 2 minutes. Add the celery, carrots, and red bell pepper and cook slowly for 7–10 minutes.

3 Add the lentils and beans and mix well. Pour in the bottled strained tomatoes and stock and bring the mixture to a boil. Season well, cover the pan, and simmer for 40–50 minutes, stirring occasionally.

4 Add the bulgur and cook for 10 minutes more, or until the bulgur is soft. Adjust the seasoning and serve hot.

nutritional breakdown per serving: calories 310, protein 14g, fat 10g (saturated fat 1g), carbohydrate 43g

cooking legumes

A 13-ounce (400g) can contains approximately 8 ounces (250g) beans, lentils, or garbanzos. To produce approximately 8 ounces (250g) cooked weight of beans, garbanzos, or lentils, you will need 4 ounces (125g) of the dried legumes. Dried beans and garbanzos need to be soaked in a bowl of cold water for at least 4 hours, then drained, and boiled fiercely in a saucepan of fresh water for 10 minutes, before being cooked over reduced heat until soft. Lentils do not need soaking but should be boiled in plenty of water for 10 minutes, then simmered until soft. It is probably worth cooking a larger quantity of legumes and freezing them for use in other recipes. See pages 91–92 for more information on cooking legumes.

sweet potato stew

This is a warming stew, both in flavor and color. It is enriched with peanut butter, which rounds out the overall taste and means that the cooking time can be quite short. This stew could be served with corn bread, rice, or whole-wheat bread. Other quick-cooking vegetables could be added, such as green beans, zucchini, or fresh peas.

serves 4

preparation: 15 minutes

cooking: 35–40 minutes

𝒱

2 tablespoons sunflower oil
1 onion, finely chopped
1 garlic clove, crushed
1 teaspoon caraway seeds
1 green chile, deseeded and chopped
2 celery stalks, sliced
10 ounces (300g) sweet potato, cubed
2 red bell peppers, cored, deseeded, and chopped
6 ounces (175g) baby corn cobs, chopped
generous 2 cups (500 milliliters) tomato purée
scant 1 cup (200 milliliters) Vegetable Stock (see page 144)
1–2 tablespoons smooth peanut butter
salt and freshly ground black pepper

1 Heat the oil in a large saucepan or flameproof casserole and gently cook the onion and garlic until soft.

2 Add the caraway seeds and green chile and cook for 2–3 minutes.

3 Add all the vegetables and cook for 5 minutes, stirring occasionally, so as to coat all the vegetables well with the chile and onion mixture.

4 Pour in the tomato purée and stock and bring to a boil. Cover the pan and cook for 20 minutes.

5 Remove 1–2 tablespoons of liquid from the pan and mix in a small bowl with the peanut butter, then return this to the stew. Season with salt and pepper to taste and serve hot.

NUT BUTTER

Nut and seed butters, such as peanut butter, can be used to enrich and thicken stews, sauces, or dressings. Always mix them first into a runny consistency with a little of the cooking liquid; otherwise, they are quite tricky to blend in thoroughly.

nutritional breakdown per serving: calories 245, protein 7g, fat 7g (saturated fat 2g), carbohydrate 34g

fava and garbanzo bean tagine

Tagine is the North African word for a slowly simmered stew or casserole and this recipe uses the aromatic spices characteristic of that cuisine. You can add extra vegetables, such as okra, cauliflower, or green beans, or even a handful of slivered dried apricots or dark raisins if you like a fruit and vegetable combination. Use fresh fava beans, which are delicious, if you can; otherwise, frozen or canned are perfectly acceptable. Serve this dish with couscous or bulgur.

serves 4
preparation: 15 minutes
cooking: 1 hour 15 minutes
suitable for freezing
(Fe) v

2 tablespoons sunflower oil
1 onion, finely chopped
3 garlic cloves, crushed
2 teaspoons grated fresh ginger
2 teaspoons ground cumin
2 teaspoons ground coriander
½ teaspoon ground cinnamon
2 red bell peppers, cored, deseeded, and
   finely chopped
2⅔ cups/13 ounces (400g) fava beans
1⅓ cups/8 ounces (250g) cooked garbanzo beans
generous 2 cups (500 milliliters) tomato purée
⅔ cup/¼ pint (150 milliliters) Vegetable Stock
   (see page 144)
2 tablespoons tomato paste
2 bay leaves
salt and freshly ground black pepper
chopped cilantro leaves or parsley, to garnish

1 Heat the oil in a large saucepan or flameproof casserole and cook the onion and garlic gently for 4–5 minutes, or until soft.

2 Add the ginger, cumin, coriander, and cinnamon and fry for a few minutes. Then add the bell peppers, fava beans, and garbanzo beans and cook very slowly for about 5–10 minutes, until just beginning to soften.

3 Pour in the tomato purée and vegetable stock and stir in the tomato paste. Add the bay leaves and season well with salt and pepper.

4 Bring the mixture to a boil, then cover the pan, and simmer gently for at least 1 hour. Adjust the seasoning and serve hot, garnished with chopped cilantro or parsley.

nutritional breakdown per serving: calories 238, protein 13g, fat 9g (saturated fat 1g), carbohydrate 28g

cider casserole with new potatoes

Tart apple and hard cider impart a clean flavor to this light vegetable casserole. New potatoes add a distinct bite, but you can use chunks of regular potato when new potatoes are out of season. This casserole is great served with chunks of rustic bread and a glass of hard cider.

serves 4

preparation: 15 minutes

cooking: about 1¼ hours

suitable for freezing

2 tablespoons sunflower oil

1 onion, chopped

1 leek, sliced

2 celery stalks, sliced

4 carrots, finely chopped

4 zucchini, finely chopped

1 pound (500g) new potatoes

1 tart dessert or cooking apple, cored and
    finely chopped

1 cup (250 milliliters) hard cider

1 cup (250 milliliters) Vegetable Stock
    (see page 144)

1 cup (250 milliliters) heavy cream

2 tablespoons chopped parsley

salt and freshly ground black pepper

1   Heat the oil in a large saucepan or flameproof casserole and gently cook the onion until soft.

2   Add the leek and celery and cook for 4–5 minutes more. Add the carrots, zucchini, and new potatoes and cook over low heat until just beginning to soften—this takes about 10 minutes.

3   Add the apple and pour in the hard cider, stock, and cream. Season well with salt and pepper and bring to a boil, then simmer for 45–50 minutes, or until all the vegetables are tender.

4   Stir in the parsley and adjust the seasoning to taste.

nutritional breakdown per serving: calories 503, protein 6g, fat 37g (saturated fat 20g), carbohydrate 36g

country casserole with spiced cheese dumplings

This tasty casserole is made from simple ingredients, which benefit from slow cooking. The leeks added late in the cooking process accentuate the onion flavor. Dumplings add extra nutrients and substance and are easy to make at the last minute. Garnish with extra grated cheese. The casserole is a meal in itself but you could serve a simple green side vegetable with it if you like.

serves 4	
preparation: 15–20 minutes	
cooking: 1½ hours	
suitable for freezing (without dumplings)	

2 tablespoons sunflower oil
1 onion, finely chopped
2 celery stalks, finely chopped
2–3 carrots, chopped
1 turnip, chopped
1 small rutabaga or sweet potato, chopped
generous 2 cups (500 milliliters) tomato purée
1¼ cups/½ pint (300 milliliters) Vegetable Stock
 (see page 144) or water

For the dumplings:
1 cup/4 ounces (125g) whole-wheat flour
2½ teaspoons baking powder
2 tablespoons/1 ounce (25g) vegetable
 margarine
½ cup/2 ounces (50g) grated cheese
½ teaspoon dried mustard powder
½ teaspoon paprika
salt and freshly ground black pepper
¼ cup (50 milliliters) low-fat milk

2 leeks, finely chopped
2–3 tablespoons chopped parsley, to garnish

1 Heat the oil in a large saucepan or flameproof casserole and gently cook the onion until soft.

2 Add the celery, carrots, turnip, and rutabaga to the pan. Cook slowly for about 10 minutes, stirring well.

3 Pour in the tomato purée and stock. Bring to a boil and season well, then cover the pan, and simmer gently for 50 minutes.

4 To make the dumplings, tip the flour and baking powder into a large bowl and rub in the fat until the mixture resembles fine bread crumbs. Stir in the grated cheese, mustard powder, paprika, and salt and pepper to taste, then pour in the milk and mix quickly into a soft dough. (The dumplings could also be made in a food processor, if you like.)

5 Add the leeks to the casserole then add spoonfuls of dumpling mixture, making about 8 dumplings. Let the casserole simmer, uncovered, for about 20 minutes, basting the dumplings occasionally.

6 Adjust the seasoning and serve, garnished with chopped parsley.

nutritional breakdown per serving: calories 328, protein 11g, fat 17g (saturated fat 6g), carbohydrate 35g

bean curd goulash with eggplant and mushrooms

This is a well-flavored supper dish. Bean curd adds to the nutritional value of the dish, as well as absorbing flavors from the cooking liquid—in this case the classic goulash spices of paprika and caraway. Top the goulash with sour cream or extra silken bean curd blended with lemon juice if you want to avoid dairy products, and serve with baked potatoes, rice, or millet.

serves 4
preparation: 15 minutes
cooking: 1–1¼ hours
Ⓒₐ 𝓋

2 tablespoons olive oil
2 leeks, chopped
2 garlic cloves, crushed
8 ounces (250g) bean curd, cubed
2 tablespoons paprika
1 teaspoon caraway seeds
1 eggplant, cubed
3¼ cups/8 ounces (250g) mushrooms, sliced
2 red bell peppers, cored, deseeded, and chopped
generous 2 cups (500 milliliters) tomato purée

scant 1 cup (200 milliliters) Vegetable Stock (see page 144) or water
1–2 teaspoon chopped dill
salt and freshly ground black pepper

1 Heat the oil in a large saucepan or flameproof casserole and gently cook the leeks and garlic until soft.

2 Add the bean curd and sprinkle in the paprika and caraway seeds. Cook for 3–4 minutes. Add the remaining vegetables and stir well; cook over low heat for 10–15 minutes, or until just softened.

3 Pour in the tomato purée and add the stock. Bring to a boil and season well with salt and pepper, then simmer for 35–45 minutes, or until cooked through.

4 Add the chopped dill and cook for 5 minutes more. Adjust the seasoning and serve hot.

nutritional breakdown per serving: calories 176, protein 10g, fat 10g (saturated fat 1g), carbohydrate 13g

garbanzo bean curry

Legumes make a good addition to curry dishes because they add texture and color, while also absorbing the spice flavors and giving a nutritional boost to the dish. This recipe is based on an aromatic spice paste made from cumin, coriander, and chiles. The paste is made in a blender or food processor and cooked thoroughly so that the spices develop in character. Serve this curry with some cooling plain yogurt and a plain or spiced rice such as Spiced Mushroom Rice (see page 235).

serves 4

preparation: 10 minutes

cooking: 35 minutes

suitable for freezing

(Fe)

2 onions, finely chopped
2 chiles (see right)
1 garlic clove, coarsely chopped
1 tablespoon ground cumin
1 tablespoon ground coriander
¼ cup (50 milliliters) sunflower oil
14 ounces (398 milliliters) canned tomatoes
1⅔ cups/8 ounces (250g) garbanzo beans
   (cooked weight)

1 cup (250 milliliters) Vegetable Stock (see page 144) or liquid from cooking the garbanzo beans
salt and freshly ground black pepper
2 tablespoons chopped cilantro leaves
juice of 1 lemon

1   Place the onions, chiles, garlic, ground cumin, and coriander in a blender or food processor and blend to a paste, adding a little water if necessary.

2   Heat the oil in a large skillet and cook the paste for 10 minutes, or until lightly browned.

3   Add the canned tomatoes, cooked garbanzos, and stock or liquid. Bring the mixture to a boil and simmer, uncovered, for 20 minutes.

4   Add salt and pepper to taste, and stir in the chopped cilantro and lemon juice just before serving.

nutritional breakdown per serving: calories 232, protein 7g, fat 14g (saturated fat 2g), carbohydrate 21g

CHILE POWER

This dish will be truly hot if you use the whole chiles, since much of the fire power is in the seeds and skin. For a milder version, remove the seeds. For a milder version still, roast and peel the chile. Freezing—although suitable for freezing, highly spiced dishes should not be frozen for longer than a month or the spices can develop unpleasant flavors.

spinach and new potato curry with coconut

Coconut adds a velvety texture to this tasty, colorful curry. Use regular potatoes when new ones are no longer in season. Serve this curry with spiced bread or rice or, for a more substantial meal, with Mixed Lentil Dhal (see page 250) or Garbanzo Bean Curry (see page 247).

serves 4

preparation: 15 minutes

cooking: 30–35 minutes

(Fe) 𝒱

8 ounces (250g) new potatoes
8 ounces (250g) spinach
2 tablespoons sunflower oil
1 onion, halved then thinly sliced
2 garlic cloves, crushed
1 teaspoon ground turmeric
1 chile, finely chopped
1 tablespoon ground coriander
1 teaspoon freshly ground black pepper
3 ounces (75g) coconut cream, dissolved in scant
   1 cup (200 milliliters) water
salt
juice of ½ lemon

1 Parboil the new potatoes in their skins for 8–10 minutes. Drain and cut in half.

2 Meanwhile, cook the spinach in a saucepan for 3–4 minutes. Drain and chop coarsely.

3 Heat the oil in a large skillet, and cook the onion with the garlic, turmeric, chile, ground coriander, and black pepper until soft.

4 Add the cooked potatoes and cook until slightly brown, about 6–8 minutes. Add the cooked spinach and coconut milk. Bring to a boil, then simmer for 7 minutes.

5 Season with salt and add lemon juice to taste. Serve hot.

spinach and new potato curry with coconut opposite

nutritional breakdown per serving: calories 249, protein 5g, fat 19g (saturated fat 12g), carbohydrate 16g

tomato raita with cumin

A rosy-colored accompaniment with an aromatic taste.

serves 4

preparation: 5 minutes, plus chilling

cooking: none

1 cup (250 milliliters) plain yogurt
1 tomato, skinned and chopped
1 scallion, finely chopped
2 teaspoons dry-roasted cumin seeds
salt and freshly ground black pepper

1 Tip the yogurt into a bowl and stir in the chopped tomato, scallion, and cumin seeds. Season well with salt and pepper and chill before serving.

nutritional breakdown per serving: calories 45, protein 4g, fat 0g (saturated fat 0g), carbohydrate 6g

mixed lentil dhal

Dhal is a legume-based Indian dish made with either lentils or split peas. Its consistency can be sloppy like soup or slightly dry so that it can be scooped up and eaten with bread. My version combines two types of lentils—the red dissolve to a purée to give an underlying texture, while the green keep their shape and give the dhal a little bite. As with all spice dishes, do cook the spices well before moving onto the next stage of the recipe. Serve the dhal with bread or Spinach and New Potato Curry with Coconut (see page 249) and a plain or spiced rice.

serves 4
preparation: 10 minutes
cooking: 35 minutes
suitable for freezing
(Fe) v

3 tablespoons sunflower oil
1 onion, finely chopped
2 garlic cloves, crushed
2 teaspoon grated fresh ginger
1 teaspoon chile powder
½ teaspoon ground turmeric
½ cup/4 ounces (125g) Puy or green lentils

mixed lentil dhal left,
tomato raita with
cucumber and **spiced**
cauliflower and green
beans right

½ cup/4 ounces (125g) red lentils
scant 2 cups/¾ pint (450 milliliters) water
salt and freshly ground black pepper

1 Heat the oil in a large saucepan and gently cook the onion and garlic until quite soft.

2 Combine the ginger, chile powder, and turmeric in a small bowl with 1 tablespoon water to make a thin paste. Add to the pan and cook for 2 minutes.

3 Add the lentils and the measured water and bring to a boil. Cover the pan and cook on low heat for 20–25 minutes, or until the red lentils have fallen to a purée and the green lentils are soft.

4 Season with salt and pepper to taste, then let cool a little before serving.

nutritional breakdown per serving: calories 282, protein 16g, fat 9g (saturated fat 1g), carbohydrate 36g

spiced cauliflower and green beans

This is a light vegetable dish that can be part of a spicy meal. The mixture is thickened with a high-protein flour made from chickpeas known as besan, or gram flour found in Indian and Asian markets. It has a dry finished texture which goes well with more moist dishes, such as the Spinach and New Potato Curry with Coconut (see page 249).

serves 4

preparation: 15 minutes

cooking: 30–40 minutes

Fe *v*

4–6 tablespoons sunflower oil
1 garlic clove, finely chopped
1–2 fresh red chiles, deseeded and finely chopped
8 ounces (250g) green beans, halved
1 pound (500g) cauliflower, divided into flowerets
½ cup/2 ounces (50g) gram flour
1 tablespoon sesame seeds
¼ cup/1 ounce (25g) cashew nuts, ground
1 teaspoon garam masala
¼ teaspoon ground turmeric
1–2 tablespoons lemon juice
salt and freshly ground black pepper

1 Dry roast the gram flour in a pan until it looks light brown and smells toasted.

2 Heat the oil in a large saucepan and gently cook the garlic and chiles for 3–4 minutes.

3 Add the green beans and cauliflower and cook gently, stirring frequently until they begin to soften, about 5–10 minutes.

4 Combine the gram flour, sesame seeds, ground cashew nuts, garam masala, turmeric, and ¼ teaspoon salt in a bowl. Sprinkle this mixture over the slightly softened vegetables. Mix well, add just enough water to cover the vegetables, and cook over a medium heat for 5–10 minutes until the vegetables are soft.

5 Before serving, sprinkle with lemon juice and salt and pepper to taste. Serve hot or at room temperature.

nutritional breakdown per serving: calories 273, protein 11g, fat 20g (saturated fat 3g), carbohydrate 14g

whole-wheat pie dough

It is not difficult to make a good, crisp light pastry with whole-wheat flour. Bear in mind the following points and you should have success every time. First, work with cool ingredients. Have the fats and water that you are using well chilled. Second, use a fine milled flour and add a little baking powder since this makes the end result lighter and crisper. Whole-wheat flour will absorb more water, not just initially but while the dough is resting so make the dough wetter than a white flour pastry. Adding a little oil helps add moisture without making the pastry tough. Sugar is used by many caterers in savory pastry since it makes the dough more elastic. If using brown sugar, you need to completely dissolve it first or it will show up as brown flecks.

makes approximately 15 ounces–1 pound (450–550g) dough

preparation: 10 minutes, plus chilling

cooking: none

suitable for freezing

𝓋

2 cups/8 ounces (250g) whole-wheat flour, plus extra for dusting

pinch of salt

½ teaspoon baking powder

½ cup (1 stick)/4 ounces (125g) chilled butter, solid vegetable fat, or a mixture

1 teaspoon superfine sugar

4–6 tablespoons ice water

1 tablespoon sunflower or olive oil

1 Place the flour, salt, and baking powder in a large bowl and cut in the fat. Rub the fat into the flour, using your fingertips, until the mixture resembles fine bread crumbs. Shake the bowl occasionally so that the larger lumps of fat come to the surface and you can make sure that the fat is evenly rubbed in. Alternatively, use a blender or food processor to achieve the same result.

2 Dissolve the sugar in the water and mix in the oil. Sprinkle most of the mixture over the flour and stir with a rounded knife. Only add as much water as is necessary to draw the mixture together.

3 Turn the dough onto a lightly floured board and knead gently until the surface of the dough is smooth.

4 Chill for 15–20 minutes, or while you prepare a filling.

nutritional breakdown per total recipe: calories 1739, protein 32g, fat 111g (saturated fat 27g), carbohydrate 164g

below **For the best pastry, measure the ingredients accurately and have everything well chilled.**

spinach and lentil turnovers

Spinach and lentils, peppered with warm spices, make a good moist filling for a pastry turnover. They do make a meal on their own but could easily be accompanied by a choice of simple salads. Make sure the pastry is made entirely with vegetable fats if cooking for a vegan. Serve tiny versions as appetizers.

makes 6

preparation: 15 minutes, plus pastry making

cooking: 45 minutes

suitable for freezing

(Fe)

For the filling:
2 tablespoons sunflower oil
1 onion, finely chopped
1 garlic clove, chopped
1 chile, deseeded and finely chopped
1 teaspoon cumin seeds
1 teaspoon coriander seeds
½ cup/4 ounces (125g) red lentils
1 cup (250 milliliters) boiling water
8 ounces (250g) spinach
1 tablespoon lemon juice

salt and freshly ground black pepper
1 quantity Whole-wheat Pie Dough (see page 252) or Quick Flaky Pastry (see page 256)
flour for dusting

1 To make the filling, heat the oil in a large saucepan and cook the onion, garlic, and chile until soft. Add the cumin and coriander and cook for 2–3 minutes, or until lightly toasted.

2 Add the lentils and stir in, then pour in the boiling water. Bring back to a boil, cover the pan, and cook for 10–15 minutes, or until all the water has been absorbed and the lentils have fallen to a purée.

3 Meanwhile, cook the washed spinach in a large pan, without adding any extra water, for 6–8 minutes. Drain if necessary and chop finely.

4 Stir the spinach into the cooked lentils and add the lemon juice. Season with salt and pepper and set aside.

5 Roll out the pastry on a lightly floured counter and cut into six 6-inch (15-cm) rounds. Spoon a little filling onto each round, then fold the pastry over to make a semicircle, and seal the edges with cold water.

6 Prick each turnover and bake in a preheated oven, 400°F (200°C), for 20–25 minutes. Serve hot or warm.

nutritional breakdown per turnover: calories 408, protein 12g, fat 23g (saturated fat 12g), carbohydrate 42g

enriched pie dough (pâte brisée)

makes approximately 12–15 ounces (350–450g) dough

preparation: 10 minutes, plus chilling

cooking: none

suitable for freezing

1¾ cups/7 ounces (200g) all-purpose flour
½ teaspoon salt
scant ½ cup/3½ ounces (100g) chilled butter
1 egg, lightly beaten
up to 2 teaspoons cold water

troubleshooting with pastry

- pastry shrinks during baking—not enough resting time
- pastry is tough—too much liquid, overhandling when drawing up to a dough
- pastry cracks when rolling out—too dry

1 Sift the flour and salt into a large bowl and cut in the butter. Rub the butter into the flour, using your fingertips, until the mixture resembles fine bread crumbs. Make a well in the center.

2 Pour the beaten egg into the well and work the pastry with a spatula or rounded knife until the mixture draws into a dough. Add the cold water, a teaspoon at a time, if necessary.

3 Bring the dough together and shape into a ball. Cover with plastic wrap or wax paper and chill for 30 minutes. Return the dough to room temperature before rolling out.

nutritional breakdown per total recipe: calories 1493, protein 26g, fat 90g (saturated fat 56g), carbohydrate 155g

Step 1 Sift the flour and salt and cut in the butter.
Step 2: Rub the butter into the flour using your fingertips.
Step 3: Pour in the egg and work the pastry with a rounded knife until the mixture draws into a dough.
Step 4: Shape into a rough ball, cover in suitable plastic wrap, and chill for 30 minutes.

griddled zucchini quiche with pine nuts

serves 4–6

preparation: 15 minutes, plus pastry making

cooking: 50 minutes

suitable for freezing

(Fe)

1 quantity Enriched Pie Dough
    (see page 254)
flour for dusting the counter

For the filling:
12 ounces (400g) zucchini, sliced
4 ounces (125g) shallots, sliced
½ cup/2 ounces (50g) pine nuts
2 teaspoons chopped rosemary
3 eggs
⅔ cup/¼ pint (150 milliliters) heavy cream
1 tablespoon pesto (see page 211)
salt and freshly ground black pepper

2 tablespoons freshly grated Parmesan

1 Roll out the dough on a lightly floured counter to
   fill a 9-inch (23-cm) quiche pan. Line with baking
   parchment and weigh down with baking beans.
   Bake in a preheated oven, 400°F (200°C), for
   15 minutes.

2 Meanwhile, to make the filling, heat a griddle
   pan or large nonstick skillet and griddle
   the zucchini and shallots until quite brown
   and softened, turning them over several times
   during cooking.

3 Add the pine nuts and cook until toasted. Remove
   from the heat and add the rosemary.

4 Beat the eggs in a bowl with the cream. Add the
   pesto and plenty of salt and pepper.

5 Combine the griddled zucchini and shallots
   mixture with the egg and pour into the cooked pie
   shell. Sprinkle with the grated Parmesan and bake
   in a preheated oven, 400°F (200°C), for 35 minutes.
   Serve warm.

nutritional breakdown per serving: calories 769, protein 18g,
fat 58g (saturated fat 29g), carbohydrate 48g

quick flaky pastry

Do start with cold ingredients and have the fats frozen solid beforehand because this makes them easier to grate in.

makes approximately 1 pound 2 ounces (550g) dough

preparation: 15 minutes, plus chilling

cooking: none

suitable for freezing

𝒱 (optional)

2 cups/8 ounces (250g) all-purpose flour, plus
  extra for dusting
⅓ teaspoon salt
1½ cups (1¼ sticks)/5 ounces (150g) butter,
  solid vegetable fat or a mixture, frozen for
  30 minutes before using
1 tablespoon lemon juice
about ½ cup (125 milliliters) ice water

below **Follow these easy stages for perfect flaky pastry. The rolling and folding will give the dough the characteristic flaky texture.**

1   Sift the flour and salt into a large bowl. Grate in the frozen fat.

2   Add the lemon juice and just enough water to draw the mixture into a dough, using a rounded knife. Draw up to a ball and knead very lightly.

3   Wrap the dough in wax paper or plastic wrap and chill for 30 minutes.

4   If very cold, leave the dough for a few minutes before rolling out. On a lightly floured counter roll it into a long oblong. Lightly mark the dough into thirds. Fold in one end third on top of the middle third, then fold the remaining third over the top. Seal the folded edges and give it a quarter turn on the counter. Repeat this process once more—done to trap air in the pastry—and chill again for 30 minutes.

nutritional breakdown per total recipe: calories 1962, protein 24g, fat 126g (saturated fat 54g), carbohydrate 196g

chestnut and cèpe pie

This is a moist, flavorsome pie, which uses the classic combination of mushrooms, walnuts, and chestnuts. The sweetness of the chestnuts with their dry texture combines well with the rich intense walnuts and woody mushrooms. Serve this pie as the hot centerpiece for a special meal on a cool evening. Serve with a mushroom or onion sauce, Roasted Root Vegetables with Caraway (see page 283) and a green vegetable. For a midweek meal, you could top the pie filling with a simple crisp topping (see page 271).

serves 4

preparation: 15 minutes, plus soaking

cooking: 45 minutes

suitable for freezing

𝓋

For the filling:
¼ cup/½ ounce (15g) dried cèpes
scant ½ cup (100 milliliters) boiling water
2–3 tablespoons sunflower oil
2 onions, finely chopped
2 garlic cloves, crushed
2 leeks, sliced
2 carrots, finely chopped
¼ cup (50 milliliters) red wine
1 cup/4 ounces (125g) walnuts, chopped
7 ounces (200g) chestnuts (cooked weight), roughly chopped
¼ cup/¼ ounce (7g) chopped parsley
2–3 tablespoons shoyu or soy sauce
salt and freshly ground black pepper

½ quantity Quick Flaky Pastry (see page 256)
flour for dusting the counter
egg yolk and water, for brushing (optional)

1 To make the filling, place the cèpes in a bowl with the boiling water and soak for 30 minutes.

2 Heat the oil in a large saucepan and gently cook the onions and garlic until very soft. Add the leeks and carrots and cook for 3–4 minutes, or until just beginning to soften. Add the red wine and cook gently to reduce the liquid.

3 Drain the cèpes, reserving the soaking liquid. Chop if necessary, then add to the vegetables with the walnuts, chestnuts, parsley, and soaking liquid from the cèpes. Cook for 2–3 minutes, then remove the pan from the heat. Stir in the shoyu or soy sauce, season well with salt and pepper, and let cool.

4 Roll out the dough on a lightly floured counter to a size at least 1–2 inches (2.5–5cm) larger than the 8-inch (20-cm)) deep ovenproof dish you will need to use. Place the dish in the center of the dough. Cut out the shape of the dish, then cut a collar about 1 inch (2.5cm) wide from the remaining pastry.

5 Spoon the cool pie filling into the dish. Moisten the edge of the dish with water, then press on the pastry collar. Brush with cold water.

6 Place the pastry lid on top, using a rolling pin to help lift it into place, then press it onto the collar. Trim the pastry with a sharp knife. Crimp the collar and the lid together, using a fork or fingertips.

7 Cut a small hole in the top of the pie to allow steam from the pie filling to escape. If you like, give the pastry a golden finish by brushing with egg yolk beaten with a little water and salt.

8 Bake in a preheated oven, 425°F (220°C), for 30 minutes, or until golden brown.

nutritional breakdown per serving: calories 660, protein 11g, fat 46g (saturated fat 10g), carbohydrate 52g

USING DRIED CHESTNUTS

If you are using dried chestnuts, soak 4 ounces (125g) dried chestnuts in plenty of water for 30 minutes. Then bring to a boil in the same water and simmer for 30 minutes, or until quite tender. Drain, reserving the stock for other uses. This should provide you with at least 7 ounces (200g) cooked chestnuts.

choux pastry

preparation: 5 minutes

cooking: 5 minutes

suitable for freezing

1 cup (250 milliliters) water
scant ½ cup/3½ ounces (100g) butter
1¼ cups/5 ounces (150g) all-purpose flour
1 teaspoon salt
4 eggs, beaten
½ cup/2 ounces (50g) grated Cheddar
egg yolk and water for brushing

1 Bring the water and butter to a boil in a saucepan.

2 When the butter has melted and the liquid is boiling, tip in all the flour and the salt. Remove the pan from the heat and beat well using a wooden spoon. Return briefly to the heat and cook until the flour forms a ball.

3 Remove the pan from the heat, add 1 egg, and beat in until completely absorbed.

4 Add the remaining eggs in the same way, beating until the dough is smooth and glossy with a soft but not runny consistency. It should drop off the spoon when shaken.

5 Stir in the grated cheese. The choux pastry can now be used in a variety of ways depending on the recipe.

VARIATIONS

For cocktail snacks and appetizers, make 30–40 puffs by spooning 30–40 small mounds or piping them using a ½-inch (1-cm) piping tip. Brush the tops with a little beaten egg yolk and water and bake in a preheated oven, 400°F (200°C), for 20 minutes, or until crisp and golden.

For gougère, spoon or pipe walnut-size amounts of the mixture around a greased ovenproof dish. Bake in a preheated oven, 400°F (200°C), for 25–30 minutes.

nutritional breakdown per puff: calories 50, protein 12g, fat 13g (saturated fat 2g), carbohydrate 3g

Step 1 Bring the mixture to a boil and tip in the flour.
Step 2 Beat well with a wooden spoon.
Step 3 Cook until the mixture forms a ball.
Step 4 Beat in the egg.
Step 5 The dough should look smooth and glossy.
Step 6 Stir in the grated cheese.

artichoke and red bell pepper gougère

Elegant enough for a dinner party, this is a colorful dish that is light but satisfying. This version focuses on the summer flavors of roasted bell peppers and artichokes. Use fresh artichokes if you can; otherwise, splurge on good-quality marinated artichoke halves.

It is easy to make a simpler gougère for suppertime treats—just fill the cooked gougère with a vegetable stir-fry or sauté, and moisten it with tomato sauce or white sauce.

serves 4

preparation: 20 minutes, plus choux pastry making

cooking: 1 hour 10 minutes

suitable for freezing (gougère only)

(Fe)

For the sauce:
4 red bell peppers
⅓ cup (80 milliliters) olive oil
2 tablespoons white wine vinegar
salt and freshly ground black pepper

For the filling:
2 tablespoons olive oil
1 onion, finely chopped
2 garlic cloves, crushed
8 artichoke hearts, halved
8 ounces (250g) cherry tomatoes
salt and freshly ground black pepper
1 quantity Choux Pastry (see page 258)
freshly grated Parmesan for sprinkling

1 To make the sauce, place the bell peppers on a baking sheet or in a roasting pan and roast in a preheated oven, 400°F (200°C), for 25 minutes. Leave until cool enough to handle, then remove the skins and seeds. Chop the flesh coarsely.

2 Using a blender or food processor, purée the red bell peppers with the olive oil until smooth. Add the vinegar and purée again. Season well with salt and pepper.

3 To make the filling, heat the oil in a saucepan and gently cook the onion and garlic until soft. Add the artichoke hearts and cook until lightly browned, then add the cherry tomatoes. Cook until these are quite soft. Pour the red bell pepper sauce over the artichokes and mix in well. Add salt and pepper to taste.

4 To make the gougère, spoon or pipe walnut-size amounts of the choux pastry around a greased ovenproof dish. Bake at 400°F (200°C), for 25–30 minutes.

5 When the gougère is cooked, pile the filling into the center of the dish, and sprinkle with grated Parmesan. Bake for 5 minutes more. Serve hot.

nutritional breakdown per serving: calories 733, protein 18g, fat 54g (saturated fat 21g), carbohydrate 48g

leek and feta parcels

These well-flavored light parcels make great party food. This version is shaped like an individual strudel, but it is just as easy to make triangles, perhaps with a contrasting filling.

makes 24
preparation: 25 minutes
cooking: 25–30 minutes
suitable for freezing

For the filling:
2 tablespoons/1 ounce (25g) butter
2 tablespoons olive oil
2 pounds (1 kg) leeks, shredded
2 garlic cloves, crushed
freshly grated nutmeg
6 ounces (200g) feta (drained weight), crumbled
salt and freshly ground black pepper

For the pastry:
¼ cup (½ stick)/2 ounces (50g) butter
3 tablespoons olive oil
24 sheets phyllo pastry

1 To make the filling, melt the butter with the oil in a large skillet, then gently cook the shredded leeks with the garlic until soft.

2 Let cool, then add a grating of nutmeg and the crumbled feta. Season well with salt and pepper.

3 To assemble the parcels, melt the butter with the oil for the pastry. Use 1 sheet of phyllo at a time and brush well with melted butter and oil.

4 Spoon a portion of filling along the central third of the sheet, leaving a border around the edges. Fold over the top edge to cover the filling then fold in the sides. Brush the folded pastry with melted fat.

5 Roll up the pastry to make a cigar shape. Brush well with more melted fat.

6 Repeat with the remaining sheets of pastry and the filling. Bake the parcels in a preheated oven, 400°F (200°C), for 15–20 minutes, or until crisp. Serve warm or at room temperature.

nutritional breakdown per parcel: calories 153, protein 5g, fat 6g (saturated fat 1g), carbohydrate 20g

phyllo pie with double mushrooms and goat cheese

Mushrooms and goat cheese are a good combination and form a rich filling for this feather-light pie. This could easily be part of a meal suitable for entertaining, served with new potatoes, a green vegetable, or salad. Begin the meal with a contrasting soup or refreshing Oranges with Red Onion and Black Olives (see page 163).

serves 4–6

preparation time: 20 minutes

cooking time: 40–45 minutes

suitable for freezing

(Fe)

For the filling:

¼ cup (½ stick)/2 ounces (50g) butter

1 pound (500g) oyster mushrooms, coarsely chopped

4 cups/10 ounces (300g) cremini mushrooms, sliced

1 teaspoon dried marjoram

⅓ cup (80 milliliters) white wine

5 ounces (150g) goat cheese, coarsely chopped

3 eggs

salt and freshly ground black pepper

For the pastry:

¼ cup (½ stick)/2 ounces (50g) butter

2–3 tablespoons olive oil

12 sheets phyllo pastry

1 To make the filling, melt the butter in a large skillet and cook the oyster and cremini mushrooms over medium heat so that they color slightly. When fairly soft, add the marjoram and white wine and season well, then cook over high heat until the liquid has reduced. Set aside.

2 Using a blender or food processor, blend the goat cheese and eggs to make a smooth sauce. Pour this over the cooked mushrooms and mix well. Season with salt and pepper.

3 To assemble the pie, melt the butter with the olive oil for the pastry. Brush the melted butter mixture over the base of a square ovenproof dish.

4 Take 1 sheet of phyllo and use it to line the base and sides of the dish. Brush with the melted butter mixture.

5 Place another sheet of phyllo on top, at an angle to the first, and brush with more of the melted butter. Continue layering phyllo in the same way until you have a base of 6 sheets, with each successive sheet at a slightly different angle.

6 Spoon the mushroom filling on top and fold over any phyllo pastry edges.

7 Cover the filling with a sheet of phyllo brushed with the melted butter mixture and tuck in the edges. Repeat this, using the remaining sheets. Mark a cross through the center of the phyllo with a sharp knife.

8 Bake in a preheated oven, 400°F (200°C), for 35–40 minutes, or until the pastry is crisp and golden. Turn the oven down a little for the last 10 minutes if the pastry is becoming too brown. Serve hot.

nutritional breakdown per serving (4 portions): calories 695, protein 22g, fat 39g (saturated fat 20g), carbohydrate 59g

potato and leek boulangère

This fabulous dish makes a wonderful meal for family or company. It is easy to make enormous quantities if you are having an informal supper party. The recipe is very quick to prepare and the dish is then slowly cooked in the oven. When ready, it needs little accompaniment other than a light salad.

serves 4–6
preparation: 15 minutes
cooking: 1 hour
suitable for freezing
(Ca)

2 tablespoons/1 ounce (25g) butter
1 pound (500g) leeks, sliced
2 garlic cloves, chopped
1¾ pound (875g) potatoes, scrubbed and sliced
4 tomatoes, sliced
1¼ cups/½ pint (300 milliliters) heavy cream
1¼ cups/½ pint (300 milliliters) milk
1 cup/4 ounces (125g) grated smoked cheese
salt and freshly ground black pepper

1 Use the butter to grease a large, deep 13 x 9-inch (33 x 23-cm) or similar size ovenproof dish. Put in half of the chopped leeks and garlic, cover with half of the slices of potato, and season well.

2 Cover with a layer of the remaining leeks and garlic, then the remaining potato slices, and season well again. Cover with the slices of tomato.

3 Mix the cream with the milk and pour over the top. Don't worry if it settles on the top because it will melt through during the cooking process.

4 Cover with grated cheese and bake in a preheated oven, 350°F (180°C), for 1 hour, or until the potatoes are cooked and the cheese well browned.

nutritional breakdown per serving (4 portions): calories 719, protein 18g, fat 51g (saturated fat 32g), carbohydrate 50g

sweet potato and zucchini gratin

This is similar in concept to the boulangère (see page 262), but with a very different look and distinctive, delicious flavor. The sweet potato and golden zucchini add warm fall tones. This dish is good enough for a dinner party, served with a simple salad.

serves 4–6

preparation: 15 minutes

cooking: 1 hour

suitable for freezing

Ⓒa Ⓕe

2 tablespoons/1 ounce (25g) butter
1 pound (500g) golden zucchini, sliced
8 ounces (250g) shallots, sliced
1¾ pounds (875g) sweet potatoes, scrubbed
 and thinly sliced
salt and freshly ground black pepper
1¼ cups/(½ pint (300 milliliters) heavy cream
1¼ cups/½ pint (300 milliliters) milk
1 cup/4 ounces (125g) grated Emmental

1 Use the butter to grease a large, deep 12 x 12-inch (30 x 30-cm) ovenproof dish. Put in half of the sliced zucchini and shallots, cover with half of the slices of sweet potato, and season well with salt and pepper.

2 Cover with a layer of the remaining zucchini and shallots, then the remaining sweet potato slices, and season well again.

3 Mix the cream with the milk and pour over the top. Don't worry if it settles on the top because it will melt through during the cooking process.

4 Cover with grated cheese and bake in a preheated oven, 350°F (180°C), for 1 hour, or until the sweet potatoes are cooked and the cheese well browned.

nutritional breakdown per serving (4 portions): calories 840, protein 19g, fat 53g (saturated fat 33g), carbohydrate 78g

roasted pecan and cashew loaf

This rich nut loaf, encrusted with roasted nuts and seeds, makes a good centerpiece for an evening or weekend meal. Serve it with a mushroom, onion, or tomato sauce (see pages 291–92), roast or baked potatoes or root vegetables, and a green vegetable or salad. Nut roasts are rich so you need serve only small portions. Leftovers will keep well and can be reheated successfully or served cold.

This recipe can be made with soy flour for a vegan alternative. Mix 2 tablespoons soy flour with water to a runny consistency and use in place of the eggs. While just as tasty, it will not hold together quite so well and is therefore better baked in a larger shallower dish. Consequently, it will cook in a shorter time so check it after 35 minutes.

serves 4
preparation: 10 minutes
cooking: 1 hour 10 minutes
suitable for freezing
(Fe) v

1¼ cups/5 ounces (150g) pecan nuts
1½ cups/5 ounces (150g) cashew nuts
1 cup/2 ounces (50g) sunflower seeds
¼ cup/½ ounce (15g) dried mushrooms
⅔ cup/¼ pint (150 milliliters) boiling water
2 tablespoons sunflower oil
1 onion, finely chopped
2 garlic cloves, crushed
2 celery stalks, finely chopped
3¼ cups/8 ounces (250g) cremini mushrooms, finely chopped
⅓ cup (80 milliliters) red wine
1 tablespoon all purpose flour
2 tablespoons chopped parsley
1 tablespoon shoyu or soy sauce
salt and freshly ground black pepper
2 eggs, beaten

1 Put the pecans, cashews, and sunflower seeds on a large baking sheet and roast in a preheated oven, 400°F (200°C), for 5 minutes, or until lightly browned. Set aside enough to garnish the top of the roast.

2 Soak the dried mushrooms in a bowl of a boiling water to make a simple stock. Drain the mushrooms and chop finely, reserving the mushroom stock.

3 Heat the oil in a large skillet and cook the onion and garlic until soft. Add the celery, fresh mushrooms, and dried mushrooms and cook until quite soft.

4 Add the red wine and increase the heat, then cook until most of the liquid has evaporated.

5 Sprinkle in the flour, stir, and cook for 2 minutes; pour in the mushroom stock, bring the mixture to a boil, then simmer for 2 minutes. Remove from the heat and season well.

6 Using a food processor, process the roasted nuts and seeds, the mushroom sauce, parsley, and shoyu or soy sauce together until fairly smooth. Season with salt and pepper to taste.

7 Add the beaten eggs to the mixture and process again. (Alternatively, add the mixed soy flour and water.)

8 Spoon the mixture into a greased and lined 8 x 4-inch (1.2-liter) loaf pan. Arrange the reserved nuts and seeds over the top, pressing in lightly.

9 Bake in a preheated oven, 375°F (190°C), for 45–55 minutes, or until quite firm to the touch. Let stand in the pan for 10 minutes, before turning out to serve.

nutritional breakdown per serving: calories 695, protein 18g, fat 59g (saturated fat 8g), carbohydrate 20g

cooking with nuts

Nut roasts have become a humorous cliché in a vegetarian diet and are seen as a poor alternative to meat. The truth is, they are not like meat, nor meant to be, but are delicious in their own right. Here are a few tips on making a great nut roast or loaf.

• A nut roast must have a moist base, made with a thin sauce or a well-flavored stock or wine, otherwise the end result will be dry.

• Roasting the nuts first highlights their flavor.

• Be bold with your use of herbs and spices since, although rich in themselves, nuts do benefit from extra flavorings.

• Mixtures of nuts often work better than using just a single variety since their different flavors complement each other.

• Make a loaf or roast look more attractive by layering the mixture with cooked vegetables, such as sliced mushrooms, thick tomato sauce, or spinach purée.

lentil layer with red bell pepper

Red lentils make a great basis for a savory baked dish because they cook to a soft but well-textured purée. Do season the dish well and don't skimp on the parsley. If it isn't at hand, then flavor the dish with lemon juice and zest instead. This can be served as an easy supper or lunch dish with a simple tomato or mushroom sauce and a selection of roasted vegetables.

serves 4

preparation: 15 minutes

cooking: 1 hour 10 minutes

suitable for freezing

(Fe)

½ cup/4 ounces (125g) red lentils
1¼ cups/½ pint (300 milliliters) water
2 tablespoons sunflower oil
1 onion, finely chopped
2 celery stalks, finely chopped
1 teaspoon paprika
1 large red bell pepper
⅓ cup/⅓ ounce (9g) finely chopped parsley
salt and freshly ground black pepper
3 eggs, separated

1 Place the lentils in a saucepan with the water and bring to a boil. Cover the pan and simmer very gently for 25–30 minutes, or until all the water has been absorbed and the lentils are tender. Beat in the pan until smooth and set aside.

2 Heat the oil in a skillet and gently cook the onion until soft. Add the celery and paprika and cook for 3–4 minutes.

3 Cut the stalk end from the red bell pepper and slice off 4 rings. Reserve for garnish. Finely chop the remainder of the bell pepper and add to the onion and celery mixture. Cook for 2–3 minutes. Stir the cooked vegetables and the parsley into the lentil purée and season well with salt and pepper.

4 Stir the egg yolks into the lentil mixture. Beat the egg whites in a bowl until stiff, then fold into the lentil mixture.

5 Spoon the mixture into a lightly oiled ovenproof dish and garnish with the red bell pepper rings. Bake in a preheated oven, 400°F (200°C), for 30–35 minutes, or until golden brown and firm to the touch. Serve hot.

nutritional breakdown per serving: calories 226, protein 13g, fat 10g (saturated fat 2g) carbohydrate 22g

spiced hazelnut and quinoa loaf

Although nuts in themselves are a rich ingredient, they can seem dry in a baked dish. I've used coconut milk in this recipe to add moisture and an extra silky texture. Quinoa cooks to quite a soft consistency and so is ideal for adding bulk to the dish. Serve with a spiced tomato sauce or a cold yogurt dip and cucumber relish, or a green vegetable.

serves 4
preparation: 10 minutes
cooking: 50–55 minutes
suitable for freezing
(Fe) 𝑣

2 tablespoons sunflower oil, plus 1 teaspoon for toasting the quinoa
generous ½ cup/3½ ounces (100g) quinoa, rinsed
scant 2 cups/¾ pint (450 milliliters) boiling water
1 onion, finely chopped
2 tablespoons sesame seeds
2 teaspoons cumin seeds
½ teaspoon ground turmeric
½-inch (1-cm) piece of fresh ginger, grated
1¼ cups/5 ounces (150g) hazelnuts, finely ground
⅔ cup/¼ pint (150 milliliters) coconut milk
salt and freshly ground black pepper

1 Heat the 1 teaspoon of oil in a saucepan and gently toast the quinoa for 1 minute. Add the boiling water and bring to a boil, stirring a few times. Cover the pan and simmer for 15 minutes, or until quite soft. Drain if necessary and set aside.

2 Meanwhile, heat the remaining oil in a large skillet and gently cook the onion. When soft, add the sesame and cumin seeds, turmeric, and ginger and cook for 3–4 minutes. Then stir in the ground hazelnuts and cook for 2–3 minutes. Let cool.

3 Combine the quinoa with the nuts and spices, and stir in the coconut milk. Season with salt and pepper to taste.

4 Spoon the mixture into a lined, greased 8 x 4-inch (1.2-liter) loaf pan. Cook in a preheated oven, 375°F (190°C), for 30–35 minutes, or until just firm to the touch.

nutritional breakdown per serving: calories 408, protein 10g, fat 33g (saturated fat 3g), carbohydrate 20g

almond croustade with Swiss chard

A classic croustade is made with very thin slices of bread baked to form a crisp shell. This version is easier because it is made with a mixture of bread crumbs enriched with almonds and cheese, which is then pressed into the base of a dish, and baked until crisp. This recipe has many variations since the base can be flavored with different nuts and cheeses. Alternatively, the cheese can be left out altogether for those wanting a dairy-free recipe.

This topping comprises a well-flavored cream sauce combined with a colorful assortment of vegetables. It is good as a supper dish, but quite elegant enough to serve at a special meal.

serves 4

preparation: 15 minutes

cooking: 45 minutes

suitable for freezing

(Ca) (Fe)

For the croustade:

1 cup/4 ounces (125g) ground almonds

1 cup/4 ounces (125g) grated strongly flavored hard cheese

3 cups/6 ounces (175g) fresh bread crumbs

1 teaspoon dried thyme

2–3 tablespoons sunflower oil

For the topping:

2 tablespoons/1 ounce (25g) butter

2 leeks, finely chopped

1 red bell pepper, cored, deseeded, and diced

12 ounces (400g) Swiss chard

2 tablespoons all-purpose flour

1¾ cups (400 milliliters) milk (low-fat)

1 teaspoon paprika

½ cup/2 ounces (50g) shredded strongly flavored hard cheese

salt and freshly ground black pepper

1 To make the croustade, combine the ground almonds, grated cheese, and bread crumbs in a large bowl or food processor. Add the dried thyme and 2 tablespoons of the oil. If the mixture seems dry, add extra oil.

2 Press the mixture into a shallow ovenproof dish and bake in a preheated oven, 400°F (200°C), for 15 minutes.

3 To make the topping, melt the butter in a saucepan and gently cook the leeks until soft. Add the red bell pepper and Swiss chard and cook for a few minutes until beginning to soften.

4 Sprinkle in the flour, stir, and cook for 2 minutes, then pour in the milk, and add the paprika. Stir well and bring to a boil, stirring frequently. Season well and simmer for 2–3 minutes.

5 Spoon the filling over the cooked base and cover with shredded cheese. Bake at 400°F (200°C), for 15 minutes. Serve hot.

nutritional breakdown per serving: calories 686, protein 28g, fat 48g (saturated fat 16g), carbohydrate 39g

fresh corn cobbler

This corn-bread style mixture on colorful vegetables makes a straightforward tasty supper dish. Use fresh corn if you can since it provides an extra springy texture in the filling. Canned corn is an acceptable alternative, however, and you can try many other combinations of vegetables.

serves 4

preparation: 15 minutes

cooking: 40 minutes

suitable for freezing

(Ca)

2 tablespoons sunflower oil
1 onion, finely chopped
1 green bell pepper, cored, deseeded, and
    finely chopped
3 corn cobs, stripped
12 ounces (400g) carrots, finely chopped
2 tablespoons all-purpose flour
1¾ cups (400 milliliters) milk
1 teaspoon dried thyme
salt and freshly ground black pepper

For the topping:
⅔ cup/3 ounces (75g) cornmeal
⅔ cup/3 ounces (75g) whole-wheat or
    white flour, plus extra for dusting
½ teaspoon salt
1½ teaspoons baking powder
1 egg
¼ cup (50 milliliters) milk
½ cup/2 ounces (50g) grated strongly flavored
    hard cheese

1 Heat the oil in a saucepan and gently cook the onion, then add the green bell pepper, corn kernels, and carrots, and stir well. Cook for 5 minutes, or until beginning to soften.

2 Sprinkle in the flour, stir, and cook for 2 minutes, then pour in the milk and add the dried thyme. Bring the mixture to a boil, stirring frequently. Simmer for 2 minutes and season well with salt and pepper. Transfer the mixture to a lightly oiled ovenproof dish or four individual baking cups.

3 To make the topping, mix the cornmeal in a bowl with the flour, salt, and baking powder.

4 Beat the egg with the milk, then pour the mixture over the dry ingredients. Mix to a dough. Working on a lightly floured counter, press the dough into a rough round about 8 inches (20cm) in diameter. Sprinkle with grated cheese.

5 Cut into 2-inch (5-cm) rounds and arrange on top of the corn mixture. Bake in a preheated oven, 400°F (200°C), for 25 minutes. Serve hot.

nutritional breakdown per serving: calories 434, protein 16g, fat 15g (saturated fat 3g), carbohydrate 63g

cottage pie

Classic, homey, and heartwarming, this substantial supper takes a little time to prepare but it can all be done in advance. The filling is good made with brown or Puy lentils, or larger green lentils, or adzuki beans. Serve with a contrasting vegetable such as cauliflower, cabbage, or broccoli.

serves 4
preparation: 15 minutes
cooking: about 1½ hours
suitable for freezing
(Fe) 𝒱

¾ cup/6 ounces) Puy lentils or brown lentils
1 pound (500g) potatoes
¼ cup (50 milliliters) milk or soy milk
2 tablespoons olive oil
1 onion, chopped
2 leeks, sliced
2 celery stalks, finely chopped
6 ounces (175g) carrots, finely chopped
6 ounces (175g) parsnips or squash, finely chopped
2 tablespoons shoyu or soy sauce
2–3 tablespoons tomato paste
1 teaspoon chopped sage
1 teaspoon chopped thyme
salt and freshly ground black pepper

1 Cook the lentils in a large saucepan of boiling water for about 20–30 minutes, or until quite soft. Drain and reserve the cooking liquid.

2 Meanwhile, boil the potatoes in another saucepan of water for 15 minutes, or until soft, then drain, and mash with the milk, seasoning well.

3 Heat the oil in a large saucepan and cook the onion until soft. Then add the leeks and celery and cook for 4–5 minutes more until beginning to soften.

4 Add the carrots and parsnips or squash and continue cooking over low heat for 10 minutes. Cover the pan so that the juices from the vegetables do not evaporate.

5 Stir in the cooked drained lentils, then add the shoyu or soy sauce, tomato paste, sage, thyme, and enough cooking liquid from the lentils to make the mixture moist but not sloppy. Simmer this mixture for 10 minutes, adding more liquid if necessary. Season well with salt and pepper.

6 Spoon the lentil mixture into a lightly oiled ovenproof dish. Cover with the mashed potatoes and bake in a preheated oven, 350°F (180°C), for 35–40 minutes, or until the potato topping is crisp and brown.

nutritional breakdown per serving: calories 360, protein 17g, fat 8g (saturated fat 1g), carbohydrate 59g

celery root and almond crisp

This tasty crisp makes a good nutritious supper dish. It could be served with red cabbage or broccoli.

serves 4
preparation: 15 minutes
cooking: 1 hour
suitable for freezing
(Fe) *V*

2 tablespoons sunflower oil
1 pound (500g) leeks, chopped
1½ pounds (750g) celery root, cubed
1 teaspoon chopped rosemary
1 teaspoon chopped thyme
generous 2 cups (500 milliliters) tomato purée
juice of ½ lemon
12 whole blanched almonds, to garnish
salt and freshly ground black pepper

For the crisp:
½ cup/2 ounces (50g) whole-wheat flour
⅔ cup/2 ounces (50g) rolled oats
½ cup/2ounces (50g) ground almonds
1 teaspoon chopped thyme
3 ounces (75g) sunflower margarine
salt and freshly ground black pepper

1　Heat the oil in a large saucepan and sweat the leeks until just soft. Add the celery root and cook slowly for 10 minutes.

2　Add the rosemary, thyme, tomato purée, lemon juice, and seasoning. Bring to a boil and simmer, covered, for 10 minutes. Adjust the seasoning and transfer the mixture to an oiled, deep ovenproof dish.

3　To make the crisp, combine the flour, oats, almonds, and thyme in a bowl. Rub in the margarine, and season with salt and pepper.

4　Sprinkle the crisp mixture over the filling. Arrange the whole almonds on the top, then bake in a preheated oven, 375°F (190°C), for 30 minutes. Serve hot.

nutritional breakdown per serving: calories 450, protein 12g, fat 32g (saturated fat 5g), carbohydrate 30g

---

CRISP TOPPINGS

A crisp topping is a very easy way to add texture and substance to a thick sauce or moist vegetable mixture. The plainest crisps can be made from a simple mixture of oats and flour, bound together with enough oil to coat the dry ingredients, which saves the job of rubbing in. An oil-based crisp mix is quite crunchy and dry so only use it with a stew with plenty of spare liquid. More traditional crisp toppings are made with a solid fat rubbed in. You can vary the flavor by adding different nuts, seeds, or herbs. Chopped blanched almonds and walnuts work well, as does chopped parsley, thyme, or paprika. Grated cheese will make sure that the mixture browns to an appetizing golden color. An uncooked crisp mixture freezes well, and will also keep in the refrigerator for up to 2 weeks.

moussaka

A traditional Greek recipe, moussaka comprises layers of fried eggplant, rich tomato sauce, and slices of potato finished with a creamy topping then baked. It takes some time to prepare, although this can be done in advance, and the end result is certainly worth the time spent. This robust supper dish needs no accompaniment other than a light crisp salad.

serves 4

preparation: 15 minutes, plus parboiling, salting, and infusing

cooking: about 1½ hours

suitable for freezing

2 eggplant, sliced
salt
8 ounces (250g) cauliflower flowerets
⅓ to ½ cup (80–125 milliliters) olive oil

For the tomato sauce:
2 tablespoons olive oil
1 onion, chopped
1 garlic clove, crushed
generous 2 cups (500 milliliters) tomato purée
1 teaspoon dried oregano
¼ teaspoon ground cinnamon
salt and freshly ground black pepper

For the topping:
scant 2 cups/¾ pint (450 milliliters) milk
½ onion
1 bay leaf
6 black peppercorns

1 sprig thyme
2 tablespoons/1 ounce (25g) butter
¼ cup/1 ounce (25g) all-purpose flour
salt and freshly ground black pepper
2 eggs, beaten
13 ounces (400g) potatoes, parboiled and sliced
½ cup/2 ounces (50g) grated hard or feta cheese

1 Put the eggplant slices in a large colander and sprinkle with salt. Let stand for 30 minutes, then pat dry with paper towels.

2 Steam the cauliflower flowerets over a saucepan of boiling water until soft. Drain, then chop coarsely.

3 Heat ¼ cup of oil in a large skillet and cook the eggplant slices, a few at a time, until brown. Set aside.

4 To make the tomato sauce, heat the oil in a saucepan and cook the onion and garlic until soft. Add the tomato purée, oregano, and cinnamon, then bring to a boil, cover the pan, and cook for 30–35 minutes. Season well with salt and pepper. Stir in the cauliflower.

5 To make the topping, steep the milk for the topping by warming it in a small saucepan and adding the onion, bay leaf, peppercorns, and thyme. Let stand for at least 10 minutes.

6 Meanwhile, melt the butter in a small saucepan. Stir in the flour and cook for 2 minutes. Strain the steeped milk into the roux and bring the sauce to a boil, stirring constantly. Simmer for 2 minutes, then season with salt and pepper to taste. Let cool slightly, then stir in the eggs.

7 To assemble the moussaka, put half the tomato sauce in the base of a lightly oiled ovenproof dish. Top with the slices of potato, then cover with the remaining tomato sauce, and top with the slices of eggplant. Cover with the white sauce and sprinkle the grated cheese over the top. Bake in a preheated oven, 350°F (180°C), for 35–40 minutes, or until golden brown on top. Serve hot.

nutritional breakdown per serving: calories 572, protein 18g, fat 40g (saturated fat 12g), carbohydrate 38g

stir-fry vegetables with cashews and chile

Chile and ginger add a kick to this simple stir-fry. Serve with rice or noodles.

serves 3–4

preparation: 15 minutes

cooking: 10 minutes

𝒱

1 tablespoon sunflower or peanut oil
3 shallots, finely chopped
1 garlic clove, crushed
1 chile, finely chopped
½-inch (1cm) piece of fresh ginger, grated
1 cup.4 ounces (125g) cashew nuts
8 ounces (250g) carrots, cut into thin batons
8 ounces (250g) snow peas
4 cups/10 ounces (300g) mushrooms, halved
juice of 1–2 limes
1 tablespoon sesame oil

1 Heat the oil in a wok or large skillet and stir-fry the shallots with the garlic, chile, and ginger. Add the cashews and stir-fry until toasted.

2 Add the carrots and cook for 1 minute, then add the snow peas and cook for 1 minute more. Add the mushrooms and cook for 3 minutes. Add the lime juice and sesame oil and steam the vegetables for 1 minute.

3 Serve immediately with freshly cooked rice or noodles.

nutritional breakdown per serving (4 portions): calories 387, protein 13g, fat 28g (saturated fat 5g), carbohydrate 21g

stir-fry vegetables and bean curd with sesame marinade

Try to plan ahead with this recipe since it is best to leave the bean curd to marinate as long as possible. For the stir-fry, I've suggested a mixture of vegetables, but many combinations are possible. Serve with rice or noodles.

serves 4

preparation: 15 minutes, plus marinating

cooking: 10 minutes

For the marinade:

3 tablespoons dark toasted sesame oil
3 tablespoons shoyu or soy sauce
1 tablespoon concentrated apple juice
juice of ½ lemon
1 chile, finely chopped
2 scallions, finely chopped
2 tablespoons chopped cilantro leaves
freshly ground black pepper

8 ounces (250g) bean curd, cut into bite-
    size pieces
1 tablespoon sunflower oil
2 scallions, chopped
1 garlic clove, chopped
4 ounces (125g) baby corn cobs,
    coarsely chopped
6 ounces (175g) sugar snap peas
1⅔ cups/4 ounces (125g) mushrooms, sliced
salt and freshly ground black pepper

1 Make the marinade by combining all the
  ingredients in a screw-top jar. Place the bean curd
  in a shallow dish. Pour the marinade over it, cover,
  and set aside for 2–3 hours, turning the pieces
  over occasionally.

2 Drain the bean curd, reserving the marinade.

3 Heat the oil in a wok or large skillet, then quickly
  stir-fry the scallions and garlic. Add the corn, peas,
  and mushrooms in order, cooking each briefly
  before adding the next vegetable. Add the drained
  bean curd and stir well.

4 Add the reserved marinade and cook for 1 minute.
  Season with salt and pepper and serve immediately.

nutritional breakdown per serving: calories 190, protein 10g,
fat 14g (saturated fat 2g), carbohydrate 7g

stir-fry vegetables with golden coconut sauce

Coconut is used extensively in Southeast Asian cuisine. It adds a rich, silky quality to this quickly prepared spicy, golden sauce. Pour it over the stir-fry vegetables to finish off the cooking, and serve the dish with rice or noodles.

serves 3–4

preparation: 15 minutes

cooking: 20 minutes

𝒱

For the sauce:

1 tablespoon peanut or sunflower oil

1-inch (2.5-cm) piece of fresh ginger, grated

1 shallot, finely chopped

2 garlic cloves, finely chopped

½ teaspoon ground turmeric

1 ounce (25g) coconut cream

1¼ cups/½ pint (300 milliliters) warm water

1 lemongrass stalk, chopped into 3 pieces

1 bay leaf

salt and freshly ground black pepper

1 tablespoon sunflower oil

4 scallions, finely chopped

12 ounces (375g) asparagus, chopped

2 red bell peppers, cored, deseeded, and sliced

1 pound (500g) broccoli, divided into flowerets

1. To make the sauce, heat the oil in a saucepan and gently cook the ginger, shallot, and garlic. Add the turmeric and cook for 1 minute.

2. Dissolve the coconut cream in the warm water in a pitcher, then pour into the pan. Add the lemongrass and bay leaf. Bring the sauce to a boil. Simmer very gently for 5 minutes, then remove from the heat and season with salt and pepper to taste.

3. Have ready all the ingredients for the stir-fry. Heat the oil in a wok or large skillet and quickly stir-fry the scallions, then add the asparagus, red bell pepper, and broccoli and stir-fry until just soft.

4. Remove the bay leaf and lemongrass from the sauce and pour it over the vegetables. Cook for 2 minutes.

nutritional breakdown per serving: calories 179, protein 10g, fat 9g (saturated fat 5g), carbohydrate 15g

stir-fry with chinese sauce

The technique in this recipe is slightly different in that the vegetables are briefly stir-fried, then finished off in a sauce thickened with arrowroot. Cornstarch could also be used as a thickening agent. Serve with rice or noodles—if using instant noodles, they can be added in step 4.

serves 3–4
preparation: 10 minutes
cooking: 8 minutes
$\mathcal{V}$

For the sauce:

⅔ cup/¼ pint (150 milliliters) Vegetable Stock (see page 144)
1 tablespoon shoyu or soy sauce
1 tablespoon lemon juice
1 garlic clove, crushed
1 tablespoon concentrated apple juice
1 teaspoon Chinese five-spice powder
1 tablespoon arrowroot

For the stir-fry:

1 tablespoon peanut or sunflower oil
3 scallions, chopped
1 green bell pepper, cored, deseeded, and sliced
7 ounces (200g) water chestnuts, halved
3¼ cups/8 ounces (250g) oyster mushrooms
4 cups/8 ounces (250g) bean sprouts

1 Combine all the ingredients for the sauce in a pitcher and set aside.

2 Heat the oil in a wok or large skillet and stir-fry the scallions. Add the green bell pepper and water chestnuts and stir-fry for 1–2 minutes, then add the oyster mushrooms, and cook for 1 minute more.

3 Pour in the sauce and bring to a boil, then simmer, stirring frequently, until the sauce thickens and becomes clear.

4 Add the bean sprouts and mix in well. Serve as soon as they are heated through.

nutritional breakdown per serving: calories 120, protein 5g, fat 4g (saturated fat 1g), carbohydrate 19g

stir-fry with japanese sauce

This stir-fry includes classic Japanese ingredients, such as strips of omelet, together with hijiki and wasabi, which add a distinctive character to this nutritious dish.

serves 4	
preparation: 15 minutes	
cooking: 15 minutes	
(Ca) (Fe)	

For the omelet:

2 eggs

2 tablespoons water

1 tablespoon shoyu or soy sauce

1 tablespoon sunflower oil

For the sauce:

⅔ cup/½ pint (150 milliliters) hot water

1 garlic clove, crushed

2 tablespoons miso

¼ cup (50 milliliters) rice wine

2 tablespoons shoyu or soy sauce

1–2 teaspoon wasabi or grated fresh ginger

1–2 teaspoon hijiki (dried Japanese seaweed)

1 pound (500g) egg or rice noodles

1 teaspoon sesame oil

2 teaspoons sunflower oil

4 scallions, finely chopped

1 pound (500g) bok choy, shredded

2 red bell peppers, cored, deseeded, and sliced

1¾ cups/10 ounces (300g) green beans, chopped

1 To make the omelet, lightly beat the eggs with the water and season with the shoyu or soy sauce.

2 Heat a little of the oil in a small skillet and quickly pour in half of the beaten egg mixture. Cook for 2–3 minutes, then remove from the pan. Make a second omelet in the same way. Let cool, then cut into shreds.

3 To make the sauce, combine the ingredients in a pitcher and set aside.

4 Cook the noodles in a large saucepan of boiling water for 3–4 minutes. Drain and toss in the sesame oil.

5 Heat the sunflower oil in a wok or large skillet and quickly sauté the scallions. Add the shredded bok choy, red bell peppers and green beans and stir-fry until just wilted.

6 Turn down the heat, pour in the prepared sauce, and toss in the drained noodles and the omelet strips. Heat through and serve immediately.

nutritional breakdown per serving: calories 699, protein 28g, fat 19g (saturated fat 4g), carbohydrate 111g

sweet and sour sauce

This is a useful sauce for serving with stir-fried vegetables and Tempura Vegetables (see below), and it is very simple to make.

Makes about 2 cups
preparation: 5 minutes
cooking: 5 minutes
v

3 tablespoons arrowroot
3 tablespoons sherry
3 tablespoons shoyu or soy sauce
3 tablespoons sugar
1 cup (250 milliliters) apple juice
12 cardamom pods, crushed and husks removed
½-inch (1-cm)) piece of fresh ginger, grated
1 garlic clove, crushed
3 tablespoons cider vinegar
salt and freshly ground black pepper

1 Combine all the ingredients in a bowl, making sure that the arrowroot is properly dissolved.

2 Tip the mixture into a saucepan and bring to a boil, then simmer, stirring constantly, until the sauce thickens and clears.

3 Adjust the seasoning and serve hot or at room temperature.

nutritional breakdown per ½ cup: calories 149, protein 1g, fat 0g (saturated fat 0g), carbohydrate 35g

tempura vegetables

Tempura vegetables are chunks of vegetable coated in a light batter and fried until crisp then served with a Japanese dipping sauce. They are best eaten within a few minutes of making, so treat this as a very informal meal and cook and eat in batches. For other Japanese recipes, see pages 277 and 281.

serves 4
preparation: 20 minutes
cooking: 5–10 minutes

For the batter:
1 egg
1 cup (250 milliliters) ice water
1 cup/4 ounces (125g) all-purpose flour
½ teaspoon salt, optional

vegetable oil for deep-frying
2 pounds (1kg) vegetables of your choice (the following work well—green beans, asparagus cauliflower, carrots, and mushrooms), chopped or trimmed into manageable pieces
Sweet and Sour Sauce (see above) or wedges of lemon and salt, to serve

1 To make the batter, beat the egg and water together in a bowl, using a balloon whisk, then whisk in the flour and salt, if using. Do not beat more than necessary since, surprisingly, a slightly lumpy batter works well.

2 Pour oil to a depth of 1 inch (2.5cm) in a small deep skillet and heat until a piece of onion dropped in sizzles immediately.

3 Coat a few pieces of prepared vegetables in the batter, then drop into the hot oil. Cook until golden brown.

4 Drain and serve with sweet and sour dipping sauce or with wedges of lemon and salt.

nutritional breakdown per serving: calories 275, protein 10g, fat 12g (saturated fat 2g), carbohydrate 34g

sweet and sour sauce top, **tempura vegetables**

satay sauce

This easy sauce is delicious served with Tempura Vegetables (see page 278) or with a stir-fry of vegetables. Its use need not be confined only to Asian dishes since the sauce also goes well with vegetable or nut burgers and barbecue kabobs. As a variation, you can use honey instead of the concentrated apple juice.

makes about 2 cups

preparation: 10 minutes

cooking: 10 minutes

v

I tablespoon sunflower oil
I small onion, finely chopped
I garlic clove, crushed
½ chile, deseeded and finely chopped
1¼ cups/½ pint (300 milliliters) water
¼ cup (4 tablespoons) smooth peanut butter
1–2 tablespoons lemon juice
I tablespoon concentrated apple juice
I tablespoon shoyu or soy sauce
salt and freshly ground black pepper

1 Heat the oil in a small skillet and gently cook the onion, garlic, and chile until soft but not colored. Remove from the heat.

2 Using a blender or food processor, blend together the water with the peanut butter, lemon juice, concentrated apple juice, and shoyu or soy sauce until smooth.

3 Add the cooled onion mixture and blend again. Season to taste.

nutritional breakdown per ½ cup: calories 198, protein 6g, fat 16g (saturated fat 3g), carbohydrate 7g

sushi

makes 20 sushi slices

preparation time: 15 minutes, plus chilling time

cooking time: 20 minutes

v

8 ounces (250g) Japanese sushi rice
1¾ cups (400 milliliters) boiling water
½–1 teaspoon salt
½–1 teaspoon sugar
2 teaspoons rice wine vinegar
salt and freshly ground black pepper to taste
4 sheets of nori, toasted
2–3 ounces (50–75g) cucumber, cut in strips
2–3 ounces (50–75g) red bell pepper, cored, deseeded, and cut into strips
2–3 ounces (50–75g) green beans or snow peas, cooked
shoyu or soy sauce, or pickled ginger, to serve

1 Place the rice and the water in a large saucepan and cook for 20 minutes or until quite soft. Let cool, then mix in the salt, sugar, and rice wine vinegar to taste. Season well.

2 Spread each sheet of nori with a portion of the rice mixture. Cover with a selection of the prepared vegetables and roll up.

3 Refrigerate for 30 minutes, then cut each roll into 5 or 6 slices.

4 Serve with shoyu or soy sauce, or pickled ginger.

nutritional breakdown per sushi: calories 47, protein 1g, fat 0g (saturated fat 0g), carbohydrate 10g

sushi opposite

Side Dishes, Sauces, and Relishes

Many main courses need little more than simple accompaniments such as steamed vegetables or straightforward salads. If you turn to the descriptions of individual vegetable families on pages 33–57 in the reference section, you'll find plenty of tips on how to cook and serve a wide range of vegetables.

The recipes on the following pages are designed to show off vegetables in a more elaborate fashion, and also to highlight some of the best cooking techniques. There are some easy sauté ideas, such as Lemon-glazed Celery Root and Cabbage and Cumin. Stir-frying, as seen in Stir-fry Shredded Leeks with Tarragon, is also a good way of preparing a single vegetable for an accompaniment. Roasting vegetables, as in the recipe featured on this page, works well for root vegetables that require a longer cooking time, and once in the oven, need little attention. The section on sauces includes a classic white sauce and a very easy tomato sauce—both recipes that can be used time and again. Do try some of the other ideas such as the tasty, dairy-free Leek and Cashew Sauce as well as the quick Pinto Bean and Red Onion Salsa with Cumin and Roasted Red Bell Pepper Coulis.

roasted root vegetables with caraway

Roasting vegetables accentuates their mellow flavors and, once in the oven, they require little attention, leaving you free to do other things. The beets "bleed" a little, so try to keep them apart from other vegetables while they are cooking.

serves 4

preparation: 10 minutes

cooking: 30 minutes

2 tablespoons/1 ounce (25g) butter
1 tablespoon sunflower oil
12 ounces (400g) raw beet, peeled and
    thinly sliced
12 ounces (400g) sweet potato, peeled and
    thinly sliced
12 ounces (400g) potato, peeled and thinly sliced
1 teaspoon salt
1 teaspoon caraway seeds
freshly grated nutmeg
freshly ground black pepper

1   Melt the butter with the oil in a large roasting pan. Mix in the vegetables and spread out in the pan. Sprinkle with the salt, caraway seeds, nutmeg, and black pepper.

2   Bake in a preheated oven, 400°F (200°C), for 30 minutes, turning the vegetables a few times during cooking.

3   Once cooked, they should be crisp and browned. Serve hot.

nutritional breakdown per serving: calories 270, protein 5g, fat 9g (saturated fat 4g), carbohydrate 46g

cabbage and cumin

Cooked cabbage should retain its crisp texture and nutty flavor. This method is part stir-fry and part steaming, and is simple and quick, keeping both the texture and flavor of the cabbage.

serves 4

preparation: 5 minutes

cooking: 10 minutes

2 tablespoons/1 ounce (25g) butter
1 onion, finely chopped
1 garlic clove, crushed
2 tablespoons cumin seeds
4 cups/13 ounces (400g) finely shredded cabbage
2–3 tablespoons water
salt and freshly ground black pepper

1 Melt the butter in a large saucepan and cook the onion and garlic gently until translucent.

2 Add the cumin seeds and cook for 1 minute, or until just toasted.

3 Add the cabbage with the water and cook for 5 minutes, stirring frequently.

4 Season well with salt and pepper and serve immediately.

nutritional breakdown per serving: calories 87, protein 2g, fat 6g (saturated fat 4g), carbohydrate 7g

VARIATION

This recipe is also great with caraway seeds instead of the cumin seeds.

lemon-glazed celery root

Fragrant and nutty, this recipe is good hot or cold. Use the same idea for other root vegetables or use orange juice as a flavoring instead of the lemon for a variation. This is good served with egg or grain dishes as well as baked dishes.

serves 4

preparation: 5 minutes

cooking: 15 minutes

1 pound (500g) celery root, coarsely chopped
2 tablespoons (25g) butter
2 tablespoons soft brown sugar
2 tablespoons lemon juice
¼ cup/1 ounce (25g) pecans, chopped
salt and freshly ground black pepper

1 Steam or cook the celery root in boiling salted water for 8–10 minutes until just soft. Drain.

2 Heat the butter, sugar, and lemon juice in a large skillet.

3 When melted and mixed, add the celery root pieces and the pecans. Cook over medium to high heat until brown. Season well with salt and pepper and serve hot or at room temperature.

nutritional breakdown per serving: calories 203, protein 2g, fat 15g (saturated fat 7g), carbohydrate 15g

stir-fry shredded leeks with tarragon

This is an extremely easy way of serving leeks and is a combination of stir-fry and braising.

serves 4

preparation: 5 minutes

cooking: 7 minutes

v

4 leeks
2 tablespoons sunflower oil
2–3 tablespoons white wine
1 teaspoon tarragon vinegar
2 teaspoons chopped tarragon
salt and freshly ground black pepper

1 Shred the leeks in a food processor or cut them thinly by hand.

2 Heat the oil in a large skillet or wok, and quickly stir-fry the leeks until just soft.

3 Add the wine, tarragon vinegar, and chopped tarragon and simmer for 3 minutes. Season well with salt and pepper and serve immediately.

nutritional breakdown per serving: calories 77, protein 2g, fat 6g (saturated fat 1g), carbohydrate 3g

pan-fried cauliflower

Crisp fried bread crumbs and a hint of mustard are a great way of livening up plain cauliflower, providing a pleasing mixture of textures and flavors.

serves 4
preparation: 5 minutes
cooking: 10 minutes

2 tablespoons/1 ounce (25g) butter, softened
1 tablespoon Dijon mustard
1 cauliflower, divided into flowerets
2 tablespoons olive oil
½ cup/1 ounce (25g) fresh bread crumbs
salt and freshly ground black pepper

1 Combine the softened butter with the mustard in a small bowl and chill.

2 Steam the cauliflower flowerets over a saucepan of boiling water for 10 minutes, until just tender.

3 Meanwhile, heat the olive oil in a skillet and cook the bread crumbs until very crisp.

4 Toss the cooked cauliflower with the mustard butter, season well with salt and pepper, immediately stir in the crisp bread crumbs, and serve.

nutritional breakdown per serving: calories 150, protein 5g, fat 12g (saturated fat 4g), carbohydrate 2g

butternut squash and carrot purée with nutmeg and mascarpone

PHYLLO PARCELS

This purée is also great in phyllo parcels. Let the purée cool, then brush individual sheets of phyllo pastry with melted butter or oil. Place a spoonful of purée on each sheet and roll up into a parcel. Brush with more butter, place on a baking sheet, and bake in a preheated oven, 400°F (200°C), for 15–18 minutes.

Rich and colorful, this purée is excellent with savory baked dishes and casseroles. It could also be used as a filling for crêpes. It can be made with other vegetables, such as pumpkin, sweet potato, parsnip, or rutabaga.

serves 4
preparation: 10 minutes
cooking: 20 minutes
suitable for freezing
V

1¼ cups/½ pint (300 milliliters) water
2 tablespoons/1 ounce (25g) butter
2 teaspoons sugar
12 ounces (375g) carrots, chopped
12 ounces (375g) butternut squash, chopped
freshly grated nutmeg
2 tablespoons mascarpone cheese
salt and freshly ground black pepper

1 Bring the water to a boil in a large saucepan with the butter and sugar. Add the carrots and squash and simmer, uncovered, until the water has all evaporated.

2 Using a blender or food processor, purée the cooked vegetables with a generous grating of nutmeg and the mascarpone.

3 Season well with salt and pepper and serve immediately.

nutritional breakdown per serving: calories 162, protein 2g, fat 10g (saturated fat 7g), carbohydrate 17g

pan-fried cauliflower top **butternut squash and carrot purée with nutmeg and mascarpone** front

rösti

This originated as a breakfast dish for hungry Swiss farmers who had generally done a morning's work before sitting down to eat. The meal was made from potatoes leftover from the night before.

If you boil the potatoes especially for this dish, cook them until firm but not soft. It is best to choose a waxy textured potato, in other words one more suitable for a potato salad than mashed potato. Rösti can also be made from leftover baked potatoes.

This is a robust accompaniment but could also make a meal on its own, served with Red Onion Marmalade with Coriander (see page 295) and a contrasting salad.

serves 4

preparation: 10 minutes

cooking: 35 minutes

𝓋

2 pounds (1kg) cooked potatoes
6 tablespoons/3 ounces (75g) clarified butter or ghee
salt

1 Grate or thinly slice the cooked potatoes into slices ⅛ inch (2–3mm) thick.

2 Heat half the fat in a large skillet. Add the grated or sliced potatoes and a little salt, and mix gently over a high heat for 1 minute.

3 Reduce the heat and press the potatoes into a flat cake, no more than 1 inch (2.5cm) deep using a wooden spoon.

4 Melt a little of the remaining fat around the sides of the skillet, letting it run under the rösti cake so that it does not stick to the pan.

5 Cook gently for about 20 minutes, shaking the skillet from time to time.

6 Turn the rösti over, either by inverting it into a second skillet or by sliding it out onto a plate, turning it over, and then sliding it back. Add the rest of the fat and let it run under the rösti as before, then cook for 10 minutes.

7 Serve hot.

nutritional breakdown per serving: calories 326, protein 5g, fat 16g (saturated fat 10g), carbohydrate 43g

VARIATION
Add onion, chopped parsley, or Swiss chard at step 2.

mushroom ragoût

This is a good accompaniment that works well with savory pastries and baked dishes and is a little more substantial than a sauce. It works well with contrasting green or orange hues.

serves 4

preparation: 5 minutes, plus soaking

cooking: 35 minutes

⅓ cup/¾ ounce (20g) dried cèpes or other
    dried mushrooms
generous 2 cups (500 milliliters) boiling water
1 tablespoon/½ ounce (15g) butter
1 leek, finely chopped
4 ounces (150g) Paris or cremini
    mushrooms, sliced
1 tablespoon brandy
1–2 tablespoons shoyu or soy sauce
salt and freshly ground black pepper

1 Place the cèpes or dried mushrooms in a bowl and cover with boiling water for 15 minutes. Strain, reserving the soaking liquid, and chop the mushrooms coarsely.

2 Melt the butter in a saucepan and gently cook the leek until quite soft.

3 Add the fresh mushrooms and cook for 2–3 minutes over high heat to soften and brown. Stir in the chopped dried mushrooms.

4 Add the brandy and cook for 1 minute, then add the reserved mushroom stock and shoyu or soy sauce, and bring to a boil.

5 Reduce the heat to a simmer, partially cover the pan, and cook for 25 minutes, or until most of the liquid has been absorbed and the mushrooms are very soft.

6 Season with salt and pepper to taste and serve hot.

nutritional breakdown per serving: calories 64, protein 2g, fat 3g
(saturated fat 2g), carbohydrate 5g

classic white sauce

White sauce is often used in vegetarian cookery as a coating for vegetables, a filling for crêpes, or as a topping on traditional dishes such as lasagne or moussaka. White sauce can be made with either whole-wheat or white flour. If you are using whole-wheat, you may need a little extra butter or margarine in the recipe to make a smoother roux. Make sure the roux is properly cooked and the finished sauce simmered or the sauce will taste floury.

serves 4

preparation: 5 minutes, plus infusing

cooking: 10 minutes

suitable for freezing

(Ca)

- 1¼ cups/½ pint (300 milliliters) milk
- ½ onion
- 1 bay leaf
- 6 black peppercorns
- 1 sprig thyme
- freshly grated nutmeg
- 2 tablespoons/1 ounce (25g) butter
- ¼ cup/1 ounce (25g) all-purpose or whole-wheat flour
- salt and freshly ground black pepper

1 Heat the milk in a small saucepan with the onion, bay leaf, peppercorns, thyme, and a generous grating of nutmeg until just warm, then let stand for 15 minutes. Strain and reserve.

2 Melt the butter in a small saucepan and, when it is foaming, sprinkle in the flour. Mix well and cook over gentle heat for 2–3 minutes to make a roux.

3 Add the milk to the roux—about a quarter at a time—stirring very well.

4 Bring the sauce to boiling point, then simmer over very gentle heat for 3–4 minutes.

5 Season well with salt and pepper and use as required.

nutritional breakdown per serving: calories 123, protein 3g, fat 8g (saturated fat 5g), carbohydrate 10g

VARIATIONS

Substitute a little cream or vegetable stock for the milk to make richer or lighter sauces. For a parsley sauce, add 3 tablespoons chopped parsley once the sauce is cooked. For a cheese sauce, add ½–1 cup/2–4 ounces (50–125g) grated cheese when the sauce is cooked and stir over gentle heat until melted.

buttered shallot and wine sauce

This is a rich sauce for special meals. It can be served with a simple pasta dish, with savory crêpes, or with pastry. Try this sauce with Chestnut and Cep Pie (see page 257) or Roasted Pecan and Cashew Loaf (see page 264).

serves 4

preparation: 10 minutes

cooking: 20 minutes

- 2 tablespoons/1 ounce (25g) butter
- 3 shallots, very finely chopped
- scant ½ cup (100 milliliters) white wine
- 1 teaspoon grain mustard
- scant 1 cup (200 milliliters) heavy cream
- salt and freshly ground black pepper

1 Melt the butter in a saucepan and cook the shallots gently until very soft—this takes at least 10 minutes.

2 Pour in the white wine and bring to a boil, then cook over medium heat until the liquid has reduced by about half.

3 Stir in the mustard and cream, season well with salt and pepper, and bring to a boil, then remove from the heat. Serve hot.

nutritional breakdown per serving: calories 298, protein 1g, fat 29g (saturated fat 18g), carbohydrate 4g

mushroom sauce

This is a delicious dark sauce with complex woody flavors. It is very important to use a mushroom stock and to sweat the vegetable base until very soft, in order to bring out the flavors.

serves 4

preparation: 5 minutes, plus stock making

cooking: 25 minutes

suitable for freezing

𝒱 (using margarine)

2 tablespoons/1 ounce (25g) butter or margarine
1 shallot, finely chopped
1 garlic clove, crushed
1 ounce (25g) all-purpose flour
1½ cups/½ pint (300 milliliters) Dark Mushroom
  Stock (see page 145)
1 tablespoon tomato paste
1 teaspoon dried thyme
1 tablespoon miso, dissolved in a little stock
salt and freshly ground black pepper

1 Melt the butter or margarine in a saucepan and very gently cook the shallot and garlic until soft and browned.

2 Sprinkle in the flour and cook, stirring constantly, for 2 minutes. Then add the mushroom stock, and bring to a boil, stirring constantly. Add the tomato paste, thyme, and miso. Simmer the sauce for 5 minutes, then add salt and pepper to taste.

3 Cook for 10 minutes more, partially covered, so that the sauce reduces slightly.

nutritional breakdown per serving: calories 88, protein 2g, fat 6g (saturated fat 3g), carbohydrate 8g

from the left **buttered shallot and wine sauce, classic white sauce, mushroom sauce**

QUICK VERSION

For a quick version of this sauce, use the soaking water from ½ cup/1 ounce (25g) dried mushrooms in place of the mushroom stock. The flavors are not so intense. A richer version of the sauce can be made by adding a mixture of very finely shredded or sliced vegetables, such as carrots, celery, or mushrooms. Cook these with the shallot and garlic at the end of step 1.

very easy tomato sauce

This is an essential recipe to have in your repertoire since it is not only easy to make but can be used in so many different ways. Smother freshly cooked pasta with it, serve it with a baked dish, such as Lentil Layer with Red Bell Pepper (see page 266), use it sparingly as a pizza topping, or spoon it over a plain risotto.

serves 4
preparation: 5 minutes
cooking: 35 minutes
suitable for freezing
(Fe) $\mathcal{V}$

2 tablespoons olive oil
I onion, finely chopped
28 ounces (796 milliliters) canned chopped
    tomatoes
I teaspoon sugar
I teaspoon salt
I bay leaf
I teaspoon dried thyme or oregano
freshly ground black pepper

1 Heat the oil in a large saucepan and gently cook the onion until translucent.

2 Add the canned tomatoes, sugar, salt, bay leaf, thyme, and black pepper to taste. Bring to a boil, then cover the pan, and cook slowly for 30 minutes.

3 Let cool slightly, remove the bay leaf, and then purée the tomato mixture until very smooth, using a blender or food processor. Adjust the seasoning to taste and use as required.

> **nutritional breakdown per serving:** calories 99, protein 2g, fat 6g (saturated fat 1g), carbohydrate 10g

VARIATIONS

For a garlic finish, add 1–2 crushed garlic cloves at step 3. For a creamy finish, add 1–2 tablespoons olive oil at step 3. For a mushroom sauce, add 5¼ cups/13 ounces (400g) thinly sliced mushrooms once the sauce has been puréed. Return to the pan, bring to a boil, and simmer for about 15–20 minutes. Season fo taste.

pinto bean and red onion salsa with cumin

This is a pretty pink-beige salsa with a creamy texture and aromatic spicing. It could also be made with black-eyed peas, black beans, or red kidney beans, and is delicious with taco shells and sour cream, plus crisp salad.

serves 4
preparation: 5 minutes
cooking: 15 minutes
suitable for freezing
$\mathcal{V}$

¼ cup (50 milliliters) olive oil
I teaspoon cumin seeds
I red onion, very finely chopped
2 garlic cloves, crushed with salt
1⅔ cups/8 ounces (250g) cooked pinto beans
freshly ground black pepper

1 Heat 2 tablespoons of the oil in a medium skillet and fry the cumin seed gently until just beginning to brown. Add the red onion and garlic and cook very gently until very soft.

2 Add the beans and stir well. Mash in the pan with a potato masher or fork to get a well-textured mixture. Add the remaining 2 tablespoons oil and pepper.

> **nutritional breakdown per serving:** calories 202, protein 6g, fat 12g (saturated fat 2g), carbohydrate 19g

leek and cashew sauce

This is an easy, high-protein, dairy-free, and wheat-free sauce, which goes well with a wide range of savory pastries and baked dishes.

serves 4

preparation: 5 minutes

cooking: 10 minutes

𝒱

2 tablespoons sunflower oil

scant 1 cup/3½ ounces (100g) cashew nuts

2 leeks, finely chopped

1¾ cups (400 milliliters) water

2 tablespoons shoyu or soy sauce

salt and freshly ground black pepper

1 Heat the oil in a saucepan and fry the cashew nuts until lightly browned. Remove from the pan using a slotted spoon and set aside.

2 Add the leeks to the pan and cook until soft.

3 Using a blender or food processor, blend the leeks with the cashew nuts, water, and shoyu or soy sauce until completely smooth.

4 Season with salt and pepper to taste and heat gently before serving.

nutritional breakdown per serving: calories 208, protein 6g, fat 18g (saturated fat 3g), carbohydrate 6g

leek and cashew sauce back **pinto bean and red onion salsa** front left **very easy tomato sauce** front right

roasted red bell pepper coulis

cucumber relish with chile and lemon left
roasted red bell pepper coulis center
red onion marmalade with coriander right

This delicious, sweet, smoky dipping sauce is great for barbecue food or as a sauce for pasta. Try spooning some into scrambled eggs or pouring over stir-fry vegetables.

serves 4

preparation: 5 minutes

cooking: 25 minutes

𝓋

4 red bell peppers, lightly oiled
⅔ cup/¼ pint (150 milliliters) olive oil
2 garlic cloves, crushed
2–3 tablespoons chopped basil
1–2 tablespoons balsamic vinegar
salt and freshly ground black pepper

1 Place the bell peppers on a baking sheet or in a roasting pan and cook in a preheated oven, 400°F (200°C), for 25 minutes, or until well charred.

2 Leave the bell peppers until cool enough to handle, then remove the skins and seeds. Do not wash them; coarsely chop the flesh.

3 Using a food processor, purée the bell peppers with the olive oil until very smooth, then add the garlic, basil, and balsamic vinegar, and blend again. Season well with salt and pepper.

4 Store in the refrigerator and use as required.

nutritional breakdown per serving: calories 293, protein 2g, fat 28g (saturated fat 4g), carbohydrate 9g

cucumber relish with chile and lemon

This lively relish is quick to make and great served with grain dishes, barbecue food, with Tempura Vegetables (see page 278) or with Spiced Vegetable Fritters (see page 168).

serves 4

preparation: 5 minutes, plus chilling

cooking: none

V

For the dressing:

I teaspoon finely chopped green chile
I tablespoon shoyu or soy sauce
I–2 tablespoons lemon juice
salt and freshly ground black pepper

I cucumber
2 tablespoons snipped chives or chopped
    scallions, to garnish

1 Make the dressing by mixing together the chile, shoyu or soy sauce, lemon juice, and salt and pepper to taste.

2 Cut the cucumber into thirds, then cut into very thin strips using a vegetable peeler. Add to the dressing and chill for up to 30 minutes.

3 Serve garnished with snipped chives or chopped scallions.

nutritional breakdown per serving: calories 11, protein 1g, fat 0g (saturated fat 0g), carbohydrate 2g

red onion marmalade with coriander

This moist, dark relish is delicious served with cheese or egg dishes. Use it on bruschetta or savory toasts, or to give sandwiches an extra kick. It is also great with Rösti (see page 288). It is worth making a large amount since it will store for several weeks in the refrigerator.

makes about 10 ounces (300g); serves 4

preparation: 10 minutes

cooking: 45–50 minutes

suitable for freezing

V

3 tablespoons olive oil
1¾ pounds (875g) red onions, coarsely chopped
I tablespoon ground coriander
I tablespoon dark brown sugar
2 tablespoons balsamic vinegar
salt and freshly ground black pepper

1 Heat the oil in a large saucepan and cook the onions gently so that they start to soften.

2 Sprinkle the ground coriander over them and cook for 2–3 minutes more, then sprinkle in the brown sugar, and stir well.

3 Add enough water to cover the onions, then bring to a boil. Simmer very gently for 35–40 minutes until the liquid has virtually evaporated, stirring occasionally at first and more frequently as the water evaporates.

4 Add the balsamic vinegar, stir well, and cook for 5 minutes more. Season with salt and pepper to taste and let cool.

nutritional breakdown per serving: calories 179, protein 3g, fat 9g (saturated fat 1g), carbohydrate 23g

Main Course Salads

alads suit a modern, lighter style of eating and they certainly needn't be confined to side dishes or eaten only in hot weather. They have a great deal to offer since they are highly nutritious, extremely colorful, and simple to put together. The salads described range from quite substantial meals constructed around ingredients such as rice, bulgur wheat, or legumes, to light vegetable concoctions that make good accompaniments or snacks.

In a lot of countries, the cuisine includes traditional salads that highlight a particular flavoring or seasoning. Many of these recipes have enormous worldwide appeal, such as Classic Tabbouleh from the Middle East, which has inspired many variations, and Gado Gado, an Indonesian bean sprout and vegetable salad with a rich dressing made from coconut and peanuts. Also included is a Greek Potato Salad and a Smoked Bean Curd and Water Chestnut Salad with Chinese Dressing from the Far East. Apart from the recipe featured on this page, you'll find the more robust salads are at the start of the chapter, and the less substantial salads toward the end. A salad would not be complete without a dressing, and the recipes here include classic vinaigrette with several variations, as well as mayonnaise and lower-fat or lower-calorie suggestions.

belgian endive and beet with mustard dressing

This robustly colored salad is great as a cool weather dish. The sweet flavor of beet complements the slight bitterness of Belgian endive and provides a colorful contrast. For extra protein, add some toasted hazelnuts; for extra flavor, add a little hazelnut oil to the dressing.

serves 4
preparation: 5 minutes
cooking: none
v

2–3 heads Belgian endive, sliced
5 ounces (150g) raw beet, finely grated
3 ounces (75g) watercress or mixed salad greens

For the dressing:
6 tablespoons olive oil
2 tablespoons white wine vinegar
2 teaspoons Dijon mustard
1 garlic clove, crushed
salt and freshly ground black pepper

1 Combine the endive, beet, and watercress in a large bowl.

2 Combine the dressing ingredients in a pitcher and season with salt and pepper to taste.

3 Toss the dressing into the salad and serve immediately.

> nutritional breakdown per serving: calories 176, protein 2g, fat 17g (saturated fat 3g), carbohydrate 4g

marinated bean salad

*It is best to make this salad from freshly cooked beans
since they soak up the marinade much better when they
are warm. If you want to use canned beans or cooked
beans that you have cooked and frozen, heat the
marinade ingredients gently so that the flavors steep, then
pour it over the beans.*

serves 4

preparation: 10 minutes, plus marinating

cooking: about 1–1½ hours

(Fe) 𝒱

½ cup/4 ounces (125g) dry garbanzo beans,
   soaked overnight
scant 1 cup/4 ounces (125g) dry red kidney
   beans, soaked overnight
1 green bell pepper, cored, deseeded,
   and chopped
3 celery stalks, chopped
½ cucumber, chopped

For the marinade:
⅔ cup/¼ pint (150 milliliters) olive oil
¼ cup (50 milliliters) red wine vinegar or
   balsamic vinegar
½ teaspoon salt
2 bay leaves
1 red onion, chopped
¼ cup/¼ ounce (7g) chopped parsley
1 teaspoon dried thyme
salt and freshly ground black pepper, to taste

1 Keeping them separate, drain the soaking garbanzo
and kidney beans. Discard the soaking water and
bring them to a boil in 2 large saucepans of fresh
water. Boil fast for 10 minutes, then cook until
tender—60–90 minutes. (Keeping the red kidney
and garbanzo beans separate when cooking
preserves their colors.)

2 Meanwhile, combine all the marinade ingredients
in a bowl.

3 Drain the cooked beans and combine them in a
large bowl. Pour the marinade over the top and
let cool.

4 When the beans are cold, add the remaining salad
ingredients and mix well. Adjust the seasoning and
serve the salad at room temperature.

nutritional breakdown per serving: calories 453, protein 15g,
fat 30g (saturated fat 4g), carbohydrate 33g

classic tabbouleh

This salad comes in many guises throughout the Middle East. It can be an equal balance of bulgur and herbs, or cam be vivid green with just a hint of grain. It is, however, invariably doused in a fragrant lemon and olive oil dressing. Additional extras for this salad could include chopped tomatoes, finely chopped cucumber, and toasted pine nuts.

serves 4

preparation: 5 minutes, plus soaking

cooking: none

𝒱

⅔ cup/4 ounces (125g) bulgur
½ teaspoon salt
scant 1 cup (200 milliliters) boiling water
2 tablespoons lemon juice
2 tablespoons olive oil
2–3 tablespoons finely chopped mint
2–3 tablespoons chopped parsley
3 scallions, finely chopped
salt and freshly ground black pepper

1　Place the bulgur and salt in a large bowl. Pour in the boiling water and soak for 30 minutes. The water should be absorbed but drain the bulgur if necessary.

2　Pour in the lemon juice and olive oil and mix in the chopped mint, parsley, and scallions.

3　Season with salt and pepper to taste and serve at room temperature.

nutritional breakdown per serving: calories 187, protein 4g, fat 6g (saturated fat 1g), carbohydrate 30g

MEZZE

There is a strong tradition of informal meals or mezze throughout the Middle East. At these meals, a large assortment of dishes is put on the table at the same time, leaving everyone to make their own selection. Tabbouleh is good served on these occasions, as are roasted vegetables such as Roasted Bell Pepper Salad with Basil Vinaigrette, (page 313), Hummus (page 167), Falafel (page 174), a bowl of cubed feta cheese, olives, marinated chiles, and roasted nuts. You could also serve some phyllo parcels or slices of Kuku with Spinach (see page 181). All go toward making a colorful and memorable meal.

beet and green bean salad with couscous

With its bold colors and a good combination of flavors, this salad is useful when you want something robust but not heavy. It is great with gratin dishes, such as Sweet Potato and Zucchini Gratin (see page 263), as well as with Frittata (see page 179) or savory quiches. The couscous is useful for absorbing some of the water that leaches out of the vegetables.

serves 4

preparation: 15 minutes, plus standing

cooking: 4–5 minutes

𝓋

¼ cup/1½ ounces (40g) couscous
¼ cup (50 milliliters) boiling water
4 ounces (125g) green beans
2 raw or cooked beets, diced
⅓ cucumber, diced
4 scallions, diced
1 red bell pepper, cored, deseeded, and diced
2 tablespoons finely chopped cilantro
¼ cup (50 milliliters) olive oil
juice of 1 lemon
salt and freshly ground black pepper

1 Place the couscous in a small bowl. Add the boiling water and set aside to soak.

2 Meanwhile, cook the green beans in a saucepan of boiling water for 4–5 minutes. Drain and chop finely.

3 Toss the beets, cucumber, scallions, red bell pepper, cilantro, cooked beans, and couscous in a large bowl.

4 Combine the olive oil and lemon juice and season well with salt and pepper. Pour the dressing over the salad and let stand for about 30 minutes.

5 Adjust the seasoning to taste and serve at room temperature.

nutritional breakdown per serving: calories 168, protein 3g, fat 12g (saturated fat 2g), carbohydrate 14g

greek potato salad

Potatoes make splendid robust salads. There are two points to bear in mind. First, choose a suitable variety—don't try to make a salad with a mealy overcooked potato, which will easily disintegrate. Second, potatoes thirst for dressings. These can be based on mayonnaise or sour cream. For a less rich result, I prefer a light vinaigrette mixed with plain yogurt.

serves 4

preparation: 15 minutes

cooking: 15 minutes

1 pound (500g) waxy potatoes
1 cup/4 ounces (125g) fava beans
   (shelled weight)
3 scallions, chopped
2 hard-cooked eggs, chopped
3 artichoke hearts, cooked and sliced or
   4 canned artichoke hearts, sliced

For the dressing:
¼ cup (50 milliliters) olive oil
2 tablespoons lemon juice
1 garlic clove, crushed
1 teaspoon dried marjoram
⅓ cup (80 milliliters) plain yogurt
salt and freshly ground black pepper

To serve, optional:
sliced large tomatoes
crisp lettuce (such as romaine)
black olives

1   Cook the potatoes in a large saucepan of boiling salted water until just tender. Drain, peel if you like, then roughly chop.

2   Meanwhile, cook the fava beans in another saucepan of boiling salted water for 5 minutes, or until tender. Drain and refresh in cold water.

3   Combine the cooked potato, fava beans, scallions, eggs, and artichoke hearts in a large bowl.

4   To make the dressing, whisk the oil, lemon juice, garlic, and marjoram in a pitcher. Stir in the yogurt and season well with salt and pepper.

5   Stir the dressing into the potato salad and adjust the seasoning. Serve at room temperature.

nutritional breakdown per serving: calories 296, protein 11g, fat 15g (saturated fat 3g), carbohydrate 33g

pasta salad

Cook the pasta until just firm-tender so that it still has some bite when you serve it. Chunky shapes, such as shells and spirals, hold the dressing better.

serves 4

preparation: 15 minutes, plus salting

cooking: 25–30 minutes

2 eggplant, cubed
salt
3–4 tablespoons olive oil
2 cups/8 ounces (250g) dried whole-wheat pasta
    shells or spirals
8 sun-dried tomatoes, chopped
3 tablespoons chopped parsley

For the dressing:
⅔ cup/¼ pint (150 milliliters) sour cream
2 ounces (50g) Roquefort
1–2 tablespoons lemon juice
salt and freshly ground black pepper
dark salad greens (such as radicchio, lollo rosso,
    feuille de chêne), to serve

1 Put the cubes of eggplant in a colander and sprinkle with salt. Let stand for 30 minutes, then pat dry with paper towels.

2 Spread out on a baking sheet or in a roasting pan, sprinkle with the olive oil, and roast in a preheated oven, 400°F (200°C), for 25–30 minutes, until browned. Let cool.

3 Meanwhile, cook the pasta spirals in a large saucepan of boiling salted water until just firm-tender. Drain and let cool.

4 Tip the pasta into a large bowl and toss in the roasted eggplant, sun-dried tomatoes, and parsley.

5 To make the dressing, place the sour cream in a small bowl. Mash in the Roquefort and add lemon juice, salt, and pepper to taste.

6 Toss the dressing into the pasta and vegetables and adjust the seasoning. Serve on a bed of colorful salad greens.

nutritional breakdown per serving: calories 713, protein 15g, fat 53g (saturated fat 13g), carbohydrate 48g

smoked bean curd and water chestnut salad with chinese dressing

Colorful and flavorsome, this distinctive salad is prepared in just a few minutes. It can be served as an appetizer to a Chinese meal, or served as a side salad with a grain dish, such as Sesame Millet (see page 228). You could also add bean sprouts, snow peas, or sugar snap peas.

nutritional breakdown per serving: calories 260, protein 12g, fat 18g (saturated fat 4g), carbohydrate 14g

serves 4

preparation: 10 minutes

cooking: 15 minutes

v

2 tablespoons sunflower oil
8 ounces (200g) smoked bean curd, drained and thinly sliced
8 ounces (200g) water chestnuts
1 tablespoon shoyu or soy sauce
8 ounces (200g) asparagus
1 yellow bell pepper, cored, deseeded, and sliced
4 scallions, finely chopped
4 ounces (125g) baby spinach

For the dressing:
3 tablespoons sunflower oil
1 tablespoon rice wine
1 tablespoon shoyu or soy sauce
1 garlic clove, crushed
1 teaspoon grated fresh ginger
salt and freshly ground black pepper, to taste

1 Heat the oil in a skillet and cook the bean curd and water chestnuts for 5 minutes, or until lightly browned.

2 Sprinkle in the shoyu or soy sauce and cook for 2–3 minute mores. Remove from the skillet.

3 Griddle or broil the asparagus for 3–4 minutes, until just softened and browned.

4 Mix the bean curd, water chestnuts, and asparagus in a large bowl with the yellow bell pepper, scallions, and baby spinach.

5 To make the dressing, thoroughly combine all the ingredients and toss into the bowl of salad. Serve immediately.

spiced rice salad with mango and cashews

Golden rice, flavored with aromatic spices, makes a wonderful base for a substantial salad. Add fruit, nuts, and vegetables for extra color and texture. For a party special, press this salad into a lightly oiled mold and serve surrounded by extra fruit and nuts.

serves 4
preparation: 10 minutes
cooking: 35 minutes
𝓋

2 tablespoons sunflower oil
3 shallots, finely chopped
I chile, deseeded and finely chopped
I tablespoon black mustard seeds
2 teaspoons cumin seeds
2 teaspoons ground coriander
I teaspoon ground turmeric
2 cups/8 ounces (250g) long-grain brown rice
2½ cups/1 pint (600 milliliters) boiling water
½ teaspoon salt
2–3 tablespoons lime juice
½ cup/2 ounces (50g) cashew nut pieces
I mango, diced
I red bell pepper, cored, deseeded, and finely chopped
salt and freshly ground black pepper

1 Heat the oil in a large saucepan and gently cook the shallots until soft. Add the chile, mustard seeds, cumin, coriander, and turmeric. Cook for 2–3 minutes, or until slightly toasted.

2 Stir in the rice, then pour in the boiling water and ½ teaspoon salt. Bring back to a boil, cover the pan, and cook for 30 minutes. All the water should have been absorbed. If necessary, drain the rice or cook it for a few minutes longer without the lid. Stir in the lime juice and let cool.

3 While the rice is cooking, roast the cashews by placing them on a baking sheet; roast in a preheated oven, 400°F (200°C), for 5 minutes, or until lightly browned.

4 When the rice is cold, stir in the mango, roasted cashews and red bell pepper and season well.

5 If the salad is a little dry, stir in 1 extra tablespoon of sunflower oil or a flavored oil, such as chile oil, to give an extra kick.

nutritional breakdown per serving: calories 403, protein 8g, fat 14g (saturated fat 2g), carbohydrate 64g

griddled vegetables with brie

Griddled vegetables are delicious in salads because they keep their freshness and color but develop a different flavor. Other vegetables suitable for griddling for salad include asparagus, artichokes, fennel, shallots, leeks, and cauliflower. Keep the pieces chunky or they will disappear to nothing. Toss the Brie into this salad at the last minute so that it melts with the warmth of the vegetables.

serves 4

preparation: 10 minutes

cooking: 10 minutes

 (Ca) (Fe)

1 red onion, cut into thick pieces
2 yellow bell peppers, cored, deseeded, and cut into thick pieces
3 red bell peppers, cored, deseeded, and cut into thick pieces
4 zucchini, thickly sliced
8 ounces (250g) broccoli flowerets
salt and freshly ground black pepper
8 ounces (250g) Brie, roughly sliced
salad greens, to serve
3–4 tablespoons Fruity Vinaigrette (see page 314)

1 Heat a griddle pan or heavy skillet until very hot. Add the onion, yellow and red peppers, zucchini, and broccoli. Cook for several minutes until the vegetables start to blister and brown. Turn them over quite frequently.

2 When cooked, season well, remove the pan from the heat, and toss the Brie into the vegetables.

3 Pile the cheese and griddled vegetables onto a bed of salad greens. Serve immediately with the Fruity Vinaigrette passed separately.

nutritional breakdown per serving: calories 360, protein 18g, fat 25g (saturated fat 12g), carbohydrate 18g

gado gado

This is a marvelous peanut and bean sprout salad from Indonesia. It is a dish of contrasts—crunchy nuts smothered in a creamy coconut dressing, cool bean sprouts, and hot spices, all bound to set your taste buds alight.

serves 4

preparation: 15 minutes

cooking: 12 minutes

(Fe)

For the salad:

4 ounces (125g) green beans or snow peas

¾ cup/3 ounces (125g) shelled peanuts

1 yellow bell pepper, cored, deseeded, and sliced

2½ cups/5 ounces (150g) bean sprouts

6 ounces (150g) Chinese cabbage or green cabbage, shredded

2 scallions, finely chopped

For the dressing:

1 tablespoon sunflower oil

2 shallots, finely chopped

1 garlic clove, crushed

½ hot chile, deseeded and finely chopped

½-inch (1-cm) piece of fresh ginger, grated

2 ounces (50g) coconut cream

scant ½ cup (100 milliliters) warm water

2 tablespoons lemon juice

scant ½ cup/3½ ounces (100g) smooth peanut butter

2 tablespoons shoyu or soy sauce

salt and freshly ground black pepper

1 Boil or steam the green beans or snow peas in or over a saucepan of boiling water for 5–6 minutes, or until just tender. Drain and refresh in cold water.

2 Place the peanuts on a baking sheet and cook in a preheated oven, 400°F (200°C), for 5 minutes, or until lightly browned. Cool slightly, then rub off the skins in your hands or using a clean dish towel.

3 Arrange all the salad vegetable ingredients on a large serving platter. Scatter over the roasted peanuts.

4 To make the dressing, heat the oil in a saucepan and gently cook the shallots, garlic, chile, and ginger until quite soft.

5 Dissolve the coconut cream in the warm water in a pitcher, then blend with the cooked shallot mixture in a blender or food processor. Add the lemon juice, peanut butter, and shoyu or soy sauce and mix to a smooth sauce.

6 Season with salt and pepper to taste and serve the salad with the sauce.

nutritional breakdown per serving: calories 425, protein 16g, fat 34g (saturated fat 12g), carbohydrate 15g

avocado and pistachio salad

This salad is richly endowed with a cool mixture of colors and exotic flavors. It is extremely simple to prepare and works well as a main course, served with a bowl of feta cheese, black olives, and cherry tomatoes; or serve it as an accompaniment to Griddled Zucchini Quiche with Pine Nuts (see page 255) or Mediterranean Galette (see page 358).

serves 4

preparation: 5 minutes, plus soaking

cooking: 5–7 minutes

(Fe) v

¾ cup/4 ounces (125g) bulgur
½ teaspoon salt
1 cup (250 milliliters) boiling water
¾ cup/3 ounces (75g) unsalted, shelled
    pistachio nuts
1 avocado, cubed
2 scallions, finely chopped
¼ cup/¼ ounce (7g) chopped cilantro
¼ cup (50 milliliters) olive oil
juice of 1 lime
salt and freshly ground black pepper

1 Place the bulgur and salt in a large bowl. Pour in the boiling water. Leave for up to 30 minutes then drain if necessary.

2 Meanwhile, place the pistachio nuts on a baking sheet and roast in a preheated oven, 400°F (200°C), for 5–7 minutes, until lightly browned. Cool and chop coarsely.

3 Stir the pistachios, avocado, scallions, and chopped cilantro into the bulgur.

4 Combine the olive oil and lime juice and season well with salt and pepper. Stir into the bulgur salad and serve.

nutritional breakdown per serving: calories 413, protein 8g, fat 29g (saturated fat 3g), carbohydrate 31g

fennel and red bell pepper salad with lemon and oregano dressing

robust tomato salad left green garden salad center **fennel and red bell pepper salad with lemon and oregano dressing** right

The fresh tang of lemon permeates this dressing and complements the crisp fruity salad ingredients. For a dairy-free dressing, use a soy yogurt instead of the mayonnaise.

serves 4

preparation: 5 minutes

cooking: 5 minutes

½ cup/2 ounces (50g) pecan nuts
8 ounces (250g) fennel, sliced
1 red bell pepper, cored, deseeded, and sliced
½ cucumber, sliced
4 ounces (75g) mixed salad greens (such as romaine lettuce, frisée, radicchio)

nutritional breakdown per serving: calories 316, protein 3g, fat 32g (saturated fat 4g), carbohydrate 5g

For the dressing:
1 tablespoon mayonnaise
2 tablespoons lemon juice
1–2 teaspoons chopped oregano
⅓ cup (80 milliliters) olive oil
salt and freshly ground black pepper

1 Spread the pecans on a baking sheet and roast in a preheated oven, 400°F (200°C), for 5 minutes, or until lightly browned.

2 Let the nuts cool before tossing with the prepared vegetables. Arrange the salad greens on a serving plate and place the vegetables on top.

3 To make the dressing, combine all the ingredients in a pitcher. Just before serving, toss a little dressing into the salad, hand the rest separately.

green garden salad

serves 2–4

preparation: 5 minutes

cooking: none

v

¼ cup (50 milliliters) olive oil or flavored oil
½ teaspoon coarse mustard
1 tablespoon lemon juice
¼ cup/¼ ounce (7g) mixed chopped herbs (such
   as marjoram, oregano, thyme, parsley)
1 tablespoon capers, chopped
salt and freshly ground black pepper
3 ounces (75g) mixed green salad greens (pick
   the more strongly flavored greens, such as
   watercress, lollo rosso, and arugula)

1 Place the oil in a small bowl and beat in the
   mustard. Stir in the lemon juice, herbs, and capers
   and season with salt and pepper to taste.

2 Just before serving, toss the dressing into the
   salad greens. (4 portions)

nutritional breakdown per serving (4 portions): calories 107,
protein 1g, fat 11g (saturated fat 2g), carbohydrate 1g

robust tomato salad

*Rich colors and aromatic flavors abound in this salad. It
goes perfectly with creamy main course salads, such as
pasta or potato, as well as working well with pastry or egg
dishes, such as Frittata (see page 179). Always try to find
the best flavored tomatoes; cherry tomatoes work well, too.*

serves 2–4

preparation: 10 minutes, plus standing

cooking: none

v

4 tomatoes, coarsely chopped
¼ cucumber, finely chopped
8 small cornichons, chopped
1 small sweet onion, finely chopped
2–3 artichoke hearts, quartered
½ cup/2 ounces (50g) pitted black olives

For the dressing:
⅓ cup (80 milliliters) olive oil
1–2 tablespoons red wine vinegar
1 tablespoon chopped parsley
1 tablespoon capers
2 teaspoons grain mustard
1 teaspoon chopped oregano
salt and freshly ground black pepper, to taste

1 Combine the tomatoes, cucumber, cornichons,
   onion, artichoke hearts, and olives in a large bowl.

2 To make the dressing, combine all the ingredients
   in a pitcher and season to taste.

3 Pour the dressing over the salad and let stand for
   30 minutes before serving.

nutritional breakdown per serving (4 portions): calories 212,
protein 4g, fat 16g (saturated fat 2g), carbohydrate 13g

red cabbage and black grape salad with orange vinaigrette

This cheerful crunchy salad adds color to cold days. It benefits from being prepared a little in advance so that the flavors have time to develop. The ingredients, once tossed in the vinaigrette, don't lose their crisp character.

serves 4
preparation: 15 minutes
cooking: 5 minutes
not suitable for freezing
v

½ cup/2 ounces (50g) walnut halves
12 ounces (400g) red cabbage, shredded
4 ounces (125g) black grapes, halved and deseeded
2–3 celery stalks, finely chopped

For the vinaigrette:
¼ cup (50 milliliters) olive oil
¼ cup (50 milliliters) walnut oil
2–3 tablespoons fresh orange juice
1 tablespoon cider apple vinegar
1 teaspoon grain mustard
2 tablespoons chopped parsley
salt and freshly ground black pepper

1 Spread the walnut halves on a baking sheet and roast in a preheated oven, 400°F (200°C), for 5 minutes, or until lightly browned.

2 Let the nuts cool before placing in a large bowl with the other salad ingredients.

3 Combine all the vinaigrette ingredients in a pitcher and season well. Toss into the salad and adjust the seasoning with salt and pepper to taste.

nutritional breakdown per serving: calories 293, protein 3g, fat 27g (saturated fat 3g), carbohydrate 10g

carrot and kohlrabi with pumpkin seeds

This refreshing salad can be made with baby turnips instead of the kohlrabi. The combination of mayonnaise and yogurt in the dressing keeps the mixture creamy but light—for a vegan alternative use the Silken Bean Curd Dressing (see page 317).

serves 4
preparation: 15 minutes
cooking: 3–4 minutes

scant ½ cup/2 ounces (50g) pumpkin seeds
8 ounces (250g) carrots, coarsely grated
8 ounces (250g) kohlrabi or baby turnips, coarsely grated
¼ cup (50 milliliters) mayonnaise
¼ cup (50 milliliters) plain yogurt
2 tablespoons chopped parsley
salt and freshly ground black pepper

1 Spread the pumpkin seeds on a baking sheet and roast in a preheated oven, 400°F (200°C), for 3–4 minutes. Let cool.

2 Combine the grated carrot and kohlrabi or baby turnips in a large bowl. Add the roasted pumpkin seeds.

3 To make the dressing, combine the mayonnaise, yogurt, and parsley in a small bowl, then mix thoroughly into the grated vegetables and pumpkin seeds.

4 Season well with salt and pepper and chill until ready to serve.

nutritional breakdown per serving: calories 359, protein 7g, fat 31g (saturated fat 5g), carbohydrate 13g

red cabbage and black grape salad with orange vinaigrette left **carrot and kohlrabi with pumpkin seeds** right

roasted bell peppers with basil vinaigrette

Colorful and succulent, roasted bell peppers make splendid salads. This type of salad is also useful for a buffet or picnic because it won't spoil on standing and can be easily transported. Bell peppers can be roasted in large batches since they will keep for several days. Eggplant, onions, shallots, and zucchini are also good roasted and used for salads.

serves 4
preparation: 10 minutes
cooking: 35–40 minutes
v

2 large red bell peppers, lightly oiled
2 yellow bell peppers, lightly oiled

For the dressing:
¼ cup (50 milliliters) olive oil
1–2 tablespoons white wine vinegar
1 garlic clove, crushed
3 tablespoons chopped basil
salt and freshly ground black pepper

½ cup/2 ounces (50g) walnut pieces, toasted
   and chopped
sprigs of basil, to garnish

1 Place the bell peppers on a baking sheet and roast in a preheated oven, 400°F (200°C), for 35–40 minutes, or until the skins are well charred and look to be lifting away from the flesh.

2 Let cool, then peel the skin off each bell pepper. It should come away easily but use a sharp knife for any stubborn patches. Remove the seeds and core. Reserve any juices.

3 Slice the bell peppers into thick pieces and arrange on a serving plate.

4 To make the dressing, combine the olive oil, vinegar, garlic, and chopped basil in a small pitcher. Add some of the juices from the roasted bell peppers. Season well with salt and pepper.

5 Drizzle the dressing over the bell peppers and sprinkle them with the walnut pieces. Serve at room temperature, garnished with fresh basil.

> nutritional breakdown per serving: calories 203, protein 4g, fat 17g (saturated fat 2g), carbohydrate 9g

dressings

These can range from a simple drizzle of olive oil to a luscious creamy mayonnaise or an aromatic vinaigrette. As well as adding flavor, a dressing helps preserve nutrients by protecting the cut ingredients from oxidizing.

There are no hard and fast rules about which dressing goes with which salad combination. In general, lighter leafier salads are usually better dressed in a vinaigrette or vinaigrette-style mixture. More robust salad ingredients, such as shredded cabbage, roasted Mediterranean vegetables, or chunky carrots, can take sturdier, thicker dressings, based on cream or mayonnaise.

A classic vinaigrette is usually in the ratio of 3 parts oil to 1 part vinegar. You can vary both the type of vinegar used and the type of oil. Obviously, the ratio can be changed if you like a sharper or, conversely, a smoother finish. Acidity can also be introduced by adding lemon or lime juice. Garlic, mustard, and herbs add flavor to vinaigrette; sugar, honey, or concentrated fruit juice sweeten the mixture.

fruity vinaigrette

makes ½ cup (125 milliliters)

preparation: 5 minutes

cooking: none

𝒱

⅓ cup (80 milliliters) olive oil
2 tablespoons wine vinegar
1–2 garlic cloves, crushed
1 teaspoon Dijon mustard
1 tablespoon concentrated apple juice
salt and freshly ground black pepper

1 Whisk all the ingredients together in a small bowl or pitcher, or shake well in a screw-top jar. Season with salt and pepper to taste.

2 Use the vinaigrette at once or store in the refrigerator and use within a week.

nutritional breakdown per tablespoon: calories 68, protein 0g, fat 7g (saturated fat 1g), carbohydrate 1g

roasted walnut dressing

This robust dressing is great with griddled zucchini or fennel, as well as with roasted bell peppers and eggplant. The roasted walnuts will permeate the other ingredients but you can intensify the walnut flavor even further by substituting some walnut oil for the olive oil.

makes about scant 1 cup (200 milliliters)

preparation: 10 minutes

cooking: 5 minutes

𝒱

½ cup/2 ounces (50g) walnut pieces
½ teaspoon grain mustard
1–2 tablespoons balsamic or red wine vinegar
1 garlic clove, crushed
⅔ cup/¼ pint (150 milliliters) olive oil or a
   mixture of olive and walnut oil
salt and freshly ground black pepper

1 Spread the walnut pieces on a baking sheet and roast in a preheated oven, 400°F (200°C), for 5 minutes, or until lightly browned. Let cool.

2 Using a blender or food processor, grind the walnuts finely. Add the mustard, 1 tablespoon of the vinegar, and the garlic and process again.

3 With the motor running, gradually pour in the oil in a thin steady stream. Season to taste with salt and pepper, and add more vinegar if required.

nutritional breakdown per tablespoon: calories 84, protein 1g, fat 9g (saturated fat 1g), carbohydrate 0g

lemon and sunflower vinaigrette

makes about ⅔ cup/¼ pint (150 milliliters)

preparation: 5 minutes

cooking: none

1 tablespoon honey
3 tablespoons lemon juice
⅓ cup (80 milliliters) sunflower oil
1 scallion, very finely chopped
1 teaspoon paprika
salt and freshly ground black pepper

1 Whisk all the ingredients together in a small bowl or pitcher, or shake well in a screw-top jar. Season with salt and pepper to taste.

2 Let stand 10 minutes before serving.

nutritional breakdown per tablespoon: calories 53, protein 0g, fat 5g (saturated fat 1g), carbohydrate 2g

green vinaigrette

This is good with tomatoes and Belgian endive.

makes about ¾ cup (175 milliliters)

preparation: 5 minutes

cooking: none

𝑣

½ cup (125 milliliters) olive oil
1–2 tablespoons lemon juice
2 cups/2 ounces (50g) chopped herbs (such as chives and parsley)
2 scallions, finely chopped
1 garlic clove, crushed
salt and freshly ground black pepper

1 Combine the olive oil and lemon juice in a small bowl or pitcher.

2 Stir in the herbs, scallions, and garlic. Season with salt and pepper to taste.

nutritional breakdown per tablespoon: calories 68, protein 0g, fat 7g (saturated fat 1g), carbohydrate 0g

mayonnaise

Making mayonnaise used to be a hit-or-miss affair since there was always the possibility of the eggs curdling. Thanks to modern electrical gadgets it is now much easier and virtually foolproof. Do remember, though, to have all the ingredients at room temperature before you start.

makes 1¼ cups/½ pint (300 milliliters)
preparation: 10 minutes
cooking: none

2 egg yolks
2 tablespoons white wine vinegar or lemon juice
½ teaspoon salt and and a pinch of freshly
    ground black pepper
1¼ cups/½ pint (300 milliliters) olive oil

1   Stir together the egg yolks, vinegar, water, salt, and pepper in a small saucepan until blended.

2   Cook over low heat, stirring constantly, until the mixture just starts to bubble. Remove from heat and let stand for 4 minutes.

3   Pour into a food processor or blender and whirl at high speed. While blending, very slowly add the oil. Blend until thick and smooth, scraping down the side of the container as necessary.

4   Scrape the mayonnaise into a bowl, cover, and refrigerate for up to 3 days.

nutritional breakdown per tablespoon: calories 105, protein 0g, fat 12g (saturated fat 2g), carbohydrate 0g

VARIATIONS

You might prefer to mix the mayonnaise with equal quantities of plain yogurt, crème fraîche, or sour cream. Flavor the mayonnaise by adding chopped herbs, such as parsley, basil, chives, or tarragon. Alternatively, add chopped roasted bell peppers and paprika to make a russet-colored dressing, or chopped chile, dried chile flakes, or crushed peppercorns for a hotter finish.

Electric blenders or electric whisks make mayonnaise production a much speedier and easier process.

warning

Since we must be cautious about eating raw egg (see page 82), it is best to buy mayonnaise or make your own cooked version. Manufactured mayonnaise is made with pasteurized egg, which avoids the problem of salmonella.

tahini dressing

This smooth thick dressing goes well with stir-fry vegetables and substantial salads of grains or potatoes. Use the dressing as a topping rather than stirring it in, so that the colors of the salad remain fresh. This dressing is also good as a dip for crudités.

makes about ¾ cup (175 milliliters)

preparation: 5 minutes

cooking: none

(Ca) (Fe) 𝒱

¼ cup (4 tablespoons) tahini
¼ cup (50 milliliters) water
juice of 1 lemon
1–2 tablespoons olive oil
1 tablespoon shoyu or soy sauce
salt and freshly ground black pepper

1 Place the tahini in a small bowl and mix with the water until well blended.

2 Add the lemon juice, olive oil, and shoyu or soy sauce and mix well. Season with salt and pepper to taste.

nutritional breakdown per tablespoon: calories 113, protein 3g, fat 11g (saturated fat 2g), carbohydrate 0g

VARIATIONS

For an aromatic mixture, add 1 teaspoon dry-roasted ground cumin. For a sharper, yet creamy version add ¼ cup (50 milliliters) plain yogurt.

low-calorie cream dressing

makes 1¼ cups/½ pint (300 milliliters)

preparation: 10 minutes

cooking: none

1 cup/8 ounces (250g) cottage cheese
1–2 teaspoons lemon juice
2 teaspoons sunflower oil
1 teaspoon chopped tarragon
½ cup (125 milliliters) plain yogurt
1 teaspoon white wine vinegar or apple
 cider vinegar
salt and freshly ground black pepper, to taste

1 Using a blender or food processor, blend everything together until smooth. Season to taste.

2 Use the dressing immediately or store in the refrigerator for up to 3 days.

nutritional breakdown per tablespoon: calories 17, protein 2g fat 1g (saturated fat 0g), carbohydrate 1g

silken bean curd dressing

Silken bean curd makes a very good base for a dairy-free cream dressing, and lends itself to all sorts of flavoring variations. Add ginger, lime, shallots, dry-roasted sesame seeds, or shoyu or soy sauce, as well as herbs and spices.

makes 1¼ cups/½ pint (300 milliliters)

preparation: 5 minutes

cooking: none

(Ca)

8 ounces (250g) silken bean curd
2 tablespoons lemon juice
2 tablespoons sunflower oil

1 garlic clove, crushed
1 scallion, finely chopped
salt and freshly ground black pepper

1 Mix all the ingredients together until smooth, using a blender or food processor.

2 Season with salt and pepper to taste. Refrigerate for up to 3 days and use as required.

nutritional breakdown per tablespoon: calories 17, protein 1g, fat 1g (saturated fat 0g), carbohydrate 0g

Bread, Cakes, and Desserts

The smell, wafting through the house, of freshly baked bread, cakes, or cookies hot from the oven is something that no one can resist and is guaranteed to boost your popularity ratings. This section shows you how to make basic whole-wheat and white bread easily, with variations on these recipes, and then goes on to look at a variety of international breads including focaccia, corn bread, griddle breads, and a bread made without wheat or other ingredients that contain gluten.

The cake recipes include an Upside-down Apple Cake with Maple Syrup and Lemon, made by the batter method, and a Classic Rich Fruit Cake. There is also an unusual Middle Eastern Pistachio Cake, as well as a Carrot Cake with a wicked Orange Cream Frosting.

Everyone enjoys something sweet to round off a meal, and it does no harm to indulge now and again. The dessert recipes include delicious treats such as Layered Fruit Pavlova and Ricotta Cheesecake. There are also some simple suggestions for using fruit, such as Broiled Peaches with Ginger Cream, and a Quick Berry Brûlée. On colder days, you could treat yourself to the Plum Crisp featured here.

plum crisp

This attractive dessert is straightforward to make. If you can't buy a fruit bread, buy a sweet plain bread and add some raisins when cooking the plums.

serves 6
preparation: 10 minutes
cooking: 30–35 minutes
suitable for freezing

2 pounds (1kg) plums or apricots, pits removed and sliced
½ cup (1 stick)/4 ounces (25g) butter or sunflower margarine
⅓ cup (4–6 tablespoons) dark sugar
zest of ½ lemon
1 teaspoon ground cinnamon
8–10 slices fruit bread

nutritional breakdown per serving: calories 385, protein 4g, fat 20g (saturated fat 12g), carbohydrate 52g

1 Place the plums or apricots in a large saucepan and simmer with 2 tablespoons/1 ounce (25g) of the butter or margarine and the sugar, and cook for about 5 minutes until just soft. Stir in the lemon zest and ground cinnamon. Taste and adjust the sweetening if necessary.

2 Spoon the plums into a buttered or greased shallow ovenproof dish or pie plate.

3 Spread the remaining butter or margarine over the fruit bread and cut the slices into triangles. Arrange the triangles over the cooked fruit.

4 Bake in a preheated oven, 350°F (180°C), for 25–30 minutes. Serve hot.

CRISP TOPPINGS

Fruit stewed in this way can also be topped with a crisp topping. Sweet crisps are made in a similar way to savory crisps (see page 271) except that sugar or other sweeteners are added. You could also add sweet spices, such as ground cinnamon, nutmeg, or allspice, as well as seeds, such as sunflower seeds.

carrot cake with orange cream frosting

This colorful, moist whole-wheat cake is straightforward to make. It can be left plain for a dairy-free version or decorated with a cream cheese frosting.

serves 12	
preparation: 15 minutes	
cooking: 1–1¼ hours	
suitable for freezing	

2 cups/8 ounces (250g) whole-wheat flour
1 tablespoon baking powder
2 teaspoons ground cinnamon
½ cup/4 ounces (125g) sunflower margarine
    or butter
¾ cup/4 ounces (125g) honey
½ cup/4 ounces (125g) light brown sugar
8 ounces (250g) carrots, grated
½ cup/2 ounces (50g) walnut pieces, chopped
⅓ cup/2 ounces (50g) golden raisins
zest of 1 orange

For the frosting:
¾ cup/175g (6 ounces) cream cheese
½ cup/2 ounces (50g) confectioners' sugar
1–2 tablespoons orange juice

1   Combine the flour, baking powder, and ground cinnamon in a large bowl.

2   Gently melt the margarine or butter in a small saucepan with the honey and sugar. Stir into the flour mixture.

3   Add the grated carrot, chopped walnuts, golden raisins, and orange zest and mix well.

4   Spoon the mixture into a lined medium 9 x 5-inch (1-kg) loaf pan and bake in a preheated oven, 350°F (180°C), for 1–1¼ hours. Turn out and let cool on a wire rack.

5   To make the frosting, cream the ingredients together in a bowl and spread thickly over the cooled cake. Eat within a day or so.

---

nutritional breakdown per serving: calories 342, protein 4g, fat 19g (saturated fat 6g), carbohydrate 42g

classic rich fruit cake

This is a useful cake because it keeps extremely well and cuts cleanly. It is great for taking on hikes and picnics, but also for serving as a festive treat.

serves 12

preparation time: 10 minutes

cooking time: 3–3 ½ hours

suitable for freezing

¾ cup (1½ sticks)/6 ounces (175g) sweet butter
¾ cup/6 ounces (175g) dark brown sugar
4 eggs
1¾ cups/7 ounces (175g) whole-wheat flour
2 teaspoons baking powder
2 teaspoons apple pie spice spice
¾ cup/6 ounces (175g) currants
generous 1 cup/6 ounces (175g) golden raisins
generous 1 cup/6 ounces (175 g) raisins
⅔ cup/5 ounces (150g) chopped candied cherries
10–12 whole almonds, to decorate

1 Place the butter and sugar in a large bowl and cream together.

2 Add the eggs, 1 at a time, and beat each very well, adding a little of the flour in between each addition of egg to prevent the mixture from curdling.

3 Add the remaining flour, the baking powder, apple pie spice, currants, golden raisins, raisins, and cherries. Mix together very well. Spoon the mixture into a greased and lined 8-inch (20-cm) round cake pan.

4 Smooth the top of the mixture and arrange the whole almonds in a circular pattern. Bake in a preheated oven, 300°F (150°C), for 3–3½ hours. Let cool in the pan.

nutritional breakdown per serving: calories 407
protein 6g, fat 16g (saturated fat 9g), carbohydrate 65g

upside down apple cake with maple syrup and lemon

serves 8

preparation: 20 minutes

cooking: 30 minutes

suitable for freezing

⅔ cup (1¼ sticks)/5 ounces (150g) butter
2 tablespoons maple syrup
zest and juice of ½ lemon
3 tart dessert apples (such as Granny Smith),
    cored, peeled, quartered, and thinly sliced
½ cup/4 ounces (125g) light brown sugar
1 cup/4 ounces (125g) self-rising flour
2 eggs
raw brown sugar for sprinkling

1 Melt 2 tablespoons/1 ounce (25g) of the butter and
   pour into an 8-inch (20-cm) loose-based round
   cake pan. Add the maple syrup and sprinkle in the
   lemon zest.

2 Arrange the slices of apple, slightly overlapping
   each other, around the base of the pan. Squeeze the
   juice of ½ lemon over them.

3 Using a food processor or electric hand-held
   beater, mix together the remaining butter, the light
   brown sugar, flour, and eggs and pour or spoon this
   over the apple slices. Smooth the top of the
   cake mixture.

4 Bake in a preheated oven, 350°F (180°C), for
   30 minutes.

5 Let stand in the pan for 5 minutes, then turn out.
   Sprinkle with raw brown sugar and serve warm
   or cold.

nutritional breakdown per serving: calories 309, protein 3g,
fat 17g (saturated fat 11g), carbohydrate 38g

deluxe chocolate and prune refrigerator cake

This is rich, scrumptious, and extremely easy to make. It is good for parties because it can be served in very small quantities. Do not take it out of the refrigerator until just before serving since it is at its best when cold and crisp. Use ready-to-eat prunes since they will be softer. If these are unavailable, soak ordinary prunes in fruit juice or alcohol for 30 minutes or so before starting the recipe.

makes 16 squares
preparation: 10 minutes, plus chilling
cooking: 6 minutes
suitable for freezing

7 ounces (200g) bittersweet chocolate, broken
   into small pieces
scant 1 cup (1¾ sticks)/7 ounces (200g) butter
⅔ cup/5 ounces (150g) ready-to-eat
   prunes, chopped
scant 1 cup/3½ ounces (100g) pecans
   roasted and coarsely chopped
8 ounces (250g) graham crackers,
   roughly crushed
¼ cup (50 milliliters) rum or brandy

1 Melt the chocolate with the butter in a large bowl
   set over a saucepan of hot but not boiling water.

2 Remove from the heat and stir in the prunes,
   pecans, graham crackers, and rum.

3 Spoon the mixture into a deep, lined 8 x 12-inch
   (20 x 30-cm) cake pan. Leave to set in the
   refrigerator for at least 2 hours.

4 Cut into 16 squares to serve.

nutritional breakdown per square: calories 294, protein 2g, fat 22g (saturated fat 11g), carbohydrate 22g

pistachio cake

*This is a traditional cake made in the Middle East. It is
sometimes known as 1-2-3-4 because, when measured in
cups, the starting point is 1 cup of oil, 2 of sugar, 3 of flour,
and then 4 eggs. In this version I have used less sugar and
added pistachio nuts and raisins.*

serves 12	
preparation: 10 minutes	
cooking: 1–1¼ hours	
suitable for freezing	
Ⓕⓔ	

1 cup/8 ounces (250g) light brown sugar
4 eggs
1 cup (250 milliliters) light olive oil
3 cups/12 ounces (375g) all-purpose flour
1 tablespoon baking powder
1⅔ cups/8 ounces (250g) raisins
2 cups/8 ounces (250g) unsalted, shelled
   pistachio nuts
3 tablespoons milk, optional

1 Place the sugar and eggs in a large bowl and whisk
   together. Whisk in the oil, then the flour and
   baking powder.

2 Stir in the raisins and pistachio nuts, reserving
   a few for decoration. Add the milk if the mixture
   seems a little dry.

3 Spoon the mixture into a lined, 8-inch (20-cm)
   square cake pan. Bake in a preheated oven, 350°F
   (180°C), for 1–1¼ hours.

4 Remove from the oven and let cool in the pan for
   10 minutes, then turn out, and decorate with the
   remaining pistachios, coarsely chopped. Cover the
   cake with a dish towel until cold.

nutritional breakdown per serving: calories 543, protein 10g,
fat 29g (saturated fat 3g), carbohydrate 64g

all-in-one banana loaf

Moist and dense, this banana loaf is good served plain or buttered.

serves 12
preparation: 10 minutes
cooking: 30–40 minutes
suitable for freezing

1 cup/4 ounces (125g) pecans
3 ripe bananas, chopped
½ cup (1 stick)/4 ounces (125g) butter, melted
½ cup/4 ounces (125g) light brown sugar
3 eggs
2 cups/8 ounces (250g) self-rising flour
⅓ cup/3 ounces (75g) dried apricots, slivered

1 Set aside half the pecans for decoration.

2 Combine the bananas, butter, sugar, eggs, flour, and apricots in a food processor and mix together until well combined.

3 Spoon the mixture into a greased and lined 8-inch (20-cm) round cake pan or medium 9 x 5-inch (1-kg) loaf pan, decorate with the reserved nuts, and bake in a preheated oven, 325°F (160°C), for 30–40 minutes.

4 Let cool in the pan.

nutritional breakdown per serving: calories 312, protein 5g, fat 18g (saturated fat 7g), carbohydrate 36g

very lemon wedges

This is a refreshing bite of lemon on a simple base. It makes a good mid-morning snack or could be cut into very tiny pieces to serve at a party.

makes 12
preparation: 10 minutes
cooking: 30–35 minutes
suitable for freezing

For the base:
¼ cup (½ stick)/2 ounces (50g) butter, softened
½ cup/2 ounces (50g) superfine sugar
⅔ cup/3 ounces (75 g) all-purpose or whole-wheat flour

For the topping:
1 cup/8 ounces (250g) cream cheese
¾ cup/5 ounces (150g) superfine sugar
1 egg
zest and juice of 1 lemon
½ teaspoon vanilla extract

1 To make the base, mix the butter, sugar, and flour to a dough, using a blender or food processor. Press into a 7-inch (18-cm) round tart pan or ovenproof dish.

2 Bake in a preheated oven, 350°F (180°C), for 15–20 minutes, or until just golden.

3 To make the topping, blend the cream cheese, sugar, egg, lemon juice, zest, and vanilla together until smooth, using a blender or food processor. Spoon the filling over the cooked base and bake at 350°F (180°C), for 15 minutes, or until just set.

4 Let cool then cut into 12 pieces.

nutritional breakdown per wedge: calories 215, protein 2g, fat 14g (saturated fat 9g), carbohydrate 22g

raisin and almond flapjack bars

There are many variations on this flapjack recipe. You can vary the type of flakes used—try barley or millet instead of oats. You could also use different dried fruits, such as chopped dates, slivered mango, or chopped apricots.

makes 12
preparation: 10 minutes
cooking: 30–35 minutes
suitable for freezing
𝒱 (using syrup)

1 cup/8 ounces (250g) vegetable margarine
½ cup/2 ounces (50g) light brown sugar
½ cup/4 ounces (125g) honey or syrup
2¼ cups/8 ounces (250g) rolled oats
2 cups/8 ounces (250g) whole-wheat flour
scant 1 cup/4 ounces (125g) raisins
½ cup/2 ounces (50g) almonds, chopped

1 Put the margarine, sugar, and honey or syrup in a small saucepan and melt together.

2 Combine the oats, flour, raisins, and almonds in a large bowl.

3 When the margarine mixture is boiling, pour it over the dry ingredients, and stir very well. Spoon the mixture into a lightly greased cake pan approximately 7 x 11 inches (18 x 28cm), and bake in a preheated oven, 350°F (180°C), for 20–25 minutes.

4 Mark into 12 pieces. Let cool in the pan before cutting into 12 bars.

nutritional breakdown per bar: calories 402, protein 6g, fat 22g (saturated fat 8g), carbohydrate 49g

apricot lattice

A cross between a cake and a tart, this colorful latticed dessert is easy to make. If you are in a hurry, you could use an apricot preserve or jelly instead of the purée used here.

serves 12
preparation: 15 minutes
cooking: 1–1 ¼ hours
suitable for freezing

1 cup/8 ounces (250g) dried apricots
1 ¼ cups/½ pint (300 milliliters) water, plus 1 tablespoon
2 cups/8 ounces (250g) self-rising flour
generous ½ cup/4 ounces (125g) superfine sugar
½ cup/4 ounces (125g) vegetable margarine
1 egg, lightly beaten
flour for dusting counter

1 Place the apricots in a saucepan with the water. Bring to a boil, then simmer for 30–40 minutes, or until quite tender. Let cool, then purée with the cooking liquid, using a blender or food processor, until smooth. Set aside.

2 Using the blender or food processor again, mix the flour, superfine sugar, margarine, and egg together to a soft dough. Add up to 1 tablespoon of cold water if the mixture seems dry.

3 Using two-thirds of the dough, press it into a 9-inch (23-cm) quiche pan. Spread the apricot purée on top.

4 Roll out the remaining dough on a lightly floured counter and cut into thin strips. Arrange the strips on top of the purée in a lattice pattern.

5 Bake in a preheated oven, 350°F (180°C), for 30–35 minutes, or until golden brown. Serve at room temperature.

nutritional breakdown per serving: calories 232, protein 3g, fat 9g (saturated fat 4g), carbohydrate 36g

ricotta cheesecake

This light cheesecake is simple to make. The dried fruit can be varied—raisins or slivers of dried pear work very well. The fruit can be soaked in fruit juice but a little alcohol does add a special flavor.

serves 8

preparation: 10 minutes, plus soaking

cooking: 45–50 minutes

suitable for freezing

⅓ cup/2 ounces (50g) golden raisins
3 tablespoons Marsala
3 eggs, separated
¼ cup/2 ounces (50g) superfine sugar
2 cups/1 pound (500g) ricotta cheese
2 tablespoons all-purpose flour
zest and juice of 1 lemon
whipped cream, to serve

1   Place the golden raisins in a bowl. Add the Marsala and soak for at least 30 minutes.

2   Place the egg yolks in a bowl and beat with the sugar until thick. Add the ricotta, flour, lemon zest, and juice and stir well. Mix in the soaked raisins.

3   Whisk the egg whites in a large bowl until standing in soft peaks. Fold into the ricotta cheese mixture. Spoon the mixture into a buttered and floured 8-inch (20-cm) ring or springform pan. Bake in a preheated oven, 350°F (180°C), for 45–50 minutes.

4   Let cool before turning out. Serve with extra cream.

nutritional breakdown per serving: calories 187, protein 9g, fat 9g (saturated fat 5g), carbohydrate 17g

layered fruit pavlova

This pavlova has a sticky marshmallow-type base, made by adding cold water to the egg white mixture. Choose colorful fruit for the topping. Here I have used mango and nectarines, but you could try soft fruits, such as raspberries and strawberries, as well as other tropical fruits.

serves 8

preparation: 10 minutes, plus cooling

cooking: 45 minutes

suitable for freezing (base only)

3 egg whites
2 tablespoons cold water
generous 1 cup/8 ounces (250g) superfine sugar
1 teaspoon wine vinegar or cider vinegar
1 teaspoon vanilla extract
1 tablespoon cornstarch
pinch of salt
1¼ cups/½ pint (300 milliliters) heavy cream
2 mangoes, peeled, pits removed and sliced
2 nectarines, pits removed and sliced
confectioners' sugar for dusting

1 Beat the egg whites in a large bowl until stiff but not dry.

2 Add the water and beat again, then add the sugar, a little at a time, beating thoroughly until the sugar is dissolved.

3 Sprinkle in the vinegar, vanilla extract, cornstarch, and salt and beat again. Spoon the mixture into a 12-inch circle onto a baking sheet lined with baking parchment.

4 Bake the pavlova base in a preheated oven, 300°F (150°C), for 45 minutes. Turn off the oven and leave the meringue in the oven to cool completely.

5 To make the topping, whip the cream in a bowl until standing in peaks. Spread over the base and cover with sliced mango and nectarines. Dust with confectioners' sugar.

nutritional breakdown per serving: calories 347, protein 3g, fat 18g (saturated fat 11g), carbohydrate 46g

strawberry yogurt ice

For special occasions, add a liqueur to the fruit; for a richer version, replace some of the yogurt with cream.

serves 4
preparation: 10 minutes, plus freezing
cooking: none
suitable for freezing

3 cups/12 ounces (375g) strawberries
generous ½ cup/4 ounces (125g) superfine sugar
scant 1 cup (200 milliliters) plain yogurt

1 Blend the strawberries and sugar together until smooth, using a blender or food processor. Pass the mixture through a strainer to remove the seeds.

2 Stir the yogurt into the mixture. Pour into a freezerproof container and freeze for 2 hours.

3 Remove from the freezer and beat until smooth with an electric whisk. Return to the freezer for 2 hours more.

4 To serve, remove from the freezer 10 minutes before serving.

nutritional breakdown per serving: calories 175, protein 3g, fat 1g (saturated fat 0g), carbohydrate 42g

strawberry yogurt
ice back carob
mousse front

carob or chocolate mousse

serves 4
preparation: 5 minutes
cooking: none
(Ca) (Fe) 𝒱 (using syrup)

7–8 ounces (200–250g) silken bean curd
3 tablespoons tahini
1 banana, coarsely chopped
1–2 tablespoons honey or syrup
1 ounce (25g) carob or chocolate

1 Blend together the silken bean curd, tahini, banana, and sweetening in a blender or food processor.

2 Grate in the carob or chocolate and blend again for a few seconds. Spoon into 4 attractive glasses and chill before serving.

nutritional breakdown per serving: calories 353, protein 12g, fat 27g (saturated fat 4g), carbohydrate 17g

water ices

For refreshing dairy-free ices, make a light sugar syrup (see page 59) and stir into a fruit purée, such as strawberries, or combine with a well-flavored juice, such as orange or lemon juice. Pour into a freezerproof container. Beat once or twice during the initial freezing process to break up the ice crystals. For children, freeze the mixture in small quantities in molds and add popsicle sticks.

quick berry brûlée

This recipe works well with fruit that doesn't need cooking, such as strawberries and other soft fruit, or with apricots, peaches, or plums.

serves 4

preparation: 5 minutes

cooking: 5 minutes

2 cups/8 ounces (250g) strawberries, halved
1 cup/8 ounces (250g) mascarpone cheese or thick plain yogurt
¼–½ cup/50–75g (2–3 ounces) superfine sugar

1 Place the strawberries in a flameproof 1-quart dish or individual dishes and cover with mascarpone cheese or thick yogurt. (The mascarpone is quite hard to spoon over but it will even out because it melts under the broiler.)

2 Sprinkle the superfine sugar on top. Place under a preheated very hot broiler and cook until the sugar caramelizes. Serve hot.

nutritional breakdown per serving: calories 328, protein 4g, fat 25g (saturated fat 19g), carbohydrate 23g

broiled peaches with ginger cream

You could also broil nectarines, apricots, and plums, as well as pears and apples, in the same way as the peaches used here.

serves 4

preparation: 5 minutes

cooking: 2–3 minutes

For the ginger cream:

1 cup/8 ounces (250g) ricotta cheese

2 tablespoons heavy cream

1 tablespoon ginger syrup

1 tablespoon finely chopped preserved ginger

For the fruit:

4 ripe peaches, halved and pits removed

1 tablespoons/½ ounce (25g) butter, softened

1   To make the ginger cream, place the ricotta in a bowl with the heavy cream and ginger syrup and blend until smooth. Stir in the finely chopped preserved ginger.

2   Brush the peach halves with the softened butter. Place under a preheated broiler and cook for 2–3 minutes.

3   Serve hot with the ginger cream.

nutritional breakdown per serving: calories 259, protein 8g, fat 19g (saturated fat 12g), carbohydrate 16g

low-fat cream

This is a useful low-fat accompaniment to baked or broiled fruits or to serve with fruit salad.

serves 6

preparation time: 5 minutes, plus chilling

cooking: none

8 ounces (250g) farmer's cheese or plain yogurt

up to ⅔ cup/¼ pint (150 milliliters) fruit juice

1 teaspoon vanilla extract

1   Using a blender or food processor, process the farmer's cheese or yogurt until smooth, adding sufficient fruit juice to give a pouring or spooning consistency.

2   Flavor with vanilla extract to taste, then chill.

nutritional breakdown per serving: calories 55, protein 6g, fat 3g (saturated fat 1g), carbohydrate 2g

VANILLA CREAM

To make a vanilla cream, follow the ginger cream recipe but use 2–3 drops vanilla extract, or to taste, instead of the ginger and syrup. Sweeten with 1 tablespoon honey or sugar to taste.

whole-wheat bread

This recipe is suitable for whole-wheat loaves, rolls, and braids. Many different savory flavorings can be added to the basic dough, for example, 1 teaspoon dried thyme, ½ cup/2 ounces (50g) grated cheese, 1 teaspoon dried chile flakes, or 1–2 tablespoons sunflower or sesame seeds.

makes 2 loaves, each makes 12 slices
preparation: 15 minutes, plus rising
cooking: 35–40 minutes
suitable for freezing
𝓋

Step 1 Add the oil to the mixture.

Step 2 Use a wooden spoon to draw to a dough.

Step 3 Knead well until the dough is smooth.

Step 4 Set aside to rise in a clean bowl.

Step 5 Punch the air out of the dough.

Step 6 Set aside to rise in greased or oiled pans.

6 cups/1½ pounds (750g) whole-wheat bread flour, plus extra for dusting
1 teaspoon salt
1 packet/¼ ounce (7g) active dry yeast
1¾ cups (400 milliliters) lukewarm water
1 tablespoon olive oil

1 Combine the flour, salt, and yeast in a large bowl. Pour in the water and olive oil. Work the ingredients into a dough and knead on a lightly floured counter for 5 minutes, or until the dough is smooth and elastic but not sticky.

2 Return the dough to a clean bowl and cover with plastic wrap or a damp dish towel. Set aside to rise in a warm place for about 1 hour—the dough should have doubled in size.

3 Again working on a lightly floured counter, punch the air out of the dough and knead again briefly.

4 Shape into 2 loaves. Place in oiled, 8 x 4-inch (1-pound)/20 x 10-cm (500-g) loaf pans and set aside to rise for up to 30 minutes.

5 Bake in a preheated oven, 425°F (220°C), for 35–40 minutes. Test that the loaf is cooked by tapping the base—it should sound hollow. If it is not cooked, replace in the pans and cook for another 5 minutes.

6 Turn out and let cool on a wire rack.

nutritional breakdown per slice: calories 102, protein 4g, fat 1g (saturated fat 0g), carbohydrate 20g

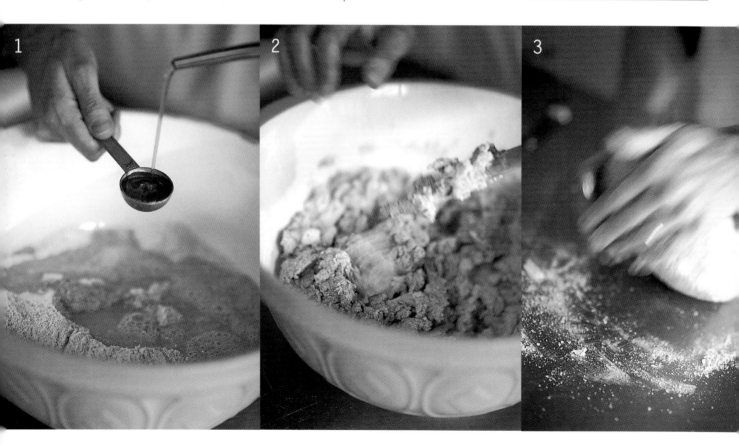

VARIATIONS

Rolls—a good-sized uncooked roll weighs about 3 ounces (75g). If you are making rolls for a party make them smaller—about 2 ounces (50g).

To make rolls, follow steps 1–3 for bread making. Divide the dough in half. Knead each half lightly to make a ball, then shape into rounds or crescents. Set on an oiled baking sheet and set aside to rise for 10 minutes. Bake in a preheated oven, 425°F (220°C), for 15–20 minutes. Let cool on a wire rack.

troubleshooting

• dense or heavy loaves may mean that the initial dough was too dry. If you notice cracks in the dough as you knead, this is definitely the case

• soggy bread is either undercooked or has been left too long to rise in the pan and it has collapsed

• lopsided loaves mean there is uneven heat in the oven. Try turning the loaf around during cooking

enriched white bread

Adding milk and egg to a dough gives a softer crust and a richer texture. Use a strong, preferably unbleached, white bread flour for the best flavor.

makes 12 slices

preparation: 15 minutes, plus rising

cooking: 35–40 minutes

suitable for freezing

4 cups/1 pound (500) white bread flour, plus extra for dusting
1 packet/¼ ounce (7g) active dry yeast
1 teaspoon salt
1 cup (250 milliliters) warm milk
2 tablespoons/1 ounce (25g) butter, melted

Step 1 To make a perfect braid, roll out three even strips.
Step 2 Line them up and start braiding in the middle toward one end.
Step 3 Continue braiding to the end of the first half.
Step 4 Turn the braid around and braid the other half.
Step 5 Tuck in the ends firmly.

1. Place the flour, yeast, and salt in a large bowl.

2. Add the warm milk and melted butter and draw the ingredients into a dough. Knead on a lightly floured counter for 5 minutes, or until the dough is smooth and elastic but not sticky.

3. Return the dough to a clean bowl and cover with plastic wrap or a damp dish towel. Set aside to rise in a warm place for about 1 hour—the dough should have doubled in size.

4. Again working on a lightly floured counter, punch the air out of the dough and knead again briefly.

5. To make a braid, divide the dough into 3 equal pieces and roll each one into a "rope," about 12 inches (30cm) long. Lay the 3 lengths side by side. To get an even braid, begin braiding from the middle toward one end, then turn the whole thing round and braid the other end. Pinch the pieces together at each end of the braid.

6. Place the braid on a baking sheet and set aside to rise until roughly doubled in size.

7. Bake in a preheated oven, 425°F (220°C), for 35–40 minutes, or until cooked—it should sound hollow when tapped on the base. Turn the loaf over and cook for 3 minutes more to crisp the base.

8. Let cool on a wire rack.

nutritional breakdown per slice: calories 176, protein 6g, fat 4g (saturated fat 2g), carbohydrate 32g

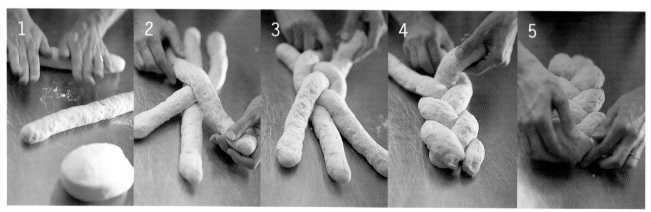

focaccia

This is a flat bread, enriched with olive oil and flavored with herbs or typical Mediterranean ingredients, such as olives, sun-dried tomatoes, and oregano. You can also use this dough as a pizza base.

makes 2 rounds, each cuts into 12 wedges
preparation: 15 minutes, plus standing, rising
cooking: 20–25 minutes
suitable for freezing
v

1 packet/¼ ounce (7g) yeast
scant 2 cups/¾ pint (450 milliliters) water
6 cups/1½ pounds (750g) white bread flour, plus
    extra for dusting
1½ teaspoons salt
¼ cup (50 milliliters) plus 1 tablespoon olive oil
1 cup/4 ounces (125g) olives
1 teaspoon dried oregano
coarse sea salt

1 Mix the yeast with the water and about one-quarter of the flour in a large bowl. Stir to make a batter and let stand in a warm place for about 10 minutes.

2 Add the remaining flour, the salt, and ¼ cup (50 milliliters) of the olive oil. Draw the ingredients into a dough. Knead on a lightly floured counter for 5 minutes, or until the dough is smooth and elastic but not sticky.

3 Place the dough in an oiled bowl, cover with plastic wrap or a damp dish towel, and set aside to rise in a warm place for 1 hour.

4 Again working on a lightly floured counter, punch the air out of the dough, then work in the olives and dried oregano. Shape the dough into 2 rounds, each about 1 inch (2.5cm) thick. Place on a baking sheet and set aside to rise for up to 30 minutes.

5 Using the end of a wooden spoon, make indentations in the dough, dipping the end of the spoon in flour each time you put it in the dough. Brush the focaccia with the remaining olive oil and bake in a preheated oven, 425°F (220°C), for 20–25 minutes.

6 Once cooked, sprinkle with coarse salt and let cool on a wire rack.

nutritional breakdown per wedge: calories 134, protein 4g, fat 3g (saturated fat 1g), carbohydrate 24g

glazing and decorating

A glaze on a loaf looks very attractive and is easy to do. Beat 1 egg yolk with a little salt and brush this over the risen loaf just before it goes in the oven. Then sprinkle with some sesame or poppy seeds. A light sugar syrup or warmed honey can be used to glaze a loaf after it has been baked.

gluten-free bread

This is a dense loaf, which slices well and can be toasted. The buckwheat flour adds an intense flavor—use potato flour if you prefer. Gluten-free breads will not rise in the same way as wheat loaves but they need not be heavy. This loaf is lightened with a mash of cooked squash—you could vary this by using carrots or pumpkin. For extra texture, add sesame seeds at step 2 if you like.

makes 20 slices	
preparation: 20 minutes	
cooking: 30–40 minutes	
suitable for freezing	
v	

1 packet/¼ ounce (7g) active dry yeast
1 cup (250 milliliters) lukewarm water
1 cup/4 ounces (125g) brown rice flour
1 teaspoon sugar
1 cup/4 ounces (125g) buckwheat flour
¼ cup/1 ounce (25g) soy flour
7 ounces (200g) butternut squash, cooked
  and mashed
1 teaspoon salt
1 tablespoon sunflower oil

1 Combine the yeast with the warm water, rice flour, and sugar in a large bowl. Mix well and set aside for 10 minutes.

2 Stir in the buckwheat and soy flour, the mashed squash, salt, and oil. Mix very well, then spoon into a greased 9 x 5-inch (2-pound)/23 x 13-cm (1-kg) loaf pan.

3 Bake in a preheated oven, 350°F (180°C), for 30–40 minutes. Turn out and let cool on a wire rack.

nutritional breakdown per slice: calories 62, protein 2g, fat 1g
(saturated fat 0g), carbohydrate 12g

soda bread

Soda bread is a yeast-free bread, which does not need to rise and can be made, baked, and eaten in less than an hour! To make a richer dough you can add melted butter; for a sweet, almost cake-like bread add some sugar and dried fruit.

makes 8 wedges
preparation: 10 minutes
cooking: 35–40 minutes
suitable for freezing

3 cups/12 ounces (375g) whole-wheat flour, plus
  extra for dusting
1 cup/4 ounces (125g) all-purpose flour
1 teaspoon baking powder
½ teaspoon salt
1¼ cups/½ pint (300 milliliters) milk
1 egg

1 Place the whole-wheat and all-purpose flours, baking powder, and salt in a large bowl. Beat the milk and egg together in a pitcher and pour into the flour. Mix until you have a soft dough.

2 Turn onto a lightly floured counter and knead very lightly to shape into a rough ball.

3 Place on a floured baking sheet and flatten to a round, about 1½ inches (3.5cm) thick. Using a floured sharp knife, mark the dough into quarters with deep cuts that go almost through the dough round. Make shallower cuts in between so that you have 8 even divisions marked.

4 Bake in a preheated oven, 375°F (190°C), for 35–40 minutes, or until the crust is well browned.

5 Allow to cool on a wire rack before cutting into wedges.

nutritional breakdown per wedge: calories 224, protein 9g, fat 3g (saturated fat 1g), carbohydrate 42g

griddle bread

These quick breads have a distinctive chewy texture and can be made with either white or whole-wheat flour, although the whole-wheat versions do not puff up in the same way. Eat them hot with a dip, or brush with a little butter and serve with dhal and spicy dishes.

makes 12

preparation: 15 minutes

cooking: 20 minutes

suitable for freezing

3 cups/12 ounces (375g) all-purpose flour, plus extra for dusting
¾ teaspoon baking powder
pinch of salt
1–2 teaspoons dry-roasted coriander or cumin seeds
scant 1 cup (200 milliliters) plain yogurt

1 Place the flour, baking powder, salt, and coriander or cumin seeds in a large bowl. Stir in the yogurt to make a soft dough. Add a little more yogurt, if necessary, but the dough should be pliable not sticky.

2 Knead briefly on a lightly floured counter, then divide the dough into 12. Roll or flatten each piece of dough into a round, about 4 inches (10cm) in diameter. The dough should be quite thin.

3 Heat a large skillet until hot and dry-fry each round for 2–3 minutes, or until it has puffed up slightly and the surface looks brown and blistered. Turn over and cook the other side for 2 minutes.

4 Once cooked, keep warm wrapped in a clean dish towel, while you cook the remainder. Serve hot.

nutritional breakdown per serving: calories 110, protein 4g, fat 1g (saturated fat 0g), carbohydrate 24g

savory cheese corn bread

makes 8 slices

preparation: 10 minutes

cooking: 20 minutes

suitable for freezing

1 cup/4 ounces (125g) whole-wheat flour
1 cup/4 ounces (125g) cornmeal
½ cup/2 ounces (50g) grated cheese
1 tablespoon sugar
2 teaspoons baking powder
½ teaspoon salt
1 teaspoon dried chile flakes
2 eggs
1 cup (250 milliliters) milk
2 tablespoons sunflower oil

1 Place the flour, cornmeal, cheese, sugar, baking powder, salt, and dried chile flakes in a large bowl.

2 Beat the eggs with the milk in a pitcher, then add the oil. Add to the dry ingredients and mix quickly.

3 Pour the mixture into a greased 8 x 8-inch (20 x 20-cm) ovenproof dish and bake in a preheated oven, 400°F (200°C), for 20 minutes, or until golden brown and firm to the touch.

4 Serve hot or warm, cut into slices or wedges.

nutritional breakdown per slice: calories 200, protein 6g, fat 8g (saturated fat 2g), carbohydrate 28g

savory cheese corn bread left **griddle bread** right

Entertaining

If you love food, it often follows that you enjoy making and sharing meals with other people. This is certainly one of the pleasures in my life. Entertaining can range from the simplest, casual supper of a plate of pasta and a glass of wine, to a full-blown formal meal with all the trimmings. This part of the book looks at a number of different special occasions, namely barbecues, picnics, buffets, and summer and winter dinner parties. Along with the recipes is a timetable that shows you what to prepare in advance. Although particular recipes have been highlighted here, there are numerous other recipes in the book that can be used for entertaining.

Here are one or two thoughts to bear in mind when laying out a special spread:

PLANNING AHEAD

Whatever you are planning, don't try to do everything on the day. Many meals, especially soups, stews, and sauces, are better cooked the day before and reheated. Alternatively, use the freezer to get things done ahead. Don't forget that, often, at least part of a recipe can be cooked ahead of time. For example, you could make the dressing for a salad, cook the rice, or make a filling for a pastry. When planning a menu, try to make sure you always offer a variety of ingredients, a choice of textures, and a good range of colors.

FORMAL MEALS

At a formal dinner party, there is bound to be a fair amount of attention on the food, so it is worth planning the menu carefully. Apart from looking for variety, spend time thinking about how to present each part of the meal, and whether to have individually plated meals or a centerpiece. Both can look equally good. It is also necessary to leave yourself enough time for putting together small details such as garnishes, salads, and bread.

INFORMAL MEALS

Don't feel you have to stick to conventional ways of serving meals—an appetizer, main course, and dessert. There is no reason why you cannot have a meal comprising several small dishes. The Middle Eastern mezze are a classic example of this. Alternatively, you can serve small dishes separately. Each course becomes a little taster in itself, and you do not have to worry about whether things go together or not.

IMPROMPTU MEALS

Keep a well-stocked pantry for impromptu meals. Dishes based on grains or pasta are very easy to throw together. Or you could offer two or three tasty snacks supplemented with cheese, breads, and store-bought pâté such as hummus. In the summer, a barbecue, where you can cook to order, can also be fun.

wines

Matching wine and food should be fun, and if it doesn't quite work as you expect, you can always eat and drink separately!

Before trying to link food with a suitable wine, spend time tasting wines on their own and learning to identify different characters and flavors. It may take years of experience and lots of tasting to absorb the complexities, but there are some basic things to look for. When tasting, pour a little wine into a large glass and swill it around. This will release the bouquet which may indicate the flavor. Does the wine smell spicy or flowery? Is it earthy or aromatic? When you sip it, take a mouthful and concentrate on both the initial flavor and the aftertaste. Is it powerful or light? Is it sweet or acidic? Zingy or lingering?

Look at the color too. Is it a deep red or almost rose? Is it a clear white or a honey hue? While color and flavor have a more subtle relationship, getting to know the look of a wine may help you build terms of reference as you start to work out what you like.

Once you have a vocabulary of flavor in your mind, try to think of wine as an ingredient that you are putting with your dish in just the same way that you have a cook's instinct for balancing texture or richness, or matching flavors, such as putting basil with tomato. When you discover a few wines that you like, you can start linking them with food.

First, consider the character of the dish. If your meal is robust and full of flavor, it will need a wine to match. Wines with plenty of flavor are described as full-bodied. This applies whether they are red or white. When looking for a full-bodied wine, remember that reds tend to have more body than whites, and wines from warmer climates, such as Australia, South Africa, California, South America, and Spain tend to have more color, body, and alcohol—in other words more weight. Labels on the wine bottles can also be very helpful. If your main dish is light and delicate, it should be partnered with wine of a similar character. Wines from cooler climates, such as New Zealand, Germany, much of France, and the US Pacific Northwest, tend to have less color, body, and alcohol. The flavors can still be intense, but are more subtle.

Secondly, think about the flavor influences in your dish. Is it redolent with herbs, hotly spiced, or aromatic? Is it characterized by earthy flavors, sweetness, or acidity? Use your choice of wine to echo these qualities or to act as a balancing ingredient. Spicy dishes can be matched with spicy wines, such as Gewürztraminer from Alsace. Similarly, you could complement robust aromas by choosing an equally weighty wine, such as an Australian Shiraz or a Californian Zinfandel. Flavors can also be used as a counterbalance, for example a crisp, acidic wine, such as a Sauvignon Blanc from New Zealand, will act as a foil for a rich, creamy dish.

Another good starting point is to serve wines from the region that inspired the dish. For example, the flavors of a Mediterranean tomato and herb dish would work well with a Hermitage from southern France.

Finally, consider the season and the time of day. Light wines are more suitable in the middle of the day (unless you plan a lengthy siesta) and your choice of wine will probably be different on hot, sunny days as opposed to the icy cold of winter. Naturally, the food you choose to serve at these times is likely to vary as well. Cold food and light summery meals are good with crisp, light wines that are delicious chilled, for example a Riesling or a delicate Chardonnay from a cool climate. If you are expecting to be thirsty, it is probably wise to go for a wine with a lower alcohol content.

Red wine

Examples of full-bodied red wines include most New World Shiraz and Cabernet Sauvignon reds, southern French reds, and many southern Spanish and Italian wines. Less weighty, but still substantial, reds embrace most types of red wines from Bordeaux, Burgundy, and Chianti. Light-bodied reds feature Beaujolais and many from the Loire, as well as most reds from Alsace, Germany, and the Pacific Northwest. Spicy reds wines include Syrrah, South American Maalbec, and Zinfandel.

White wine

For a full-bodied white, try an oak-aged Chardonnay or Semillon from the New World. For a medium-bodied white wine, try Australian Riesling, Pinot Blanc from Alsace, or Soave or Frascati from Italy. Light white wines made from Sauvignon Blanc, Riesling, or local grape varieties can be found in the Loire, northern Italy, Switzerland, Germany, New Zealand, Washington State, and England. New Zealand and the countries of northern Europe produce a number of delicate whites.

It is very helpful to go to informal wine-tastings offered by specialist wine merchants, because it gives you the opportunity to sample different varieties. It isn't true that vegetarian food automatically has to be paired with white wine! If you have personal favorites, that is fine, but if you want to branch out, give your palate time to develop. Above all, enjoy!

fruit punches

It is useful to have some tantalizing nonalcoholic drinks to serve at parties and special occasions. These drinks can be made from bought or freshly extracted juices. They are less intense than the pure fruit and vegetables juice recipes on page 138 because they use a significant amount of water.

cucumber and orange cooler with mint

serves 6

preparation: 5 minutes

cooking: none

v

1 cucumber
1¼ cups/½ pint (300 milliliters) orange juice
sprigs of mint
still or sparkling mineral water to taste
crushed ice, to serve

1 Set aside one-quarter of the cucumber. Peel, seed, and chop the rest and place in a blender or food processor with the orange juice and blend until smooth.

2 Slice the remaining cucumber thinly and stir in. Add the sprigs of mint, then dilute to taste with mineral water. Chill well and serve poured over crushed ice.

nutritional breakdown per serving: calories 20, protein 1g, fat 0g (saturated fat 0g), carbohydrate 5g

pineapple punch

This is delicious made with freshly extracted juices if you have a juicer, otherwise buy ready-made fruit juice and make the passion fruit juice by pressing the flesh through a sieve. You need only a small quantity but it does make a big difference to the overall flavor.

serves 6

preparation: 5 minutes, plus chilling

cooking: none

v

1 cup (250 milliliters) pineapple juice
1 cup (250 milliliters) apple juice
juice of 2 passion fruit
juice of 1 lemon
2 oranges
⅔ cup/4 ounces (125g) raspberries

1½ cups/½ pint (300 milliliters) sparkling
    mineral water or to taste
edible flowers or sprigs of mint or lemon balm

1 Mix together the pineapple, apple, passion fruit, and lemon juices. Peel the oranges, then slice them thinly on a plate so that you retain all the juice. Add to the fruit juice with the raspberries and chill well.

2 Just before serving, stir in chilled sparkling mineral water to taste and garnish with edible flowers or sprigs of mint or lemon balm.

nutritional breakdown per serving: calories 63, protein 1g, fat 0g (saturated fat 0g), carbohydrate 15g

cucumber and orange cooler with mint right **pineapple punch** left

345

barbecues

A barbecue is a lovely way to enjoy food and, if well organized, it should be a leisurely affair. When planning a barbecue menu, bear in mind that it is good to have either a couple of contrasting kabobs, or a kabob and a vegetable, such as the stuffed mushrooms on page 348.

If you intend serving platters of grilled vegetables, have ready slices of baguette or warm pita bread to add substance. Use ready-made vegetarian sausages and burgers to supplement the meal, as well as interesting breads and a variety of cheeses.

It is a good idea to have a choice of nibbles and snacks to keep your guests or family happy while the food is being cooked. Keep salads chilled until ready to serve.

preparation and equipment

Light a charcoal barbecue about 45 minutes before you want to start cooking. Don't start cooking until the flames have died down and the coals are glowing with a powdery gray surface. Make sure you have plenty of fuel; if you do need to liven up the fire during the barbecue, put fresh coals around the sides rather than on top.

Vegetables that take up a fair amount of space will need to be cooked in batches unless you have an enormous cooking area. Wipe metal skewers with oil so that the food does not stick; soak wooden skewers in water for up to 30 minutes before use so that they don't scorch. Hand-held grills and hinged wire baskets are useful for holding odd-shaped vegetable pieces, as well as being an easy way to turn over batches of food. Long-handled tongs are also useful items. After your barbecue, leave everything to cool down before disposing of ashes and cleaning the grid.

barbecue safety

- Wear a thick protective apron and potholders
- Do not use gasoline, kerosene, or paint thinner to light the barbecue
- Do not leave a barbecue unattended
- Have ready a bucket of sand or soil in case of fire
- Do not leave picnic food in the sun
- All food that has been out of the refrigerator for more than an hour or two is best thrown away at the end of the party

menu

Bean Curd Kabobs

Haloumi, Sweet Onion, and Apple Kabobs

Corn with Herb, Shallot, and Olive Butter

Stuffed Mushrooms with Walnuts
and Sun-Dried Tomatoes

Sliced Eggplant with Yogurt Dip

Mixed Vegetable Platter

bean curd kabobs

Bean curd is an excellent ingredient for a kabob. It provides a contrast to the vegetables, as well as adding nutrients. Here it is marinated in an Asian-inspired marinade.

makes 8
preparation: 15 minutes, plus marinating
cooking: 10 minutes

For the marinade:
juice of 1 lemon
2 tablespoons dry sherry
2 tablespoons shoyu or soy sauce
2 tablespoons concentrated apple juice
1 tablespoon sesame oil
2 garlic cloves, crushed
1-inch (2.5-cm) piece of fresh ginger, peeled
    and grated
1 chile, deseeded and chopped

For the kabobs:
8 ounces (250g) bean curd, cut into bite-
    size pieces
2 pounds (1kg) mixed vegetables (such as bell
    peppers, pearl onions, mushrooms, cherry
    tomatoes, zucchini), chopped

1 Combine all the ingredients for the marinade in a large bowl.

2 Mix the bean curd and the vegetables carefully into the marinade and set aside for at least 2 hours, longer if possible.

3 Thread the pieces onto oiled metal or presoaked wooden skewers, alternating the bean curd with pieces of vegetable.

4 Grill for several minutes so that the vegetables char and the bean curd is heated right through. Brush on a little of the marinade residue while the kabobs are cooking.

nutritional breakdown per kabob: calories 76, protein 5g, fat 3g (saturated fat 0g), carbohydrate 7g

Serve a choice of kebabs, supplemented by salads, bread, and cheese.

haloumi, sweet onion, and apple kabobs

Haloumi is a great cheese for grilling since it softens, rather than melts, and the heat of the cooking brings out its full flavor. It partners well with most vegetables and is mixed here with a sweet variety of onion and slices of apple.

makes 8
preparation: 10 minutes, plus marinating
cooking: 10 minutes

For the marinade:
¼ cup (50 milliliters) olive oil
1 tablespoon apple cider vinegar
1 garlic clove, crushed
1 tablespoon whole-grain mustard
salt and freshly ground black pepper

For the kabobs:
1 pound (500g) haloumi, cubed
3 sweet onions, each cut into 8 wedges
2 apples, each cut into 8 wedges

1 Whisk the marinade ingredients together in a bowl and season to taste. Add the cubes of haloumi and pieces of onion and apple. Set aside for 1 hour.

2 Thread alternate pieces of haloumi, onion, and apple onto oiled metal or presoaked wooden skewers and grill until the vegetables brown slightly and the cheese is hot. Baste with a little more marinade and serve hot.

nutritional breakdown per kabob: calories 270, protein 14g, fat 21g (saturated fat 10g), carbohydrate 8g

corn with herb, shallot, and olive butter

makes 4

preparation: 10 minutes

cooking: 15–20 minutes

½ cup (1 stick)/4 ounces (125g) butter, softened
1 shallot, very finely chopped
1 cup/1 ounce (25g) pitted olives, finely chopped
1 tablespoon chopped thyme
juice of ½ lemon
4 corn cobs
salt and freshly ground black pepper

1 Combine the softened butter with the shallot, olives, and thyme in a small bowl, then mix in the lemon juice, and chill well.

2 To cook the corn, either wrap the cobs in foil or roast in their husks on the barbecue for 15–20 minutes.

3 To serve, dot with the flavored butter and sprinkle with a little salt and pepper.

nutritional breakdown per ½ cob: calories 162, protein 2g, fat 14g (saturated fat 9g), carbohydrate 8g

stuffed mushrooms with walnuts and sun-dried tomatoes

Choose large flat mushrooms for this easy recipe.

serves 6–8

preparation: 10 minutes

cooking: 10–15 minutes

For the filling:
¾ cup/3 ounces (75g) walnuts, roasted
8 large sun-dried tomatoes
1 teaspoon fennel seeds
3 scallions, finely chopped
1 garlic clove, crushed
1–2 tablespoons olive oil
salt and freshly ground black pepper

6–8 large flat mushrooms

1 Place all the filling ingredients in a blender or food processor, reserving a little oil to coat the mushrooms, and blend to a coarse paste. Season well with salt and pepper.

2 Wipe each mushroom with oil, then cover with the filling.

3 Place the mushrooms on the barbecue grill and cook for 10–15 minutes, or until really well done.

nutritional breakdown per serving (6 portions): calories 246, protein 3g, fat 25g (saturated fat 3g), carbohydrate 2g

sliced eggplant with yogurt dip

Remove the seeds from the chile unless you want a particularly fiery dip.

serves 4

preparation: 10 minutes

cooking: 10 minutes

1 cup (250 milliliters) plain yogurt
2 scallions, finely chopped
1 mild green chile, very finely chopped
½ teaspoon cardamom seeds, crushed
2 tablespoons olive oil
salt and freshly ground black pepper
1 large or 2 medium eggplant, thinly sliced

1 Pour the yogurt into a bowl and stir in the scallions and chile. Add the cardamom, season well, and chill before serving.

2 Season the olive oil with salt and pepper and use it to brush the slices of eggplant. Grill on the barbecue for 10 minutes, turning once, until well cooked.

3 Serve the grilled eggplant slices and hand the dip separately.

nutritional breakdown per serving: calories 114, protein 5g, fat 7g (saturated fat 1g), carbohydrate 10g

sliced eggplant with yogurt dip above back **stuffed mushrooms with walnuts and sun-dried tomatoes** front

mixed vegetable platter

Huge platters of grilled vegetables, redolent with color and flavor, make a stunning presentation. Bell peppers and onions work particularly well, but many other vegetables are worth a try. Cook a contrasting mixture of vegetables each time so that there is a choice while waiting for the next batch. Before grilling vegetables, toss them in a well-seasoned oil or a special oil, such as walnut or chile oil, which adds a lively flavor. Serve platters of vegetables with hot pita bread or split grilled baguettes, creamy cheese, or roasted nuts.

Below are ways to prepare some of the most suitable vegetables for a barbecue.

Bell peppers—The three sweeter bell peppers—red, orange, and yellow—work very well, while the green variety can be bitter. Remove the seeds, then cut into halves or quarters. For kabobs it is best to use chunks.

Celery—this is best marinated before cooking (see below) since it can be rather dry. Trim individual stalks, then split them lengthwise or cut diagonally.

Baby corn cobs—trim and leave whole if cooking for a platter with dips; otherwise, cut in half for threading onto skewers, making it easier to turn.

Fennel—this can be quite dry, so marinate first (see below) or brush well with a good oil. Trim off the feathery tops and slice lengthwise thinly or leave in wedges.

Mushrooms—white mushrooms and small cup varieties can be left whole and are good for kabobs. Portobello mushrooms can also be thickly sliced and cooked and added to vegetable platters or served with dips. They are very good stuffed (see page 348).

Onion—use both the red and the sweet onions since they are milder and delicious when grilled. Trim off the root leaving enough so that the layers of the onion do not fall apart. Then cut into 8 wedges.

Potatoes—these don't grill as such, but if you have a decent supply of charcoal, you can wrap them in foil and bake among the coals. My tip with these is always cook one extra since inevitably one seems to get lost in the fire!

Zucchini—look for sweet baby zucchini that you can simply trim and leave whole. Turn while cooking. Larger zucchini can be sliced into ovals or chunky sticks—don't cut them too fine or they shrivel to nothing.

Corn cobs—like potatoes, corn cobs can also be roasted very successfully among the coals. They take about 20 minutes and taste great—even the burned bits!

Squash and sweet potato—these can be grilled but need to be cut into quite small chunks and cooked over a slow fire if possible. They are particularly good for adding color contrast to kabobs.

FOIL WRAPPED

Some vegetables are best grilled in foil. For large tomatoes, halve them, season with salt and pepper, a little balsamic vinegar, and basil. Wrap in foil and cook for about 10 minutes. New potatoes can be wrapped in foil with butter and garlic cloves. Cook for about 20 minutes and sprinkle with snipped chives to serve.

GRILLED FRUIT

Grilled fruit can be served as a separate course or mixed with vegetables and served as kabobs or on a platter. Brush fruit with lemon juice or lemon and honey, or add to a savory marinade before grilling. Serve with yogurt, cream, or silken bean curd for a sweet course. The following fruits grill well: apricots, nectarines, peaches, pineapples, apples, and pears.

vegetable marinade

Use this marinade with grilled vegetables (see above).

Sufficient for about 2 pounds (1kg) vegetables; serves 8

preparation: 5 minutes

cooking: none

v

⅔ cup/¼ pint (150 milliliters) olive oil
¼ cup (50 milliliters) red wine vinegar
1–2 tablespoons balsamic vinegar
juice of ½ lemon
1 teaspoon grated lemon zest
1 tablespoon chopped rosemary
1 tablespoon chopped oregano
4 garlic cloves, thinly sliced
salt and freshly ground black pepper, to taste

1 Combine all the ingredients for the marinade in a bowl.

2 To marinate vegetables, stir in the chosen vegetable pieces, cover, and set aside for 1–2 hours. Spread out on the barbecue grill and cook well, turning occasionally.

3 To serve with hot pita bread, split open the pita, brush with a little marinade, and sprinkle with some crumbled cheese or freshly grated Parmesan. Warm the bread through on the grill, then fill with vegetables, adding extra grated cheese.

nutritional breakdown per serving (not including **vegetables**: calories 125, protein 0g, fat 14g (saturated fat 2g), carbohydrate 7g

picnics

Picnics can range from the elegant to the robust and very much depends on the circumstances and what is required. In this section you'll find food that travels well and benefits from standing.

menu

Onion Braid with Mustard Seeds

Watercress Roulade with Asparagus and Crème Fraîche

Cheese and Potato Turnovers

Blueberry Summer Pudding

**Other recipes
that make good
picnic fare:**

Avocado Gazpacho
(see page 143)

Poached Vegetables
with Herbs and Wine
(see page 162)

Roasted Eggplant
and Garlic Dip
(see page 167)

Hummus
(see page 167)

Kuku with Spinach
(see page 181)

Leek and Feta Parcels
(see page 260)

Greek Potato Salad
(see page 301)

Beet and Green Bean
Salad with Couscous
(see page 300)

Red Cabbage and
Black Grape Salad
with Orange
Vinaigrette
(see page 311)

Classic Rich Fruit
Cake (see page 321)

Pistachio Cake
(see page 324)

onion braid with mustard seeds

This lightly textured bread has a gorgeous aroma and is delicious with a soft or semisoft cheese, such as goat cheese or Brie.

makes 10–12 slices

preparation: 15 minutes, plus rising

cooking: 35–40 minutes

suitable for freezing

𝒱

2 tablespoons olive oil

1 tablespoon black mustard seeds

8 ounces (250g) onion, finely chopped

3¼ cups/13 ounces (400g) white bread flour, plus extra for dusting

generous ¾ cup/3½ ounces (100g) whole-wheat flour

1 packet/¼ ounce (7g) active dry yeast

1 tablespoon dark brown sugar

1 teaspoon salt

1¼ cups/½ pint (300 milliliters) warm water

1 Heat the oil in a skillet and gently fry the mustard seeds for 1 minute. Add the onion and cook until soft and colored. Let cool.

2 Place the white and whole-wheat flours, yeast, sugar, and salt in a large bowl and pour in the warm water.

3 Add the onion mixture and stir the ingredients into a dough. Add more water if necessary. Knead on a lightly floured counter for at least 5 minutes, so that the dough becomes smooth and elastic.

4 Return the dough to a clean bowl and cover with plastic wrap or a damp dish towel. Set aside to rise in a warm place until it has doubled in size.

5 Again working on a lightly floured counter, punch the air out of the dough and knead again briefly, then divide into 3 equal pieces. Roll out each piece into a sausage shape, about 10 inches (25cm) long. Lay the lengths side by side and braid together, pinching the pieces together at each end.

6 Place the braid on a baking sheet and cover with plastic wrap. Set aside to rise until roughly doubled in size.

7 Bake in a preheated oven, 425°F (220°C), for 30–35 minutes, or until cooked—it should sound hollow when tapped on the base.

8 Turn the loaf over and cook for 3 minutes more to crisp the base. Let cool on a wire rack..

BRAIDING A LOAF

When braiding a loaf it is best to start the braid in the middle and then braid toward either end since this will make the braid more even, and avoids stretching the dough too much (see page 336).

nutritional breakdown per slice: calories 206, protein 7g, fat 3g (saturated fat 0g), carbohydrate 40g

watercress roulade with asparagus and crème fraîche

This impressive dish makes a welcome alternative to pastry-based savories and will travel well if properly wrapped. It will keep in the refrigerator for 24 hours.

serves 4

preparation: 20 minutes

cooking: 12–15 minutes

(Ca)

8 ounces (250g) watercress or 4 ounces (100g) watercress and 4 ounces (100g) arugula
5 eggs, separated
⅔ cup/2 ounces (50g) grated Parmesan
freshly grated nutmeg
4 ounces (125g) asparagus
3 scallions, finely chopped

4 ounces (125g) crème fraîche
salt and freshly ground black pepper
fresh watercress and Parmesan shavings,
    to garnish

1   Place the watercress or watercress and arugula in a bowl and cover with boiling water. Let stand for 30 seconds, then drain. Squeeze dry, then chop very finely.

2   Beat the egg yolks in a bowl with the watercress and grated Parmesan. Grate over some nutmeg and season well.

3   Whisk the egg whites in another bowl until they stand in soft peaks.

4   Stir 1 tablespoon of egg white into the egg yolk mixture, then gently fold in the remaining egg whites.

5   Spoon the mixture into a lined, 9 x 13-inch (23 x 33-cm) jelly roll pan. Shake slightly to even out the mixture.

6   Bake in a preheated oven, 400°F (200°C), for 12–15 minutes, or until just firm. Turn out onto a sheet of baking parchment and let cool completely.

7   Meanwhile, to make the filling, steam the asparagus over a saucepan of boiling water for 5 minutes, or until just tender. Drain and chop finely. Place in a bowl.

8   Stir in the scallions, then the crème fraîche. Season well.

9   Spread the filling over the roulade. To roll it up, start by folding in one short edge of the roulade, then use the baking parchment to help you ease it into a roll.

10 Wrap the roulade in plastic wrap for traveling. Serve garnished with watercress and shavings of Parmesan, if liked.

nutritional breakdown per serving: calories 310, protein 16g, fat 24g (saturated fat 13g), carbohydrate 7g

cheese and potato turnovers

These are great for a picnic or outdoor meal, full of flavor and very satisfying. Serve on their own or, if you have plates and cutlery, add a salad or two to provide color.

makes 6
preparation: 20 minutes, plus pastry making
cooking: 30–35 minutes
suitable for freezing

8 ounces (250g) potato, coarsely chopped
8 ounces (250g) squash or rutabaga,
   coarsely chopped
2 tablespoons/1 ounce (25g) butter
1 onion, finely chopped
3 tablespoons chopped parsley
scant 1 cup/3½ ounces (100g) grated cheese
1 teaspoon Dijon mustard
1 quantity Quick Flaky Pastry (see page 256)
flour for dusting
salt and freshly ground black pepper

1 quantity Quick Flaky Pastry (see page 256)

GLAZING

To give the turnovers a glaze, use an egg wash. Beat 1 egg yolk with 1 tablespoon water and a little salt. Brush over the turnovers before baking.

1 Cook the potato and squash or rutabaga in a saucepan of boiling salted water for 10–15 minutes until soft. Drain and set aside.

2 Meanwhile, melt the butter in a large saucepan and cook the onion for 10 minutes until soft and lightly browned. Remove from the heat.

3 Mash the cooked vegetables with the onion and all the residue of butter. Add the parsley, grated cheese, and mustard and mix well. Season with salt and pepper to taste.

4 Roll out the pastry on a lightly floured counter and cut into 7-inch (18-cm) rounds.

5 Put a portion of the cheesy vegetable filling on each round. Moisten the edges with cold water, then fold over each piece to make a semicircle, and crimp the edges together.

6 Place the turnovers on a baking sheet and prick with a fork. Bake in a preheated oven, 425°F (220°C), for 20 minutes, or until golden brown.

nutritional breakdown per serving: calories 480, protein 10g, fat 31g (saturated fat 15g), carbohydrate 42g

VARIATION

Other vegetables can be added to turnovers, for example carrots, parsnips, or beet. You could also add a few cooked beans or lentils to make a hearty filling.

blueberry summer pudding

Ideal for using soft summer fruits, this easy, colorful pudding makes a good picnic or buffet dish. All manner of berries can be used, but blueberries add a light clean flavor. Make this recipe in a glass bowl so that you can check on how well the juices are soaking into the bread. Turn out the pudding only when you arrive at the picnic.

serves 6

preparation: 20 minutes, plus standing

cooking: 3–4 minutes

𝒱

3 ¼ cups/13 ounces (400g) blueberries
generous 2 cups/13 ounces (400g) raspberries
1 ¾ cups/7 ounces (200g) red currants
¾ cup/5 ounces (150g) superfine sugar
1 medium loaf (white or soft whole-wheat bread)
extra fruit and cream, to serve, optional

1 Place the blueberries, raspberries, and currants in a large saucepan and sprinkle with the sugar.

2 Heat the fruit for 3–4 minutes until the juices begin to run, then let cool.

3 Cut the loaf into slices and remove the crusts. Cut a small disk of bread to fit the base of a 5-cup/ 2-pint (1.2-liter) glass bowl. Line the sides of the bowl with more slices of bread, reserving a few slices to cover the top.

4 Pile all the fruit into the center of the bread-lined bowl and pour the juices over the top.

5 Place the reserved bread on top of the fruit, trimming to fit. Cover with a plate that just fits inside the bowl and put a 2-pound (1-kg) weight on top so that the fruit is pressed down and the juices are pressed into the bread. Let stand overnight in the refrigerator—stand the bowl on a tray to collect any juice that may ooze out.

6 Turn the pudding out just before serving and serve with extra fruit and cream, if you like.

nutritional breakdown per serving: calories 348, protein 9g, fat 2g (saturated fat 0g), carbohydrate 79g

buffet for 12

This is a cold buffet with plenty of variety in terms of texture, color, and flavor. You can add extra appetizers according to the number of people for whom you are catering. For dairy-free alternatives serve a Saffron Onion Pizza (see page 198) and Spiced Hazelnut and Quinoa Loaf (see page 267). Substantial salads, such as Marinated Bean Salad (see page 298) and Spiced Rice Salad (see page 304) are also good for buffets and have the advantage that they can be prepared well ahead.

suggested timetable

One or two days before:
Make the filling for the grape leaves and store in the refrigerator
Make the filling for the phyllo triangles and store in in the refrigerator

The day before:
Fill and cook the grape leaves
Make the vegetable terrine and chill

On the day:
Make the galette
Assemble the phyllo triangles and cook

menu

Stuffed Grape Leaves with Spiced Bulgur

Mediterranean Galette

Layered Vegetable Terrine

Red Bell Pepper and Parmesan Phyllo Triangles

Choice of salads

---

mediterranean galette opposite back
stuffed grape leaves with spiced bulgur opposite front

mediterranean galette

This tasty galette is baked in the oven rather than fried and flipped over in the classic manner. It is certainly more foolproof when prepared in this way. As with all egg dishes, be bold with the flavoring so that the finished dish is not bland. The galette can be served hot but I think the flavors are more evident once the dish is cool.

serves 12
preparation: 10 minutes
cooking: 40 minutes

2 tablespoons olive oil
1 onion, finely chopped
1 garlic clove, crushed
3 zucchini, sliced
1 red bell pepper, cored, deseeded, and chopped
2 cups/10 ounces (300g) fava beans (shelled weight), steamed or boiled until just tender
6 eggs
⅔ cup/5 ounces (150g) cream cheese
1 teaspoon dried thyme
2 tablespoons chopped basil
salt and freshly ground black pepper
2 tablespoons freshly grated Parmesan

1 Heat the oil in a saucepan and cook the onion and garlic until soft. Add the zucchini and red bell pepper and cook for 4–5 minutes, then add the cooked fava beans, and stir well. Remove the pan from the heat.

2 Lightly mix the eggs in a large bowl with the cream cheese, thyme, and basil. Season well with salt and pepper. Stir in the cooked vegetables. then pour the mixture into a lightly buttered ovenproof dish.

3 Dust with the freshly grated Parmesan and bake in a preheated oven, 375°F (190°C), for 30 minutes, or until well browned and firm in the center. Let cool.

4 Cut the galette into wedges or slices and serve at room temperature.

nutritional breakdown per serving: calories 148, protein 7g, fat 11g (saturated fat 5g), carbohydrate 5g

stuffed grape leaves with spiced bulgur

Grape leaves stuffed with bulgur or rice make pretty packages that look good as part of a buffet spread. This filling also contains apricot. Tiny currants are good, too, as well as versions that use just herbs. Make a meal of these by serving them with a bowl of plain yogurt and some crisp salad.

makes 50

preparation: 25 minutes

cooking: 45–50 minutes

𝑣

For the filling:
1 tablespoon olive oil
1 onion, very finely chopped
½ teaspoon ground cinnamon
½ teaspoon ground turmeric
¼ cup/2 ounces (50g) dried apricots, sliced
¾ cup/3 ounces (75g) pine nuts
⅔ cup/4 ounces (125g) bulgur
scant 2 cups/¾ pint (450 milliliters) Vegetable
   Stock (see page 144) or water
2 tablespoons chopped mint
salt and freshly ground black pepper

50 grape leaves
juice of 1 lemon
2 tablespoons olive oil
2 tablespoons chopped mint, to garnish
plain yogurt and wedges of lemon, to serve

1 To make the filling, heat the olive oil in a saucepan and cook the onion for 10 minutes over very gentle heat until it is really soft. Add the cinnamon and turmeric and cook for 2–3 minutes, then add the apricots, pine nuts, and bulgur. Mix well.

2 Pour in 1¼ cups/½ pint (300 milliliters) of the stock, bring to a boil, and simmer for 5 minutes. The bulgur will still be firm at this stage. There may be some liquid left in the pan but this will probably be absorbed on standing. Stir in the mint and season well with salt and pepper.

3 Rinse the grape leaves if using brine-packed ones and trim the stalks. Put a dessert spoonful of filling on each leaf, tuck in the sides, and roll up.

4 Arrange a layer of the stuffed leaves in the base of a deep ovenproof dish, seam-sides down. Cover with more layers of parcels until all the leaves and filling

are used. Pour in the remaining stock with the lemon juice and olive oil.

5 Cover and bake in a preheated oven, 350°F (180°C), for 30 minutes. Let cool.

6 Remove the parcels from the dish using a slotted spoon and serve at room temperature, garnished with mint and accompanied by plain yogurt and wedges of lemon.

nutritional breakdown per stuffed leaf: calories 29, protein 1g, fat 2g (saturated fat 0g), carbohydrate 3g

USING FRESH GRAPE LEAVES

If using fresh grape leaves, blanch them in boiling water for 1 minute, then refresh in cold water and drain. This makes them pliable.

layered vegetable terrine

A beautiful concoction of layered vegetable purées, which is baked until set, then served, thinly sliced, for an elegant addition to a buffet. Although there is work in the preparation, it can all be done well ahead of time, leaving a simple assembly. This recipe will also serve 6–8 as an appetizer for a special meal.

serves 12
preparation: 30 minutes
cooking: about 1 hour
suitable for freezing

1 pound (500g) carrots, chopped
1 pound (500g) fennel, chopped
1 pound (500g) spinach, chopped
6 eggs
6 tablespoons heavy cream
salt and freshly ground black pepper

1 Cook the carrots in a saucepan of boiling water for 15–20 minutes, or until soft. Drain well and let cool.

2 Meanwhile, cook the fennel in another saucepan of boiling water for 15–20 minutes, or until soft. Drain well and let cool.

3 Steam the spinach in its own juices for 3–4 minutes, or until the leaves have wilted. Drain well and let cool.

4 Place the cooked carrots in a blender or food processor and purée until smooth, adding 2 eggs and 3 tablespoons cream. Season well with salt and pepper, remove from the blender, and set aside.

5 In the same way, purée the fennel in the rinsed blender or food processor until smooth, again adding 2 eggs and 3 tablespoons cream. Season well with salt and pepper and set aside.

6 Lastly, again using the rinsed blender or food processor, purée the spinach until smooth, adding 2 eggs. Season well with salt and pepper.

7 Prepare an 8 x 4-inch (20 x 10-cm)/4–5-cup (900-milliliter–1.2-liter) loaf pan by lining it with baking parchment or foil. Place one-third of the carrot purée in the base, cover with one-third of fennel purée, then one-third of spinach purée. Repeat the layering to give 3 layers of each purée, finishing with the spinach.

8 Bake in a preheated oven, 350°F (180°C), for 35–45 minutes, or until the terrine feels firm to the touch. Let cool in the pan, then lift out and transfer to a serving plate. For a buffet it is preferable to serve the terrine already sliced as it can be tricky for your guests to do—use a very sharp knife.

nutritional breakdown per serving: calories 146, protein 5g, fat 11g (saturated fat 6g), carbohydrate 6g

red bell pepper and parmesan phyllo triangles

Savory parcels and packages make simple quick meals and phyllo pastry is an ideal wrapping. Be liberal with the brushed oil and butter or the end result will be papery and dry. As for fillings, almost any vegetable, nut, or cheese combination can be used—especially tasty leftovers—just choose something that is not too sloppy.

makes 24 small triangles
preparation: 15 minutes
cooking: 40–45 minutes
suitable for freezing

For the filling:
4 large red bell peppers, lightly oiled
7 ounces (200g) sun-dried tomatoes
⅓ cup/1 ounce (25g) freshly grated Parmesan
salt and freshly ground black pepper

For the triangles:
24 sheets phyllo pastry
⅓ cup/4–6 tablespoons (50–75g) butter, melted
¼ cup (50 milliliters) olive oil

1 To make the filling, place the bell peppers in a roasting pan and place in a preheated oven, 400°F (200°C), for 20–25 minutes, or until well charred.

2 Set the bell peppers aside until cool enough to handle, then remove the skins and seeds. Do not wash them.

3 Chop the bell peppers coarsely and place in a blender or food processor with the tomatoes and Parmesan. Blend to a coarse paste. Season well with salt and pepper.

4 To make the triangles, work with 1 sheet of phyllo pastry at a time. Take a sheet and brush well with a mixture of melted butter and olive oil. Fold lengthwise to make a strip and brush again with the melted butter and oil mixture.

5 Place a dessertspoonful of filling on one end of the strip. Fold the end over at an angle to cover the filling and make a triangular shape. Continue folding the pastry over the filling, always keeping the triangle shape, until the pastry strip is rolled up. Brush well with more melted butter and oil.

6 Repeat the process with the remaining sheets of pastry and filling.

7 Place the triangles on a lightly greased baking sheet and bake in a preheated oven, 400°F (200°C), for 20 minutes, or until crisp. Serve warm or at room temperature.

nutritional breakdown per triangle: calories 190, protein 5g, fat 9g (saturated fat 3g), carbohydrate 24g

VARIATION

For a dairy-free option, substitute pitted black olives for the Parmesan cheese in the filling and use olive oil only to brush the phyllo pastry. It gives the pastry a slightly dryer finish but is still very appetizing.

finger food buffet for 16

Finger food is a great way of entertaining. Plan a selection of ideas, some of which you can make in advance. Choose a range of textures and lay the savories on large trays and garnish with fresh fruit and vegetables. For 16 people allow about 6–8 different items. Double quantities as necessary and supplement with some of the additional suggestions in the menu box.

suggested timetable

One or two days before:
Make the bruschetta bases and store in an airtight container
Roast the almonds and store in an airtight container

The day before:
Make spiced new potatoes and dip; cover, and store in the refrigerator

Prepare toppings for bruschetta and store in an airtight container in the refrigerator

On the day:
Assemble the bruschetta
Make the tartlets

menu

Asparagus Tartlets

Spiced New Potatoes with Sharp Cream Dip

Roasted Almonds with Shoyu

Bruschetta with Fresh Tomato and Basil

Bruschetta with Roasted Walnuts and Black Olives

Other finger food savories could include:
Savory Choux Puffs with Avocado and Pesto
(see page 164)
Dips with Crudités (see page 166–7)
Falafel (vegan) (see page 174)
Baked Bean Curd and Cremini Mushrooms (vegan)
(see page 175)

asparagus tartlets

These little tartlets, with their rich pastry base, make mouthwatering savories.

makes 36
preparation: 15 minutes, plus pastry making
cooking: 25–30 minutes
suitable for freezing

For the filling:
¼ cup (½ stick)/2 ounces (50g) butter
4 shallots, finely chopped
1 pound (500g) asparagus, coarsely chopped
¼ cup (50 milliliters) white wine
1 cup (250 milliliters) heavy cream
4 eggs, beaten
2 tablespoons chopped tarragon
salt and freshly ground black pepper

Double quantity Enriched Pie Dough
(see page 254)
flour for dusting

spiced new potatoes with sharp cream dip
opposite top and right

asparagus tartlets
opposite bottom

1 To make the filling, melt the butter in a saucepan and cook the shallots over gentle heat until translucent. Add the asparagus and cook for several minutes until beginning to soften.

2 Add the wine to the pan, increase the heat, and cook until the liquid has reduced, then remove the pan from the heat.

3 Combine the cream, eggs, and tarragon in a bowl, and season well with salt and pepper.

4 Roll out the chilled pastry on a lightly floured counter to fill 36 individual muffin pans. Arrange pieces of cooked asparagus and shallot in each shell. Pour in the cream and egg mixture.

5 Bake the tartlets in a preheated oven, 400°F (200°C), for 15–20 minutes, or until firm to touch. Serve warm or at room temperature.

nutritional breakdown per tartlet: calories 138, protein 3g, fat 10g (saturated fat 6g), carbohydrate 9g

spiced new potatoes with sharp cream dip

These flavorsome potatoes make a substantial appetizer for a finger food party. As they cook, they take on a gorgeous rusty glow from the mixture of tomato paste and red wine vinegar, as well as absorbing the spices and herbs. Prepare well ahead so that the flavors develop.

serves 16
preparation: 10 minutes
cooking: about 1 hour
𝒱 (excluding dip)

¼ cup (50 milliliters) sunflower oil
1½ pounds (750g) baby new potatoes
1 tablespoon red wine vinegar
2 garlic cloves, crushed
1 tablespoon tomato paste
⅔ cup/¼ pint (150 milliliters) Vegetable Stock
   (see page 144) or water
1 medium hot chile, chopped
1 teaspoon ground cumin
1 sprig thyme
salt and freshly ground black pepper

For the dip:
scant 1 cup (200 milliliters) sour cream
3 tablespoons chopped fresh herbs (chives,
   parsley, or tarragon)
1 scallion, finely chopped
1 garlic clove, crushed
1 teaspoon apple cider vinegar
salt and freshly ground black pepper, to taste

1 Heat the oil in a large skillet and cook the potatoes, in batches if necessary, until lightly browned. Use more oil if necessary. Remove from the skillet and place in an ovenproof dish.

2 Combine the red wine vinegar, garlic, tomato paste, stock, chile, cumin, and thyme in a pitcher. Season well with salt and pepper and pour over the potatoes. Add a little water if necessary.

3 Bake in a preheated oven, 375°F (190°C), for 35–40 minutes until tender. Turn the potatoes once or twice during the cooking. Let cool in the dish.

4 To make the dip, blend everything together in a small blender or food processor until you have a very smooth consistency. Season to taste. Serve the potatoes at room temperature with the sour cream dip in a separate bowl.

VARIATION

For a dairy-free version of this recipe, replace the sour cream with bean curd. Blend the bean curd with 6–8 tablespoons water so that it has the consistency of plain yogurt. Then add 1–2 tablespoons sunflower or olive oil to the dip to give it a creamy texture.

nutritional breakdown per serving: calories 84, protein 1g, fat 5g (saturated fat 2g), carbohydrate 8g

OUT OF SEASON

When new potatoes are not in season, make this recipe using larger potatoes, cut into bite-size wedges.

roasted almonds with shoyu

Roasted almonds make a delicious nibble. They can also be tossed in spices, such as cumin or paprika, as well as coarse rock salt and ground pepper, right after cooking.

serves 16

preparation: 2 minutes

cooking: 40 minutes

4 cups/1 pound (500g) whole blanched almonds
2–3 tablespoons shoyu or soy sauce

1 Roast the almonds in a preheated oven, 300°F (150°C), for 30 minutes or so, until they are light brown.

2 Sprinkle with 2–3 tablespoons shoyu or soy sauce and roast again for 10 minutes more.

3 Let cool. Keep in airtight jars.

nutritional breakdown per serving: calories 193, protein 7g, fat 17g (saturated fat 2g), carbohydrate 2g

bruschetta

Bruschetta are toasted slices of rustic bread or focaccia topped with a variety of flavorings. They make very simple snacks and great nibbles prior to a meal. You can obviously vary the toppings to fit in with whatever else you are serving. Whole-wheat bruschetta take longer to bake.

makes 16

preparation: 5 minutes

cooking: 10 minutes

𝑣

1 loaf rustic bread or baguette, cut into 16 slices
1–2 garlic cloves, peeled and halved, and 2–3 tablespoons olive oil, or 2–3 tablespoons Garlic Oil (see page 196)
2–3 tablespoons freshly grated Parmesan, optional

1 Arrange the slices of bread in a single layer on a baking sheet and bake in a preheated oven, 400°F (200°C), for 5–7 minutes.

2 Rub the surfaces with garlic, then brush with olive oil. Alternatively, brush liberally with garlic oil.

3 If using Parmesan, sprinkle the bruschetta with a little cheese and bake again briefly. Serve as they are or topped with one of the toppings given below.

nutritional breakdown per bruschetta (with no topping): calories 69, protein 2g, fat 2g (saturated fat 1g), carbohydrate 11g

fresh tomato and basil topping

This topping is good on toast baked with Parmesan cheese.

sufficient for 16 bruschetta

preparation: 15 minutes

cooking: none

𝑣

2 pounds (1kg) tomatoes, skinned and finely chopped
2 garlic cloves, crushed
1 shallot, finely chopped
3–4 tablespoons chopped basil leaves
salt and freshly ground black pepper
1–2 tablespoons olive oil

1 Combine the finely chopped tomatoes, crushed garlic, shallot, and basil leaves. Season well with salt and pepper and sprinkle with the olive oil.

2 Pile the topping on top of the bruschetta toasts just before serving.

nutritional breakdown per serving: calories 21, protein 1g, fat 1g (saturated fat 0g), carbohydrate 2g

roasted walnut and black olive topping

For a lively extra, add some flakes of dried chile to the topping.

sufficient for 16 bruschetta

preparation: 10 minutes

cooking: 5 minutes

1 cup/4 ounces (125g) walnut pieces
2 tablespoons white wine vinegar
1 garlic clove
⅓ cup (80 milliliters) olive oil
2 tablespoons chopped parsley
1 green bell pepper, cored, deseeded, and
    finely chopped
2½ cups/10 ounces (300g) pitted black olives,
    finely chopped
salt and freshly ground black pepper

1 Roast the walnuts in a preheated oven, 400°F (200°C), for 4–5 minutes, or until well browned. Let cool, then chop finely, and place in a blender or food processor.

2 Add the wine vinegar and garlic to the nuts and grind the ingredients to a paste. With the motor running, pour in the oil in a thin steady stream, as if making mayonnaise.

3 When thoroughly blended, scrape the walnut mixture into a clean bowl. Mix in the parsley, chopped green bell pepper and 2 cups (250g) of the finely chopped olives. Season to taste.

4 Pile the topping on top of bruschetta toasts just before serving. Garnish with the remaining black olives.

nutritional breakdown per serving: calories 106, protein 1g, fat 11g (saturated fat 1g), carbohydrate 1g

bruschetta with fresh tomato and basil topping left **walnut and black olive topping** right

QUICK AVOCADO TOPPING

Avocado also makes a great topping for bruschetta. Mash the flesh of 1 avocado with some crème fraîche, chopped cilantro, and lime juice. Season well and pile it on bruschetta just before serving.

summer dinner party for 8

This pretty meal, bursting with color, captures the essence of summer. Start with a light but tangy goat cheese soufflé, impress with a glossy tarte tatin full of roasted Mediterranean vegetables, and end with glistening nectarines and refreshing raspberry coulis. An added bonus is that this dinner party really is stress-free entertaining—most of the preparation for the meal can be done in advance, and all you need to do on the evening is relax and enjoy yourself.

suggested timetable

Several days before:
Make the Mascarpone and Amaretti Ice
Make the pesto
Roast the almonds (optional)
Make the Falafel and freeze (optional)

Two days before:
Make the tomato sauce for the soufflés
Prepare the raspberry coulis
Make the vinaigrette

The day before:
Make the soufflés and chill
Make the flaky pastry and chill

On the day:
Finish the tarte tatin
Assemble the soufflés ready for reheating
Prepare the nectarines
Make the salad
Make sure the cheese has time to come to room temperature
Fry the falafel (optional)

menu

Appetizers (optional)—Roasted Almonds with Shoyu
(see page 364) or miniature Falafel with yogurt
(see page 174)

Twice-Baked Goat Cheese Soufflés with Tomato Sauce and
Walnuts

Tarte Tatin with Roasted Mediterranean Vegetables

New Potatoes with Pesto
(or Avocado and Pistachio Salad, see page 307)

Garden Salad with Green Olive Dressing

Bowl of cherry tomatoes

Broiled Nectarines with Fresh Raspberry Coulis

Mascarpone and Amaretti Ice

Cheese and crackers (I suggest a blue and a hard cheese
with a good tang)

twice baked goat cheese soufflés with tomato sauce and walnuts

Choose a well-flavored goat cheese so that the tang comes through. You could also use Gruyère or fontina instead. Twice-baked soufflés are prepared in the same way as regular soufflés, except they are baked in small dishes such as ramekins or cups. Let them cool completely in the dish, then chill them. Don't worry that they collapse at this stage. When required, heat them in the chosen sauce. They will puff up a little and make a tasty light appetizer.

serves 8

preparation: 25 minutes

cooking: about 1 hour

suitable for freezing (tomato sauce only)

¼ cup (½ stick) 2 ounces (50g) butter
½ cup/2 ounces (50g) all-purpose flour
1 cup (250 milliliters) milk
7 ounces (200g) well-flavored soft goat
   cheese, crumbled
4 extra large eggs, separated

For the tomato sauce:
1 tablespoon olive oil
1 onion, chopped
1 garlic clove, chopped
28 ounces (796 milliliters) canned chopped
   tomatoes or bottled strained tomatoes
1 bay leaf
1 teaspoon dried thyme
½ teaspoon granulated sugar
½ teaspoon salt
1–2 tablespoons walnut oil
salt and freshly ground black pepper

2 tablespoons chopped walnut pieces
2 tablespoons freshly grated Parmesan
garnish of salad greens, to serve

1 Lightly grease 8 ramekin dishes or cups. Line the base of each with a small piece of baking parchment.

2 Melt the butter in a small saucepan. Stir in the flour to make a roux and cook for 1 minute. Add the milk and, stirring constantly, bring the sauce to a boil. Simmer for 2–3 minutes—it should be very thick. Season well and add the goat cheese.

3 Stir the egg yolks into the goat cheese sauce.

4 Whisk the egg whites in a large bowl until stiff. Stir 1 tablespoon of egg white into the cheese sauce. Then fold in the remaining egg white, using a metal spoon.

5 Spoon the mixture into the prepared ramekins and bake in a preheated oven, 400°F (200°C), for 15 minutes. Let cool completely, then remove from the molds and chill in the refrigerator until required.

6 To make the tomato sauce, heat the oil in a saucepan and gently cook the onion and garlic until translucent.

7 Pour in the canned chopped or bottled strained tomatoes and add the bay leaf, thyme, sugar, and salt. Bring to a boil and simmer, covered, for 20 minutes.

8 Let the tomato sauce cool, remove the bay leaf, and then, using a blender or food processor, blend until smooth, adding the walnut oil and salt and pepper to taste.

9 Meanwhile, spread the walnut pieces on a baking sheet and roast at 400°F (200°C) for 4–5 minutes. Set aside.

10 To assemble, place the soufflés in a greased ovenproof dish and cover with tomato sauce, reserving scant 1 cup (200 milliliters). Sprinkle with grated Parmesan, then bake at 400°F (200°C), for 15 minutes.

11 To serve, heat the reserved tomato sauce gently. Spoon a couple of tablespoons of sauce on each plate and place a soufflé in the center. Sprinkle with a few roasted walnuts and serve hot with a garnish of salad greens.

nutritional breakdown per serving: calories 293, protein 11g, fat 23g (saturated fat 8g), carbohydrate 11g

tarte tatin with roasted mediterranean vegetables

This classic pie is baked with the crust on top, then turned upside down to serve. The end result is a light base topped with a mouthwatering selection of dark glazed vegetables. Use either flaky pastry or pie dough for the base. You can simply lay the pastry right over the roasted vegetables but I think it is safer to line a clean dish with baking parchment so that you can be sure the pie will turn out. This pie is also great as a picnic dish; vary the vegetables to suit and serve it with Avocado and Pistachio Salad (see page 307). For more information on making pastry, see pages 252–58.

serves 8

preparation: 45 minutes, plus chilling and standing

cooking: about 1 hour

v

For the pastry:

2 cups/8 ounces (250g) all-purpose flour, plus
   extra for dusting

½ teaspoon salt

⅔ cup/5 ounces (150g) butter, solid vegetable fat,
   or a mixture, frozen for 30 minutes before use

1 tablespoon lemon juice

8–9 tablespoons ice water

For the filling:

1 large red bell pepper, cored, deseeded, and
   sliced lengthwise

1 large yellow bell pepper, cored, deseeded, and
   sliced lengthwise

1 eggplant, cubed

1 red onion, sliced

¼ cup (50 milliliters) olive oil

1 tablespoon balsamic vinegar

salt and freshly ground black pepper

1 To make the pastry, sift the flour and salt into
   a large bowl.

2 Grate in the frozen fat, then add the lemon juice
   and just enough ice water to draw the mixture into
   a dough, using a rounded knife. Draw up to a ball
   and knead very lightly.

3 Wrap the dough in wax paper and chill for
   30 minutes.

4 Roll out the dough on a lightly floured counter to
   a long oblong. Lightly mark the pastry into thirds.

Fold in one end third on top of the middle third, then fold the remaining third over the top. Seal the edges of the folded pastry and give it a quarter turn on the counter. Repeat this rolling and folding process once more and chill again for 30 minutes.

5 Meanwhile, to make the filling, toss the red and yellow peppers, eggplant, and onion in the olive oil and season well with salt and pepper.

6 Spread the vegetables out in a large roasting pan or flameproof dish. Bake in a preheated oven, 400°F (200°C), for 30 minutes, or until well browned.

7 Remove the vegetables from the roasting pan with a slotted spoon. Add the balsamic vinegar to the roasting pan and place the pan on the stovetop to deglaze, then scrape out the juices, and reserve.

8 Line a shallow ovenproof dish or plate with baking parchment and spoon in the juices from the roasting pan. Spread the roasted vegetables over the base, arranging them in an attractive pattern.

9 Roll out the pastry on a lightly floured counter to a size to fit over the vegetables. Place the pastry on top of the vegetables and tuck in the sides.

10 Bake at 425°F (220°C), for 30 minutes. Let stand for about 10 minutes, then turn out. Serve warm or at room temperature.

> nutritional breakdown per serving: calories 306, protein 4g, fat 21g (saturated fat 8g), carbohydrate 28g

new potatoes with pesto

serves 8

preparation: 5 minutes

cooking: 15 minutes

2 pounds (1kg) new potatoes
2–3 tablespoons pesto (see page 211)
salt and freshly ground black pepper

1 Boil the new potatoes in a large saucepan of boiling water for 15 minutes, until just tender.

2 Drain and toss in the pesto while still warm. Season with salt and pepper to taste and serve warm or at room temperature

> nutritional breakdown per serving: calories 126, protein 4g, fat 4g (saturated fat 2g), carbohydrate 20g

garden salad with green olive dressing

serves 8

preparation: 5 minutes

cooking: 3–4 minutes

𝑣

For the dressing:
¼ cup (50 milliliters) olive oil or flavored oil
juice and zest of 1 lemon
10 pitted green olives, finely chopped
1 teaspoon chopped thyme
1 teaspoon chopped oregano
1 garlic clove, crushed
salt and freshly ground black pepper

⅔ cup/2 ounces (50g) pumpkin seeds
125g (4 ounces) mixed salad greens

1 Combine the oil, lemon juice, and zest in a pitcher and stir in the chopped olives, thyme, oregano, and crushed garlic. Season well with salt and pepper.

2 Spread the pumpkin seeds on a baking sheet and roast in a preheated oven, 400°F (200°C), for 3–4 minutes.

3 Just before serving, toss the dressing into the salad greens. Sprinkle the roasted pumpkin seeds over the top.

> nutritional breakdown per serving: calories 95, protein 2g, fat 9g (saturated fat 1g), carbohydrate 1g

tarte tatin with roasted mediterranean vegetables opposite

369

mascarpone and amaretti ice

If you prefer not to use alcohol, soak the golden raisins in fruit juice instead.

serves 8

preparation: 10 minutes, plus soaking and freezing

cooking: none

suitable for freezing

1 cup/8 ounces (250g) mascarpone cheese
generous 2 cups (500 milliliters) plain yogurt
¼ cup/2 ounces (50g) superfine sugar
¼ cup (50 milliliters) milk
4 amaretti, crumbled
2 ounces (50g) golden raisins, soaked for at least
    30 minutes in 2–3 tablespoons brandy or
    Marsala

1 Combine all the ingredients in a large bowl.

2 Pour the mixture into a freezer container and freeze for 2 hours, then beat vigorously for 2–3 minutes, and freeze again for 2 hours more. Alternatively, use an ice-cream maker and follow the manufacturer's instructions.

3 Remove from the freezer and place in the refrigerator 15 minutes before serving. However, if you have made the ice some time in advance, it will need longer than 15 minutes in the refrigerator to soften before serving.

nutritional breakdown per serving: calories 247, protein 6g, fat 15g (saturated fat 10g), carbohydrate 22g

broiled nectarines with raspberry coulis

It is important to have very ripe, good-quality nectarines for this dish. If they are not in season, use peaches, which can be broiled in the same way. Alternatively, make a fresh berry compôte with red currants, blueberries, and strawberries. Dust with confectioners' sugar and serve in a pool of coulis.

serves 8

preparation: 10 minutes

cooking: 3–4 minutes

For the coulis:
2 cups/12 ounces (375g) fresh or frozen
    raspberries, thawed
scant ½ cup/3 ounces white superfine sugar
1–2 tablespoons kirsch

8 ripe nectarines, halved and pits removed
juice of ½ lemon
1–2 tablespoons/½–1 ounce (15–25g) butter,
    melted

1 To make the coulis, purée the raspberries with the sugar using a blender or food processor, then press the mixture through a sturdy, preferably conical, sieve. Add the kirsch to taste.

2 Place the nectarine halves, cut-side up, on a large baking sheet and sprinkle with lemon juice.

3 Brush with melted butter and place under a preheated broiler. Cook for 3–4 minutes, or until just soft. Let cool.

4 To serve, arrange the nectarines on serving plates, drizzled with the raspberry coulis.

nutritional breakdown per serving: calories 158, protein 3g, fat 3g (saturated fat 2g), carbohydrate 30g

broiled nectarines with raspberry coulis bottom left
mascarpone and amaretti ice top right

winter dinner party for 6

This is a sumptuous menu, suitable for special meals and festive occasions. It is easy to double the quantities if you are entertaining on a grander scale. I have chosen two moist vegetables to accompany the brioche. However, you could make a sauce instead, such as the Buttered Shallot and Wine Sauce (see page 290) or the dairy-free Leek and Cashew Sauce (see page 293).

A dairy-free brioche is not possible since the eggs and butter give the dough its distinct character. Instead make Quick Flaky Pastry (see page 256) and use smoked bean curd in place of the mozzarella, which works very well. A suitable dairy-free alternative to the soup would be Carrot and Parsnip Soup with Coconut and Tamarind (see page 151).

suggested timetable

Two days before:
Prepare the Chestnut and Chocolate Petits Fours

The day before:
Prepare the soup
Prepare the brioche and the filling, but do not assemble

Make the brûlée base
Slice and chill the citrus fruits to accompany the brûlée

On the day:
Assemble the brioche
Prepare the side vegetable dishes
Finish the brûlée

menu

Cream of Fennel Soup with Saffron

Wild Rice and Mushroom Brioche

Roast Shallots with Almonds

Hot Red Cabbage with Beet

Lemon Brûlée and sliced citrus fruits

Chestnut and Chocolate Petits Fours

cream of fennel soup with saffron

This is an attractive delicately flavored soup.

serves 6
preparation: 40 minutes
cooking: 20 minutes
suitable for freezing

2 tablespoons/1 ounce (25g) butter
1 onion, finely chopped
12 ounces (365g) fennel, finely chopped
½ cup (125 milliliters) white wine
pinch of saffron threads
4 cups/1¾ pints (1 liter) Vegetable Stock (see page 144)
¾ cup (175 milliliters) crème fraîche
salt and freshly ground black pepper

1 Melt the butter in a large saucepan and gently cook the onion until soft. Add the fennel, cover the pan, and cook very gently for about 10 minutes, or until tender. Stir occasionally.

2 Pour in the wine and increase the heat, then reduce until the liquid has mostly evaporated.

3 Grind the saffron, using a pestle and mortar, then steep in a little of the vegetable stock.

4 Combine the steeped saffron and remaining vegetable stock and pour over the fennel. Bring to a boil, stirring well.

5 Cover the pan and simmer for 15–20 minutes, or until the fennel is very soft.

6 Cool slightly then, using a blender or food processor, purée the soup to a smooth cream, working in batches. Sieve for a very smooth finish, if you like. Stir in the crème fraîche and salt and pepper to taste. Return the soup to a clean pan and heat through before serving.

nutritional breakdown per serving: calories 173, protein 1g, fat 15g (saturated fat 10g), carbohydrate 4g

hot red cabbage with beets

Beets and red cabbage are a happy partnership, intensifying each other's color. When beets are out of season, use dessert apples instead.

serves 6

preparation: 10 minutes

cooking: 40 minutes

suitable for freezing

𝓋

2 tablespoons sunflower oil
1 red onion, finely chopped
1½ pounds (750g) red cabbage, shredded
8 ounces (250g) raw beets, grated
2 tablespoons concentrated apple juice
2 tablespoons red wine vinegar
salt and freshly ground black pepper
2–3 tablespoons water

1 Heat the oil in a large saucepan and gently cook the onion until quite soft.

2 Add the cabbage and beet and stir well. Cook over slow heat for 5 minutes, then add the concentrated apple juice and wine vinegar. Season well with salt and pepper.

3 Add the water and cover the pan. Cook over low heat, stirring occasionally for 30 minutes, or until the cabbage is very well cooked.

4 Adjust the seasoning and serve hot or cold.

nutritional breakdown per serving: calories 95, protein 2g, fat 4g (saturated fat 0g), carbohydrate 13g

wild rice and
mushroom brioche
served with **roast
shallots with
almonds**

wild rice and mushroom brioche

serves 6

preparation: 25 minutes, plus rising and chilling

cooking: 1 hour–1 hour 10 minutes

suitable for freezing

(Ca)

For the pastry:
2 cups/8 ounces (250g) all-purpose flour, plus
   extra for dusting
1 teaspoon golden superfine sugar
1 packet/¼ ounce (7g) active dry yeast
pinch of salt
3 tablespoons milk at room temperature
2 eggs, beaten
scant ½ cup/3½ ounces (100g) butter, softened

For the filling:
scant ½ cup/3 ounces (75g) wild rice
¼ cup/ (½ stick)2 ounces (50g) butter
4 shallots, chopped
6 cups/14 ounces (425g) mushrooms, chopped
3 tablespoons chopped parsley
salt and freshly ground black pepper
4 ounces (125g) mozzarella, cubed

1 To prepare the pastry using a food processor or
electric mixer, put the flour, sugar, yeast, and salt
into the bowl, mix well, then mix in the milk and
eggs until evenly combined.

2 Beat in the butter, a piece at a time, to make a
smooth glossy dough. Add a little more flour if
the dough is very slack. Transfer the dough to a

clean bowl and cover with plastic wrap. Leave the
dough to rise for 1½ hours.

3 Punch down the dough, add a little more flour if
necessary, then return it to the bowl. Cover with
plastic wrap and chill well, preferably overnight.

4 To make the filling, put the rice in a saucepan.
Add twice its volume of water and cook for
35–40 minutes. Drain if necessary.

5 Meanwhile, melt the butter in a saucepan and gently
cook the shallots until soft. Add the chopped
mushrooms and cook for 10 minutes until well
softened, then remove from the heat. Stir in the
parsley, season well with salt and pepper, and let cool.

6 Stir the cooked rice into the mushroom mixture
and add the cubes of mozzarella. Adjust the
seasoning if necessary.

7 Roll out the brioche dough on a lightly floured
counter to a large oblong to cover a baking sheet. Pile
the mushroom filling along the center, then fold the 2
long edges of the pastry oblong over the filling so that
they meet in the middle. Moisten the edges and press
together. Make diagonal cuts in the dough along either
side, using a sharp knife. Bake the brioche in a preheated
oven, 400°F (200°C), for 25–30 minutes, or until
golden brown and crisp. Serve hot with vegetables.

nutritional breakdown per serving: calories 479, protein 15g,
fat 28g (saturated fat 17g), carbohydrate 44g

roast shallots with almonds

*This is an easy dish to make and the moist shallots
complement the brioche.*

serves 6

preparation: 5 minutes

cooking: 45 minutes

2 tablespoons/25 g (1 ounces) butter, melted
2 tablespoons olive oil
1 ounce (25g) blanched almonds, coarsely chopped
1 tablespoon dark sugar
pinch of cayenne pepper
salt and freshly ground black pepper
30–36 shallots or pearl onions, peeled

1 Melt the butter with the oil, pour into a gratin dish,
and stir in the almonds, sugar, cayenne, salt, and
pepper. Stir in the shallots.

2 Cover with a lid or sheet of foil and bake in a
preheated oven, 350°F (180°C), for 20 minutes.

3 Remove the lid and bake for 20–25 minutes more.
Serve hot.

nutritional breakdown per serving: calories 160, protein 2g,
fat 13g (saturated fat 5g), carbohydrate 10g

lemon brûlée

serves 6

preparation: 15 minutes, plus chilling

cooking: 20 minutes

6 egg yolks
3 tablespoons superfine sugar
zest of ½ lemon
2½ cups/1 pint (600 milliliters) heavy cream
1 vanilla bean

For the citrus platter:

selection of contrasting citrus fruits, such as pink and white grapefruit, orange, Ugli fruit
½–¾ cup/4–5 ounces (125–150g) granulated sugar

1 Place the egg yolks, superfine sugar, and lemon zest in a bowl and beat until light and fluffy.

2 Heat the cream in a small saucepan with the vanilla bean until hot but not boiling.

3 Remove the vanilla bean and pour the cream into the egg mixture, beating constantly.

4 Pour the mixture into a double saucepan or a bowl set over a pan of hot but not boiling water, and cook very gently until the mixture thickens. This takes about 10–15 minutes—if you try to rush it the eggs will scramble.

5 Once thick, pour into 6 ramekins or 1 shallow gratin dish. Cover with plastic wrap and set aside in the refrigerator to set.

6 Meanwhile, to prepare the citrus platter, peel and segment the fruit and arrange on a serving plate. Chill well.

7 Two hours before serving, sprinkle granulated sugar over each ramekin. Place under a preheated hot broiler and brown until caramelized. Let cool before serving with the platter of citrus fruit.

nutritional breakdown per serving: calories 663, protein 6g, fat 54g (saturated fat 32g), carbohydrate 42g

chestnut and chocolate petits fours

Exquisitely rich and so simple to make, these petits fours make the perfect indulgent finish to this meal. You may find that there are enough here for two meals—but that will depend entirely on the appetite of your guests.

makes 36

preparation: 10 minutes, plus chilling

cooking: 2 minutes

suitable for freezing

3½ ounces (100g) bittersweet chocolate, broken
   into small pieces
scant ½ cup (100 milliliters) crème fraîche
½ cup/3½ ounces (100g) superfine sugar
14 ounces (400g) cooked chestnuts (see
   page 257)
2 tablespoons Grand Marnier
1 teaspoon orange zest

1 Melt the chocolate carefully with the crème fraîche in a bowl set over a saucepan of hot but not boiling water. Remove from the heat and beat until smooth.

2 Using a blender or food processor, purée the chestnuts finely, then add the remaining ingredients, and blend again.

3 Spoon the chocolaty chestnut mixture into a lined, lightly buttered 6-inch (15-cm) square pan. Set aside in the refrigerator for at least 4 hours, preferably overnight. Cut into 36 small squares before serving.

nutritional breakdown per petit four: calories 46, protein 0g,
fat 1g (saturated fat 1g), carbohydrate 9g

Index

An italic page reference indicates an illustration.

Acknowledgments

This book took up a good part of my life and involved a large number of people. I am very pleased with the end result and so to all those who played a part, however small, I would like to say thank you.

There are also some key people who deserve a special mention. A huge thank you to Rachel Anderson for making all the testing of the recipes so enjoyable with her enthusiasm and generous spirit. My thanks also go to Ann Halsey, Antonia Halse, Marco, and Monica Bonafini, Cherry Wilson, Kay Denny, Caroline Moran, Ann-Marie Kjof, and Amal Rashid for contributing recipe ideas.

I would also like to thank Shirley Patton who was mainly responsible for managing this project and who drew together the many threads of this book in a highly focused and very supportive manner.

At Ivy Press I would like to thank Peter Bridgewater, Terry Jeavons, and Sophie Collins for keeping this book alive; Caroline Earle, for picking up the final editing; Alistair Plumb whose design really brought the text to life; and Jacqueline Clark and Marie-Louise Avery, who respectively made and photographed my recipes.

Picture Credits

The publishers wish to thank the following for the use of these pictures:

Cephas: 45 bottom left, 117 top.
Bruce Coleman Collection: 24 bottom, 87 top right.
Corbis UK Ltd: 24 top, 27 top, 62 bottom right, 76 bottom left, 108 top right, 118 bottom.
Garden Picture Library: 13 bottom, 30 bottom, 64 bottom right, 73 bottom left, 115 top, 119 bottom right.
Science Photo Library: 18 top, 28 bottom, 30 top, 88 top right, 90 left, 112.